SILHOUETTED AGAINST THE MISTY MOON

She could see without mistake the swirl of black cloak and the broad width of his shoulders, the proud lift of his head, and the crowning touch—she could see he wore a mask.

Across the distance, he sensed her presence. He turned and stared at her in return. Then he moved straight for her.

She could feel the intensity of the moment as she waited, trembling. He came to a halt and looked her over, beginning at her feet and moving slowly upward. At last his gaze made contact with hers. His eyes glittered like diamonds through his mask, piercing her soul.

Suddenly he stripped away his molded leather gloves, reached for her, and pulled her into his embrace. The heat of his fingers shocked her bare arms. A shudder shook her as the truth flooded in on her. The secret—known to her and her alone—sprang on her in its entirety. The man who'd dared put a torch to her heart was the most dangerous pirate in England.

ANNOUNCING THE
TOPAZ FREQUENT READERS CLUB
COMMEMORATING TOPAZ'S 1 YEAR ANNIVERSARY!

THE MORE YOU BUY, THE MORE YOU GET

Redeem coupons found here and in the back of all new Topaz titles for FREE Topaz gifts:

Send in:

 2 coupons for a free TOPAZ novel (choose from the list below);
- ☐ **THE KISSING BANDIT**, Margaret Brownley
- ☐ **BY LOVE UNVEILED**, Deborah Martin
- ☐ **TOUCH THE DAWN**, Chelley Kitzmiller
- ☐ **WILD EMBRACE**, Cassie Edwards

 4 coupons for an "I Love the Topaz Man" on-board sign

🔹 6 coupons for a TOPAZ compact mirror

🔹 8 coupons for a Topaz Man T-shirt

Just fill out this certificate and send with original sales receipts to:

TOPAZ FREQUENT READERS CLUB-1ST ANNIVERSARY
Penguin USA • Mass Market Promotion; Dept. H.U.G.
375 Hudson St., NY, NY 10014

Name_____

Address_____

City_____State_____Zip_____

Offer expires 5/31/1995

This certificate must accompany your request. No duplicates accepted. Void where prohibited, taxed or restricted. Allow 4-6 weeks for receipt of merchandise. Offer good only in U.S., its territories, and Canada.

PIRATE'S ROSE

Janet Lynnford

A TOPAZ BOOK

TOPAZ
Published by the Penguin Group
Penguin Books USA Inc., 375 Hudson Street,
New York, New York 10014, U.S.A.
Penguin Books Ltd, 27 Wrights Lane,
London W8 5TZ, England
Penguin Books Australia Ltd, Ringwood,
Victoria, Australia
Penguin Books Canada Ltd, 10 Alcorn Avenue,
Toronto, Ontario, Canada M4V 3B2
Penguin Books (N.Z.) Ltd, 182–190 Wairau Road,
Auckland 10, New Zealand

Penguin Books Ltd, Registered Offices:
Harmondsworth, Middlesex, England

First published by Topaz, an imprint of Dutton Signet,
a division of Penguin Books USA Inc.

First Printing, June, 1995
10 9 8 7 6 5 4 3 2

Topaz is a trademark of Dutton Signet,
a division of Penguin Books USA Inc.

Printed in Canada

This book is dedicated
to the following important people in my life:

First, to the women of Central Ohio Fiction Writers,
wonderful, supportive friends
especially

Beverly Shippey, who insisted I rewrite many scenes until I got them right. To Becky Barker, Connie Dimattilleo, Mel Jacobs, Laurie Grant, Karen Harper, Judie Hershner and Deb Simmons, published authors who tirelessly lent their advice and support. To Vickie Batte, Ann Bouricius, Sharon Hillis, and Linda Miller, who never failed to urge me on. And to the many others too numerous to name, you know who you are.

To Audrey LaFehr, without whom I would not be where I am today. And to Leah Bassoff, her hardworking assistant.

To Andrea Cirillo, a very special lady who guides and supports.

To the five bouncing children of the Johnson family: Sam, Anna, Simone, Silvia, and baby Paul, who inspired me to create the Cavandish family.

To my beloved friend and scholarly mentor, Professor Elizabeth M. Burns, international expert in neurophysiology, Alzheimer's disease, and the addictions, and to my faithful colleague Kathy Slone, both of whom encouraged me.

To Suzanne Barrett and Lesley Payne, my California supporters.

To my paternal grandmother, Lynnferd Lucy McMahon, from whom I took my pen name.

And of course to Dana, David, and my mother, who patiently put up with the writer's odd hours, a messy house, and incessant chatter about books, authors, and other people they never heard of.

To each of you, I send my love.

PART ONE

—

The Town of West Lulworth, Dorset, England, June 1573

Chapter 1

In the late morning of a sunny June day, Rozalinde Cavandish heard the bell on the door of her father's drapery establishment jingle as someone came in. Kneeling on the floor before a huge wooden crate, she did not look up.

"John," she called to her father's apprentice, "someone comes at the door."

She *must* get this crate open. It was critical she check the latest shipment of goods from Antwerp. Wrinkling her brow in concentration, Roz worked her lever into an opening and pried. The lid groaned dismally but refused to come off. "Please, God," she prayed as she worked. "Let it not be ruined. Let me for once be wrong."

The customer's footsteps echoed in the silence of the empty shop behind her. Someone in heavy boots, Roz thought absently, her gaze locked on the crate. "The apprentice will be with you straight," she called over her shoulder, sensing more than seeing the man at the counter just behind her. Jamming the lever into another crevice, she tried again.

Still it wouldn't budge. Roz worked her way around the crate, searching for a weak spot in the lid. Once she wouldn't have done this sort of work. But these days she tackled any job that presented itself. Since her mother was again with child, managing the household fell to Rozalinde. And since her father's serious illness, he trusted no one but her with the business. Roz plunged into the work gladly, determined to show how much she cherished them. Finding a likely gap at last, Roz fit her lever in the space and flung her weight against it. The nails yielded with a loud crack.

Inside the crate, ells and ells of precious lace nestled. There! she thought with triumph, scanning the contents.

She'd had no reason to worry. It all seemed in order, it all seemed perfectly—

She froze, her eyes riveted to one spot. A blackish stain covered the entire right side of the goods.

A moan escaped her lips as Roz lifted the first layer of lace, then the second. Did the stain go all the way down? Plunging deeper, she burrowed head first into the depths of the big crate, one foot braced against the wooden side, the other stuck in the air, half out of her shoe.

She straightened and stood a second later, spluttering from the lint. Ruined! Their ninth shipment in the last six months. This crate had cost them a hundred and fifty pounds, and there were six more like it in the warehouse at Poole. They would all be damaged, just like last time. The captain had let seawater destroy them.

She piled the pieces back willy-nilly, her anxiety turning to despair. They couldn't take any more losses like this. Their profits were shrinking daily. Expenses were becoming hard to meet. The captain would have to be dismissed. She thought of going to the quay to confront him, willing to have it out with him on the spot, but John had not appeared from the back room.

"Troth," she muttered, realizing she could not leave now, "where is John when I need him?" The customer still waited. Pushing back her thick brown hair, she righted the practical coif she had tied on earlier to keep out the dust. Her father usually drew the line at her serving customers. He had Master Gray for that, as well as John and the other apprentice.

But they were not here, so she would do it. Resolutely she turned.

Her "How may I serve you?" died an unexpected death half out of her mouth as she beheld the man before her— a man who commanded her attention. His black cloak hung by a silk cord knotted across his broad chest. A finely wrought, black doublet emphasized a tapering torso that narrowed to a trim, black-belted waist. Everything he wore was black: black trunk hose, black hat; even his beard and hair were black. No splash of white or any other color broke the solemnity of his imposing figure.

Involuntarily, her eyes dropped to high leather boots that accented his muscular thighs, and to the gilt sword—not a useless, ornamental rapier, but a heavy one with a jeweled pommel—that swung in the hanger at his side. Done with her study, she let her gaze travel back to his face—a lean countenance, exquisitely modeled and thoroughly stern. He studied her intently in return.

"God's greeting to you, little maid. At last you honor me with your attention." Doffing his Milan bonnet with its curling black plume, he drew together his booted feet till the heels clicked, saluting her with an eminently correct bow. "As to serving me, are you quite sure you can?"

His blue eyes were so challenging, she looked away with irritation. She had enough problems to deal with, so let him get on with his purchase. "Why should you think I cannot?"

"Well . . ." He chose that moment to smile at her, baring astonishingly white teeth. Instantly his face changed—so dramatically that Roz almost gaped at him. Gone was the stern, lean profile, the look of hard command. She was so surprised, all thought of the lace evaporated. Her hurry to return to the house was temporarily arrested as his smile sent her its pure, dazzling warmth.

"I was watching you examine that crate," he went on, sure that he had her attention, "when you up and dived into it headlong. I said to myself, 'Either 'tis something of vast import down there, or she has gone completely daft.' As I can see quite well you are not daft, I wonder what is in the bottom of that box?" His voice gentled. "Is it something that troubles you?"

"It does," she said, puzzled as to why he should care. "But I shall manage. I always do."

"And the person who caused it?"

"I shall manage him, too."

She jumped when he laughed suddenly, throwing back his head and letting his mirth resonate through the shop.

"Why do you laugh?" she demanded. Attractive men always thought too much of themselves. He was probably just like the rest. Catching up a bolt of cotton frieze, she snapped the loose cloth tight. "I have managed far worse."

"I do not doubt that you have. And I shouldn't wish to be in this man's boots when you, er, manage him. Determined little lass, are you not?"

"Yes." She banged the bolt back into its place. "And I am not so little."

He stroked his beard. "I agree you are not. I should have said 'determined' and stopped there."

His gaze stroked her body, lingering on her tightly laced waist, on the low-cut neck of her smock.

Instinctively she tugged the smock higher, searching for a polite way to tell him to go. But none of the words popping into her head were polite. There was nothing she could do short of walking out, and that would surely lose them a sale. "I am here to sell goods," she said brusquely, "so what is it you wish to buy?"

He grinned at her, and she was surprised to find herself staring at his wide, attractive lips, thinking they were pleasant to look upon, so sensual . . .

She gave herself a firm mental shake. He was trying to provoke her, that was all, and she would not stand for it. She was mistress here. "I am waiting, sir." She put on an expression that showed she would brook no nonsense, but she couldn't help feeling curious about this man. What would he say next?

He shrugged. "If you insist. I wish to purchase a fan. A lady's feather fan, if you have some of quality."

Roz caught up the keys from the ribbon at her waist and moved to the case where the fans were kept. Unlocking it, she withdrew two white ones. "These are our finest. The feathers are ostrich from the Americas to the south. But I see you are all in black. Is the lady, too, in mourning?"

"She is. She has lost her husband, so I thought to cheer her with some pretty knack." He gestured toward the fans. "I know nothing of these trifles for ladies. Tell me, which should I choose?"

Roz studied the fans she had placed on the case top, becoming caught up in the merchandise. Her father had told her all about the new fans when they first arrived. She knew more about them than any of the apprentices. "If she is a lady of quality—"

"She is."

"Then I would recommend this one." She turned again to the case and drew out another fan—a black one this time with a silver handle, the feathers spread elegantly, each one sprinkled with fine silver oes. Holding it before her to demonstrate, Roz waved it gently to and fro, making the oes sparkle as they caught the light.

The man regarded her solemnly. "A beauty, for certain."

Roz almost dropped the fan; his gaze was locked on her face. Did he mean her or the fan? His words, his vibrant blue eyes, filled her with an anticipation so great, so overwhelming, she could not understand it. Who could he possibly be?

"I will take the fan, and can you wrap it well? I wish to present it to the lady this day."

"Certes." Roz put away the other two fans and moved shakily toward the front counter. "Is there anything more?"

"Mayhap ... some lace."

She eyed him skeptically. "Ours is all ruined, and well you know it."

"I did not know," he said gently. "Let me see."

Wordlessly she led him to the back of the shop, showed him the crate. He studied the lace for several minutes, handling it with strong, capable-looking hands. Straightening, he turned. "I will buy it. The entire box."

Rozalinde's jaw almost dropped. "But you cannot. 'Tis all of it ruined, clear to the bottom of the crate. See." To show him, she burrowed down to bring up a blackened piece from the bottom. "So you understand you cannot—" She stopped, beset by an explosive sneeze.

"You have lint on your nose, mistress." He extended a pristine linen handkerchief. "I will give you a hundred and fifty pounds. Are there more of these crates? I will buy them as well."

"All of them?" Her eyes widened as she stared at him over the cloth clutched to her nose. " 'Twould be robbery for me to let you."

"Come, come, I intend to buy at least this one. What should I pay?"

She handed back the handkerchief and named a price for the one crate.

"Too low," he argued. "You will make no profit."

She shook her head adamantly. "We cannot expect a profit on ruined goods."

"Then at least accept what you paid. Without profit, but without loss."

Rozalinde wanted to agree. She struggled to get some

word, any word at all, out of her mouth, but none came. She hadn't meant to let it happen. She'd fought it until now. But she was caught fast in the snare of his gaze.

Apparently that wasn't enough for him. Now that he had her, the contagious curve of his mouth insisted she answer with a smile of her own. Slowly, she let the expression creep over her face.

Christopher Howard took that smile willingly, gathering it to him like treasure, marveling at its sweetness. For a full minute he indulged himself, giving in to her beauty—the sweet tuck of her slender waist, the swell of her shapely breasts against the plain linen of her smock, the limpid depths of her autumn brown eyes. Cascades of curling brown hair escaped the coif she had tied on in a futile attempt to confine it. Oh, she was marvelous in form, without question. But it was something he saw in the perfect oval of her face, the quality of her smile, that made him want to stand all day and look at her.

Of course it couldn't continue. Being made earl was a blasted nuisance. It claimed his time in ways he resented. Even now he was expected elsewhere, instead of here, feasting his gaze on this girl. Reluctantly he broke the trance.

"I believe," he coughed, still smiling at her, "I am expected to pay?"

Mustering her self-control, Rozalinde snapped out of her stupor. Briskly she forced herself to walk to the front counter and set about wrapping the fan. Such weakness, wanting to stare overlong at him. What was wrong with her today? An ordinary man walked into the shop and the next thing she knew, she was acting like an idiot. Yet he wasn't so ordinary. He'd bought all that lace.

"What will you do with it?" The words sprang unchecked from her lips.

"What? Oh, the lace." Christopher pensively stroked his perfectly trimmed marquisette beard. "I shall give it to the lady who will have the fan—at least the good parts. The rest, well, mayhap the maids at Lulworth Castle will be better arrayed than most."

The maids? Rozalinde's jaw almost dropped for the second time that day. "That is so generous ... of course 'tis not my affair," she corrected herself hastily. "But you will want to cleanse the damaged parts, which can be done with plenty of lye and hot water, only you must have a care it does not steep too long in the lye—"

He waved at her to stop. "Do not trouble to explain." His voice soothed her. "Surely you have cares enough without more to add. You must scarce have time to think of yourself."

She stopped wrapping the fan and looked perplexed. "But of course I do not think of myself. That would be selfish."

"Not if you examine your soul. Or what you would make of your life. But I see you have little time left for such things. It is something we all lack."

Rozalinde regarded him in astonishment. "I cannot think what you mean. My father provides well for us, and I lack for nothing. I examine my soul in church of a Sunday. No one is expected to do more than that. Besides, I have my duty. What else should there be?"

He said nothing in return, but his gaze seemed to bore a hole straight into that soul she had just named.

She looked away quickly, put industrious energy into wrapping the fan. While she busily avoided his provocative eyes, she could hear the clanking of coins on wood as he counted out the proper sum.

Suddenly, the sound of coins ceased. His warm presence loomed behind her. Turning her head slightly, she could see the solid barrier of his black-clad chest just touching her right shoulder. His hand reached out.

For a split second Rozalinde thought he was going to embrace her. It was a mad idea, born out of nowhere. Indecent, even to think it. She sought his face with her gaze, wanting an explanation, and discovered again his eyes—as blue as the Dorset sea—locked upon her. As if in slow motion, his hand continued to advance . . .

. . . and captured hers. Fascinated, Rozalinde examined his fingers, covered with calluses from rapier practice. He turned her hand upright and, with a tinkling sound, showered the golden coins into her palm.

"No," he agreed, " 'Tis not money you lack, but something else." His voice was husky. "I'll tell you about it some time."

Never had she liked a man's closeness, but this one smelled tantalizingly of musk and leather mingled with an exotic scent she couldn't quite name. The complex barrage of feelings that welled up inside made her stomach tighten as he closed her palm over the money, then stepped away.

She clutched the coins, realizing her heart pounded with excruciating pleasure beneath her ribs. "Kindly explain yourself," she demanded, striving for her customary control. " 'Tis impolite to hint."

Christopher tilted his head to one side and considered. What had he meant? Nothing he could utter in feminine company, of course: that she was ripe and unplucked as a new-formed bud, hidden away in the shop as if waiting for him on this clear June morning, a maid clearly unwed and uninitiated to the pleasures of love.

He struck the thoughts aside. He had vowed to resist every female in the last year and he'd done it. But this one moved him, with her face like a solemn angel and her ruined crates of lace—they made him want to do things he couldn't begin to explain. "You are in the right," he answered finally. "But then I am seldom polite. I find politeness a useless trait." He shrugged apologetically. "My worst fault."

At that, her lips longed to curve into a smile again. They tried, yet she refused to let them.

"I'll vow you don't smile near enough. Nor laugh." He reached out to trace her brow with one finger. "When I first came in, I could see the lines of worry here."

"I smile if there is something to smile about—"

"And that is seldom," he finished for her. "A pity, for one so young."

"I am not a child. You speak as if I were." She turned away from him and began counting the coins he had paid, letting each one rattle loudly into her father's little money box. "I am one and twenty," she said as she counted, her face feeling as stiff as the wooden box.

"Are you?" His blue eyes drilled for where she hid her truths.

"I . . . well . . . I shall be come fall."

He chuckled at her amendment. "Your frown belongs to someone decades older. I think it is not yours. But your smile ..." He allowed a pregnant pause. "It is all your own."

Her gaze darted to him, suspicious that his statement would be followed by an avowal. She'd had too many men swear love within minutes of their meeting. But his face betrayed no ridiculous ardor—only that enfolding warmth. "Pray do not mock me," she said uncertainly.

"I am not mocking. I only wish to see you happy."

She stiffened. "You presume to know too much about me."

"Don't be offended." He pulled one of her hands into his two big warm ones and chaffed it tenderly. "It's only that a person's face is an open book, if one cares to read."

Rozalinde turned her head away, overcome with confusion. "Your words are not of reason."

"You mean you think I am a rogue and you shouldn't trust me. Yet I have done nothing untoward."

She had no idea what to say. She, who was never at a loss for words.

"Trust me, mistress," he coaxed.

"Trust you to do what?" She jerked away her hand and began to tidy the counter. "To be a knave, like all men? You speak in riddles, and I am not in the mood for riddles today. Why will you not go away?"

"Do you dismiss all things that baffle you? Most unwise, mistress. Someday you must face certain facts. I would like to acquaint you with a few choice ones." He laughed deep in his throat. "But I cannot today. I must go. After I have named you."

He scrutinized her for a minute, pacing around her as she stood looking at him, amazed. He didn't ask her name. He presumed to name her. It made her so uncomfortable, his attention, that she clasped both arms across her chest and twisted her neck, first one way, then the other, to watch him go round.

"Rose," he said at last, having made a complete circuit and stopped where he began. "Skin soft like the flesh of the flower, eyes luminous as the dew. No other name suits you so well." He stood there looking satisfied with himself.

"Are you quite finished?" she asked sharply. "If you fancy yourself a poet, you are a poor one. And Rose is not my name."

"Ah, there are the thorns. You see I am right—"

"I am not what you say, just because you choose to say it." Thoroughly enraged by his presumption, confused by his earlier kindness of buying the lace, Roz caught up a heavy wooden bobbin wound with ribbon and clutched it tightly.

"Angry?" He nodded to indicate the bobbin.

"Yes," she ground out.

"Then throw it at me."

"Nonsense."

"Do," he urged. He lunged forward, as if threatening, and she jumped back so quickly, hurled the bobbin so fast, she hardly knew what she'd done.

Laughing, he put up both hands to ward it off, so that it fell with a clatter on the floor. Abruptly her anger ran out of her like dry meal from a rough frieze bag.

"Feel better?" Cheerfully he retrieved the bobbin.

Strangely, she did.

"Ah, I am relieved." Christopher swiped at his brow. "If you are done with anger, you must know that I would like greatly to kiss you." He eyed her appreciatively.

"What?" She stared at him, aghast, realizing she'd been thinking the same thing. "You *are* impolite."

"I told you I was." His eyes laughed merrily at her. "But then I'm also honest. Don't be angry again. I should be sorry if you were."

"I am not angry, but you must not say such things."

"Not ever?"

His face showed disappointment. In fact, he looked so sorrowful, she could hardly bear it. His entire body slumped, became dejected. He crushed his hat in both hands and looked at her, his bewitching blue eyes mirroring his pain. They made her feel guilty, as if she had hurt him sorely. "Well, of course, 'tis not that it's such a fault, as long as you do not follow the words with the action, as you said yourself, but you must remember that in polite company, one does not ordinarily, that is, you must see, people do not talk of such things when they have just met ..." Groping for words, she looked at the floor in bafflement, then turned back, convinced he really did not understand.

His attractive face wore a look of pure devilment, and it slowly dawned on her that he was teasing. What could she possibly be thinking, stumbling out an explanation when he meant to bait her? With a rush of anger, she grasped the wrapped fan and almost threw it at him. "You, sir, are a rogue and a knave. There is the door. Be gone at once!"

He was chuckling as he caught the package midair. Holding the fan carefully within its coarse cotton wrapping, he swiveled lightly to obey. Halfway to the door, he turned back. "I shall still call you Rose when we meet. Agreed?"

"We shall not meet . . . except on business," she amended lamely, feeling ungrateful. But his roguish grin forced her to snap at him again. "You are insufferable."

"In truth, my red-cheeked Rose?" He said the words as carefully as he protected the fan, nodding to himself. "I shall send someone for the crate of lace, then find a buyer for the rest." He held up one finger and winked at her. "Remember, I have made you smile. Next time, I shall make you laugh." He gave her a bold glance. "And perhaps something more."

With that, he was gone. The bell on the door seemed to clang harshly as he went out.

Roz pressed one hand to her hot cheek, wondering just how red her face was. But after a second, a new thought came to her in a rush—the scent that clung to him, she knew what it was. Cloves. The lingering fragrance twined around her senses and buried itself deeply in her subconscious as she watched him mount his huge black horse and ride rapidly away.

Chapter 2

When he was well gone, when there was not the slightest chance he might return, Roz gave in to temptation. Going to where her father kept a looking glass for customers, she lifted it down and scanned her reflection, trying to think what had just happened. Her own brown eyes gazed back at her, and she touched her now-pale cheek in disbelief. Was it possible? She who never blushed ... had turned so red?

Tilting the glass, she surveyed her simple kirtle and smock, trying to make out how she must have looked. Troth, she thought, pushing back a stray tendril of hair, her feelings swirling, rough as the eddies of Lulworth Cove. Everything was upside-down today. First the ruined lace. Now this man, suggesting ... She should have slapped his face. She always had before when a man went too far.

But she hadn't wanted to slap him. Not as she had the others. Perhaps it was because no man had ever bought her ruined cargo before. That alone was enough to make her love him.

Love? Nonsense, she chided herself. What in heaven made her use that word? She'd never been in love, and she didn't intend to be now. Just because her body responded in such an unusual way didn't make the man trustworthy. In fact, quite the opposite—it made him dangerous.

Best forget him, she told herself sensibly. He would prove to be like the others who courted her—mouthing words about her beauty, thinking that a fair exchange for her dowry. None of them cared what *she* wanted. Only her father did that.

A sadness descended upon her. Her cherished papa, the bulwark of her childhood, the center of her existence, he was so ill now it frightened her. The physicians had sug-

gested a quieter life, the sea air. They had left their fashionable house in London to come here. She hadn't minded.
She would do anything for him. No one else in her life
mattered so much.

"Ah, Mistress Rozalinde, what do you here?" The errant
apprentice interrupted her reverie by entering at last,
scratching his back and yawning hugely.

"John!" Roz whirled around and put away the glass before he could see her examining herself. "Where have you
been? A customer came."

He goggled at her. "What? Where is Master Gray?
And Tom?"

"Gray left for his half day off, and well you know it.
And Tom," she shrugged, having heard her father complain
about this problem before, "has disappeared. You," she
said accusingly, "were left in charge."

"Pardon, mistress." The young man hung his big head
on its lanky neck. "I fell asleep in the back room. 'Twill
not happen again."

Roz looked at him sternly for a minute, then melted.
"You have served us long. I'll overlook it this time. Now
then," she held out the broom with authority, "sweep up
and tidy the stock. Especially the ribbons. They are all in
disarray." She indicated the brightly colored silks half un-
wound from their bobbins. One in particular was a hopeless
tangle from its earlier roll on the floor. Roz looked away
from it guiltily, trying to forget what she'd done.

John took the broom and swept the floor industriously,
gathering scraps of cloth and dirt. "Who was the customer?" he ventured to ask while he worked.

"I don't know," she admitted as she tallied the latest
income in her father's account book. "A gentleman of some
means, though I've never seen him before."

John was just opening his mouth to question her further,
but at that moment the back door slammed. A plump lass
in a stiffly starched coif and apron bounced in and curtsied
before Rozalinde, panting from her haste. "Oh, Mistress
Rozalinde, your pardon, but we need you sore up t' the
kitchen, what with all them folk your pa hired to make up
our revel. The one's got lice, I'd swear to it, and Cook's in
such a titter about 'em. You'd best come."

"Troth! I forgot the time." Roz draped her cloak around

her, frowning with worry. "I hope they've done the tasks I set them. The revel begins in just a few hours." Moving quickly, she led Margery out the back door.

The two girls hurried up the steep steps cut in the hill behind the shop, making for the fine timbered house overlooking the street. Roz could have outdistanced her maid easily—Margery was winded from her climb—but she waited patiently before slipping in a side door and leading the way to her chamber.

Roz indicated her best gown, laid out on the bed. "I'd best dress now, for I'll get no chance later. You must lace my busk tighter, if I'm to wear that."

Deftly Margery stripped off her mistress's plain kirtle skirt and bodice, and began tightening the laces of Roz's busk. "Any customers in the shop?" she asked, tying the laces and reaching for the bodice to the gown.

"One," Roz answered, standing still so Margery could hook the bodice up the back. "He didn't look travel worn so he must be local. I sold him a fan and—"

"*You* sold him a fan!" Margery frowned in disapproval. "You're not to do that. Where were Tom and John?"

Roz sized up her maid. No one would benefit if she told on the apprentices. "Why shouldn't I help a customer?" she said carefully. "I'm a shopkeeper's daughter."

"Faugh," Margery scoffed, taking the bait and forgetting the boys. "You're no such thing. You're the daughter of the richest master merchant in London. No, the richest in England, I'd wager. How many times have I said, you're not to be alone with strange men in the shop. What would your pa think? Worse yet, what did that gentleman think?"

"He thought nothing at all. Why should he?" Roz said sharply, feeling the blood rise unexpectedly to her face.

"He did, I'll vow. I know what I know about men, mistress." Margery clucked her tongue as she came around to straighten the bobbin lace on the front of Roz's bodice. "A minute alone with a lass as looks like you, an' ... well, I never said so before, but I always thought all 'twould take is the right man to come along and then heaven help us all! So what happened? Did he try to take liberties?" Margery held out the matching blue brocade kirtle skirt guarded with lace.

Roz shook her head with irritation as she stepped into

it. "Nothing happened. I made the sale and he went away. I'll probably never see him again. It's late, Margery. The guests will be arriving for the revel as soon as dinner's done. I'd best go down like this."

"Oh, no, you don't. Not with today being what it is, special and all. You'll wear your sleeves and overgown or I'll get scolded for being lax."

"Oh, troth." Fuming, Roz held up her arms so Margery could help her into the separate gown. "Bother all these clothes. They take too much time. Are the children all arrayed?"

Margery rolled her eyes while she tied on a beribboned, lacy sleeve. "As arrayed as I could get 'em. At least Angelica is."

"Tell me the truth, now—how are things in the kitchens?"

This time Margery grimaced. "I didn't want to say in front o' John, but them folk your pa hired to bring the pasties and meat and all—they're all mad."

"How so?" With both her elaborate sleeves and gown tied in place, Roz sat down, loosened her hair, and looked at her maid in the glass.

"Can't stop talking, that's what." Margery picked up the brush and began to arrange her mistress's long, curling hair. "Jabbering and gossiping fit to drive you witless. All this nonsense about pirates, saying as they're goin' to land on our coast." She harrumphed as she divided the hair and began braiding. "Got the stable lads and spit turn so stirred up, they're ready to run off wild in the night. Such a muddle I never did see."

Roz reached for her sapphire earrings, the only baubles she would let her father buy her, and slipped them on. "I shall tend to the kitchen folk. Is Papa resting as the physician ordered?"

"He is, and your ma's with him. So you'd best see to things," Margery grumbled, "before half our folk run away this very night. The chief caterer—the one what gives Cook fits 'cause he claims his sauce is the best in Dorset—why, he says they'll be giving things away."

Roz flashed Margery a sharp glance. "The pirates around Lulworth don't give away things. They land up Lulworth Creek, and everything they bring is sold for a pretty price."

"Aye, I know." Margery sighed as she finished Roz's braids, then wrapped them around her head like a coronet. "But they're *our* pirates, our locals. We know what to expect of them. But these others are the Sea Beggars, the Netherlands pirates. And Lord knows what they'll be up to. Seems they give away goods from the Spanish ships they capture."

Roz stopped, her hand poised with her left earring, and stared at Margery in surprise. "The Sea Beggars? They won't come here. Not to West Lulworth."

Margery folded her lips smugly. "You tell that to those gossips."

Rozalinde turned back to the mirror and closed the catch on her earring as she thought it over. Everyone had heard about the Sea Beggars, men from the Netherlands who sailed the North Sea and the channel. They were more than pirates, really, commissioned by their rebel leader, the Prince of Orange, to fight the Spanish king who ruled their land. All she needed was for them to land, put everyone in town and in her household in a frenzy. "They won't come," she told Margery firmly. "I'm sure they won't."

"They might," Margery went on, warming to what was actually her favorite subject. "Just think, the Sea Beggars. Here, in Dorset. Noblemen thrown off their land because they wouldn't pay the King of Spain's taxes. Isn't that right?"

Roz eyed her braids critically. "I don't know. Alderman Trenchard says King Philip has been fair to them. Look, Margery, don't loop my hair so. I prefer it plain."

The maid obediently rewrapped the braid.

"Besides," Roz went on resolutely, "it's none of our affair. The queen requires us to be neutral, and so we are. And the Beggar King may be a noble, but he's the only one."

"Ah, the Beggar King." Margery grinned broadly and held out the looking glass so Roz could examine her handiwork. "There's a subject of great import to many a maid. Said to be a dashing gallant, their leader. Lord of the sea and brave as they come. Now there's a man for you, mistress. A king among men."

"What a nonsensical thing to say, Margery." Satisfied at

last with the simplicity of her shining braids, Rozalinde got up to change her shoes. "An outlaw, no less."

"Ah, but they say he's courageous. And handsome, in his black swirling cape and mask, comin' to seek the fairest woman in Dorset. If he was to sweep *me* into his arms, I know I'd—"

"Trash, Margery, stop talking trash." Roz straightened and looked around the room.

"That's the trouble with 'e," the maid complained as she tidied the dressing table. "You work too hard and you don't like men. Look at the proper suitors you've turned away."

"They just wanted my dowry," Roz insisted, looking under the bed. "I can't find my girdle, Margery. Where can it be?"

The maid pulled it from beneath a cushion. "Angelica hid it. What about Master Trenchard?" she persisted. "He has money of his own and he's sore enamored of you."

"He's no such thing," Roz said with finality, reaching for her pomander. "He's a man of business. He gives me the latest news on prices and products. Here," she instructed, "you hold the girdle while I fasten this on."

Margery looked skeptical, but she held the chain without saying anything while Rozalinde clipped her scent-filled pomander to it. "What about these other men your mother's chosen," Margery asked. "The ones coming to the revel?"

"Bother the revel."

"But 'twill be grand, sure. All those gentlemen wooin' you."

Rozalinde wrinkled her nose in profound disgust, but there was no time to argue. "You see to Lucina," she instructed. "I'll see to the boys." And taking the belt from Margery, she clasped it around her waist and hurried out the door.

A minute later she entered the room where her three younger brothers slept. The place was utter chaos. Jonathan, a tall lad of sixteen, lounged against the window casement. He, thank goodness, was ready, wearing a new doublet and velvet-paned trunk hose. He winked at her as she entered the room, daring her to make sense of the mess.

Matthew, who was thirteen, sat fiddling with a pair of

torn netherstocks. And Charles, just eight, was fighting with his nurse.

"I won't wear it. 'Tis devilish nasty." He twisted away from the old lady as she tried to pull the heavy doublet over his head. "The day is too hot."

"For shame, Master Charles," admonished the nurse, struggling for a grip on his squirming body. "You are going to a great revel and must practice your manners at table before. You must show respect."

"I'll show you . . ." Charles made a rude gesture with his hand.

The nurse let go of him and shrank back with a gasp. "Where did you learn that?"

Jon and Matthew were suddenly busy looking out the window, talking about something else. Rozalinde whisked into the chamber and took Charles in hand.

"Come dear, you must dress yourself." She took the doublet and put it in Charles's hands. He gaped at her with surprise, now that he controlled the hated garment. Rozalinde dropped a kiss on his head and showed him how to hold the doublet. "If you hurry, there will be sweet suckets after dinner."

Charles regarded her with big brown eyes. "In truth? Even raspberry?"

"In truth." Roz coaxed the garment over his head while still convincing him he was in control. "Matthew, let Nurse help you with your stocks."

"They're torn," Matthew whined in his worst childish voice. " 'Tis Jon's fault."

"No matter." Done with Charles, Rozalinde pulled a clean pair of stockings from a coffer, tossed them at her middle brother, and shook her finger at Jonathan. "You might help rather than holding up that window. And where were you last night? Mother was asking for you."

"I prefer to let you manage things. 'Tis unfailing pleasant when you do." Jon purposely avoided her question. "You keep *them* well in hand." He gestured at his younger brothers.

Before Roz could contradict him, to say it was not unfailing pleasant for *her,* Lucina, who was six, ran into the chamber crying and cast herself into Rozalinde's arms. She was followed by a frazzled-looking Margery. "She won't let me wear my new red ribbons," sobbed the child, pointing at Margery. "Mama would have let me."

"There now, poppet," soothed the nurse, "your yellow ones are fine. And if you do not hasten, your dinner will be cold. 'Tis already nigh on one."

"But the yellow ones aren't new," insisted Lucina, bursting into fresh tears. "I want my red ones."

The nurse rolled her eyes at Margery. The maid heaved a sigh of defeat. Both turned to Rozalinde.

"Fetch the red ribbons, Margery. Let us sit, love." Rozalinde sat on a stool and patted her lap. The little one went into her arms and nestled close, her eyes now suspiciously dry.

"You may wear the red ribbons tonight, Luce," Roz told her, "but after they must be laid away until next month. The yellow were to last all through June, and only then might you wear the red. So 'tis just this once. Do you understand?"

"Aye, sister," the little wench whispered meekly, having got her way. "But could I not wear them on Sunday as well?"

"No, you may not." Roz touched the child's nose with one fingertip in a teasing gesture, but accompanied it with a firm glance. "And tomorrow, you will do an extra figure on your sampler to earn the privilege of wearing the new ribbons tonight."

"Extra!" moaned Lucina, puckering up to cry. " 'Tis uncommon cruel."

But Rozalinde was not fooled. "It's a fair exchange," she admonished. Lucina sat docilely as the nurse came in with the red ribbons and Roz tied up the child's glossy hair. "Where," she asked of Margery as she worked, "is Angel?"

"I did dress 'er earlier, as I told 'e," said Margery, who had gotten Matthew into his stocks and fastened his garters. "I sent her down to see Cook. For a tidbit or two."

"Then pray she has stayed out of mischief." Rozalinde finished Lucina's ribbons and prepared to leave the room. She had to check the kitchens before she might sit down to dine. The house servants had fought unceasingly with the hired caterers ever since they'd arrived. 'Twould be a wonder if they didn't come to blows. And her mother was having a hard time keeping her father off his feet, making him rest. His color was bad these days. She would definitely have to hurry.

She had just let Luce up and turned for the door when three-year-old Angelica toddled in and stood in the entry, grinning from ear to ear. The nurse let out a shriek of dismay. Margery just stood and stared, her mouth hanging wide. Angelica had a jam spoon in one hand, which she waved at everyone in greeting. And the entire front of her best kirtle was stained the bright purple of plums.

Rozalinde let out an audible groan. Everyone in the room was eyeing her, as usual, waiting to see what she would do. Well, there was no help for it. Briskly she took her sister in hand. "Angel, you were to stay out of mischief, but here you are in trouble again. How did this come about?"

"Jam did it," insisted the diminutive lass, toddling willingly after Rozalinde.

"But now I shall have to wash you," Roz protested, entering her own chamber and wetting a cloth at the ewer. "Did you ever stop to think of the mess? I'll never understand how you are always in trouble. Do you go looking for it?"

"It looks for me."

Roz bent over to mop her sister's hands, shielding her face to hide her smile. Her second one that day, it surprised her.

"Rosie wroth?" Angelica lisped, coaxing with the pet name she had used when younger because she could not get her mouth around *Rozalinde.*

Roz shivered as she heard it, instantly reminded of the stranger in the shop who had called her Rose. "No, dear," she told her, straightening up and kissing her sister's soft cheek. "I was only thinking about nicknames."

"What about them?"

Roz shook her head soberly, willing herself to forget the stranger. "Nothing," she said gently, leading her sister from the room. "Nothing at all. I was only wondering how it happened we were mad enough to nickname you Angel."

Chapter 3

It was nigh on two of the clock before Rozalinde had cleaned up the mess and redressed Angelica, then admonished all the kitchen staff several times over about gossiping, especially on the subject of pirates.

Everyone was worse than usual, it seemed, whispering in corners about the Sea Beggars. But finally things seemed in order, and Roz entered the dining parlor to kneel before her father. Master Henry Cavandish, in his high-backed carved chair, murmured a blessing in his old-fashioned manner, then gestured for Jonathan to follow with the others, bidding them take their places at table.

Roz slid into her seat on the bench and looked solemnly at her trencher during the lengthy prayer, hoping to avoid discussion about the lace, but she had no luck.

"You were long in the shop, daughter. I trust the lace was brought from the storehouse, as required." Smoothing his long gown over his paunch, her father gave her a fond look.

Roz lowered her eyes, thinking. It was no use upsetting him. "Your pardon, Papa. A customer came and I forgot the time. The lace has been ... taken care of. You needn't give it another thought."

"Taken care of? How's that?" Joan Cavandish spoke for the first time, her chubby face distressed beneath her neatly starched coif. "Mercy on us, did those boys do as they're told? Your father pays ever so much for those 'prentices and they're always shirking. If we still lived in London, it would be the worse for them ..." Her speech trailed off as if she'd forgotten the apprentices. She was too busy shaking her finger at Angelica who squirmed on the bench. She had just turned back to Roz when Angelica's soup

spilled, staining her clothes for a second time that day. It
dripped thickly over the tablecloth and floor.

Just in time, Roz thought, thankful for the diversion.
While she and her mother were busy cleaning up, Jonathan
kicked Matthew under the table till he shouted, Charles
pulled Lucina's hair so that she threw her bread at him,
and their father stood up and roared. "Matthew, Jonathan,
enough of this. Charles! Lucina! I should banish you all
back to the nursery. A man can't even sit at table and
enjoy his food." He waved with irritation for the footman.
"Fetch the nurse, straight."

When the youngest had been removed for yet another
change of clothing and all was quiet again, the subject of
the shop was replaced by other business.

"Rozalinde, dear," her mother began earnestly, "you
know why we're giving tonight's revel?"

Roz instantly put on a disinterested expression and became absorbed in her soup. Usually she would look forward
to such a party with food, dancing, and players. But not
tonight.

"Please, daughter," her mother pleaded. "We have chosen several eligible men for you to consider. We would like
you to look them over . . . perhaps accept one."

"I am needed here by you and Papa." Rozalinde put
down her spoon decidedly. "Surely you do not wish me to
go. You've never urged me to wed."

"You're good as gold to us, child. How I would get on
without you, I don't know. But, well, there are reasons you
should wed. Your father can explain them." Her mother
stopped, cleared her throat, and looked uncomfortably at
her husband.

"Mmm. The mutton is excellent tonight." Her father
wiped his chin with his linen napkin and averted his eyes,
also looking uncomfortable. "Tell her, my dear."

"Oh." Her mother was suddenly crestfallen. "There's yet
another prospect." She paused, biting her lower lip. "You'll
never guess who it is."

"Who?" Rozalinde warily examined the orange she
peeled.

"George Trenchard. The chief alderman of our town."

Instantly the orange was abandoned. "Trenchard!" Her

eyes widened with disbelief. "You jest, Mama. He must be nigh on thirty, and he's only just buried his wife."

"Indeed, indeed." Her mother tried to make light of the subject, though she squirmed anxiously on the bench. "But he's mourned a full year and now he thinks to seek another. A young woman, mayhap, who can give him sons."

"I don't want a husband. I prefer to stay single," Roz said decisively, shaking her head.

"My stars, my stars," her mother wrung her hands. "It's better you wed, and he is the chief alderman. Not as highly placed as your father, of course, who is a London master merchant and one of the Company of Merchant Adventurers—"

"*Was* a London merchant," her father insisted glumly. "Was."

"Well, 'tis naught," her mother went on with forced blitheness, "that we bide here awhile so your father can benefit from the sea air. And you could do worse than Master Trenchard. His butcher shop is earning gold in piles, I hear, what with his supplying the London market. And he cuts a handsome figure, 'tis sure. The lasses like him well."

"There's another the lasses like well." Her father looked up, stroking his long gray beard. "Who is he? The one at the castle. What do they call him?"

"Christopher Howard?" Roz's mother frowned. "He's the new Earl of Wynford, come to inherit since his brother died. But he's not to be considered for our Rozalinde." She turned back to her daughter and shook her ever-busy finger at her. "No, indeed. He'll be high and mighty like his brother was, not mixing with us common folk because he's an earl, treating us like dirt under his feet. You'll see. Best listen to your father and look to one of these other boys. If you don't fancy Trenchard," she stopped as her husband gave her a warning look, "take one of the others. Do, Rozalinde. This earl—your father only invited him out of courtesy, him and the dowager countess. Everyone else is invited, so 'twas only right."

"True." Her father nodded gloomily in agreement. "You must listen to your mother, Rozalinde. I have applied for my coat of arms, and if it's granted we'll be gentry—"

"Even so we'll be upstart merchants in his eyes, like as not," her mother cut in. "His brother was ever high and mighty, him and his lady." She sniffed at the thought of past slights from the Howards. "Why, it's said the new earl spoils her, buying her all manner of gifts."

Rozalinde had been listening carefully to all this. "This new earl, he buys the dowager countess presents?"

"Indeed," snorted her mother. "So I hear."

"He must be the one who bought the lace," Roz said without thinking, "even though it was ruined—"

"Ruined?" Her father sat up in his chair. "The lace was ruined? How's that?"

"Oh, 'twas n-nothing, Papa," Rozalinde stammered. "Just a little water."

But her father's countenance had darkened. "The whole crate of Flemish lace, that expensive stuff from Antwerp? Ruined you say? The whole thing?"

"Do not concern yourself, Papa." Desperately she strove to placate him. "It has been sold—"

But her father leaped from his chair and slammed his fist on the table. "That no-good, cony-catching, puling whoreson of a sea captain. He's ruined another cargo, hasn't he? I knew he would. Knew even before I saw the goods. Irresponsible devil, destroying one load after another, no matter how many times I tell him it's got to stop. What does he do? Drill holes and let the water in? Toss 'em off the longboat on the way from the quay?"

Roz jumped to her feet and rushed to her father's side. If he got angry, he might have one of his spells. "Please, Papa, sit down. You must not let this upset you. I'll speak to the captain. I'll see to the lace. A whole crate's been sold, and he promised to see about a buyer for the other crates."

The rest of the family sat staring at both of them. No one save Roz dared approach the master when he was angry. And there was no question he was getting angrier still.

"You'll not speak to him!" he roared, flinging down his napkin and trampling it underfoot. "It's my place and I'll speak to him. In fact, I'll do more than speak. I'll have his head, that's what. I won't put up with this another moment. Nine shipments he's ruined. I've never had losses like this. It's getting so bad, there's only so much a man can take—"

Roz jumped as her father stopped in midsentence,

swayed, and reached out to grip his chair. His face, previously red from his anger, now turned an unnatural shade of gray.

"Henry, Henry, are you ill?" Joan ran to his side, caught his one arm while Rozalinde grasped the other. Together they supported his sagging form to his chair. Margery hurried in from the passage and herded the younger children out.

Bending over him, Joan loosened his collar button, fanning him with her handkerchief. He leaned back his head, eyes closed. "Speak to me, Henry, speak. Can you get your breath, dear? Are you all right?"

"Aye," he managed to pant, opening his eyes, giving them a wan nod. "A moment of dizziness overcame me. I could do with some water, please, my dear."

Joan rushed away.

"Come here, my child." Her father motioned weakly to Rozalinde, as if he'd only been waiting for his wife to be gone. She hurriedly knelt by his chair. "Help me, daughter. You must help." His voice was barely a whisper.

"I shall, Papa, I promise I'll not leave you." Taking his hand, she held it against her cheek as she struggled against the tears.

"No." He shook his head, able to manage only the barest movement. "It's not what you think. I've asked too much of you these last years. Ever since we moved from London, I've let you manage too much. It was my mistake, but I trust you so. Now my time grows short. Promise me you will consider Master Trenchard . . ." His voice tapered off.

Rozalinde couldn't believe her ears. "You can't want me to marry him," she cried, aghast. "He's much older than I—"

"I am much older than your mother," her father said firmly in something like his normal tone. "Twenty years older, and we have suited well. Love can take a while to come."

She looked at him in anguish, realizing he meant what he said. "But why, Papa? Why? You've been ever happy to have me at home. You've never pressed me to wed. What has made you change your mind?"

Her father evaded her gaze. "I know you don't want to marry, Rozalinde. You're so independent, so good at managing things. And I've let you—nay, I've encouraged you to take over the business in my stead." He gave a dismal groan. "Blast, but it's my fault really, treating you the way I have. Now you're too willful ever to obey a husband—not the way most men would expect. I delayed making a decision for this very reason."

Tears gathered in her eyes at his words. Roz couldn't stop them. Angrily she wiped them away before they could run down her cheeks. "I couldn't obey some strange man, Papa. I wouldn't! Not if he had such foolish ideas as all those ... those buffoons who offered for me in London. Not one of them knew a thing about the business, and when I quizzed them about it, they gave answers that were all wrong. Please, Papa," she pleaded, "I would far rather stay here."

A shadow of anguish flickered across his face as she spoke. She knew her words pained him. She had always been his favorite child; she had adored him from the time she could toddle. A sob gathered in her throat, but she refused to let it out. Its pressure tightened like a cramp. If only she could throw herself into his arms as she had when she was small and had been frightened. But it wouldn't solve the terrible troubles of their business. As if guessing her thoughts, he reached out, gently smoothed her hair with his big, wrinkled hand.

"I know you will hate leaving home, Rozalinde. I confess I hate to let you go." His gaze was tender and full of pain. "If I thought you loved him, it would be easier for me."

"I don't love him, Papa."

"I know, I know." He stroked her hair again, his voice gruff. "But we have to face facts. The problems of the business grow too great for even you to handle. Nay." He shook his head, dropped his hand away as she began a protest. "I mean it as no criticism. But we need a strong man to take over—someone who can stop this ruin." His head drooped wearily. "Then there are the practical problems of my will. I can't pass the business to you, you're not yet one and twenty. Even if you were, only widows are expected to own things in their own right. Either way, it would be difficult. Men would try to cheat you. You would be so vulnerable. No, I've made up my mind. I must appoint a man in my will and I'm going to do it—someone who can be legal guardian to your brothers and sisters and can manage our interests until Jon comes of age. I've considered the possibilities, and Trenchard seems right. He'll take care of you and put the business back together."

"He might not have me," Rozalinde began hopefully.

But her father cut her off, shifting in his seat, a tired expression on his pale face. "I have every reason to expect he would. Despite your strong will. And your temper," he added, shooting her a stern gaze. "I've appraised him carefully and he seems to have the qualities we require. He's strong, capable, he's rising quickly in the town and holds a great deal of power. Everyone turns to him for advice and information. You do yourself. And he has shown you marked attention since we moved to West Lulworth. If we can't find a man you care for, at least let us take one who cares for you."

"But will he care for our *business*, Papa. Never mind me. I cannot think—"

"As your husband, it would be in his best interest to do well by the business. Come now, Rozalinde, you must think of your mother. If I died tomorrow, she would have no one to care for her. A woman alone with six children, not to mention another on the way—"

Roz's mother came back into the room. Overhearing, she put down her jug of water and set up a wail. "Oh, do not talk of dying, Henry! Aren't things bad enough? Rozalinde, Rozalinde, you put me beside myself, always wanting to do things your way. This time you must obey us and set our minds at ease." She burst into tears.

Roz looked at her father in anguish. The words he said were sensible. But, oh, it hurt to hear them. Yet inside she'd known this was coming. Every day, as his health worsened, she was haunted by the specter of the troubles he described. He could die at any moment, leaving them unprotected. The idea was so frightening, it didn't bear thinking. Much worse than marrying, although marrying meant letting some strange man relegate her to the kitchens and the nursery.

Gently she helped her father drink the water, then sponged his face with a wet napkin, unable to chase the painful thoughts from her mind. She must do something to solve the problem before the family's living disintegrated.

These people in her life, father and mother, younger siblings who depended on her—they were so dear to her. She would lay down her life for them if necessary.

But of course it wasn't. All she had to do was marry her father's choice. And repellent as the idea was to her, she gritted her teeth and steeled herself for the evening ahead.

Chapter 4

Dozens of candles burned in silver sconces that night, making the great chamber of the Cavandish house blaze with light. In the adjoining dining parlor Rozalinde sat with her mother, watching the guests lining both sides of the long table, their laughter rippling in bright cacophony around her. The many delicacies she had labored to create had made a brilliant entrance earlier, borne by the hired yeomen of the table—a swan done up in its green and blue plumage, a roast pig browned and succulent with an apple in its mouth, a cherry pasty as big as a cart wheel. In the space of a few minutes the table groaned with an abundance of food. In equally short order the edibles dwindled, consumed by their ravenous guests.

Gazing into the high-ceilinged hall next door, Rozalinde toyed with her dish of custard. The heat had grown in both rooms when the dancing started. Those who were done eating and didn't care to dance ranged along the wall, clapping and singing to the tune of the three-stringed rebec, pipes, and crumhorns. Couples perspired on the dance floor, laughing and capering their way through a galliard. The evening was a success. Everyone, it appeared, was having a wonderful time.

"My thanks, but I cannot possibly eat more." Rozalinde shook her head as politely as possible at her mother, who urged her to take more of the fruit pasty offered by the yeoman.

"You've hardly touched your food tonight." Her mother helped herself to a large piece, licked her fingers as she placed it on her trencher. The sight of the thick red syrup dripping from the knife made Rozalinde's stomach shift uneasily.

Unable to sit still any longer, Rozalinde jumped up,

bumped the table leg in her hurry. Her Venetian flagon of malmsey trembled, sloshing its contents over the rim so it wet the cloth. "I believe I will ... dance."

Two young men leaped to their feet.

"I will partner you, gracious mistress ..."

"I would be proud ..."

Embarrassed to have spoken in tandem, the two stopped and eyed each other. Rozalinde paid them no heed. Someone else had risen deliberately and the chatter in the parlor dropped to a murmur as the most influential man in West Lulworth, George Trenchard, planted his substantial figure before his host's daughter.

"Permit me, Mistress Rozalinde."

His bow was correct, his expression neutral. She blinked at him, surprised as always by the easy way he carried himself, completely at odds with the size of his lumbering frame. Her gaze rose to scan his face, taking in the way his thick, dark hair lay straight across his forehead like a schoolboy's. But there was nothing boyish about the face below. The broad, flat cheekbones sloped to a massive, square jaw, held in such a way as to denote stubbornness at worst, a firm will at best. Meeting his gray-green eyes, she assessed them. They were quick and alert, also at odds with his size.

But his looks didn't matter. He was solid and capable, and that was what was required. Stretching out her hand, she placed it on the arm he offered. The heat of his skin rose to her fingertips, startlingly real through the rich brocade of his sleeve.

"I have waited patiently for this moment," he said softly, so that only she could hear.

Rozalinde's gaze slid away, ranged around the room. A hush had fallen over the guests and every eye seemed to bore into her. She continued her search until she found her father gracing the head of the long dining table. Her gaze locked with his. With an almost imperceptible movement of his head, he nodded.

Roz's heart contracted sharply. She turned away. It was decided, then—what she must do to save her family's livelihood. Without a word, she tightened her grip on Trenchard's arm. They moved in the direction of the dance floor.

They joined the others in the pavane. As the stately

music began, Roz looked down at her hand where it disappeared into Trenchard's huge fist and felt a twinge of rising panic. She fought it down firmly. It made her angry, that she found her duty distasteful when she had always loved the tasks given by her father. "We're supposed to be conversing," she said to Trenchard. "You begin."

"That's an odd way of putting it." Trenchard's features, florid from the heat of the dance floor, were set in an inscrutable expression as he led her down the length of the room. "I should hope you want to converse with me."

"Yes, yes," Roz said impatiently. "But you choose the topic. I can't just now."

He glanced at her swiftly, a shrewd, appraising look in his eyes. "A topic of discourse for the lady. Very well, we'll speak of business."

Roz let out her breath in a long sigh. The Lord was merciful. Trenchard had chosen the one topic that could divert her. She nodded her assent.

"What would you hear?" He loosed her hand so they could execute a turn. They completed their circuits and he recaptured her hand. "Prices in Antwerp, or the latest news about Italian silks."

"Oh, prices in Antwerp," she urged.

He smiled, showing a row of fine teeth in a generously cut mouth. "I am pleased I can amuse you."

"Oh, it's more than amusement," Roz assured him, wondering why those teeth bothered her, along with other things about his person. "I must decide what to buy for our next shipment."

Trenchard's face grew solemn. "Are you in some kind of trouble, Rozalinde? I have asked you before. You can confide in me."

She shook her head staunchly. "Just tell me what is selling well."

Trenchard was silent for a few minutes, concentrating on the dance. "Sugar is doing well," he said finally as he passed directly behind her in one of the movements. "You cannot go wrong with sugar. Prices are solid in Antwerp, not fluctuating as in other cities."

"Then Antwerp is still the best place to trade?"

"Unquestionably."

"Sugar, then." Rozalinde relaxed slightly at his assurance, then began the tally in her head. How many chests could they carry? If she dismissed the present captain, she could hire a larger ship and transport a huge cargo. Gratefully she plunged into the refuge of numbers.

"I know something sweeter to me than such cargo," Trenchard whispered, his voice gone husky as he completed a step that brought them face to face. "Allow me to tell you of it."

"Not just now." Rozalinde concentrated as hard as she could on the numbers. Her wandering gaze fell upon a thin line of dirt under the nails of his left hand. Quickly she averted her face. She must not look at him, or she would fail to do what she must. "Sugar seems promising. What else sells well? Meat? I hear butchers do well."

"*I* do exceedingly well," Trenchard corrected her, abandoning his intimate tone. "Other butchers don't have the knack I do. Rozalinde." A trace of exasperation edged his voice. "I am trying to speak to you of a serious subject."

Rozalinde leaned over to catch up her kirtle skirts for the next movement. "So am I. Please tell me of this other product. You said there was one more."

She heard Trenchard exhale harshly. "Wool," he barked at the back of her head as he circled her. "Its price has risen to an unprecedented level this summer in anticipation of a harsh winter." He returned to face her, executed the bow required, then recaptured her hand. "You can purchase and have it woven cheaply in Wiltshire, then ship it out by way of London. Stock heavily and ship as soon as possible. You will make a pretty profit."

"Stock heavily and ship soon," Roz repeated, half to herself, absorbing the information. "Yes, I'll do that. I hope 'twill be in time."

"You are foolish not to confide in me," he stated as they again moved forward to the music. "You don't seem to realize I can help."

"You already have. Wool will be just the thing." Roz narrowed her eyes speculatively as she ran another mental column of figures. The final tally formed in her mind, vast and comforting. Yes, wool was the right choice.

"You've had another shipment ruined."

Roz stopped short on the dance floor, startled by his bald

statement. Her head whipped around. "Your pardon?" Her voice was cold as she raised her chin haughtily.

"Admit it, Rozalinde. You and your father have tried to hide it. And I have kept silent out of respect for your family's reputation. We must not have business failures ruining your everyday custom. But I know about your losses, all eight of them. And this one makes nine. How much was it this time?"

His words vibrated in Roz's ears as she assessed him. Who had told him? she wondered bitterly. The captain? Mayhap the apprentices? Defiantly she returned his stare, noting how his sharp little eyes watched her—those eyes that saw everything. "I did not say—"

Trenchard snorted impatiently. "Enough dissembling." He grasped her hand, drew her back into the procession. "I know everything that happens in West Lulworth."

Displeasure surged through Rozalinde. This was private family business—hers and her father's. But if she wed with George, she would be forced to share it. She wanted to pull her hand away and leave him on the dance floor. With great effort she managed to suppress the impulse. "There's nothing to confess," she said coolly. "We will earn back our investment on this trip. I found a buyer for one of the crates of lace and a promise to help sell the rest."

"A buyer?" A flicker of surprise lighted Trenchard's gray-green eyes. "For ruined goods? Who in West Lulworth can afford such a thing?"

"I don't know." Roz slowed in the dance. She didn't want to tell George about the man in the shop. Besides, she thought defiantly, in a way she spoke the truth. She knew nothing about him other than his name. "He said he would send someone for the crate."

"He won't." Trenchard dismissed the idea with a bored shrug. "Probably a knave and a swindler, telling you a tale because of your pretty face."

Doubt chilled Rozalinde's blood.

"You must guard against such men, my sweet. He didn't attempt to take liberties, did he? In exchange for his offer?"

"Of course not!" Roz felt suddenly, irrationally furious with him—more furious than she'd been at having to dance with him. Heat rushed to her face.

"I am glad to hear it," Trenchard went on dryly, leading

her on through the dance, not letting her tarry. "I would
be distressed to hear of some rogue disturbing your peace
of mind. I should have to challenge him."

Roz inadvertently scanned his huge bulk, unable to
stop herself.

He noticed. A scowl darkened his face as he led her in
a circle with the rest of the couples. "I am excellent with
a rapier. Don't encourage this man so I have to prove it."

The dance separated them. The men went to one side of
the floor; women, to the other. The men executed their
steps, dancing to impress their partners, like the peacock
for which the pavane was named.

George had been studying with a fencing master, Roz
decided, able to examine him now that he was somewhat
removed. He didn't have the rank to wear a rapier on the
street, but he could still learn to use one. It also explained
why he moved so lightly, his big-boned form seemingly all
muscle—firm, impenetrable.

The woman next to her jostled Rozalinde, murmured an
apology. With irritation Roz glanced at the other females
in her row, noted how they all watched George, particularly
the unmarried girls. The married ones stole covert glances
at him. He was far from the most handsome man in the
group, but he was unquestionably their leader.

She was thoroughly aggravated by the time the dance
rejoined them. This must end soon, for she was running
short on tolerance. "There will be no duels," she said firmly
to George.

"Then that rogue better not come near you."

"He has to come near me, to pay for the lace."

"As I have said before, no one buys ruined lace."

Outrage erupted inside Rozalinde. "Are you saying I'm
a poor judge of character? I think I am experienced enough
to know when a customer tells the truth."

Trenchard gave her a reproving stare. "You seem on
edge tonight, Rozalinde. Are you unwell?"

Roz jerked her hand away. "This will never work."
Abruptly she whirled around and left the dance floor.

She retreated behind the screens at the end of the hall.
Here the light was dim, the air less stifling. Stopping just
inside the screens' passage, Roz leaned against the wall,
feeling the cool plaster against her right temple. Her anger

fell away. Despondently, she noted that George had followed, was standing at her elbow. "My father said I should consider you as a suitor," she said to the wall. "He thinks you the best choice. But I'm not sure I can marry anyone."

Trenchard put his hand on her shoulder. She could feel the heat of his short, thick fingers, splayed wide. He sighed deeply. "You *are* lacking in subtlety, Rozalinde. I've debated whether this was a good thing or bad." He sighed again when she didn't answer. "But you are also determined when you want something." He paused. "In that we are alike. We could go far together. I am situated to rise in life, Rozalinde. I can offer you much."

"You wanted to speak of love."

"I don't recall mentioning the word."

It was true, he hadn't. He also hadn't touched her the whole time, except for his hand on her shoulder, and it seemed impersonal, now, despite its heat. Roz breathed steadily, trying to keep her composure. "I don't expect love."

He was silent for a minute. "Then let us make a bargain," he said at last. "I can solve your problems with your business. If you will agree to wed with me, I will do it forthwith. I will care for you and your family and see you lack for nothing."

She turned around slowly, feeling a small measure of relief. "Papa said you would."

"He is a sensible man, your father." Trenchard nodded gravely. "He and I see eye to eye—I believe in the importance of caring for family. And we are much alike, Rozalinde, you and I. I admire you for your reason, your sensible approach to things. We will rub along well together, in my rise to prominence in this town and beyond. Come now, say you agree."

He towered over her, large and imposing, and she looked desperately at the wall again. It seemed reasonable. He offered the solution she needed. Why did she hesitate? "I-I agree."

"Then I shall announce our wedding date tonight, here at the revel." He smile broadly.

Roz felt a tightness in her chest, cutting off her breath. This was what the family needed. But her heart pained her so, beating so hard she thought it would rupture her chest.

"No," she burst out, unable to stop herself. "Do not announce it yet. I agree," she went on hastily. "We will ... do just as you say. We will wed. But let us have a private betrothal. Then we can decide the marriage date. And no public announcement. Please, not tonight." A terrible sinking feeling roiled in her stomach.

"Agreed. The betrothal immediately, the wedding date to be set later. It will be an excellent arrangement, I promise. Come, let us seal our agreement with a kiss."

"I-I ..." She didn't want to kiss him. She'd never kissed a man before, never wanted to except perhaps in the shop this morning. Troth, she thought angrily at herself, if she could want to kiss a perfect stranger, she could kiss this man. She at least knew him. Turning to Trenchard, she put up her face determinedly.

He placed one hand on each of her shoulders, leaned close. The heat of his touch burned into her bones. Suddenly the intense odor of his hair pomade swept over her, making bile rise in her throat.

Trenchard came closer and closer, until his face went out of focus. She closed her eyes and clenched her fists. His lips brushed hers, then drew away.

And she felt ... nothing.

Relief washed over her. It was done and he would go away now. That was how it would be between them—emotionless, businesslike. She felt like collapsing as he stepped back. Her mind and body were drained.

"Would you care for refreshment? Perhaps some wine?"

"No, no," she assured him. "I'll wait here while the musicians take their rest." She leaned her back against the cool plaster wall. "I will speak to you anon."

He bowed correctly and left her. As he disappeared beyond the screens, she finally let out her breath.

"Any progress?" Trenchard's dark-complected steward, Paul Sutton, greeted him at the door to the dining parlor, his wide mouth drawn back into a grimace that was supposed to be a grin. He seemed nervous, for he shifted his weight constantly back and forth, from one foot to the other. Much smaller than Trenchard, he had the same light way of moving, suggesting a wiry agility and strength compared to Trenchard's brawn.

Trenchard scowled fiercely at the flagon he'd just drunk from, thrust it back at his steward. "This ale you gave me is terrible. Take it away."

Sutton took the wooden flagon, handed Trenchard another flagon of crystal. "Your pardon, sir. 'Twas a new preparation. The brewer insisted I ask you to try it."

"And you complied, for a small sum." Trenchard gave Sutton a scornful look as he took the new glass of wine and quaffed it. "Everyone has their price," he muttered. He allowed his gaze to rest on Rozalinde where she stood alone by the back screen.

Sutton's gaze followed his. "And what is the price for Mistress Cavandish?"

Trenchard narrowed his eyes. "I think I have discovered it."

"Hah, which means you have gotten nowhere." The servant lowered his voice as a lady squeezed past him on the arm of a gentleman. "I tell you, you are being fainthearted about this. You have succeeded in business for nigh on eleven years since your father died, and for the first time you hold back from something you want." He wrinkled his face, which was scarred by small pox, into a sneer. "You hesitate over a girl who is as hard and stubborn as ... as this flagon." He snapped the wooden vessel he held with one finger.

Trenchard eyed him coolly over the rim of his flagon. He took another swallow of wine. "About your choice of words, Sutton—" He raised his eyebrows warningly. "Temper them. You tend to forget your birth."

The reprimand had the desired effect. Sutton's face turned a dangerous shade of red. "I do not take kindly to your bringing my mother into this. She was an honest woman, hardworking. Just because my father failed to wed her before I was—"

"Enough." Trenchard's tone switched from cool to glacial. He turned a bored shoulder on his servant and regarded the crowd. "You forget your place from time to time and it offends me. If you will concentrate on your task of aiding me in my goals, you will be rewarded."

Sutton muttered something under his breath.

"What was that?" Trenchard asked sharply, twisting his head to look around.

"I said," Sutton made an angry noise in his throat, "I still don't understand what you see in her. I'll grant you she's got a face and figure ... but there's no welcome in her."

Trenchard's gaze flicked back to Rozalinde. He studied her carefully. "She doesn't flirt and simper like the other girls in Lulworth, if that's what you mean. Or those in London, for that matter. But I say she is capable of anything I could ask of her. She's well-bred, industrious, clever in business, loyal to her family. I've considered many others, but they were flighty things, thinking of nothing but gifts and gowns and how many they could get of each in exchange for their bodies. No, I prefer Rozalinde Cavandish just as she is. She will serve me well in any position I should require of her."

Sutton snickered at the double meaning in his master's words. "She's rich, that's what I'd say you like about her. You've been acting like a man obsessed in the last year, skulking about town on the chance you'll meet her, following her everywhere, visiting her father's house and shop."

This time Trenchard took no notice of his servant's impertinence. He went on calmly. "I've learned to know her in this last year. She must be approached with consideration and helped to understand the benefits I offer her and her family. Tonight we passed the first hurdle."

"You mean ... ?" Sutton began.

"We will be betrothed." Trenchard paused to read his servant's face, noted with displeasure the surprise. "If you thought she would refuse me, you underestimate me, sirrah."

" 'Tis not that." Sutton's sullen expression had vanished. "But being from a long-standing London merchant family, she outranks you socially."

"In birth, perhaps," Trenchard replied, letting his gaze return to Rozalinde. "But not in position. Not anymore."

Sutton's mouth broadened into a wide grin that did nothing to improve his ugly countenance. "You got the appointment! At last! Deputy lieutenant of Dorset, under the direct authority of Sir Christopher Hatton, himself." He started to turn.

"Stop." Trenchard arrested him with the single word. He knew where Sutton was going—to blab the news to everyone. He didn't want that until he'd told the mayor and other aldermen. "I have a task for you," he told his steward. "A message to deliver."

"To whom?" Sutton halted again, his eyes turned curious.

"The Spanish ambassador in London. I want you to leave directly. Take him that leather wallet sitting on my desk. The letter is inside, addressed and sealed, I might add. Here is his direction in London."

Sutton took the small piece of paper. "What business do you have with him?"

Trenchard examined Sutton carefully before answering. "Official government business. The Queen's Privy Council wishes me to join with the other southern counties to keep the English Channel safe for Spanish shipping."

At that, Sutton's face took on an even more respectful expression.

Trenchard laughed indulgently. "There will be work aplenty for you, now that I have the commission. And plenty of extra payments from supplicants to the crown, in exchange for my words of intervention with Her Majesty and her council."

"We've waited long for this. Shall I tell the others at the house?"

"You may," Trenchard said, knowing Sutton would do so, with or without permission. "But no one else. I will inform the mayor and the other aldermen first. They will appreciate the honor. As for those in my household, anyone who spills it will suffer."

Sutton grinned. "No fear it will go beyond."

Trenchard eyed him grimly. "Discretion first."

Sutton nodded, then slipped away into the crowded dining parlor and disappeared.

Trenchard stood for several moments, finishing his wine and searching the crowd for Rozalinde. She'd left her place by the screen. He shifted his gaze with irritation, looking for her. As he took another swallow of wine, he happened to glance down. His fingernails still had dirt under them. Angrily he whipped out his dagger and pared it away, hoping no one had noticed. Rozalinde would be somewhere nearby. He would find her.

*   *   *

Rozalinde longed to speak to her father. To tell him she'd done what he wanted, to receive his praise. But he was busy. She could see him in the dining parlor, sitting next to a fat dowager who plied a fan to cool her plump cheeks, all the while talking voraciously. Roz knew the woman. It would be impossible to interrupt her.

Trenchard was the other difficulty. He stood at the entry to the dining parlor, blocking the path to her father. She didn't want to encounter him again. The thought made her giddy. With an effort, she searched for something stable in the maelstrom of changing winds. Her eye lit upon her brother, lounging by. With a sigh she hurried after him.

"Jon, walk with me."

Jon crooked his arm to accommodate her hand and gave her his usual, nonchalant grin. "I see you have quitted the company of good Master Trenchard. Everyone is whispering about you and the alderman. Does he regale you with stories of pork sides and beef joints?"

But Jon's mirthful expression changed, became serious as he perceived Rozalinde's sober look. "What is it, Roz? What's wrong?"

"I've made a decision, Jon. I'm going to wed."

"With him?" Jon shook his head and clucked his tongue. "Everyone knows he's smitten with you, Rozalinde. But he's hardly worthy of you. He may be chief alderman, but he started as a butcher, for heaven's sake."

"There's no use arguing." Roz studied her brother's face, surprised at his unusual sympathy. "Father and I feel it will be a suitable match. He'll solve our problems with the business. And he's not smitten with me. He's not like that."

Jon scoffed. "What do you know about men? Nose stuck in your ledgers all day."

"I know he'll solve our problems. I admit I would rather not wed, but we have to be practical. What if Papa should die?"

Jon's face grew instantly grave. "I don't like to think of it. We would be in terrible trouble. But if you do wed, your husband, whoever he is, will rule the business since I am underage. We have to remember that. And I, for one, don't want Trenchard."

"Why not?" Roz looked at her brother curiously. Jon didn't usually speak so definitively.

"Well, for one thing . . ." Jon glanced about and found Trenchard standing at the entry to the dining parlor, his back turned. "For one thing, he doesn't treat his servants well."

"That's just gossip. You have no proof. He's well respected," Roz said firmly, wanting to ignore her brother. "You'll have to do better than that."

"All right." Jon took a deep breath. "I will if you promise not to tell Father. He wouldn't approve if I even hinted at such things to you."

Roz started to withdraw her hand from his arm. "If you're going to say George was untrue to his wife, I won't believe you. Papa wouldn't accept him if he'd done that."

But Jon captured her hand with his own, held it tightly, his face suddenly stern, reminding her of their father. "There are worse things a man can do to his wife than be untrue to her," he said vehemently. "Oh, he didn't beat her or abuse her. It was something more private, but I heard it from a reliable source and it appears to be true. And I say a man's habits reflect his character. I'm telling you, Rozalinde, I don't want you making this sacrifice. We must find another way."

Roz's eyebrows went up. She took another look at him. "I hardly know how to answer you, Jon. You've never talked like this before."

"We've never had problems like this before. God's heartlings, it's time for drastic measures." Jon gave her hand a firm squeeze. "If Father dies, I might be his heir, but it wouldn't make any difference. No one would consult me about the business, and you wouldn't be allowed to have a say, either."

Rozalinde shook her head worriedly, realizing he was serious. "You're right, of course. But I don't see any other alternative."

"Use your imagination," Jon chided. "You're not usually so obtuse."

"I'm not obtuse," Roz snapped, feeling her temper flare. He said such thoughtless things at times. "I refuse to listen to any more nonsense. Papa isn't going to die. Why does everyone insist he's half in his grave? Look! He's as well as anyone tonight."

They both looked toward the far dining parlor where

their father sat. Their mother sat at his side, and he smiled and jested with his neighbors, tapping his foot to the music that had turned lively and gay.

"He does look better than usual." Jon's voice assumed an unaccustomed gentleness. "You and mother prepared the revel so he could rest. He looks even better than last week."

"Of course he does," Roz insisted. But she grew silent, thinking of her agreement with Trenchard.

Jon nodded congenially. "Come now, goose, cheer up. This is a revel, after all. You'll not want to spoil it for our guests. And I have someone to show you." Peering around the pillar, he gestured across the hall. "Look who's come." He grinned broadly.

Reluctantly Roz followed his gaze. A tall lady in an elaborate black gown stood beside the lord mayor's wife, obviously dominating the conversation. In her hand, Roz could see a magnificent black feather fan.

Roz let out a low groan. "The dowager countess of Wynford. Thinks she's so grand just because she's an earl's lady."

"*Was* an earl's lady," Jon reminded her. "She's probably looking for another husband right now, which accounts for her coming out tonight." Turning to regard himself in a darkened window, Jon adjusted his doublet that was decorated with ornamental slashes.

Rozalinde stared moodily at the dowager countess. "Do you think she came alone? She should be escorted by the new earl."

"She should." Jonathan slicked down his hair. "But I hear he had business. He didn't come."

Rozalinde was silent. The sinking in her stomach renewed itself. Suddenly someone in the crowd caught her eye. "Look there." She shook her brother's arm to get his attention. "It's Margaret. I thought her mother wouldn't let her come tonight."

"Ah, where?" Jon turned around, a glad smile lighting his face.

The girl saw him, too, for she tossed her golden head and smiled his way, an engaging, provocative smile.

Roz didn't miss the exchange. "That was a 'come hither' look if ever I saw one. I suppose you may go. But don't forget you are to help clear up after. We must count the plate to be sure nothing's missing. So I want no excuses tomorrow, about falling asleep in a corner or some such trash."

"As God is my witness," Jon grinned happily. "You're such a dullard sometimes, beauteous sister, always counting things. Don't you like to have fun?" He made a face at her, trying to coax her to laugh.

Rozalinde gave him a severe look. But then let her expression soften. "Not the kind you like, but I do appreciate a rest when I've been working hard. I'm so tired."

"Go lie down if you wish it," Jon said. "You've done more than your duty today." But he seemed to forget her as he stared, entranced, at the far end of the hall. A brightly dressed man juggled a whirling mass of balls. "Look, the players have begun. I must learn how he does that." He looked distractedly back and forth between Margaret and the performer, as if unsure which intrigued him more. "Whatever you do, be sure to come back for the play, sister. It's going to be exceeding fine. Complete with battles."

"I will," Roz promised halfheartedly, watching the crowd assemble for the players, knowing Trenchard would be among them.

"Then wish me luck. Do I look well enough?"

Margaret had apparently won out. Roz gave him a critical look. "I won't wish you luck. Not the kind you want. I'll wish you a chaste kiss and no more. Straighten your falling band."

Jon righted the lace at his throat, gave her a peck on the cheek, then slid away through the crowd in pursuit of his maid.

After he'd gone, Roz continued to lean against the wall, thinking. The things Jon had said bothered her. Normally she didn't listen to him—he was often such a lackwit. And he'd called her obtuse, something she didn't appreciate. But his words hung in her memory, suspended on the strength of her fear: *I don't want you making this sacrifice.*

She could stay at the revel no longer. Everywhere she looked, there was either one of her suitors, or her mother or father. And at the far end of the hall, there was Trenchard. She must have time to think, to review her earlier decision.

Quietly she went out the nearest door, slipped up the stairs.

"I'm so vexed with him!" shrilled a voice, just inside the chamber set aside for ladies to adjust their gowns. "I'm so vexed I could die."

"There, there, my lady," soothed another female voice, evidently a maid. "Let me arrange your hair. You will feel better in a trice."

Rozalinde stopped, her foot poised above the last step, and leaned against the carved handrail. She hadn't meant to eavesdrop, but that had to be the dowager countess of Wynford, Lady Mary Howard, and Roz couldn't help but hear.

"What a ridiculous revel this is," complained the countess. "Tumblers and jugglers, such rustic stuff."

"At least there will be a play," the maid said agreeably. "That will surely be amusing."

"Bah, you've got my cap crooked. Take your hands off." There was the sound of a cuff. "Leave it alone and straighten my ruff. 'Tis loose in the back."

Silence ensued while they worked. Then the countess raised her voice again. "I am still angry at Kit. He was to escort me, but no, he goes out instead, on a night like this. On business, he says. What business could that be? I tell you, I don't know what ails him, Annie. He's the oddest man I've ever known."

"But you knew him as a lad, did you not?" protested the maid. "And he wasn't odd then. Besides, I find him . . . most agreeable."

"I'll wager you do," came the terse answer. "And he'll keep being agreeable till he's had you to warm his bed. 'Twas the only thing on his mind when he was a lad, and I have no reason to think he's any different now. This so called 'business' of his is probably chasing after some wench. He up and goes away at the strangest hours. Out all night, he'll be, and comes home weary to death. One night, I was still up. He obviously didn't expect me, for he tried to slip away without talking to me, but not before I saw he had blood on his shirt. It was dark and dry, but I swear it was blood."

The maid made a sharp intake of breath. "Blood, madam! Do you think he's in danger for his life?"

"Maybe." Mary laughed harshly. "From some cuckolded husband, like as not."

Roz chose this moment to peek around the corner of the door, confirming her belief that it was the dowager countess she overheard. So he was called Kit, she thought, trying to deny her interest, and he went about at odd hours. But blood on his shirt? She waited silently, hoping they would go on.

"I shall certainly avoid him, madam," the maid said with conviction. "It would not do to be involved with a rogue. Nor any other gentleman," she added hastily.

"But he does have his good points," Lady Howard mused, her voice softening. "Look at this fan he bought me."

The maid admired it.

"He brings me such gifts often. I expect he knows how dreary things have been for me since Harry died. But then he leaves me alone, too. If it's not trips at night, he's away to London to see to those cursed ships of his. Though of course they've made him astonishingly rich." Her voice lowered. "His own money makes his share of Harry's estate look pitiful. I could scarce believe my eyes when he showed me his ledgers. And now that he's earl, he needn't lift a finger."

The maid oohed and ahhed over this revelation. "I'd never have thought him so well off. He doesn't dress. I'm surprised some girl hasn't snapped him up. He's not a youth."

"He's six and twenty," Lady Mary informed her. "And I hope he doesn't wed. At least not soon. I intend to stay on at Lulworth Castle as long as possible."

Roz could hear the swish of silk skirts as the lady stood. Thinking they might come out, Roz made her way quietly down the passage.

Blood on his shirt. The words repeated themselves uncomfortably in her head. She padded to her chamber and changed swiftly out of her elaborate gown and into a plain kirtle skirt and bodice. Pulling on her oldest cloak, she went back to the passage, found a side door, and slipped out into the night.

Chapter 5

The night was dismal. Roz didn't care. Once away from the trimmed gardens of her father's house, the land of Dorset was rugged and swampy. She welcomed its rough terrain tonight. Turning her face south, she made her way toward the sea.

She had to cross an area of bracken and heath first, then descend the chalk cliffs, but once on the sands of Lulworth Cove, she felt better. Here, in this magical little basin where sea had carved away stone, she vowed to puzzle through the troubles besetting her: the mystery of the ruined cargo, her promise to her father, the many unruly events of the day.

But as the moon slipped in and out of black storm clouds, her mind felt as foggy as the mist hovering over the waves. Everything was out of focus. Out of control. Where once she had firmly ordered the things in her life, now all was confusion. Never before had she doubted a decision made by her father. Nor had she doubted him earlier in urging her to marry, and Trenchard was the logical choice.

But Trenchard was somehow repellent to her, and now this vague feeling was reinforced by her normally dreamy brother. He'd spoken decisively against George tonight. More unsettling still, Jon had contradicted their father, something she would not ordinarily tolerate. Yet she had tolerated it. Because in her heart, she *wanted* to believe Jon. Still, doubting her father was foreign to her nature, and Roz found she trembled.

Pausing on the sand, she remembered the last on her list of the unruly—the man in the shop, Christopher Howard. His words, his manner of speaking, his person—everything about him intrigued her. That had never happened before, not with any man. It flung her orderly life into chaos, and she stared out to sea, longing to escape her confusion. It was then she saw the figure. A phantom shape striding across the sand, his dark cloak billowed by the wind.

Instinctively she sank to her knees behind some rocks, waiting for him to pass.

But he came straight toward her. "Who are you? What do you do here?" His voice was clipped, abrupt. Reaching out, he grasped her upper arm and hauled her from behind the rocks.

"Loose me!" she cried, struggling to break free. "This cove belongs to everyone. I have as much right here as you." A cloud drifted past and she saw by the light of the moon that he wore a mask. The thought stuck doggedly in her mind and refused to go away. Ceasing her struggle, she stared at him intently, trying to make out who he was.

It was his touch that told her. Looking down at his hand, she could see it was molded by a black leather glove cut with a wide gauntlet. And despite the glove, despite the mask, despite the dark, his anger and coldness, she recognized him. It was the Earl of Wynford.

"Maids do not walk out at midnight. Not at Lulworth Cove." He'd grown still as a statue, seemed to study her in return. "Not unless they're meeting lovers or hoping to get their throats cut. I ask you again what you do here. Say quickly and be done."

"I came to walk and be alone." She ignored his commanding tone, finding that heat flared within her. Looking down at where his gloved hand touched her, she felt his warmth permeate the material and puzzled at her reaction.

"All alone?" He seemed suspicious of her explanation. " 'Tis not a night for walking." His eyes roamed over her.

Roz tingled at his touch. Fire seemed to leap through his gloved fingers into her flesh, stoking the furnace that drove her pulses. Firmly she stuffed the feeling down. " 'Tis simple enough," she informed him. "There was a revel tonight. Everyone enjoyed themselves save me. I left to get away. It's what you would have done yourself, *milord*."

He cocked his head to one side, emitted a rough laugh. "Now how would you know who I am? Dare I guess?" His voice grew soft as he moved closer. He stripped off his gloves and clasped her shoulders with lean fingers. Bared of their covering, they seared radiant paths down her arms.

"So you recognize me, my Rose. Just like that. Though I have covered myself well." He indicated the mask, his cloak that fell to the ground. "My own seamen wouldn't recognize me, but you do. How is that? Are you a fairy? Or mayhap a witch?"

"Nonsense." Rozalinde choked out her answer, her heart beating a relentless rhythm against her ribs. Troth, she thought dimly, she must be falling sick. She felt as hot as if she were standing in the summer sun.

But it wasn't sickness. She knew it as she admired the sensual curve of his lips beneath black velvet, the glitter of his eyes through the mask. Her heart throbbed, filled her body with a strange ache as she watched the play of moonlight on his raven black hair. "You wanted me to know you," she whispered, steeling herself against her response to him. "You've come too near."

"I fear you are right, sweetling. I should have kept my distance." His voice was husky with suggestion, his arms tightened around her. "But since we *are* near, let us enjoy it. Calm yourself, Rose. You are safe with me."

Roz truly doubted that. *I would like to kiss you,* he'd said that morning. And tonight she'd learned of his reputation with women. Somewhere, in a corner of her brain, her good sense warned her, but for the first time in her life she ignored it. The exotic spice of cloves, the masculine scent of leather mingled with sea air that hung about him, both were too appealing to resist. His hair felt crisp and clean to her fingertips as she unthinkingly reached up and brushed a stray lock from his face.

As if she had requested it, he bent down and touched his mouth to hers.

Surprise leaped through Rozalinde. Her hands flew up to ward him off. Many had tried to kiss her, but first they had repelled her with clumsy avowals of love and gauche attempts to woo her. Each time she'd made sure they didn't succeed.

But this man gave no warning. And his lips . . . they were different from the others, unexpectedly tender. Her arms fell helplessly to her sides. The warmth of his mouth feathered against hers, lulling her eyelids to flutter and close. As his fingers meandered lazily down her spine to discover her waist, a host of sensations rose up inside her. Excitement at his closeness. Pleasure at his touch. They were such alien feelings, she felt astonished by how well she liked them as his lips traveled across her cheek to nuzzle her ear. From a secret place deep within her, a pulse of desire bloomed, throbbed awake and threatened to spread.

Against her better judgment, her one hand reached to his shoulder, the other came to rest against his chest. There she encountered the pleasing symmetry of his muscles, his warmth penetrating to her through the linen of his shirt. A new feeling burgeoned within her—the outrageous impulse to explore the lean body pressed against her. Without thinking, she indulged it—let her palms journey beneath his cloak.

Hard planes of muscle. Smooth contours of flesh meeting bone. The cords of his powerful arms bunched and tensed beneath her fingertips. He was beautifully made, his body in prime physical condition. Without looking she knew it, could feel it. It made her want to explore further. So intrigued was she by her discovery, she failed to notice his response.

Without warning, he pulled her hard against him. Her body collided with his, her breasts crushed against his chest. Their hips ground together, the impact startling awake a new burst of feeling deep in her belly. Again his lips sought hers—his tongue a swift messenger girded with clove, darted forward to invade her mouth. She gave a sigh of pleasure and let her head fall back against his encircling arm. Never had she liked a man's closeness, but now her heart pounded in her chest at a wild pace. His breath had quickened also. She could hear it rasp in his throat as she slid both arms around his torso, let her head tilt yet farther to accept his deepening kiss.

Then, suddenly, it was over.

He disengaged himself almost roughly, stepped back. Giving her a look over, he rearranged her cloak. "Impetuous wench," he muttered, pushing one of her sagging braids back into place. "I'm not known for my control." He still held her by one arm.

Fury reared up in Roz as she realized what he meant. "How dare you suggest ... you are as rude as ever!" She jerked herself away from him, groping for words. "Why do you insist on plaguing me? Just ... go away."

His chuckle was even more maddening. "This morning I was impolite. Now I am rude."

Rozalinde grimaced as she straightened her kirtle skirt. "That is because you go too far. Each time I see you, you do or say something indecent. You are nothing but a knave."

He shrugged nonchalantly. "You must give me a chance to redeem myself. Come, you're a charitable lass. Walk with me. Properly, along the shore. I'll not kiss you again," he added as she recoiled.

Roz hesitated, wanting inexplicably to say yes. She should not. She should return to the house, help with the revel, stand by her parents. This man was an earl, a man of the upper class. Nothing good could come of spending time in his company. But there was Trenchard to be reckoned with at home, and that thought canceled all the others. She held out one hand. "Very well." She rested her fingertips lightly on his arm, ready at his least advance to retreat.

They walked along the shingle. As she felt the crunch of stones beneath her feet, Roz decided she wouldn't look at him. It was too dangerous. She kept her eyes fixed ahead.

"This revel you attended," he began as they walked, "I see it gave you little pleasure. In fact, I think it's worse than that. You seemed agitated when I first saw you. Tell me why."

"I was not," Roz told him, flustered at the personal turn to his question. "The revel was fair enough as such things go."

Kit grinned down at her. "You *are* distressed. I can see the signs. Who has upset you, Rose?"

Roz stopped in her tracks and studied him, then removed her hand from his arm. She tossed her head to hide her consternation. One of her braids had come loose and she flung it over her shoulder. "It really is not worth mentioning."

Kit stepped forward swiftly, closing the gap between them and grasping her by one arm. "Tell me who was troubling you," he ordered. "I insist on knowing, so you'll not escape before you say."

Roz tried to shake loose, caught off guard by the anger in his voice. "You're not my kin, so why should I tell you?

Why should you even care?" But he grinned that devilish, endearing grin of his, took her in his arms, and held her tightly so that tides of weakness swept over her at his touch.

"I care a good deal when a person has difficulty in business." His callused right hand smoothed a wisp of hair away from her face. "If someone is causing you problems, I would be pleased to rid you of him." He made a careless gesture. "I assure you, 'twould be no trouble at all."

"And if he did not wish to be gotten rid of—if he fought you—wouldn't *that* be trouble?"

The earl gave his maddening chuckle again. "He wouldn't be causing trouble in the first place if he weren't capable of fighting back."

Rozalinde shook her head in confusion. "Do you always laugh in the face of danger?"

"It's better than giving in." His hands couldn't seem to stop touching—they brushed her cheek, her hair, her neck. "Come, you must tell me," he whispered. His voice had a deep, hypnotic timbre. "Who is it that destroys an entire cargo of fine lace?"

Roz frowned, thinking hard. If only she knew. "We haven't been able to tell whether it's deliberate or ... or just a series of accidents," she admitted. "And yet ..."

"And yet?"

"And yet, I thank you for your offer," she said primly, drawing away, deciding not to mention the suspect captain. "If I discover who it is and wish to be rid of him, I'll think of you."

Kit was watching her closely. Her expression was rigid and unsmiling, but when her eyes crinkled at the corners his mouth curved in a grin. "Is that the only time you'll think of me? You'll not think of how well I amuse you?"

Immediately she frowned. "You're not as amusing as you imagine."

"You thought so," he insisted, his voice as supple as kidskin. "Enough to make a jest. But I really don't wish to argue. I would prefer to serve you. When I take a cargo to the Netherlands or France, I might be able to learn something of import."

"You have your own ships?" She warmed to the subject instantly. "What do you trade, and what type of ship do you have? We hire the ships we require, though I wish we had our own. I've often asked my father, but he'll not buy even one. He says they are too expensive in upkeep. How long does it take you to sail to Antwerp? And where did your navigator train? Where was his astrolabe made, and what does he think of the shoals off—"

"Stop—" Kit held up his hands, laughing. "I cannot answer so many questions at once. Let us take them one by one. What does a lass know of astrolabes?"

"More than most people, I'll wager," she answered, bristling at his question. "I've talked to many ships' navigators and learned from them how to read a latitude and plot a course. I can do it as well as anyone," she told him, placing both hands on her hips. "I've been to Amsterdam forty times. More than that to France."

"Not of late, though." Kit eyed her with renewed interest. "The seas are unsafe."

"No, not of late." She looked suddenly downcast. "I've not sailed in two years. My father is ill. But we send wool and cotton to the Netherlands," she said, brightening, "and receive Italian silks on the return voyage. I shall go again sometime soon."

Kit looked at her slyly. "These astrolabes you've consulted," he began, "Am I to believe your father approved? That you should meet with the chief navigator and take lessons from him? Especially since the astrolabe, which measures the sun *and* stars, must also be used at night."

"Well, not always." She looked uncomfortable.

"And you went behind his back when he didn't. Tell me I'm right." Kit could see her wrinkling up her forehead as she had in the shop. "Out your window at all hours, no doubt, and slipping down to the wharves."

"Something like that," she admitted sheepishly, "when Mother was fretting and I just had to get away. It was quite safe, I promise you. Master Jenkins always saw me safely home."

"I would wager he did." Kit imagined how deeply in love this ship's master must have been. "But what of all the ciphering involved? I cannot think it an occupation chosen by a maid."

"Then you know nothing," she replied tartly. "Ciphering is an excellent occupation. *I* find it useful if people are being tiresome." Her loose braid had crept forward, and she flipped it impatiently over her shoulder again. "My brother in particular. When he has been vexing, I go work with my charts and instruments. They, at least, are reliable. After, I feel much improved."

Just as he had that morn, Kit threw back his head and laughed. But he stopped a second later, seeing her accusing face. "My apologies. Trade is serious business."

He tried again to probe gently, but she stubbornly refused to reveal more about her father's business. Obviously the man placed his trust rightly; the maid gave nothing away. Kit examined her soberly. She had mounted some rocks and balanced on one jagged peak, poised to leap to the next, her arms outstretched for balance. She clutched a corner of her cloak in each hand so it billowed behind her in the breeze like giant wings. The light from the moon shone on her hair, highlighting its rich chestnut hue, and he felt a rush of pleasure looking at it, but her frown from the morning had returned. It troubled him to see it, for well he knew the turmoil of the mind when business went awry.

Rozalinde continued her progress along the rocks, and Kit meandered slowly after her, watching while she leaped from one smooth spot on the rocks to another. Her balance was good, but she was too impetuous, taking chances she shouldn't. She'd almost missed that last leap, and if she wasn't careful, she would. . . .

Simultaneous with his thought she skipped for the next rock and missed.

Instantly Kit lunged toward her. She fell against his right shoulder, forcing him off balance. Somehow he managed to stay upright. Despite his six feet in height and considerable weight, she fell harder than he'd expected. Any other position and they both would have taken a tumble. Stumbling slightly, he wrapped one arm around her ribs beneath her billowing cloak.

Instead of thanking him, she convulsed against him with a faint scream. "Sir, loose me."

He tried, but his arm tangled in her cloak. Twisting the other way, his hand again contacted her ribs.

She wiggled and shrieked. "Stop it," she cried. "Your hand . . . you . . ." Caught in a spasm of some violent emotion, she bent over from the waist.

Kit's mouth widened in a grin as he realized she was laughing. "Ticklish little thing, aren't you."

"No!" Roz wriggled in his grasp. "Fiend from hell," she cursed as his fingers sought the place again. It was her worst tickle spot. No one had touched her there in years— not since she'd been young enough to wrestle with her brother. "Stop that. You're doing it on purpose."

But he was grinning down at her in the most outrageous fashion. He skittered his fingers insectlike, across her ribs. "I told you I would make you laugh and I did," he said, following her struggles so he could tickle her anew. "Though not in a way I expected. You should be merry more often, Rose. You have a beautiful laugh."

"I . . . you . . . insolent dog," Roz cried, laughing harder. "You really must stop . . . oh, I beg you!" Another fit of laughter convulsed her. Her sides hurt from it, and she bent over to clutch her stomach. "Loose me," she panted frantically, "please. I'll do anything you say."

"Anything? Anything at all? You swear?"

"Aye, aye, truly," Roz almost shrieked. She hadn't laughed this hard in all her life.

"Then I'll stop."

He was as good as his word. The tickling stopped, but as Roz recovered herself, she felt him link his arms around her waist. If she'd had the strength, she would have pulled away. As it was, she needed him—or she would probably have fallen down.

And it felt wonderful, standing there, locked in his embrace. What alien feelings these were, caused by the dizzying thrill of his touch. He would probably demand another kiss, would take gross advantage since she'd promised to do anything he said. A promise was a promise. But she wouldn't like it. She swore she would not.

"Your cloak is falling off." He caught it as it began to slide.

"Whose fault is that?" she said, jerking it back around her shoulders.

"Your hair is coming down."

Roz caught the loose braid, skewered it in place with a hairpin. "I'm surprised it's no worse than this. You could have simply said something clever to make me laugh."

He chuckled at the suggestion. "I don't think so. I believe in a sure thing."

"Tickling is a sure thing?"

"With you, yes. You're far too logical to laugh at a verbal sally. Besides, I have a strong preference for the physical."

"Clearly." She sniffed, pulling her cloak closer around her. "I suppose there's more of that to come. Get on with it, will you? Tell me what you want."

"Want?" he queried, touching her hair where she'd stabbed it with the pin. "What do you mean?"

"You know what I mean," she snapped, summoning her dignity. "I made you a promise. I expect you'll want a kiss or something equally coarse. But that's as far as I go, so you'll have to be content with that."

Kit didn't answer for a second. Then he broke into that maddening laugh of his. It went on and on, tantalizingly low. "You may keep your kisses," he said, leaning to whisper in her ear. "I want something different, and since you promised, you must do as I bid."

"I said I would." She felt half afraid of what he would ask. "As long as it is harmless."

"Then you must promise to laugh each day, or if not that, to smile. It's good for your soul, Rose."

She stared at him, dumbfounded, realizing he was right. He was so confusing, this man. She never knew what he would say or do next. Here he was thinking of her soul instead of kisses. She didn't know what to say.

"Promise, my Rose," he urged her. "Promise you'll laugh. Or think of me and smile. That's all I ask."

He was casting his spell again, and Roz felt herself slipping. "Why do you talk this way?" she mumbled. "You say such nonsensical things."

"Do I?" His voice was low, and he let his fingers slide down the length of one of her plaits. "As when I say you are a flower, fragrant and sweet?"

Rozalinde looked at the ground and nodded dumbly, afraid to meet his eyes.

"Or when I say your lips are the richest shade of rose?"

"Yes," she blurted out, looking at him against her wishes. "When you go on with all that trash."

"Why is it trash, my Rose? Why?"

"Well, I—because . . ." She found herself stammering,

tried to pull herself together. "Because it's a waste of time. We mean nothing to each other, so why annoy each other with such things? It's of value to no one, and there are more worthy subjects to discuss."

He put one finger under her chin and raised it tenderly, forcing her to meet his eyes. "It is hardly a waste of time for me to admire your beauty. You *are* a beauty, you know, yet you continually deny it, and I cannot think why."

"But what is the purpose?" she insisted, determined to argue. "Beauty is not useful. It doesn't feed my family, nor can it cure the sick. It cannot help my business—"

"It gives folk pleasure," he interrupted, "to gaze upon your lovely face." His hand shifted to cradle her cheek.

"Which ones?" She held his gaze uneasily, unable to look away from him. Holding her breath, she waited, in mortal terror of what he would do. Not because of him, but because of her—of how she would feel.

"This one." He leaned nearer, one hand caressing her cheek, the other encircling her waist. She looked deep into his eyes—they were a dark, stormy blue, like the waves of the Dorset sea she loved so well. Transfixed, she let this gaze engulf her, while thrills of pleasure raced up and down her spine.

The shrill cry of a gull shattered the moment. An odd thing. Gulls seldom came out at night.

Instantly Kit turned toward the water, letting her go. The unexpected move jolted her. She stared at his back, feeling bereft.

"It seems, Rose, I am called to my duties." He turned back to her. His face wore a preoccupied look. "My work awaits me. You, my dear, must hurry directly home."

"I'll not!" Roz wrinkled her brow at him, his words evoking hot fury inside her. How dare he kiss her one minute, then turn away the next. "I came here for a walk, if you recall, and I wanted it alone. You, sir, have interfered."

"I have. Forgive me." He pivoted back to her, knelt suddenly before her on the sand. "I most humbly beg your pardon."

"You should beg my pardon," she told him with a shiver, her fury cooling abruptly. "You do the most horrible things to me. Things I don't like."

Kit regarded her intently. "Perhaps I should not tempt

you with these private meetings. I'll not, if you send me away. Is that what you honestly desire? Think carefully before you answer, for it is not my wish." A faint sound of water splashing drifted in from the mist to where they stood on the darkened shore.

"I do wish it," she told him firmly, though her blood sang desperately otherwise. "I need no more trouble in my life. I have enough as it is."

"Then I shall cease to bother you." He rose swiftly, looking suddenly mysterious in the black cloak. "But before I go, I'll have your vow. You'll keep my secret. I know you will. But I'd hear it from your lips."

"Secret?" she echoed dismally, thinking only of how she was sending him away. "I'll not say a word. Not to anyone."

He studied her face thoroughly before he indicated the mask in his hand. "I never asked for this masquerade, yet it is my duty. No one else of West Lulworth knows. I place my trust in your care."

Roz gulped, wondering exactly what he meant. Clearly it was important, or he wouldn't swear her to secrecy, wouldn't want to hide the fact that he was on the shore at night, wearing a black mask, about to rendezvous with someone at sea. She felt overwhelmed by his trust. Or was it something else that overwhelmed her? "I won't tell a soul I saw you here," she whispered, reaching out to touch his face, tracing the hard angle of his cheekbone softly with her fingers. "By my troth. And I will aid you, if you have need."

"I shouldn't think that necessary. But I thank you." Clasping her hand, he pressed it for a long, fervent moment to his lips. Then he spun around and went away.

Rozalinde sat down abruptly on a stone, frozen in place as she watched his retreating back. The fog thickened, then swallowed up his form. She heard the sound of oars splashing in the water, pulling out to sea. Soon even that was gone.

Chapter 6

Christopher Howard watched the waves beat against the side of the skiff and his man heave away at the oars as they floated out to sea. Just at the mouth of the encircling cove, he discerned one faint point of light deep in the fog. It was straight toward that light they rowed.

Soon a ship reared up before them, a sleek, one-masted pinnace, its sails reefed. Kit gave the shrill cry of the gull as they approached. At his signal, a rope ladder came hurling over the side. He clambered up, vaulted over the rail, and landed with a thud on the deck of *The Raven.*

"Faith, 'tis about time. I thought you'd never come." Captain Courte Philips thrust his hand into Kit's in a hasty greeting.

Kit headed for the stern cabin, letting Courte issue orders for the first mate to take them out of the cove. When the two of them were inside, he calmly bolted the door.

"Do you think we'll make the rendezvous?" Courte asked anxiously. "What if we miss them in this fog?"

Kit removed his hat and cloak, tossed them with his mask on the bunk. "Calm yourself. Now's not the time for nerves."

Courte sat on a stool at the table and held his callused hands before the lantern. They shook slightly. "I am nervous, especially now. Why were you late? Does anyone suspect?"

Kit reached for a wooden box where bread was stored. His hands, Courte noticed, were steady. Selecting a chunk of hard biscuit, Kit bit into it.

"How can you eat at a time like this?"

Kit regarded him darkly. "I did not dine tonight—too many things to attend." He shook his head grimly and finished eating, then got up and moved to the porthole, taking the ship's roll in his stride. "Rumors fly everywhere. In the town, in all the shops. Even my servants gossip in the kitchens. All this talk about the Beggar King."

Courte's face registered skepticism. "I've heard it, too. Everyone saying he'll land in Dorset—saying he's done it before, giving away heaps of goods to the poor. He's quite the hero to our Lulworth friends. But I can't think why he would bother to come here."

"He will, though."

Courte searched his friend's face quickly, wondering how much he knew. "You haven't seen or met him, have you?"

Kit shook his head in the negative. "No, but I received this." From a small box on the table he produced a square of paper, handed it to Courte.

Courte shot him a questioning glance as he took the paper. He unfolded it and scanned the contents, squinting as he struggled with a few words. "Where did it come from?" he asked finally.

"One of my regular crew of *The Raven* brought it, along with this." Kit pulled a bag from the pouch at his waist, let it fall beside the note on the table. It released the pungent scent of cloves. "Another sailor on the wharf passed it to him—someone he didn't recognize, who said it was for me. The cloves are from the Canary Islands. Pirated."

"Pay it no heed." Courte dismissed the message. "Probably a hoax."

Kit merely looked at him.

"There you go again, so trusting," Courte broke out in exasperation. "Assuming this Beggar King sent it when it might be a trap—a note from someone who doesn't address you directly." Holding out the paper, Courte read aloud. "He wants to 'discourse with Her Majesty's favored servant.' Signs himself 'a loyal subject of the Prince of Orange.'" Courte threw the note on the table. "Doesn't even sign his name."

Kit remained silent, his jaw set.

Courte tugged on his jerkin belt in a frustrated gesture. "All right, let me put it another way. What if you're right? What if it is from the Beggar King? He's nothing but a pirate, who could end up in the noose, same as anyone."

"If *he's* a pirate, *we're* the same." Kit's warning was terse. "It seems you forget that fact."

"But *we* serve the queen."

"And he serves the Prince of Orange, as lord admiral of his navy. It's Spain who sees him as a rebel and a pirate. And if that's the case, how do you think they see us? We could all, as you say, end up in the noose. Or at the point of a sword." Kit gave Courte a compelling stare. "I would have you understand my decision. The Beggar King has long been my inspiration—as well you know. I do talk about him as if he were godly. It seems to me he is—a nobleman who gave up everything he held dear—even his identity—to take the mask of the Beggar King and fight for something he believes in. We don't know his real name or anything about him. Nothing but rumors. Now, since the queen has asked me to work against Spain, it would make sense for me to join forces with him. In truth, I relish the opportunity. I intend to meet with him, as he requests in the note."

"When? How?" Courte writhed on his seat, discomfited by Kit's statement, still worried about a trap. "I don't like the queen giving you this mission. 'Tis uncommon hard."

"I agree." Kit was silent for a moment before he went on. "When the queen asked me this favor a year ago, we were at Whitehall. I almost said no, that place reminded me of so many things." He grimaced. "My father took me there when I was seven; my brother, thirteen. Harry was presented to Her Majesty. I was left in a stable courtyard all day, where naturally I played in the dust and dirtied my linen. Earned a whipping for it." He gave a short, bitter laugh. "My father believed childhood was a disease. Only when I got over it would I be worth anything. And manners were taught with a cane. He was the coldest man alive."

"You never told me about him," Courte said quietly, realizing Kit's mood had changed.

"I try not to think about him." Kit stroked his beard, expression fierce. "He beat me for every infraction, real or imagined. I wasn't the only one. The servants were thrashed daily for their errors. My brother was spared; being the heir, his hide was precious. He taunted me about it. Probably hoped it was because our father loved him. But that was highly unlikely; the Earl of Wynford didn't love anyone. He didn't know what the word meant."

Courte shuddered at the hostility in Kit's voice. There

was much he didn't know about Kit, despite their eight-year acquaintance. "You're the Earl of Wynford now," he said.

"I know." Kit stared out at the waves, clenching one fist around the hilt of his sword, wanting to squeeze the life out of that reality. "Here I am, following in his footsteps, when I swore never to be like him."

"You're not," Courte assured him quickly. "Not in the least—"

"Not in obvious ways." Kit rubbed his brow, puzzled by his own statement. He wasn't like his father, was he? He looked down to where he still clutched the sword hilt, forced himself to loosen his grip. Slowly he moved away from the porthole, stood before his favorite pilot's chart while drawing a deep, calming breath. "Forgive me, Courte. I'm not myself tonight. It's coming back to West Lulworth after all these years, and taking on this damned title. I find myself doing things I don't understand." Like buying all that ruined lace, he thought darkly. And so desperately wanting that girl.

"You're more deserving of the title than either your father or brother," Courte insisted. "They served themselves, but you—you serve the queen faithfully, protecting England against invasion by Spain. Philip is the most powerful ruler in Christendom and Her Majesty fears him."

"Aye, he wants to rule England just as he does the Netherlands. If he hadn't inherited that land from his father, he'd not rule it, either. With his Inquisition and high taxes, no wonder the people turn to the Prince of Orange to lead them in rebellion."

Courte nodded. "At least they aid us by rebelling. As long as King Philip must subdue them, he is distracted from conquering England." He paused. "That reminds me. You didn't say why you were late."

Kit went back to the porthole, stared moodily out into the blank darkness. "I was delayed by . . . certain business."

Courte made a face. "A woman. I should have known. They're always after you—"

"Not one of those." Kit cut him off sharply without looking around.

Courte laughed, trying to sound nonchalant. "I've nothing against bedding. You know that. Though you get more than your share, if you ask me." He shook his head earnestly at Kit's questioning glance. "Nay, I'm not jealous. I wouldn't know what to do with so many women. But tell me then, what's she like? Is she from these parts?"

Kit shrugged evasively and stood for a long moment, making Courte wait for an answer. He thought of Rose. She was not one of *those,* that was sure. So why he bothered with her, he couldn't fathom. Yet he'd had enough of the other kind—women who craved seduction. Skilled strumpets and bawds, noblewomen with lust as voluptuous as their figures, comely servant maids, all intent on the same thing—what he could give them. Some wanted his money; others, the pleasure he offered in bed. Images of the many he'd had blurred in his mind's eye, making them all seem the same, especially in the dark. He was tired of them. Jaded. He'd vowed to be aloof now that he was earl, and he had. For a full year.

But then he met this girl. Once he would have wooed her, taken her to bed, forgotten her. Pure and simple. But nothing was pure and simple anymore.

Kit rubbed his forehead, trying to clear his thoughts. What was it about her? She was sweet as the flower he likened her to, yet she bristled when he said so. How did she expect him to seduce her, acting like that? It was most odd. As was the way she spoke of astrolabes and chartbooks. He thought again of her smile, the way it illuminated her face when released, and it burned in his memory like a magi's gift.

Behind him Courte cleared his throat, urging an answer to his question. "The maid is from these parts," Kit told him gruffly, annoyed at having to let the memory fade. He stepped over to the table, consulted a map. "Enough. We have work at hand."

Ever obedient, Courte moved the lantern nearer and they bent to their task.

"This is the expected course." Kit traced a path with his hand. "My informant tells me to look for the *Santa Maria de la Rosa.* A war ship, so she's armed. But she's also doubling as a trade ship carrying cargo. There are also King Philip's dispatches to the Duke of Alva, the governor of the Netherlands. The important thing is this—when we've taken the ship, I must search the captain's cabin to find the secret communiqué."

Courte groaned. "Will it take as long as last time? We have to get rid of the ship."

"I'll make haste," Kit promised, looking sober. "The dispatches are sheaves of paper covered with seals and easy to find. But the communiqués are always hidden in different places. This time it will be concealed in a lady's trinket. That *should* make it easier. What captain would carry a lady's trinket in his cabin?" He laughed mirthlessly before changing the subject. "The crew? Are they all agreed? They'll dispose of the ship?"

"Aye." Courte nodded vigorously. "I've hired men to do the job. 'Tis a great nuisance, these ships. Why don't we just take the communiqués and leave the ships be?"

"Then they'd know we're not pirates, as I've explained before. We must appear to be after their goods. Besides, if we leave the ship to drift, the Spanish could retake it."

Courte gulped and nodded before continuing. "The men are in agreement. They'll take the ship south and land her at The Brill."

"Good." Kit's answer was terse. "The Prince of Orange will benefit from the goods."

Courte bobbed his head in agreement. "I put Ned Ruske in command, as you instructed. He'll get her to the coast. He always got the *Swiftsure* through on trading voyages, dodging Spanish patrols, and ... oh, your pardon, I didn't mean to remind you."

Kit turned away, trying to block Courte's words, but memory seized him with a vengeance. The vision from the past swooped down to haunt him—his entire ship's crew taken by the Spanish navy and put to the sword. Bracing his hands against the table, he leaned on it for support. God help him, but he'd sworn revenge against them. They'd accused him of smuggling when he ran an honest trader's ship. Men had died that day—men he'd held dear. He'd scarce escaped himself, and only with help from the English ambassador.

"I swore to be revenged in some honorable way," he muttered. "Now I have it." He raised his head, stared at Courte. "But we sail only with men who have no families. You are sure of this?"

"As best I can tell," Courte assured him. "Of course they have their doxies at port, those who can afford 'em."

"That can't be helped." Kit sank into a chair. "I can only do so much. I trust you've warned them of the danger. If they're caught by the Spanish with a Spanish ship, they can't plead a merchantman's rights."

Courte nodded as he bent dismally over the map, worrying.

Kit turned away. The mention of doxies had brought other images flashing through his mind—Rose, with her graceful form and her heavenly kisses. Like a vision of the angels, she was, with her quantities of brown curling hair, slender figure, and perfect oval face. But what could he have from a woman like her—clearly a merchant's daughter, thoroughly respectable.

Despite that, he craved her body. From the instant he'd met her, he'd known she was hiding something. She appeared prim and proper, yet there was a secret side, a hidden fire to this flower, lurking behind the severe demeanor and plain clothes. The kiss she'd given him at the cove revealed it, as did her laugh, rippling like silk, undulating in the night wind. He paused, remembering the pleasure he'd felt to release it. She needed to laugh more. For some unknown reason it troubled him to think she did not. No one's business should give them such problems as hers. That knowledge had moved him, by God. So much so ... he'd agreed not to see her again. Sheer madness, for him to play the part of the honorable gentleman. It fit him like a poorly cut glove.

Two hours later they were on deck, peering through the night, occasionally drenched by spray. Courte shivered as he leaned against the whipstaff, steering their course, but Kit stood stark still at the rail, swathed in his cloak, feet planted wide, staring straight ahead.

"There she is, off the starboard." Kit pointed just as the lookout cried the sighting.

Courte squinted. "Is she ours? That's the important thing."

Minutes later they knew she was. The huge galleon was signaling them. Well over three hundred tons, she was one of the new, swift, low-charged English designs. She carried eight great sixty-pounder cannons, four demi-cannons, and numerous smaller culverins. A man-of-war, she belonged to Kit.

The first mate lumbered up for instructions. "His lordship and I will board the *Swiftsure*," said Courte tersely. "We'll not need you more tonight. Return to Lulworth Cove and anchor. One man to the watch should be plenty. The rest can go home." With that, he relinquished the helm to the mate and hurried after Kit, who was headed for the starboard.

Leaning against the rail, Courte shuddered and tried not to think of the waves crashing below as he gripped the rope tied to one of the yards and watched the *Swiftsure* draw near. Pray they did not collide and one of them spring a leak.

A split second before they were close enough for his taste, he saw Kit mount the rail in one fluid motion and spring into the air. He swung out over the water on his rope. The thud of his landing on the neighboring deck resounded in the dark.

Damn, Courte thought, knowing his turn had come. He looked resolutely at his destination, reset his grip on the rope, and shoved off. He landed on his backside, got up cursing. Why the devil had he let himself be talked into these things?

Kit paid him no heed. He was already deep in conversation with the captain of the *Swiftsure*. Ruske was a short, stout man, but the girth of him was all muscle and he knew his business. Together they stood at the whipstaff, guiding the ship on its course.

Within the hour they were navigating in Channel waters, on the lookout for the Spanish. Kit had gone forward to stand at the forecastle rail, unable to keep the surge of exhilaration from coursing through his veins. Always the sea wind honed his wits to a fine edge of clarity. Always the tossing of the spirited galleon conveyed to him its power. He loved the sea and he loved this bold, beautiful ship. The hands who did not work the sails or stand lookout clustered around him in stalwart silence.

Kit scanned the sea until he spotted their adversary—the lumbering *Santa Maria de la Rosa*—on her way to Antwerp. She was much heavier than the *Swiftsure,* perhaps by several hundred ton. But the *Swiftsure* was quicker. The other, loaded as she was with sugar, cinnamon, and cochineal, would have trouble outrunning them.

Kit called Ruske to him. "Run out the cannon in their ports and load them. I want you to ease the *Swiftsure* forward till we're within range. When I give the signal, fire both the forward cannon and demi-cannon. Then reload and stand at the ready. If they don't surrender after a few volleys, close in and clear their decks with the culverins. Use the hailshot and crossbow shot. Then we'll grapple and board."

Ruske saluted and returned to the helm, where he gave orders to the first mate. The man ran off to alert the gunners.

Courte came up and joined Kit on the forecastle. "Do you want a heavier sword?" He showed the one he'd brought from the cabin.

Kit shook his head. Pulling his rapier from its scabbard, he inclined his head toward the *Santa Maria.* "We are almost ready to begin."

Courte nodded but kept his eyes riveted on the neighboring ship. For the life of him he wished he had Kit's courage. The man knew no fear—else it was crushed by his sense of past outrage. Courte found it a daunting task. Together they must board the other ship, find the captain, and make him surrender. Or fight him to the death.

Minutes later they closed with the Spanish ship. Shouts in Spanish went up on the neighboring deck as the lookout and crew spotted the English galleon. Kit gave the order to run up the red flag showing they would attack. Then he gave the signal to fire.

The opening salvo of the huge English cannon boomed in the night. Instantly the air was befouled with smoke. For a minute Kit could see nothing. Then the air cleared, and he observed with satisfaction the two gaping holes in the *Santa Maria* just above water line.

He waited for what seemed an eternity. The captain could come out and surrender or run up the white flag. It often happened after the initial bombardment.

Only a few Spaniards ran to and fro on the deck. As Kit waited, scrutinizing the *Santa Maria,* he became aware of another ship, smaller than his, about five cables off to portside.

"What's that off the larboard?" he asked Courte, his gaze locked on the Spaniard.

Courte squinted, trying to make out the flag. "Can't tell. She doesn't look Spanish."

The *Swiftsure*'s culverin began from the quarterdeck then, effectively clearing the *Santa Maria*'s decks. It was almost time to board her. Kit decided to ignore the strange ship. Moving forward, he ordered the grappling hooks used, the boarding nets thrown out. Courte followed, preferring to use the net for the perilous crossover while Kit swung over on his rope. The English swarmed over the ship, meeting virtually no resistance.

It was then the unthinkable happened. The *Santa Maria* fired back. With a tremendous crash the Spanish cannon spoke, opening a massive hole in the hull of the *Swiftsure*.

"Damn!" Kit spun around to see what had happened. Suddenly they were attacked. Spaniards swarmed from every direction, swords and daggers drawn. At once Kit and Courte closed with attackers who swung at them furiously. Kit had just dispatched his man when there was a renewed thundering of hand weapons. Everyone dropped to the deck.

Before the air cleared, Kit was up and fighting his way along the ship's waist. A vibrant strength surged through his limbs. He felt infallible tonight as he made his way toward the stern cabin, seeking the captain. The deck was perilously slippery, but Kit made speedy progress, dealing this man a crashing blow, another a thrust of his rapier. At the stern cabin he rammed the door open with his shoulder. The Spanish captain came at him as if he'd been waiting, sword in his right hand, a dagger in his left.

The cabin was small, low ceilinged. Kit confronted the captain, his chest heaving, their gazes locked. The Spaniard was tall and muscled, every bit an even match.

"Surrender," Kit growled in Spanish, his voice low but piercing.

"No, by God." The captain lunged at him, dealt him a blow with his rapier. Kit parried, edging left to force the captain into tighter quarters.

Again the man attacked, attempting an imbroccata. The sound of metal rang out as Kit blocked him, then forced him back with a rapid staccata. A minute later he caught the Spaniard in the wrist with a mandritta, accompanying the swift horizontal cut with a curse. His rapier pierced a

vulnerable muscle. The wounded hand reacted, causing the
captain's weapon to leap from his grip. Instantly Kit's
sword was at his neck, threatening. Slowly, slowly, the
Spaniard lifted his face to stare at Kit with all the rage of
impotence in his eyes.

Kit stared back at him, laboring for breath. The man had
been limber and skilled in his defense, but Kit was better.
For good reason he had practiced many hours in a London
school of defense. Under the insistent pressure of Kit's rapier point, the man sank to his knees.

"Surrender," Kit barked in Spanish between hard gasps
for air. "I claim your ship and cargo. You may take your
men and go."

"Go?" the captain demanded in angry disbelief. "How?"

"Take the longboats." Kit crossed himself piously, took
a rosary from the pouch at his waist and kissed it. "I'll not
have your deaths on my soul." He regarded the captain
intently, feeling the full extent of his revenge. They would
be thoroughly humiliated, arriving at a French port in longboats. Better still, Kit would be reported a religious fanatic
of a pirate. They would never guess that he served the
English queen. As a Catholic, he could not. They would
assume their communiqués lay undiscovered.

"English whoreson," the captain spit back. "England will
pay for this outrage."

Kit narrowed his eyes angrily, stared through the slits of
his mask. "Save your breath." He tossed the captain's
sword to Courte, who caught it deftly. "You'll need it for
rowing."

The captain got up heavily, holding his arm where Kit
had drawn blood. Under repeated urgings from Kit's rapier,
he left the cabin, gave orders to cease fighting. Kit saw the
entire Spanish crew into the longboats. They were packed
in tightly.

"May the wrath of God fall on you and your brethren."
Standing in the boat, the captain shook his fist at Kit. "English pirates. Even if you are Catholic."

Kit grinned at him ruthlessly. "I should have thought you
would prefer this treatment to death." He bowed, his hands
clasped as if in prayer. "I give you a fighting chance. You
are not so far from land. It lies that way." He gestured
toward the south.

As the longboats drifted, taking the Spanish away from the *Santa Maria,* Kit turned his back on them to observe the night. Overhead the wild canopy of stars churned in a shifting maelstrom of mist. Thrusting his rapier back into its hanger, Kit gave orders to rope the *Santa Maria* for towing, all the while reveling in his triumph. He'd humiliated Philip of Spain's navy. And he meant to do it again and again.

Wheeling around, he headed for the captain's cabin. It was time to find the communiqué. Inside, he closed the door and leaned against it, taking a long, slow breath. He would start by searching the desk.

Ah, here were the dispatches. Carefully he handled the papers with their dangling seals. On top of the desk were a compass box, a pot of ink, some quills. But no lady's trinket. He riffled the drawers, didn't find it. Straightening, he searched every nook, corner, and cranny of the tiny chamber. Nothing. Not a bauble, not a trinket, not even a trinket box.

Restlessly Kit paced the floor, staring at the boards by dim lantern light. Outside he could hear the shouts of his men as they divided valuables, taking the shares he had promised them. Still no communiqué. He gritted his teeth as he rummaged through a trunk of clothes. He didn't even know what he was looking for.

The enormity of the task grew slowly in his mind as he worked. It had sounded easy, finding a lady's trinket, but its execution was more formidable than he'd dreamed.

With rising impatience Kit tore the blankets from the bunk, forcing himself to work methodically, to probe the straw-stuffed mattress for hidden objects. Nothing. Stymied, he glared at a portrait hanging on the wall between two ornaments, only half seeing them. Slowly his eyes focused on them—two fans, one on either side.

Of course! Eagerly he reached for them, searched the first one, looking between each feather, inside the hollow handle. No communiqué. He put it down and searched the other one—this time separating the handle from the feathers so he could look inside the hollow quills. It was a shame to ruin the fans, but the communiqué must be in one of them.

It wasn't. Unable to believe it, Kit broke both handles

in two and examined the fragments. Mayhap there was a double chamber, with the communiqué secreted between the walls. He found nothing.

Frustrated, Kit slammed out of the cabin and locked it with the key he'd found on the desk. At the forecastle, he planted himself with crossed arms and watched through the slits of his mask while his men brawled over cones of sugar and sacks of cinnamon.

Something caught his eye—the ship he'd spied earlier. Patiently it waited, like a wraith shimmering in the mist. She'd ventured closer since they'd set the Spaniards afloat, so that now he recognized her as a Dutch carrack. The thought lodged in his brain with needling insistence. He pushed it away. Flagging down Courte, he went to check the cannon hole in the *Swiftsure*. They studied it from the deck above.

A seaman approached, touched his cap, and waited to be noticed.

"Not now," Courte admonished him. "We are assessing damages."

"For the master." The man held out something.

"I said not now." Courte's rebuke was acrid.

"What is it?" Only half turning, Kit took the thing, meaning to stuff it in his pouch. As his hand closed around it, the bag released the wafting scent of cloves.

Kit wheeled around to confront the messenger. "Where did this come from?"

The man pointed at the smaller Dutch ship. The name, painted in white on the hull, showed clearly in the dark. *L'Esperance. The Hope.*

"Pay no heed," Courte warned Kit, grasping his arm. "Let them send to us if they want something. Here, then," he demanded of the man, who was preparing to leave them. "Who is your master?"

The old fellow grinned. He looked vaguely sinister, Courte thought, with his missing and blackened teeth. The scraggly hair and lined features made him resemble a death's head, leering at them in the night. The macabre vision beckoned to Kit.

Courte could do nothing. He watched Kit go to the rail, stand as if transfixed while the old man dragged himself over the side and disappeared. When Kit moved to follow, Courte arrested him, one hand on his arm.

"Don't go. It could be a trap."

"I must. He's sent for me. Don't you see?"

"Now just a minute," Courte insisted, clutching at his friend and managing to turn him around. "Even if this is one of the Sea Beggars, how do you know the Beggar King's on board? And look, the wind's rising. Don't go, I tell you. Stay here."

Kit shook his head and directed his gaze back to the Dutch ship. "I néed answers."

"Are you sure you'll find them?" Courte shuffled his feet in agitation, realizing Kit hadn't found the communiqué.

"I must take the risk," Kit rasped hoarsely. He moved away from Courte, went quickly over the rail.

Courte stood alone on the deck and squinted at the other ship, then shook his head anxiously, not understanding. His friend sat in the skiff as it crossed between the two ships, his gaze fastened on *The Hope*.

On board the Dutch ship, the old fellow waited. He led Kit to the stern cabin and bid him go in alone.

The room was sunk in darkness. As the door swung shut behind him, Kit made out by the light of a solitary lantern a shadowy figure draped in a long cloak, seated at the table. The hood of the cloak obscured his face so that Kit could tell nothing about him, yet he sensed power emanating from him, a force that was almost audible, like a voice speaking in the dark. Instinctively Kit took a step forward. A feeling that was not quite fear roiled in his belly.

The figure unfolded itself from the stool and stood. The man, whoever he was, possessed a towering height, with powerful shoulders and a stance of muscular strength. Yet there was something about his movements that bespoke age.

Blood pounded in the vein at the side of Kit's temple. He exalted in his victory tonight, yet something essential was missing. Here, whispered his roving heart, was meaning.

As he stared, the figure came forward into the frail light, planted himself firmly before Kit, and thrust back his hood. With a jolt of shock, Kit looked straight into the passionate eyes of the man he knew had to be the Beggar King.

Chapter 7

The two men stood face to face for some moments, staring at each other in silence.

"Why?" Kit whispered at last, unable to tear his gaze from the depths of those fathomless eyes. "Why did you send for me?" He stopped, remembering the many mysterious tales spun in alehouses and at Elizabeth's court about the Beggar King and his fleet. "Though I'm glad you did. I confess your name and deeds have inspired me since I was a lad. I wanted to be like you, to know your secrets, especially who you are." His voice rasped with emotion. "Forgive me that last."

The tall figure turned in the lantern light, illuminating a regal face framed by long locks turned silver by time. Beneath his fierce brows, the Beggar King's aged eyes were a keen blue, and they bored their way into Kit's mind to where he kept his deepest thoughts.

"You seek answers." The sage swung away from Kit, bent to hold his hands before a brazier whose burning coal's sent pricks of heat into the cold sea air. "I, too, have sought them over the years, still I find myself asking—as you do. Tell me what it is you truly seek."

Kit stood silent, knowing he was errant to pry. No one knew the Beggar King's true identity except his prince. He existed as a legend, sometimes exaggerated, often romanticized, but a secret just the same. Now the pirate's pointed question resonated through Kit's soul, setting off deep fibers of feeling—and a confusion as wild as the rising wind outside.

"You don't really know. *Goeie hemel,* I'm not surprised." The man's English was heavily accented by his Dutch and German origins. "You are young yet, and like many young men you seek me because of what I am represent. Freedom—the casting away of the bonds of society. Believe me, my secret does not spare me the indignity of having to search for answers." He gestured to a black mask on the table Kit had not noticed. "I have sailed these waters for years craving enlightenment. Often, I learn the important thing is to ask the right questions."

"And have you found these questions?" Kit could not stop the new query from rising to his lips.

"Some of them."

The Beggar King raised his gaze to meet Kit's, and again Kit felt the surge of attraction. Something so deep, he could not resist.

"But others remain unanswered," the Beggar King went on, "mayhap we are not meant to know. Or we are meant to wait. I am waiting now, marking time." He seemed to scrutinize Kit, assessing him. "You took that ship tonight. You did it as if you were used to such things. I know you are not."

"Nay, you are wrong," Kit told him, a cavalier smile coming to his lips. "I am a pirate, bound to take goods. And I know how to best my enemy. At sea or on land."

The sensuous mouth of the Beggar King curved into a smile. "Pirate?" He gave a curt laugh. "*Niet gij.* A pirate puts the captured crew to the sword and thinks naught of it. You put them in the boats. Since you are no pirate, tell me why you take a Spanish ship."

Kit's smile vanished. This man saw through him as easily as if he were transparent. And for some reason Kit didn't fully understand, he hungered for it—to be seen and understood. "You are right," he said, bowing his head. "I serve the Queen of England. I was bid take this ship and I took her. Would that I fulfilled all my vows so well."

The Beggar King's eyes now blazed with recognition. "You seek the Spanish secrets that pass between shores."

It was no question. Kit gazed back at him, enthralled.

"You wonder how I know. 'Tis because we both seek them. Our grail is the downfall of the Spanish."

"Aye." Kit's heart suddenly lifted, he felt buoyant and light as he recognized this man acted under the same orders as he. "King Philip grows too strong. He abuses his strength. I have heard what he lets the Duke of Alva do in your country. Torturing honest merchants before killing them, sending men, women, even innocent children, to violent deaths. He wishes to do the same in England."

"We must continue to fight him." The Beggar King was silent a moment. Slowly he moved to the brazier, took a shovel of coal, put the pieces on the hot embers, one by one.

"See how they burn," he said darkly. "I, too, burn, with my life's shame. Often I have wished to give up. To lay down my arms and ask God to grant me rest. I cannot know peace." The confession floated to Kit from the depths of the dim room.

"How could you feel shame?" Kit started forward, confused by the unexpected despair in the man's voice. He felt a longing to banish it. "Look at all you have done and what you represent. You are the only hope of the people who pray the Prince's navy should rule the sea and free them from Spanish laws. You cannot give up. Not now, when victory lies so close."

The Beggar King's answering smile rippled with pain. "How can I make you understand? You are *onervaren*—how would you say, young and impulsive. Once I was like you, the life inside me straining to get out. I believed my goals were pure. Yet over the years, I lost much, by my errors, those of others." He shrugged. "Some were small; I did not realize their loss. But others were such . . . You cannot know how it is, to feel the age creep up—to know your time grows short. Still, I do not give up. I have sworn not to forsake the quest."

Kit scrutinized the grim-faced man before him, trying to guess how many years he had seen. Two score and ten? More? "I honor you for your strength." He spoke boldly, knowing the respect he felt shone in his eyes. "For fighting on. I, too, have fought . . ." He stopped, wondering what he was about to say, surprised to find he fought something. He'd thought he was completely free.

"What is it you fight? Tell me." The Beggar King's words sliced into Kit's thoughts, forcing him to share them.

Kit looked at him and was again overwhelmed by the feeling of transparency. "I think it is my past. It burdens me, but I cannot give in to it."

"What is your past?" The older man approached, looked deeply into Kit's eyes. With a wrinkled hand he reached out, took Kit's fingers in a compelling grip. "I must know everything. Say thy name."

Kit spoke his name, unable to hold it back. But as he said the words—told his family of origin—a change came over the Beggar King. The craggy features stiffened, his eyes glazed with pain. The change aged him, made him seem to carry an even heavier burden.

"Howard." He pronounced the name distinctly, then let the silence deepen around them. "I thought so. Go on, lad. Tell me from whence you come?"

"Dorset."

Again the Beggar King's face contracted with agony. "Dorset. Yes, I knew. Tell me, Christopher, where is thy father?"

"In his grave."

"And your elder brother?"

"Dead, too," Kit answered, feeling torn asunder by this man's anguish. "Just over a year ago."

"And you . . . you are the Earl of Wynford," the Beggar King went on, raising a tormented gaze to meet Kit's.

Kit nodded mutely, wanting to help, but feeling so much pain himself, he could not. What was the source of this man's suffering?

The Beggar King turned away, fell to pacing. His strides devoured the space in the tiny chamber as he muttered to himself, his tones confirming something. It went on for several moments, this internal struggle. Kit watched, fascination warring with respect. He wanted to interrupt but felt he had not the right. At last the Beggar King stopped before him. "I shall give you my name in exchange. 'Tis only fair."

Kit wanted desperately to hear it, and yet . . . "Do not tell me. It is too dangerous. You must guard your identity."

As the Beggar King's gaze locked with his, Kit felt himself drawn into the other man's dark communion.

"I have my reasons for what I do. If I wished to hide my identity, no power could force me to reveal it. But you, I trust, Christopher Howard. I know you'll not betray me."

His words vibrated in Kit's mind, reminding him of another such promise. The one made at the cove by Rose.

The Beggar King bowed his head for a moment, toyed with a small cross he wore around his neck on a chain.

Then he dropped it, straightened, and drew himself up to his full height. "I was born Phillipe de Montmorency-Nivelle, and when I grew to be a man, I became the Count of Hoorne." He regarded Kit, appearing to measure how he took this information. "*Ja*, I was Knight of the Golden Fleece, Stadtholder of Gelderland, Admiral of the Netherlands, and supposed friend to Philip the Second. 'Twas I who took him to Spain in my own ship, after his father, the Holy Roman Emperor Charles the Fifth, gave Spain and the Netherlands to him. I was a trusted confidante."

Kit's mind reeled. He sat down hard on the bunk, stunned by what he'd just heard. "But Philip killed you. Everyone knows that. You were accused of treason. The Duke of Alva had you beheaded in the town square of Brussels, along with the Count of Edgmont. Even though you were—that is, are—Catholic. It was to make an example so the populace would obey him. At least 'twas what I heard years ago."

"It was 1565, to be precise." The count's voice was raw with emotion. "Eight long years ago. But I was not beheaded, as you can see. Some poor devil died in my place. I never knew who he was, but I owe him my life." He crossed himself quickly. "I was spirited out of Brussels by Prince William. Do you see now why I serve him?"

Kit did not bother to hide his amazement. "It's a miracle. Your life is blessed. I did not know . . . did not in my wildest imaginings think—"

"Think you would meet someone snatched from the jaws of death." The count laughed roughly. "*Niet*, I am not sacred. Look at what I have lost. My ancestral home, my lands, my income, all forfeited to the Spanish crown. Someone else lives in my family home, someone else sleeps in my bed. Others collect rents from the people who served me. And my heir . . ." His voice lowered. "My heir is dead."

Kit felt the impact of the count's sorrow pierce him like cannon shot. "You are bitter. For that I do not blame you. I, too, would be—"

"No! Not bitter."

The count's voice resonated in the tiny cabin, and for a second Kit thought he was furious. But he tempered his voice, controlled it before he went on.

"Never allow yourself to be overwhelmed by bitterness.

It avails you naught. In the beginning I felt it, but I learned I had to rise above it, to search for other things." He laughed wryly. "I know it sounds foolish. Like a schoolboy's lesson. Or the ideals of some moldy philosopher who spends his time thinking but has never lived. But bitterness breeds nothing but more of the same, and I had already tasted the depths of despair when I thought I was to die. I refuse to live with it."

The count's pain had lifted. His eyes were now clear. He crossed the room, swung a wrinkled hand and brought it down on Kit's shoulder in a gesture of warmth. "Together we will do our work. You shall keep my secret, and I shall give you aid. Come. We must find that communiqué."

"I shall find it," Kit protested, suddenly wary at the change of subject. He drew back. "I need no help."

"Neen?" The Beggar King's invasive gaze tore into Kit. "Why are you here then? Let me tell you. Because you are seeking. Let me lead you." He held out one hand in a simple gesture.

They went on deck into the vast bowels of the night. The wind had changed direction. Kit turned his masked face into it, judging its strength. They dared not tarry longer. Soon that same blustering wind would blow their ships apart, scattering them across the North Sea.

The *Santa Maria de la Rosa* rode low in the water, waiting like a false courtesan, promising but refusing to deliver. By this time the two crews of the Dutch and English ships were wrangling furiously, the Dutch mad with jealousy that the others had the goods.

"Let them share it all around," Kit told Courte and Ruske as he swept past them, following the masked Beggar King. "Each with equal parts. And do not let us be disturbed. The Beggar King and I wish to discourse."

They entered the captain's cabin and Kit locked the door. For two full minutes the count surveyed the quarters, his craggy features fixed.

"A lady's trinket," he muttered as he turned, spending a minute at each point of the compass.

Kit gave him a strange look.

"Of course I know how 'tis hidden." The count's mouth formed a bleak line as he returned Kit's scrutiny. "Have I not sought these communiqués as well as you? You pre-

sume to be alone in this task, but you are not. There are
many after these valuable messages, even beyond us. But
we shall have this one."

Intensely he inspected the cabin, then turned to Kit.
"You cannot find it?"

"I searched the entire room. Every inch. These trinkets,"
Kit indicated the two demolished fans, "were all I found.
And they do not conceal the communiqué."

"Think, Christopher." The count's eyes bored into him.
"Think of a lady's trinket. But not one that would be ap-
preciated by most of the females you know."

Kit removed his mask and squinted at him, not sure what
he meant. But he moved around the room obligingly in
search, while the count talked.

"Most ladies would prefer the fans, naturally. But imagine a different sort of woman. One who likes things both
practical and clever. One who—"

"Women aren't practical," Kit interrupted, pausing by
the desk. "Nor do they put their cleverness to any sensible
use. They're self-centered creatures, in love with foolish
gewgaws."

The count made an impatient gesture. "Then *imagine*
this other sort of woman, if you can't believe she exists.
What sort of trinket would she like?"

"A woman who prefers things both practical and clever
would like ..." Kit turned to the desk, snatched up the
compass box and held it aloft, "something like this. If it
were made properly, a place beneath the compass chamber
could conceal things. She could use the compass for its
usual purpose, but in reality it would carry a secret.".Kit
looked in surprise from the box to the count. "There's a
crack here, my lord."

"Open the box."

The box separated into two pieces in Kit's hands. But
the little chamber under the compass was empty. Kit examined it. "Just as I thought. There's a false bottom." He
pried at the delicate piece of wood, removed it, then held
out the box in triumph.

They had found the prize.

The count took the folded piece of paper in his hand. "I
am pleased to see it is in the usual code. I will teach you

how to decipher it. And you must call me Phillipe, Christopher. I do not stand on formality with you."

"Phillipe, then." Kit still marveled over the compass box. "Clever little thing. Beautifully constructed, the way it goes together—the join is almost invisible. I see now how I missed it. Most women wouldn't like it for storing their trinkets. They like these things covered with ribbons or lace or jewels if they can get them."

Phillipe chuckled. "Not all women are the same. You should know that."

Kit grimaced. "You have the right of it. Her Majesty, for instance, is certainly unlike other women. I must take this message to her immediately."

"I will make a copy," Phillipe told him, "and you may take this one to Elizabeth. You will give her the Prince of Orange's greetings and request England's aid? We have urgent need of her assistance."

"I shall," Kit promised.

"And this ship?" Phillipe gestured around the cabin. "What have you done with the others you've taken? As you are no pirate, I imagine you do not sell the cargo."

Kit shook his head, slightly embarrassed, irritated with himself for feeling so. "I only wanted the communiqués, so disposing of the ships became an inconvenience. I could not bring myself to sell them—to profit seemed wrong in this situation. I took some prizes of value for the queen, but she cannot accept anything recognized as Spanish. Leaving the ship adrift was too dangerous. It might be recaptured by the Spanish and they would discover I took the communiqué. So I have sent the Spanish crew with a message to King Philip. Informal, of course. The ship itself will be taken to—"

"You must take it to Dorset," interrupted Phillipe, "give away the goods to the poor, After we have our share of food and payment for my crew, that is, and your men, theirs. You can help our cause by letting the English know the Dutch are their friends. Your country must side with us, or we'll never survive."

"I?" cried Kit, surprised. "I cannot take this ship to Dorset. Why don't you go yourself, if you wish it?"

Phillipe sighed and again grew remote. "I have not been

to Dorset in over five years. There are memories there . . ."
He shook his head heavily. "I'll not go. 'Tis you who must."

"But they'll mistake me for you," Kit protested. "You've
not been there of late, so you cannot know, but the people
are wild with the legend of the Sea Beggars and their rebel
leader, the Beggar King. You have no idea how such a
story can spread."

At these words, Phillipe's mood changed abruptly. He
threw back his head and laughed vibrantly. For the first
time that night he displayed genuine pleasure, and it emanated from him with passionate abandon. "Let them mistake you," he cried joyously. "You are so full of lusty
health, I want them to mistake you. Tell them the Beggar
King has been reborn, that each time the Spanish seek to
crush him with their torture and death, he will rise again
like the phoenix, young and strong. You are the embodi-
ment of our cause, Christopher. Go and spread our friendship, so we people of the Netherlands will no longer
stand alone."

His joy was contagious, and Kit found himself caught up
in it, overwhelmed by the thought that they must stand
together or die separately and alone. Kit found himself
kneeling to the old man's hand, though he'd not meant to
be won so easily. "You give me a sacred trust." He knew
his voice throbbed with feeling, but he didn't care. For the
first time since he'd become earl, he felt he moved toward
a long awaited goal. "I do not know if I am worthy. But I
accept. I will keep your secret. And I swear by my own
honor to fight for England and the Netherlands, for our
mutual cause."

"And I," whispered Phillipe. "I swear to fight for thine."

Chapter 8

For a long time after the earl left, Rozalinde sat on the rock and wondered. The darkness seemed to thicken around her, growing heavier like the secret of his destination. Where had he gone, this Lord Wynford? One did not just row out to sea in the middle of the night without a good reason. Shifting on the cold stone, she felt inexplicable curiosity about him rise within her. It confused her abominably, but she felt it just the same.

He must be meeting a ship. Lady Mary had said he went off at all hours. True, she'd suggested he was up to something different. But there could be no woman to seduce in the middle of Lulworth Cove. And there was his mask.

He would be navigating the channel by now, she thought with jealousy. It was where she belonged. Roz's thoughts leaped to her father's business—here was the earl, going off in the middle of the night, when no one could stop him. . . .

She sat bolt upright on the stone, stuck by an idea. *She* could sail to Antwerp for her father; *she* could handle the business.

Immediately she stopped, gripped her knees. Her father would not like it; he would not agree . . . Well, she would ask him. Be entirely forthright. But if he didn't approve, she would go anyway—slip off in the night when no one could stop her. She had done it before in London. The daring of the idea made her shiver with delight.

Roz stood, squinted at the sky and tried to tell the time by the position of the moon. Clouds masked its silver face, but now it didn't matter. The night seemed full of magic, because she had done as Jon suggested, she'd found another way. *Antwerp,* she thought, stretching out her arms to it across the water. She would sail for her family's redemption.

Exhilarated by these thoughts, memory of the earl's kiss
returned. For what reason, she couldn't imagine, but her
heart rose up on thrilled, throbbing wings.

She began to walk. Back up the cliff path, along the
heights. So much about Christopher Howard baffled her—
for instance, his uncanny insight. Was he right to say
George frightened her? Impossible! He wasn't frightening.
She just preferred not to marry. She liked to manage her
own life, and with a husband like Trenchard, that would
be hard.

Again her thoughts flew to the earl—why did she continually think of him? So much about him enraged her. He
had too much experience with women, that was obvious,
and he was a noble—a class her parents had taught her
was useless. On top of it all, he had a secret.

Trudging across the meadow of waving sea grass at the
top of the cliffs, Roz pondered this secret, wanting to share
it. Oh, he enraged her, but he intrigued her as well, and
never had she met a man who kept her interest for longer
than a minute. This one did. And because of that, because
his kiss aroused so many intriguing feelings, she yearned to
know what he was up to in his black mask. Suspicion tickled her brain, and she turned west, taking the path that led
to Lulworth Creek.

Thirty minutes later she was crouched behind some
bushes, looking down on the wilds of the creek where it
joined with the sea. Over the years the creek had carved a
wide bed to rest in, leaving a deep cleft through which a
great galleon could be towed. This was the place she and
Margery had spoken of—where local pirates unloaded their
spoils, spirited them away to the town to be sold.

"Hist, this way."

Rozalinde's head swiveled at the sound of a voice—a
woman's voice—calling her softly. Then a woman's form
approached her through the brush.

Taking her by the arm, the woman urged Rozalinde to
her feet, pointed toward the north end of the creek. "You
don't want to wait here. Come, we'll sit with the others."

A shock ran through Roz, then another as she recognized
the weaver's wife, who had eight children and lived in a
tumbled-down cottage in West Lulworth's poorest part. She
knew because the lady had once begged at their back door,

saying her children starved. Rozalinde had bid the cook give the lady three loaves of fresh manchet bread. Later she'd had a large basket of food delivered to the weaver's home. Now, hurrying after her across the rough hillside, Roz felt growing excitement. Mayhap she would share Christopher's secret tonight.

As they picked their way through wet undergrowth along the creek, Roz struggled with the branches and bracken. When her shoes stuck in the mud, she stopped to pull them out, peering around her, trying to discern who these other people were. But she saw no one. They climbed the steep hillside, around huge rocks jutting up from the earth. Far below, the creek lapped nervously against its banks.

"Come along. Be quick with ye." The woman scolded her good-naturedly. "You've never done this afore, have ye? Did the chandler send ye? Well, well, we'll have plenty of victuals for all tonight, you'll see. 'Tis a rare night, mark ye." Motioning for Roz to hurry, she disappeared around an outcropping of rock.

Roz climbed after her, emerging at last onto a flat shelf cut in the hill. Before her yawned a black, gaping hole. With a shudder Roz examined it. Sure and the woman had not gone in there! Dark and dirty it looked, and heaven knew where it led.

But the woman *had* gone in, Roz realized with a stab of fear. She stood there, frozen, not daring to follow. Panic gripped her, and suddenly she felt four years old again— tiny and alone in the nursery, frightened because a storm had blown up and the nurse was gone, leaving her alone to face the roaring dark. As a child the dark had immobilized her. Now fear came back with clarity—she felt like that little girl cowering in her bed, praying for light of day.

Stop this instant! Taking a firm grip on her fears, Roz cast about with her gaze and found the moon. There *was* light here, and she was a woman grown, not four years old. She would handle her problems and not be afraid of them, as she'd once been afraid of the dark.

Turning back to the cave, she extended both arms and prepared to feel her way. *I will go in. I must know.* Trusting blindly, she took a deep breath and crossed the cave's threshold, giving herself up to the all-engulfing dark.

Instantly she halted. Just beyond the entrance huddled a

mass of people, standing and sitting, pressed tightly together in the cavern of rock. She felt rather than saw them
in the pitch blackness, the minute sound of their breath,
their pungent, warm smell.

"Sit," someone whispered, touching Roz on the arm. Roz
plunked down where she was bid and leaned against the
chilly clay wall.

Hours might have passed. But for Roz, time stood still;
she was suspended in unreality. All day she'd fought to
banish the earl from her mind. Now she ceased her struggle. His mystery beckoned, and she gave in to it like a ship
guided by the wind.

Around her the presence of many people crowded close,
and she felt tension leave her body. She, who was never a
dreamer, drifted, escaping from what was real, inviting what
was not. A sense of unspoken kinship hung on the air
among these people who gathered for an urgent purpose.
Amid their warmth, Roz drowsed. Her eyes grew heavy,
almost closed.

"He's come!" The two words, spoken in no more than
a whisper, reverberated through the crowd, chanted over
and over. "He's here. Hurry."

Rozalinde's eyes snapped open as people scrambled to
their feet, groped for the way out. She scrambled, too, getting her legs under her as they began to move, taking her
with them. Emerging into the open night, Rozalinde inhaled deeply of clean, wet air and looked around. Towed
by longboats, a ship approached, its great hull touched by
the many whispering tongues of the creek.

Swiftly she glanced around her, seeking a hint of what
she should do. Men hurriedly descended the hill, wading
out into the water knee deep to launch small boats and
row them to the ship. Around her she recognized the poor
from both West and East Lulworth.

"We wait here." A different woman behind her spoke.
"The men'll bring the stuff and we'll help cart it off.
There's many as'll eat tonight who've had naught the
week long."

"We'll not be caught?" Roz asked. This was piracy, and
though she'd heard of it, she'd never given it much thought.
In the past she was not interested in the stuff of high
romance.

"The aldermen would like to catch us," a man chimed in as he passed. "And the queen's customs men. Because o' the Spanish, Her Majesty's had to pretend we don't like the Sea Beggars. She forbids 'em to land i' our ports, and the aldermen must enforce her word."

The Sea Beggars? Roz almost blurted the name aloud, she was so taken aback. "Sure an' he's wrong," she remarked to a girl waiting beside her. "That is no Low Countries ship."

"You're right, but ye're also wrong if ye think 'tis English . . ." The girl chuckled low in her throat. "I heard 'twas Spanish, but the men be from the Netherlands. Hark and ye'll hear."

Roz listened. The sound of Dutch speech, mingled with English, floated to her across the water. The Sea Beggars were here on English shores although she'd told everyone they wouldn't come.

But she hadn't long for contemplation. The first ladened boat pulled near, followed by another, and another after that, their oars dripping as they were shipped in their locks. All along the steep, slippery banks, people surged forward in answer, reaching out to take bags and bundles, small casks and crates.

Roz moved with them, watching them take up their burdens and hurry away. She could see sugar in bags and casks, she could smell pungent spices, pepper and cinnamon brought from the New World. She had just selected a bag to carry when a voice rang out.

"My friends, here are more goods. Sell them and give the profit to the sick and the needy."

Roz spun around, looked urgently for the speaker. The familiar magnetism of the sound made her heart skip in her breast, then race urgently ahead. Searching the boats, her gaze was drawn and held by a tall man who beckoned to the others nearby.

Two burly men came at his summons, began taking the bags he handed off. They were followed by a stream of others coming to do his will. Each took a burden and hurried away, then returned to await his direction in other tasks. She felt herself drawn closer, all the while noticing how naturally he commanded, giving a word of encouragement here, a correction there, though his English was sprinkled with words from the Dutch. Unable to take her eyes from him, she stared, mesmerized.

For an instant his straight form was silhouetted against the misty moon. She could see without mistake the swirl of black cloak from the broad width of his shoulders, the proud lift of his head, and the crowning touch—she could see he wore a mask.

A shiver ran through her body, tingling all the way down into her toes, shaking her to the very core of her being. There was no mistaking who he was.

"Aye, he be something to look at." A saucy wench flounced by Roz with a huge gammon of bacon on her shoulder. "But I'd rather touch, if you take my meanin'."

"Who is?" Rozalinde spun around, pretended not to understand.

"Why, him." The girl stopped to poke Rozalinde in the ribs and gestured at the pirate. "You're not the only one to stare tonight. 'Tis more than a year since he set foot in West Lulworth, but we don't forget him, the way he gives everything he has to others. All because he was once robbed of his own. For that alone we love him." She sighed hugely.

"Does he give his favors so freely, then?" Roz asked resentfully of the girl, who had put down her burden to tuck her skirts higher out of the way.

The wench laughed softly as she displayed plump calves. " 'Tis said he has a way with women." She lowered her voice conspiratorially. "But none of us would know. We can't get close enough, neither man nor woman. He's careful o' that."

"But he must go to other parts of Dorset. Doesn't he stop at Poole or some of the other towns?"

"Nay, only Lulworth," the girl insisted, taking up her burden again. "He never went anywheres else, but here he came oft. At least he did some years ago. Now he's back, which proves the old legends right. They say he comes aseeking his lost love."

With that, she moved off. Rozalinde stood, people swirling around her as they hurried about their tasks. She trained her gaze on the creek below, staring at the dark-cloaked figure alone on the shore, apart from the others. Slowly she moved toward him, her heart protesting. *No,* it cried, *he cannot seek another. He seeks me.* By light of day, it was an absurd thought, but tonight, by the light of a mystical moon, it became the stuff of logic.

She edged closer, pretending to look over the goods, deciding which item to carry. When she was within several yards of the pirate, she stopped and let herself gaze at him. The real world receded, with its cares and problems. The dream took her tightly in its grasp.

Across the distance, he sensed her presence. He turned and stared at her in return. Then he moved straight for her.

Activity around Rozalinde ceased as the Beggar King approached. A hush fell over the crowd. Every eye fastened on Roz—she could feel the intensity of the moment as she waited, trembling, for the Beggar King. He came to a halt and looked her over, beginning at her feet and moving slowly up. At last his gaze made contact with hers. His eyes glittered like diamonds through his mask, piercing her soul.

Suddenly he stripped away his molded leather gloves, reached for her. The heat of his fingers shocked her bare arms. The blossom of delight swirled in her belly as he pulled her into his embrace. A collective sigh went up from the women in the crowd as he leaned over and placed his mouth against hers.

Inside Rozalinde, joy bloomed. Life quickened in her veins, awakening the thrill inside her. His lips did a slow, sensuous dance against hers, much different from his earlier kiss at Lulworth Cove. Now he probed, seeking answers. Her body softened, gave in to his magic. Stretching luxuriously, she reached up to lock both arms around his neck.

Too soon it was over. The Beggar King released her, stepped back and saluted her with a bow, a gesture of his hand. In a whirl of black cloak he moved toward his ship, leaving Rozalinde alone. The empty feeling from the cove assaulted her. Tears welled in her eyes.

People stirred, gathered up their burdens. The last goods were handed off, and the crews arranged themselves in the longboats, preparing to tow the galleon back to open sea.

Quickly Roz caught up a sack and puffed her way up the hillside, realizing she was thoroughly tired from her long day. As she climbed, her bodice stained with sweat and her feet ached. The others stayed at a respectful distance. She was charmed tonight. She had been singled out by the Beggar King.

Only when Rozalinde reached the top of the hill did she stop and drop her burden in the waiting cart so the apprentices holding the traces could take it away. Still breathing heavily from her climb, she looked back at the ship as it moved on the dark water, heading out to sea.

A shudder shook her as the truth flooded in on her. The secret—known to her and her alone—sprang on her in its entirety. The man who'd dared put a torch to her heart—the man who was the Earl of Wynford—was secretly the Beggar King.

Chapter 9

Rozalinde slept poorly that night. She tossed and turned. Everything was changing in her life, and she was haunted by dreams of the Beggar King that robbed her of precious rest.

Things looked different with morning. Reality bore down on her. Rising early, Roz directed the last cleaning up from the revel. Amazingly, she had little to do. Jon had handled everything the night before. Breathing a silent thanks to him, she hurried to her father's cabinet and began to cast accounts. Later, she would praise Jon for his efforts, but just now she must see how a shipment of wool broadcloth would offset their losses.

By the time her father came seeking her, she felt only a little better. The magic of the night had dissipated. Again she had to face the truth of their difficulties. If she could convince her father to approve her journey to Antwerp, they might see some profit. She would have to persuade him. Once he saw the books, he was sure to agree.

"Come in, Papa." Rising from her seat as her father entered the chamber, Roz threw down her quill. "You must look at the latest accounting. Even with the lace I just sold, we are in terrible straits."

"Well, well, child, Trenchard will handle it. You mustn't worry." He lumbered in and took the chair across from her. His face was pale except for dark smudges beneath his eyes. "You did go to bed last night?" He stretched across the table to cup her chin in his hand.

Rozalinde cast her gaze down guiltily, knowing he had heard her come in late, that she'd kept him awake worrying about her. "I—I couldn't sleep, Papa. I went for a walk." It was a lie. They both knew it. Yet he said nothing. His hand dropped away.

"Papa, I have been thinking," Roz began hesitantly. Dared she hope he would agree? "You must let me sail with the next shipment of goods to Antwerp," she continued more boldly. "No one would dare harm our cargo with me on board." There. She'd said it. Roz squared her shoulders and waited for his response.

"No! I cannot permit such a thing," he snapped. "You belong here, at home." The words had no sooner left his mouth than he seemed sorry for his harshness. His tone softened. "Rozalinde, I'll not have you going all the way across the Channel and the North Sea by yourself. We have ever traveled together, you and I, and in such circumstances none would dare dishonor the master's daughter. But alone, you invite all manner of trouble."

"But, Papa, we need the profit. Our goods are still being ruined by this captain, who is a complete bungler." She stopped for a second, aggrieved by the extent of their losses. "And we have the London cargo expected within a sen'night. Will it be ruined, too?"

"I don't know." Her father groaned, put one hand over his eyes. " 'Tis every bit as bad as you say, but we must rely on George to correct it. He will take action . . ."

"You must let me discharge the captain," Roz urged. "I can do that. He won't be surprised, Papa. Say you agree."

Her father shook his gray head heavily. "You should not be doing these things, Rozalinde. I should do them myself." He paused, put one hand to his chest. "But I don't feel my best today."

"Why did you not say you were ailing?" Wresting aside her own fears, Roz hurried around the table to him. "You must rest, Papa. Don't pretend you are well if you are not."

He leaned against her tiredly and let her fuss over him, seeming grateful for her concern.

"I thought you were better of late," she said tenderly, bending to kiss his balding head. "You looked well last night."

"That I was." He caught her hand, gave it a quick squeeze before releasing it. "I wanted to be well. This revel meant so much to your mother and the children. I wanted to be well for all of you. But there are so many troubles."

Roz started to protest, to say she would handle them, but he quieted her with a look. "Nay, it's my duty to care for you and I have not done it. I said it unkindly at table yesterday, but only because I am ashamed of not doing my part. Do not mistake me. I'm grateful to you, Rozalinde."

She was down on one knee beside him, and he put his arm around her shoulders to gather her close. "I trust you more than anyone I know. But it's time for you to fulfill your role as a woman, time for you to wed."

"I still don't wish it," Rozalinde said softly, trying to hide the burning fear that ground deep in her stomach when she thought of marriage.

He shook his head ponderously. "You're a woman grown, and dear as you are to me, we must look to your future. You must wed, and George—"

"—is not in that much of a hurry," Roz interrupted firmly. "I spoke to him last night and we came to an agreement. He's in no haste."

Her father drew back so he could see her face better. "He seemed so to me last night when he insisted on a betrothal date. He wanted it a sen'night from today."

"A sen'night?" Rozalinde sucked in her breath. "Are you sure? It makes no difference," she hurried on, not wanting to hear his answer. She roused herself instead, went to the small table by the fireplace. Briskly she mixed wine and water in a tall flagon. "I will ride to Poole tomorrow to prepare the next shipment. You must drink your wine. The physician said a little in the morning would strengthen you."

Her father took the flagon obediently and began to sip. "What shall we sell this time? I'd thought of cotton—"

"Wool broadcloths," Rozalinde interrupted crisply as she caught up the little broom and began tidying the hearth. "The prices are excellent just now in Antwerp. I have calculated the cost and the expected profit. It is our best choice."

" 'Tis exactly what Trenchard advised me last night." Her father nodded approval over his wine.

Roz turned to face him, broom in hand. "Trenchard may have given me the idea, but he offered another as well. I decided on the wool. I have planned the purchase and how we'll advance the funds. I've also got a captain in mind. His ship is large enough to carry a goodly cargo so we'll make the profit required."

"Hmm, 'tis well." Her father nodded, sipped his wine, then stopped. A spasm crossed his face, causing his expression to contort.

"Are you in pain, Papa?"

"A . . . a passing twinge. It's gone now." He raised his head and smiled at her. "I meant to tell you—I sent for the lawyer early this morning and had him revise my will. He did it on the spot and I signed it. The guardian I've appointed will be your husband, which will be settled as soon as you're wed."

Roz turned away. She didn't want to think of his death. She must distract herself, think of something else. Busily she swept the hearth. It was a small one compared to some people's—Trenchard's, for instance, who had built himself an ostentatious new house in the center of town. She didn't much care for it, but she would have to live there. His fireplaces were so huge they more befitted a castle, with chimney stacks to match.

A sharp crash startled her. Rozalinde whirled just in time to see her father slump in his chair. The flagon had fallen from his hand and shattered into a million pieces on the floor.

"Papa!" Flinging down the broom, Roz rushed to him and grasped his hands. They felt cold and lifeless to her touch. With heart in her throat, she pressed one finger against his neck, searching for his pulse. A faint flutter moved beneath her fingertip.

"Margery!" she shouted. "Come quickly. Bring the footman."

The maid ran into the cabinet, her face white and scared. Everyone in the Cavandish household feared this sort of summons, knowing what it meant.

"Send the spit turn for the physician," Roz ordered the footman who appeared. "Then help Margery fetch a pallet from the bedchamber as fast as you can to make my father comfortable. Hurry!"

Margery and the footman jumped to obey. Rozalinde bent over her father, chaffing his wrists and dabbing his face with a damp handkerchief.

"Hurts . . ." Her father moaned, stirring.

"There, there, 'twill be all right, Papa. We're going to lie you down in a minute, and you will feel more comfortable,"

Roz soothed, speaking clearly so he could understand her. "Don't fret yourself. You are going to be fine. Like last time."

Margery and the footman entered dragging a pallet and the other footman hurried in to help her. He was followed by her mother, who took several shaky steps into the room, then stood with eyes big in her terrified face. "Is he . . ."

"Come, Mama." Rozalinde held out her hand. "Hold him steady while I ready the pallet. Someone has gone for the physician."

A short while later Master Cavandish had been examined by the physician and was moved upstairs, where they made him comfortable in his huge four-postered bed. Rozalinde and her mother sat, one on either side of him, while the maids drew the window draperies, arranged the linen, plumped the pillows.

Rozalinde examined her father. His skin was an unhealthy gray that frightened her.

"He will get better, Rozalinde." Her mother's voice quivered. "Just like last time."

Roz nodded tremulously. As she watched, her father's eyelids fluttered, then closed. His expression softened. His steady breathing indicated he'd fallen asleep.

Roz backed away from the bedside. Let him rest, regain his strength. He would be up and around in a few days. As her mother said, just like the last time. Excusing herself, she slipped from the room.

Closing the door, Roz leaned against the polished oak, let her body sag. For the first time since the crisis, she let herself feel. A rush of pain swept over her. Her father was dying. Burying her face in her hands, she began to sob, her body shaken with her silent grief. Turning, she fled down the passage.

Rozalinde ran through the house, her breath catching painfully in her lungs, her heart full of despair. Wanting to be alone, she headed for the family solar, which was isolated and quiet. Flinging herself on a settle, she gave in to a rare display of tears. He must not leave her. Her father was the one person who gave her life meaning. If she lost him, she didn't know what she would do.

Her grief was so intense, for several minutes Rozalinde

forgot everything else and gave in to her weakness. But she was never one to linger over sorrow. She preferred to act rather than wait passively for fate to decide for her. So after a few minutes she sat up determinedly. Drying her face, she lectured herself.

Enough of this nonsense, she told herself sternly. Enough! If something was to happen, she must be the one to bring it about. She would busy herself with her plans—the goods they would ship, her trip to Antwerp. Surely she could succeed, and then there would be no reason to wed with Trenchard.

Resolutely Roz stood and walked to the solar table, picked up de Vault's treatise on navigation and thumbed through it absently, put it down and turned to her astrolabe. Lifting it reverently, she stroked its beautifully joined brass parts, adjusted the pinhole sighting vanes for the stars. It was her own astrolabe. Her father had commissioned it for her, after catching her at twelve sneaking out at night to learn from his ship's navigator. He'd even engaged a man trained in the best navigator's school in Portugal to teach her. And when she'd used it later, they'd been at sea together. Those were the times she liked to remember, and today of all days, when her father seemed most precious to her, she could not shake them from her mind.

There was something else she could not shake from her mind—the earl, how he'd looked at the cove last night. She supposed she hadn't been quite honest with him, saying she could use an astrolabe, for she could do a great deal more than that. She had her own pilot's chartbooks of the shores off England, France, and the Netherlands. She had her own precious maps. But it was more than the skill of navigation that intrigued her. It was the numbers themselves. Whenever she looked at a calculation, the answers rose up in her mind like whispers, forming themselves unbidden like delicate traceries in her thoughts. She could not tell how it happened. Only that it did. And it was her destiny to heed them.

Sighing deeply, Rozalinde held up the instrument and sighted through the vanes out the window, pretending to measure the altitude of a star.

There were no stars just now. It was full day outside. But suddenly the dream returned to her in full force—the one she'd had last night. It was dominated by the Beggar King.

A shiver racked Roz's body. Gooseflesh rose on her arms as memory of the earl and the Beggar King merged. Again she felt his kisses, saw in her mind's eye his dark figure poised on the Spanish galleon's deck, haunting in his black swirling cape, his face hidden from the world by the velvet mask. The moon of her dream gilded him with silver.

What could the others understand of him? Nothing! For there, on the shores of Lulworth Creek, only she, Rozalinde, had known him. In the dream, she clutched his secret tightly in her palm. Looking down, she'd seen it, pulsing like a star, burning vibrantly into her flesh. His secret— given to her alone. The pain of it filled her with a new, inexplicable desire.

It ruined her sleep, this dream. Angrily she'd awakened, sat up in bed vowing to forget it, to forget him. But he crept silently into her thoughts. Insistently. Sweetly. By day the dream images merged with those of the real earl, and she felt confused, afraid for him. They were one and the same man. The earl lived a double life. And realizing it, she would be lost again, swept away by unfamiliar sensations tearing at her heart.

Shaking her head in tired bafflement, Roz put down the astrolabe and took up her quill, began scratching calculations on a piece of vellum. It was a mere pastime, measuring the height of the parish steeple using her instruments, yet the numbers soothed her, and she bent over them intently, letting them speak their silent language to oust the dream.

"Rozalinde, can I come in?"

Roz whirled guiltily at the sound of a voice, at the same time wondering why she should feel guilty. Jonathan lounged gracefully at the door. "You don't usually bother to ask my permission. I suppose you'll come in if you want." She pointed to a chair. He entered slowly and sat down.

"Is Father all right?" Jon asked hesitantly, seeming aware she was angry. "Don't be cross, Rozalinde. I'm sorry I wasn't here to help."

Roz shut her eyes tightly and pressed her fingertips to her temples. "It's not your fault you were at the shop. But it's hard to manage everyone when Papa is ill. He will survive, it seems, but I would have had you here."

"Like last night?"

"Yes, like last night," Roz admitted, realizing why she felt guilty. For once she had been the lazy one, not Jon. "I thank you for taking my tasks," she forced herself to say.

"I didn't mind." Jon got up and strolled to the window, hands thrust deep in his pockets. "It was the least I could do. What I did mind was Father. He had hell to pay."

"What do you mean?" Roz whipped around to look at him. "Hell to pay for what?"

"It was odd, really." Jon went on, staring out the window. "I heard Trenchard speak to Father, thought for certs he would give him trouble when you disappeared. He never mentioned it, though I know he was insulted you'd left."

"How did you know?"

"I hear things." Jon looked at her pointedly. "I told you before. Anyway, Trenchard insisted on a date for your betrothal. Then he urged Father to change his will and appoint him our guardian. He wanted the lawyers to do it today."

"What did Papa say?" Rozalinde's chest felt so constricted, she could hardly breathe.

"He put him off. You know how Father can be—vague when someone bothers him. Trenchard didn't take it kindly. He hinted that Father would be ... well, he didn't actually say he would be sorry, but he made it sound that way. He's determined to get his due."

"No!" Rozalinde sank back on her stool and clasped her hands, greatly upset at this news. "No one told me."

Jon shrugged, but his gesture bore none of his usual nonchalance. "Father made us promise not to. He said you had worries enough." Turning, he confronted her, his face intent. "What I want to know is, are you going through with it? The betrothal, I mean."

Her answer stuck in Rozalinde's throat, refusing to come out. To say yes, to say no, both choices were impossible—the one put her in the arms of Trenchard, the other would cause her to go back on her word to her father. She fiddled with the quill in her hand, stroking it against her palm.

Jon's voice interrupted her as these thoughts warred in her head. "You're afraid to tell me, aren't you? You're

planning something Father won't like. What is it, Rozalinde? I'll not tell. I swear."

"You're right, Papa won't like it." Roz looked away,
feeling a rising discomfort as she thought of her plans. She
stole a peek at Jon's face, but his questioning expression
hadn't changed. Hands clasped behind his back, he continued to study her.

"If you wed with Trenchard, I won't approve."

"If my plan succeeds, I won't have to," Roz told him
firmly. "But you can't help, so there's no use my telling
you."

"Now just a blasted second." Jon brushed his hair backward with one hand, something he did when aggravated.
"Look here, sister mine. I know I've not always worked as
hard as you, and I know Father relies on you first. But I
don't like the look of our future and I'll do whatever I
must to change it."

Rozalinde lifted her gaze to study her brother, taking in
his chiseled features that still held the beauty of boyhood,
the way his thick brown hair fell across his high, intelligent
forehead. His brown eyes were so intense, so earnest, she
could not meet them. Her gaze fell away. "I've wanted
your help, Jonathan, but until now you've been so—"

"—immature and selfish," Jon finished for her, sarcasm
creeping into his voice. "Thinking only of my own pleasure.
I know, you never said so, but you thought it. Well, I intend
to change. I want to help. I see you can't do everything
alone."

Roz gripped the table edge tightly and looked up at her
brother. Though Jon could say and do astonishing things
at times, this was surely the most astonishing. "What did
you say?" she asked, staring at him.

Jon shuffled his feet and looked uncomfortable. "Stop it,
Rozalinde. It's hard enough saying it once. I mean to do
better by you and Father. I swore last night I would. After
hearing the way Trenchard spoke to Father, I know he
wants to control our business. And I don't want that. So
tell me how to help you, Rozalinde, and I swear I will."

There was a long silence, during which Rozalinde kept
her eyes fixed on the table, examining its walnut grain. He
seemed serious, at least as serious as this younger, impish

brother of hers had ever been. "There is something you could do," she began tentatively.

"What?" Jon started forward eagerly. "Shall I challenge Trenchard to a duel? I've been practicing with my blade."

"You mustn't do that. He's skilled with a rapier." Rozalinde shook her head in sudden fear. "He's been studying with a master. Besides," her voice took on its old chiding tone, "haven't you given up that nonsense, thinking you'll be made a nobleman? We belong to the merchant class. Why do you aspire to more?"

"The queen will knight me some day." Jon picked up three bright balls of wool from his mother's workbag and began to juggle them, emulating the players he'd seen last night. "So I intend to be prepared if the occasion presents itself. You said it yourself, Rozalinde—if you want something, you have to fight for it." As he finished speaking, he missed a ball and it rolled away under the settle. Getting down on his knees, he groped for it in the dark recess.

"You just want Margaret," Roz said, her many fears making her snappish. "Though her parents say no. Her father's a squire. He doesn't want Margaret marrying a merchant's son. Even if Papa gets his coat of arms, we're still nothing to them with all their land."

"I do want Margaret." Having recovered the wool, Jon straightened and set the balls spinning again. He had all three whirling perfectly before he caught them each neatly in his left hand. He grinned at her recklessly. "And I intend to win her in the end. I'm willing to do anything I must to have her."

"Anything at all?" Roz queried, deciding to test him.

"Yes, but I need your help. What must I do to have it? Manage the shop and not be lax?" He put the wool back where he'd found it. "Sit with Father and hold his hand? Though you know I hate it. Direct the maids and footmen? Just give me something that will make a difference. I won't settle for nonsense work."

Roz looked at him, feeling touched. "You really mean it? You'll do anything I ask?"

"I swear I will."

He seemed so sincere, she believed him. "I must say I'm glad." Her face softened, and she smiled at him, something that would never have happened a day ago. "I could use your help, Jon. You could manage the shop tomorrow while I go to Poole. You can inventory the fabrics from the recent shipment, at least the parts that were not destroyed."

"Aye, sister." Jon was obviously disappointed. "I was hoping for something more exciting, but I'll do your bidding. I promised I would. Only you must help me with Margaret."

"I suppose it's only fair," Roz agreed reluctantly.

"I'll do the same for you."

Looking up quickly, Roz caught a wicked glint in his eye. "I don't know what you're talking about," she began warily, telling herself to be on guard.

"You do," he told her cheerfully. "I'll help you; you help me. If you want to meet your ... whoever he is, I'll tell a tale for you." Jon laughed mischievously as Roz stared at him, trying to keep the shocked expression from her face. "Don't be an addlepate and say no," he went on in a wheedling tone. "Of course I can tell you've met someone. It shows."

Roz put both hands to her temples and squeezed her eyes shut, feeling confounded. Self-centered as he was, Jonathan could be astonishingly observant at times. Apparently this was one of them. Something about her was different after last night. And apparently even she didn't know in what way. "Well ..." she began, wishing she could trust him.

"Look here, Rozalinde." Jon slid around and sat facing her on the settle. "I need your help; you may need mine. Father won't approve of your sneaking off at night. He said nothing this time, but for certs he'll not keep silent again."

"I won't be slipping off," Roz protested.

"That's what you think." Jon gave her a knowing nod. "It pays to be prepared."

"Oh, there's no arguing with you." Roz crossed her arms and glared.

"Then don't argue," Jon said cheerfully. "Stop using that confounded reason of yours. It's not always useful, Rozalinde. Say yes to my proposal. Say it and have done."

His words, his coaxing, both reminded her hauntingly of someone else. "Yes," she said unexpectedly, not knowing why she said it. "When do you want to see Margaret?"

"Tomorrow," Jon said determinedly. "When you return from Poole. I'll mind the shop and be everything correct and proper. You've not misplaced your trust."

And somehow, for the first time in their lives, Rozalinde believed him.

Chapter 10

True to her word, Rozalinde went to the quay at Poole the next day to meet with her father's captain. By midday, she had severed their working agreement, met with two new captains, and inspected each of their ships. Making tentative plans to hire one of them, she completed her business and returned to where her horse waited outside her father's warehouse.

The day was hot and Rozalinde paused before mounting, fanning herself with a simple paper fan she kept tied at her waist. This last captain was her best choice, and he'd agreed to accept the commission. He was a devoted family man, a native of West Lulworth. His ship was of adequate size, seventy-five ton with a dozen cannon. If he could successfully get this shipment of goods to Antwerp and bring back another to sell in England, they could make thousands of pounds. The thought was an encouraging one.

Turning to tighten her horse's girth, Roz congratulated herself at how well the day had gone. First a man had come from Lulworth Castle, paid for the earl's crate of lace and hauled it away with the assurance that his lordship was working on a second buyer. Now she'd made arrangements with a new captain. Straightening her safeguard to protect her kirtle skirt, Roz sprang lightly into the saddle and gestured to the accompanying stable boy. They would return home so she could tell her father. Her heart lifted with a surge of hope.

When her horse disappeared along the road leading back to West Lulworth, Kit Howard slid behind the tall stack of crates that had concealed him. Sinking back into his previous seat, he stared at the cloud-punctuated sky, musing.

It was an ordinary task, overseeing the revictualing of

The Raven. He'd been loitering on the quay, waiting for a delivery of salt meat, when he'd heard voices from the other side of the high-piled crates.

"I'm sorry, Captain," a female voice had insisted. "I regret having to discharge you, but to date you have ruined forty-six bales of calico, two hundred ells of cambric, and two hundred and sixty loaves of sugar. Should I itemize the rest of the goods you've managed to destroy in the past six months? I'm sure you understand we cannot continue to employ you."

At the first number, Kit had leaped to his feet and peered through the barrier. One look and a strange constriction seized his heart—the girl he'd named Rose stood opposite a sea captain twice her size, not the least intimidated. She wore a plain white smock overlaid by a severely cut bodice of dull green weave. The sun glinted on her chestnut hair, burnishing it with a halo of gold highlights. It was drawn back from her face, the heavy braids bundled at the nape of her neck, making Kit remember how it felt to kiss that slim neck the other night, those soft lips. Her answering kiss had seared his senses beyond relief.

In the daylight of the docks, her beauty dazzled the eye even more than in the dim draper's shop. The captain she addressed, however, was intent on begging her for another chance. Absorbed in their discourse, Rose had noticed nothing else.

Kit reached for a piece of driftwood, began to shape it absently with his dagger. Mistress Cavandish, the captain had called her. Mistress Rozalinde. He hadn't been far wrong when he'd named her Rose. And she was the daughter of the draper, though he'd guessed that. She'd argued like a man with the captain—a trait incongruous with her beauty. *Rozalinde.* Lass with a name like a rose.

Kit swung his booted foot against the crate, let the name create images in his mind. He saw the vivid roses flowering in the gardens at Lulworth Castle. They reminded him of his mother, of course, since she'd planted them, but he usually avoided thinking of her. He focused instead on Rozalinde—her lips capturing the pale blush of the Alba rose before he kissed them. Later, they reddened like the damask after his mouth ravished hers. His thoughts meandered blissfully among these pictures.

But a second later he pulled himself to attention. Enough forbidden lusting. He was bothered by something. What was it? Ah, yes, her discourse with the last sea captain. From it he'd learned the Cavandishes traded at Antwerp. He hadn't liked hearing that. She'd told him as much the other night at Lulworth Cove, but he'd had other things on his mind. Now, he was forced to consider. They did business with England's enemy. Not everyone knew it, but Spain exerted increasing force on Antwerp, bending the populace to its will.

Standing, Kit stretched in a leisurely manner, strolled down the dock toward the longboat that would take him to *The Raven*. His casual movements belied his internal tension. Someone was ruining Cavandish cargo. And it wasn't that foolish captain Rozalinde had dismissed. He would wager money on it.

Suddenly his business with *The Raven* seemed unimportant. He would have the first mate handle it. Purposefully he turned away from the docks and went to seek Courte Philips. He had an assignment to make.

"What think you, shall we hawk today?" Courte crossed his legs carefully, unaccustomed to wearing silk netherstocks. He took a Venetian crystal wine flagon from the footman who offered it. It felt splendid to sit in the great parlor at Lulworth Castle, dressed in his best and imagining he belonged here. Perhaps he did, now that Kit was earl.

Sitting across from him in a red velvet X-chair, Kit stared out the window, worlds away. At least, thought Courte, he wore something besides black today. He eyed the earl's somber gray costume, the unadorned doublet, the gray trunk hose and netherstocks. Not even a ruff around his neck, as might be expected of an earl, especially one who visited the queen's court. There was nothing splendid about his dress at all, though he looked distinctive, Courte reflected, wishing he could do the same.

"We might hawk later," Kit answered at last, getting up from his chair and tearing his gaze from the window. It wasn't the view that held him—it was his thoughts, and they were troubled. "First, I have a task for you." He sipped his own wine. "It's nothing hard, so I would be grateful if you would do it yet today."

" 'Twill be my pleasure," Courte assured him.

His sincerity brought a smile to Kit's lips. "I wish you to call on Master Henry Cavandish, draper, and do two things. First, he has several crates of lace for sale that I wish to purchase. Fine quality stuff recently arrived from Flanders, but it was partially damaged in transit. It's stored in his warehouse at Poole. Buy it all." He reached for the purse at his waist and pulled out several gold coins of large denomination. "Give him the first payment and agree to three more installments after." Kit named a total he thought the lace was worth.

Courte whistled. "That's a lot of lace. What will you do with it?"

Kit handed him the coins and made an impatient gesture as he tucked his purse away. "The cost is low for goods of their quality, and I believe it's not all ruined. We'll sell it by the piece in London, which will make our money back plus some in the bargain. But that's not my point. I want you to buy it from Master Cavandish and refuse to take no for an answer. Then offer him the services of *The Raven*," Kit went on. "I hear he requires a ship to take goods to the Netherlands. He wishes to depart about three weeks hence. Do not mention that *The Raven* belongs to me. In fact be careful not to mention me at all throughout this entire business. Simply offer your services as captain of the ship."

Courte nodded in agreement. "Nothing easier. What do you think the cargo will be?"

"Wool broadcloths," Kit told him. "Coming back, it may be some other finery such as the laces. Stress your ability to reach port safely and the number of cannon on board."

"Cannon?" Courte sat up straighter and raised his eyebrows. "Mayhap I should offer the *Swiftsure*, do you think? *The Raven* has only six cannon. He might not be impressed."

Kit brushed aside his protests. "He would find the *Swiftsure* too expensive if I charged an honest price. And if I didn't, he would be suspicious of why it was offered. I don't want that. *The Raven* will suit his needs. But there's something else. This is the hard part."

"What is that?"

"You must convince him not to sail to Antwerp. Offer

to take him to Haarlem or Edam. Or to any other city that
has declared for the Prince of Orange."

"If he is set on trading at Antwerp," said Courte, looking
unsettled, "how can I change his mind? What should I say?"

"Tell him about the excellent rates for goods at Edam.
Tell him he can buy more at lower prices to bring back.
Tell him anything you can think of, but he must not trade
at Antwerp. Otherwise, you know I would be obliged to
stop him. Now that I have the trust of the Sea Beggars, I
could not in good faith let him set off."

Courte nodded his head in understanding. He felt sure
he could succeed at this task.

Courte presented himself at Cavandish's drapery an hour
later, just as he'd been told. He entered the shop and
looked around, admiring the neat rows of fabric, the clean
smell of the goods. A thriving business, he thought to himself, noticing the floor was swept meticulously clean, the
beam ceiling free of cobwebs. He would be most pleased
to associate with the owner of this establishment. Straightening his doublet, he prepared to speak to the shopkeeper
who left the other customers with the apprentice and came
to see what he wanted.

"I wish to speak to Master Cavandish," Courte told him,
respectfully doffing his cap. "I understand he requires a
ship for transporting goods. I should like to offer mine."

The man took his name politely, sent the other apprentice up to the house. "I have sent to ask if the master is at
leisure to attend you. If he is not, the lad will ask when
he might."

Courte thanked him and set himself to wait. He amused
himself by watching the remaining apprentice sell ribbon
to a rustic country maiden. The girl hesitated over her
choice while the lad showed to her first blue ribbon, then
yellow, then green.

"How may we serve you, Captain Philips?"

The sound of a sweetly modulated, feminine voice caused
Courte to whirl. He was confronted by the most beauteous
lass he'd ever laid eyes on. Her face, which was a pure,
perfect oval, bore a calm, noble expression, and she appraised him with deep brown eyes the color of rain-
drenched autumn leaves. Her figure was slim and perfectly

formed, shown to advantage in a kirtle skirt and bodice that were plain to the point of austerity. But their simplicity only enhanced her blinding beauty. Courte clutched his cap and began to sweat.

"You must pardon me, sir," she said gently, noticing his discomfort, "for coming in my father's place. He takes his ease each day after dinner. The physician requires that he rest. I am Mistress Cavandish. You may state your business to me."

Courte stammered something in answer. He wasn't sure what. "I understand," he went on, trying valiantly to keep his wits about him, "that you are ... that is your father, has for sale a quantity of lace. Fine stuff from Flanders. I wish to make a purchase."

The girl's face saddened. "I am sorry, sir. We have some lace, but very little and it's French, not Flemish. If you would be so good as to follow me, I will show it to you."

Courte squirmed uncomfortably but did not budge. "Not wishing to contradict you, Mistress Cavandish, but I was told you have some Flemish lace, stored in the warehouse at Poole. I hear I might get it at a good price."

Her brown eyes widened. "You wish to buy that? 'Tis all of it ruined, you know."

"I know," Courte told her, feeling recklessly happy to please this fair beauty. "I've a plan to sell it. Here is the first payment." He produced his purse and showed her the gold.

"Are you quite sure?" She did not touch the coins or make any move toward them. "I would not wish you to make an error."

"Quite sure," Courte insisted. "I intend to cut it up into short lengths and sell it in London to women who cannot afford full lengths of such things. They will cherish the chance to acquire some lace, yet not pay more than they can afford. And I shall make back my gold."

"Very well." She gave him the faintest of smiles. "If this is your first payment, the total would be what we paid for the lace."

That smile, modest as it was, gave Courte immense pleasure. He swelled out his chest. "The other payments will be forthcoming. Now then, my other business is to offer you my services. I understand your father seeks a ship and captain. I have a strong, well-fitted pinnace that will carry your goods to the Netherlands."

"I have sought a new captain," she answered in those same serene tones, emphasizing the fact that *she* did the seeking. "And you seem a responsible seaman. Tell me about your ship."

" 'Tis a fifty tonner," Courte said, as proud as if *The Raven* were his own. "With six guns. The best brass there is, forged in Germany."

"Fifty ton." The girl looked skeptical. "I am sorry. That would be too small for my purposes. But thank you kindly for your interest."

She poised to go. Courte realized he was dismissed. "Madam, I mean mistress," he spluttered, thrown off balance by her rejection, "my ship is well fitted. She can run like the wind." You must not refuse me, he wanted to shout. I have promised Kit.

The girl turned back, regarded him with those fathomless brown eyes. "I'll be heavily ladened," she informed him simply. "I'll not need a ship that can run—no ship can with a heavy cargo. What I need is more cannon. But I give you my thanks."

Courte was desperate. There seemed nothing he could do. He'd thought this would be simple, until he ran up against her impassable will.

"If I ever need a ship such as you describe," she said, seeming to take pity on his distress, "I shall think of you. I promise."

"You sound as if you were going personally," he said bluntly, finding the words out of his mouth before he realized it.

"I am." She nodded briskly.

" 'Tis a harsh trip. Not one for a maid."

"So the men like to tell me," she replied evenly. "But I've traveled it before."

"You must not go to Antwerp," he ventured, realizing he might still fulfill part of the earl's bidding.

"Why is that?"

"The Spanish hold it. You must not trade with them."

She seemed to anger at that, and her reaction surprised him.

"I'll trade where I must to get my price. We do not take

sides in this quarrel between Spain and the Netherlands. England is neutral. 'Tis the queen's policy."

"Aye, mistress." Courte gulped, knowing better but unable to say so. He gave his best bow to her in parting, but he felt defeated, realizing he'd botched the job.

He went straight to the door, intending to leave, but the temptation to look back was great. With a hand on the door, he looked over his shoulder.

She had paused at the counter to talk to someone—a young man who had the look of her, the same brown hair and flawless skin. They were, by all appearances, deep in conversation. But she looked up unexpectedly, focused directly on him, sent him a brief, faint smile.

Courte tripped at the door and almost fell. God, she was a beauty! Could Kit possibly know her? In a daze of confusion he stumbled out of the shop and into the sunlight, thinking he would never forget that perfect, angelic face.

Rozalinde forgot him within the moment. She had more immediate things pressuring her. But as she went about her day, directing the laundry, overseeing the meals, energetically conquering the household duties, one thought piqued her and would not go away. It was the earl. The image of him crept insistently into her mind.

By evening she was tired of fighting it. She'd been thinking of him and fighting it all day. Now she stood on her aching feet and counted the family silver, set out before her cleaned and dried in the dining parlor. Her father owned much silver, and to each piece she had assigned a number. As a child she had memorized them, in order. Now they seemed like old friends. Mayhap if she took a moment while she counted, she could banish all other distracting thoughts. She would think of the earl, then be done with the man.

Seventy-three was the number of the big silver soup tureen. Seventy-four was the salver received at her parents' wedding. Then she began on the unusual set of silver forks. Not many people had forks to use at table, but her father did. Seventy-five, seventy-six. He was not so very unusual, this earl. Seventy-seven, seventy-eight. Handsome, yes, but he was just a man. Seventy-nine, eighty. But then why did she always think of him? Seventeen times she'd thought of him today. No, eighteen, counting this time. Eighty, eighty-one, she went on counting the forks. No, that wasn't right. Troth! With irritation she stopped and scolded herself for being distracted.

Leaning against the table she stopped counting entirely, remembered instead how he had looked that night at the cove, his face when he'd trusted her with his secret, then again when he'd kissed her at the creek. Now that secret lay within her, burning its way to her heart.

Though she tried hard to stop it, her mouth *would* quirk at the corners whenever she thought of him: the way he'd learned she was ticklish and made her laugh; the way he'd looked standing on the deck of the Spanish ship, mysterious and proud. She knew he was involved in serious dealings, and that worried her. But even those practical worries washed away as soft feelings overwhelmed her. The details of the Antwerp trip, the cargo she must buy, and her other duties all vanished, replaced by the image of his face, which rose up in her memory till she could think of nothing else.

Uncharacteristically she stood doing nothing, gazing off into space, imagining the touch of his lips, the feel of his hands, the hard sinews of his arms as he molded her close to his warmth. How she longed for more of him—the strange, new feelings he aroused.

Voices sounded down the passage, the servants in the kitchens, and they brought Rozalinde back to reality, reminding her of her tasks. Enough nonsense. She'd meant to think of him for a moment to satisfy her need, then banish the thought permanently. Instead, here she was daydreaming like Jonathan, or worse yet, one of the maids.

Snapping her attention back to the forks, she counted all twenty-four, arranged them in their felt-lined storage box, and placed it on the top shelf of the court cupboard. Then she counted the silver serving plate. Usually the counting, the handling of the familiar items, soothed her. The numbers moved methodically through her head—the five great platters, the six silver dishes with their ornamented covers, the silver saltcellar with its bowl and festooned lid. But tonight her smile kept rising.

She must not let the way she felt get in the way of business, she told herself as she worked. Making a living was a serious thing. Her father's wealth came from a lifetime of hard work, and without that work, the money, their house, the food they ate, would all disappear. There were so many expenses to drain away the shillings. Dowries must be put aside for her sisters, shares in the business must be built up for the boys.

Turning, she automatically arranged the huge platters in their usual places, forced herself to think ordinary thoughts. But she drifted off again a minute later, unable to stop recalling the pleasant things about the earl—the way his hair waved so thickly, blue-black under the moon, his smile as his lips hovered above hers. The memory of him worked its way deeper into her brain and stuck there, obstinate, like him.

Bending over a platter, she scrubbed furiously with her apron at a mark that marred the surface, though she knew well enough it was a permanent scratch. Straightening, she regarded her face in the silver surface and exhaled despairingly. Brute force would never accomplish her aim. Try as she would, she could not forget.

The front bell rang. Roz heard the footman answer it. Absently she listened while she propped the silver in place, each piece precisely on the shelf where it belonged.

"Mistress Rozalinde, a visitor." The footman hesitated at the doorway. He was overshadowed by a larger figure who stepped in, blocking the candlelight.

Roz turned, wondering who called so late. She beheld Master Trenchard. Surprise flared within her. Her heart began to pound.

"Leave us." Trenchard stepped into the room, snapped his fingers at the footman. "Rozalinde, my dear. I am pleased to find you unoccupied."

"I am occupied." She turned away, wishing he hadn't come. Her father, who was up and around for the first time in days, must have invited him. "I am counting the plate."

He sauntered into the room and gave the lone plate left on the table a pointed stare. Flustered, she snatched it up and set it in the court cupboard, knowing her work was done. It could not be used as an excuse to keep him at bay.

"My poor darling," he soothed, caressing his beaver hat which he had removed when he entered. "Something troubles you. Tell me what it is."

Rozalinde stared at the hat where it lay in his hands. The

hat seemed so fragile, so easily crushed between his strong
fingers. "Anyone in business has troubles from time to
time." She crossed her arms before her, wanting to hide
her sudden shiver.

"Tell me about yours."

His eyes, eager for details, bore into her. She felt them
search her person, questing for secrets. "Troth," she said
testily, turning away to pull the heavy draperies over the
windows. "Things are improved. They get better by the
day. In fact ..." She stopped, not sure where to begin.

"Rozalinde." Trenchard clucked his tongue in reproof
and abandoned the hat on the table. "You continually use
that expression." Straightening his trunk hose, he meandered around the room inspecting things. "It does not become a lady."

Rozalinde felt her back go up. His words, spoken in so
civil a manner, grated on her nerves. "I wish to postpone
our betrothal," she said abruptly. "At least two more
months."

Trenchard stopped where he was before her father's portrait. His low, broad forehead creased into a frown. "We
are set to visit the church two days hence."

Roz moved behind a tall dining chair and gripped its
lathe-turned spindles with her hands, watching him warily.
"I know. But something has happened. My father is taken
a turn for the worse. We must wait—"

"Nonsense!" Trenchard's voice cut a sharp swath
through the calm of the room. "What possible reason could
we give for changing the date? We'll have the betrothal,
Rozalinde. I'll not be put off."

Rozalinde clenched her teeth in vexation. She'd been
afraid of this. As he took a step toward her, she moved
back, pulling the chair with her. "I'm not putting you off.
But with my father's illness, it is unseemly to celebrate a
betrothal. Don't you see, our house is full of physicians
..." She gripped the chair spindles hard.

He seemed to take pity on her. "Your business is ailing,"
he said gruffly, calming down. "That's the real trouble.
How do you expect me to help when you continually resist!" He came no nearer, but watched her, those keen eyes
focused on her, as if reading her thoughts.

"I am willing to wait," he said at last. He flashed her

a faint smile, showing his even, pointed teeth. "But you understand an alliance between our houses will be for the best. I will give you three extra days to consider. Three days beyond the original betrothal. I will call on you that morning. Then we can repair directly to the church."

Roz nodded, afraid to say anything. She'd got him to agree to three extra days. She had five days in all, though it wasn't near enough. Leaving the chair, she caught up the broom from the corner, began to sweep up the supper crumbs.

"Of course I cannot help with your business until we are wed. At least not directly—"

"Truly, we are doing much better," Roz insisted, concentrating on her sweeping. She rushed into the new topic feverishly. "The ruined lace was paid for, and someone else bought the rest."

Trenchard's face remained sober. Only his eyes changed. "All of it, you say?"

"All," Rozalinde declared staunchly. Pulling out the bench, she reached her broom for the crumbs surrounding Angelica's place. "At any rate, we have the money from those sales, which has helped tremendously. Then there's one of my father's company ships due by week's end in London. Those have never been troubled, and we shall have a small profit from it, though most of it is for shareholders."

Trenchard smoothed his soft leather jerkin across his broad chest. From the corner of her eye, Roz saw his left eyebrow twitch. It jumped queerly, making her pause in her work.

"I did not know your father had ships putting in at London. That is good. Ah, and Rozalinde, I had meant to tell you. I have a betrothal present for you."

"A present?" Roz put away her broom. "It isn't necessary."

"Ah, 'tis no ordinary present." Trenchard's lips curled into a satisfied smile. " 'Tis a pleasant piece of news. I've been made deputy lieutenant of Dorset by Her Majesty. I will work directly for the lord lieutenant of Dorset, Sir Christopher Hatton."

Rozalinde looked at him, astonished. How had he acquired such a high position? Everyone knew most lord lieutenants were too busy at court to do their work in the counties. So their deputies wielded the power. And that power had to do with everything military in the county—recruiting men for service, handling money, making the queen's proclamations and enforcing them, defending the country against invasion. The power—and the opportunity—was endless. "Such an honor," Roz said, trying not to show her surprise.

Trenchard chuckled low in his throat, seeming to sense her amazement and liking it. "I told you I would rise, Rozalinde. Here is proof. This is just my first step up the ladder. Think how advantageous this will be to your father's custom, to be allied with the deputy lieutenant of Dorset. And with you the lieutenant's lady."

Roz shook her head wonderingly. It was true. As wife to the deputy lieutenant, she could move in higher circles of society. She could meet hundreds of new customers in the course of her husband's business, many of them knights and nobles. It was very tempting.

But she was in no hurry to wed, she reminded herself. Power meant nothing to her. And her father's business could thrive without the contacts. She would go to Antwerp. Her mind was set.

"I've told no one yet," he said in a confiding tone. "I wanted you to be the first."

Solicitously he pulled out a chair, motioned her to sit. "I will divulge my good news to your father shortly. He, the lord mayor, and the parish priest will come tonight so that I can inform them." He placed one hand on each of her shoulders from behind the chair, began massaging, moving his hands in rhythmic motion.

She was tired, and his big hands had a light touch she had not anticipated. They soothed her weary muscles, especially the ridge of tension at the base of her neck.

Leaning back against the cushioned chair, she released her breath. She should not worry. He'd given her extra time, and she would put him off again in five days. By then it would be easier.

"In my new capacity," he explained, "I will control the seas around Dorset. If your shipments are ruined, we can find out why. We will do all this when you are my wife, of course."

She was feeling so languid, she wanted to relax. But his words made her think of their troubles. "I know you don't believe me, but our prospects are much better. They will continue to improve."

"Rozalinde, you are optimistic. A worthy trait." Trenchard's hands moved on her tense shoulders. "But remember, things may not go quite as you predict. A woman managing a business alone is bound to have difficulties. Look at your present state of affairs. Under your care, your troubles grow worse."

"It is not because I'm a woman!" She twisted around in the chair to confront him, arresting his hands in their motion. "You make it sound as if it's my fault."

"I'm sure it is not," he consoled her, turning her around and resuming the rhythmic kneading through her smock. "But remember I have offered my aid. Of course until we are wed, I will be busy with the official duties of my position. I could not possibly post a special patrol unless you were my wife. If you were, it would be understood . . ."

He gave a final rub, then removed his hands from her shoulders and circled around to stand before her. "I must meet with your father now. Five days hence, Rozalinde, I will call on you in the morning. God willing, we will go straight to church. God-den, my love." His smile was smooth. "May you have pleasant dreams."

With a last caress of her hand, he left the room.

Roz sat for some time in the chair, leaning against the cushioned back, her eyes closed. His touch had surprised her. For a few minutes it had cast a spell on her, making her think it might be acceptable, to be wed to someone who could use his hands like that.

But no, that was not a reason to wed. She preferred her freedom, with no husband to tell her what to do. Her father sometimes told her, but that was different. He loved her, so her needs and desires came first.

From down the passage she heard a knock at the front door, which one of the footmen answered. The mayor had arrived, no doubt. Voices sounded in the entry. She could make out her father's deep bass as he greeted the visitors. The door to the best parlor creaked as the visitors and her father entered. Roz could hear the men talking, greeting each other, settling down to business. They must have left the door half open, she concluded. Rising from the chair, she went and looked into the passage. The door stood just as she had imagined it, only partially closed, shielding her from their view. Trenchard was speaking, telling the others about his appointment. They congratulated him, good-naturedly jesting.

She went back into the dining parlor, retrieved her candle. She might as well go to bed. For certs she was tired, and Trenchard would not expect her to wait.

She was leaving the dining parlor a second time when Trenchard's voice stopped her.

"We shall apprehend the Sea Beggars if they land again in Dorset. The queen says they put the nation at terrible risk. We must do our duty. Gentlemen, are you prepared?"

She hadn't meant to eavesdrop, but she couldn't help it. At Trenchard's words, a violent shiver raced down her spine. Her heart unaccountably quickened. Freezing in her footsteps, she strained to hear.

"Her Majesty has issued a royal proclamation promising King Philip of Spain there will be no safe harbors in England for the Dutch pirates. That is why if the Sea Beggars land here, with or without our consent, we can be accused of breaking our word. Such a thing could precipitate war with Spain."

"That is unthinkable," interposed another whom Rozalinde recognized as the lord mayor. "England would never win such an encounter. You are right, George. We must catch these Sea Beggars when next they come to our coast. If we make an example of them, they will never dare come again."

Roz heard the conviction in his voice. She started to tremble.

"Precisely," she heard Trenchard answer. "I wish you to be the first to know that I have accepted the deputy's position from the queen for this very reason. I spoke with one of her privy counselors about it last week. It is my duty to enforce this ousting of the Sea Beggars from our ports."

Roz heard the others congratulate him again on the splendid post.

"The queen's counselors have confided their fears to me," Trenchard went on. "She is worried that if the Spanish know of such goings-on along our coast, if they even suspect we grant safe harbor, they would use it as an excuse to attack. And where do you think they would attack first?"

"Here, for certes." That was her father answering. "But the question is, what can we do? I appreciate your zeal for the problem, my friend, but the Dutch have not landed. At least not in recent years."

Silence reigned in the room, and Roz could imagine her father, sitting pale and ill between these men who demanded his support. She could tell he was not fond of his role.

"You are uninformed, Henry." Trenchard broke the silence with authority. "They landed a stolen ship here scarce a sen'night past. Did you not hear the gossip? I saw some of the goods myself. Spanish pepper, cloves from the Canary Islands—"

"How do you know 'twas stolen?" queried the parish priest anxiously. "Might have been legitimate. I myself have a liking for fresh pepper—"

" 'Twas stolen, I tell you." Trenchard's angry voice bit through the other calmer tones. "They landed right here in Lulworth Creek, which they're plotting to use as a permanent base. They must revictual and repair somewhere, and they've chosen a place within my jurisdiction. I've set a watch at the creek, but I'll need your help. I expect funds, as well as men. I will also begin a patrol of the coast. The lord admiral himself has pledged me the use of a ship should I deem it necessary."

A ship! Roz stopped listening while their voices droned on. For a second she stood paralyzed, an agonizing thought creeping into her brain. If they watched Lulworth Creek, if they patrolled the coast, they might well catch the man who had recently landed there. Her heart plummeted sharply as she thought of who that was.

Making up her mind abruptly, Roz turned from the stairs and went down the passage. When she peeked into the kitchen, she could see the cook bent over the hearth, muttering to herself as she banked the coals for the night. The back door stood ajar, letting in the smells and sounds of night, and Roz crept silently toward it. Outside, the stablemen and lads would be about their business. They would come in only after the visitors were gone.

Stealthily, Roz crossed the room, slipped through the door. Outside, she breathed deeply, glad the cook had not heard her. Raising her skirts to keep from tripping, she rounded the corner of the house, went down the garden path and out the front gate. As she dived into the shadows of the dark street beyond, her sense of foreboding grew. What was she doing skulking around her own house? She had duties to perform, yet here she was ignoring them.

Behind her the front door of the house opened. Light flared. Roz leaped into a doorway, pressing herself flat against the wall. She could hear them—the mayor, Trenchard—conversing while they waited for the horses to be brought around. They had not seen her, she told herself breathlessly, listening to the wild throbbing of her heart. She could wait here until they passed. They could not know someone hid in the shadows. They would never suspect.

George Trenchard felt conflicting emotions about his evening's work as he stepped through Cavandish's front door into the garden. The minute he did so, a warning sprang at him out of the dark. He whipped around, fastening his hawklike eyes on the street.

All was quiet. He could see the neat houses of the chandler, the shoemaker, the other tradesmen, lined up along the road, casting their shadows on the hard-packed earth. Nothing moved save the wind in the trees, but still he stared, not knowing why. The stableman came with the horses, accompanied by lads carrying glowing lanterns. Ignoring them, he stepped out of the bright circle and into the darkness, squinted down the road.

He could have sworn he saw something: a flick of a woman's skirt, a bounce of a loose braid disappearing into a doorway. Nothing more than that, but instantly his guard went up.

Affecting congeniality, he turned back to his host, bid him and the others god-den, then heaved himself into the saddle. He would find out who hid there. His time with Rozalinde tonight had made him suspicious. He wasn't quite sure of what. But she had tried to postpone their betrothal, and that boded ill. He sensed a reluctance in her. Applying his spurs more sharply than necessary to his animal, he passed by the doorway and went on down the street.

Chapter 11

Hugging her arms around her, shivering from the night's chill, Rozalinde flew up the slope toward Lulworth Castle. As she ran, she examined the few lights visible and wondered which one was the earl's. She knew the castle layout, having been to a reception there over a year ago, given by the former earl. Her father had been invited and brought both Rozalinde and her mother. Now Roz entered the garden and began to count the windows. Fourth set in from the left tower—they had to be the ones. The earl's private rooms, where she could see a light burned.

Something else burned—the blood, singing sinfully in her veins as she thought of him. Was she mad to come here? The mere image of Christopher Howard thrilled her.

But that wasn't important. The task ahead of her was. She had to get him this information. Entering the castle gardens, she picked her way among blooming hedges and flowers, rapidly approaching the massive structure.

Lulworth Castle wasn't medieval. It had been built earlier in the century by some Howard relative, so there was no moat around it, no cumbersome walls, not even a gatehouse. Only clean broad pathways and winding gravel walks leading through an intricate garden to the south. It was quite impressive, but Roz was in a hurry. Leaving the path, she headed for one particular window, drawn irresistibly to its light.

The darkness outside, the illumination within, afforded her a clear view of the room's interior. Rows of books, a portrait against paneled wood, a great marble chimney piece—all glowed by candlelight. A huge silver sconce of candles dripped with hot wax on a draw table, and before it sat Christopher Howard. He was bent over some work, writing. As she watched, he stopped and leaned back in his chair, running his fingers through his hair, flexing the muscles of his shoulder and arm. Standing outside his window, she could see those muscles, rippling beneath the taut linen of his shirt.

A matching ripple ran down Roz's spine. She remembered the feel of those arms, how they ignited such alien feelings within her the other night. Once more she was at the cove, reaching for him, touching him like she'd never touched a man—in ways she'd never wanted to before. She had thrilled to the warmth radiating from his skin. He'd kissed her thoroughly that night, and to her surprise, she'd exalted in it, wanting him to touch her all over while she explored the wonder of his male body—letting her hands play across his chest, permitting them to twine in his hair.

Christopher stopped stretching abruptly. He dipped the quill in the inkhorn and bent back over his work.

Roz came back to the present. She must get down to business. With bated breath she drew closer, squashing several marigolds in her haste. Troth, she thought, surveying the plants grouped with artistic precision in the beds. Someone had planted a rosebush so it blocked access to the window. Getting around it would be a trick.

Circling warily, she approached the window from the side, intent to pass behind the massive shrub. It sprawled in dense profusion, a fierce tangle of canes ladened heavily with buds. Their fragrance permeated the night, deceptively sweet. But as she tried to slide behind the foliage, flattening herself against the window ledge, thorns grabbed her kirtle. Digging into the cloth with insidious persistence, they hooked themselves fast.

"Troth!" She swore audibly as the sharp points went through the cloth to pierce her skin. "Troth and damn." Why did this stupid bush have to be here? Most women liked roses. But she didn't. Furious, she glared at the bush. The blasted things were good for rose hips in winter, rose vinegar in summer, and that was all, as far as she cared. And this one was making her life hellish. Given a spade, she would dig it up. Squinting in the dark, she tried to free herself, ignoring the beauty of the pale pink flowers. "Oh! Troth!" She groaned as a particularly long thorn thrust deeply into her skin. Determinedly she detached the thorns from her garments, forced them to release their hold. In

the narrow space between the plant and building, she
gripped the window ledge with both hands and pressed her
nose against the mullioned glass.

Kit gazed at a long inventory of tenants he'd visited that
day. With a stroke of his quill he wrote the last name, then
sat back to contemplate the list. The steward must compare
these names to the rent roles tomorrow, to verify where
each man stood. Some flourished, he noted. Others did not.
He would work with those whose profits were poor, seek
a remedy to turn them around.

Satisfied, Kit let the quill drop on the table. He stretched
again, flexing his right shoulder and shaking out the writer's
cramp in his hand. What a day it had been. He'd ridden
the entire estate with his new steward, learning everything
he could—what crops were planted, where the estate sheep
and cattle grazed. There was so much to know, so many
details to oversee, and now it was evident his brother had
been lax. He had delegated most duties to the old steward
and gotten cheated in the bargain. But then Harry had
always had a poor head for business, accepting whatever
anyone told him as God's truth, never bothering to look
beneath the surface. Kit looked beneath the surface—beneath people's often dissembling outward appearances.

He'd begun this practice as a child, watched his mother,
his brother, the servants, wanting to know why they did
what they did. Most of all, he'd watched his father, studied
him like a lesson—a painful one, resulting in agonizing
awareness. His father wounded his family with his total
indifference, his coldness. He set stringent rules and insisted on their enforcement. There were rules instead of
kindness, rules instead of love. The servants suffered less,
but they had their share of difficulty, being punished for
every infraction. The Earl of Wynford cared nothing for
his family. Discipline was everything. He established a strict
regime throughout the day—a set time for rising and eating,
a set time for prayer, a time for work or study, and a set
time for sleep. This schedule was followed ruthlessly, and
whenever Kit violated it, as he often did, he was punished.

No matter how hard he tried, Kit couldn't understand it.
When he'd fled West Lulworth, swearing never to return,
he'd found his freedom on the open ocean and used his
keen sense of observation there instead. He had thrived

because his ability to read men translated into gold. As a merchant he plied this skill until eventually it became second nature—to watch, to listen, to learn everything about a person. You could make men do many things if you knew them well enough. Or women. Many women had succumbed to him, since he knew just what they liked.

Reaching for the silver sandcaster in his writing set, Kit sprinkled a liberal dose of sand on the document and watched the ink dry. His efforts to control certain people hadn't worked today. He'd wanted Cavandish to hire his ship, but it hadn't happened like that.

"*She* agreed to meet with me," Courte had reported back about Rozalinde. "Not Master Cavandish, but the young Mistress Cavandish. Can you imagine? *She* turned me down. She refused *The Raven*." Courte was clearly outraged. " 'Not enough cannon,' she said. 'To small.' "

Kit's eyes had widened in surprise. Then he'd broken into hearty laughter. Wasn't that just like Rose to refuse his best ploy. All he'd wanted was to protect her, but naturally she'd refused. Almost as if she'd known he was behind the offer.

Now he sobered, stared at the scattered sand on his list and thought of her ship—the one she'd used for her last cargo. After overhearing her, he'd gone to see it. It was hidden away in a secluded cove, as if someone didn't want others to see it. An ugly cannon hole gaped in its side. 'Twas that which ruined her cargo. The captain and his crew scarce escaped with their lives. And it wasn't just this once, but several times in the past. "Who attacked you?" Kit had asked the captain as he sat morosely on the dock. The answer had been evasive. Clearly the man was afraid to tell. Just as clearly, Rozalinde Cavandish had enemies. Or her father did. Someone who meant business.

Kit smoothed his beard and pondered the problem. He had sent Courte and his new steward, Browne, to listen around town, and what did they hear? Rozalinde Cavandish was courted by the master alderman, a butcher who was making gold in piles from supplying the London market. This was assuredly the man who'd troubled her at the revel. Kit made a decision to keep an eye on him in the weeks to come.

Then there was Rozalinde's plan to take cargo to Ant-

werp. She'd told Courte as much, and it made Kit furious.
She wouldn't do it, of course. She wouldn't dare after he
warned her not to, as he intended. She was too damned
independent, this maid, an unacceptable trait. Then why did
he still feel interest? She was impossibly stubborn, drove a
hard bargain, and insisted on her rights. Just like a man,
she was. Kit stopped abruptly in midthought, astounded at
the idea. Could *that* be what he liked about her?

Picking up the paper before him, he blew at the sand
vigorously and watched it scatter across the table. His feelings, too, were scattered tonight, and he puzzled over them.
If he found her attractive, and there was no question about
that, then why did he act the way he did around her? Not
at all like he would around a beddable wench. But then he
had to admit he got more satisfaction from one of her
smiles than from a hundred beddings. Still, it was odd. He'd
wager his father had never felt like that, about Kit's mother
or anyone else.

The thought of his father turned Kit's mood sour again.
His mouth went down at the corners in a sullen grimace,
just as it had during his childhood when his father accused
him of some transgression. Never would he let himself be
bound in the suffocating ties of marriage and family. It
destroyed a man's character, forced him to do and say
things he didn't enjoy. He'd hated his father for being an
unbending tyrant. Yet he could not believe, did not wish
to believe, the powerful earl had chosen consciously to live
like that. Something must have driven him.

But what? Kit shook his head and put down the piece
of vellum before him, smoothing the fiber of its rough edges
with his fingertips. He would never know. His father had
talked to him not at all during his childhood, and by the
time he was grown, it was too late. There was no opportunity to understand him. Yet marriage had unquestionably
had a bad effect on him. And having children was the
worst part.

Then there was his father's opposite, the Beggar King.
Since their meeting the other night, Kit had felt exultant.
Courte had warned him not to meet with the pirate, yet he
had done it and they had become allies. His own daring
made him feel as buoyant inside as a new-filled sail. The
queen didn't authorize his joining forces with the Nether-

lands. But Gloriana often said one thing while meaning another, and Kit knew, in his heart, this was one of those times. She wanted to aid the Netherlands but not be caught doing it. So he undertook the task, on his own incentive, at his own expense. But to him, the reward was more than adequate.

Opening a drawer in a small rosewood table, Kit pulled out the bag of powdered cloves and inhaled deeply. The forceful grip of the Beggar King's hand on his warmed his memory. Nay, not the Beggar King. No need to think of him by that name anymore. He was Phillipe, Count of Hoorne. A man to be admired for his courage, a man of flesh and blood, with a history and a name. And now that the pirate proved to be a real person, Kit could assume his mysterious identity, become the fascinating Beggar King who roamed the sea and knew no master. Again the exhilaration of the night at the cove claimed Kit's consciousness. He had been worshiped by the people of Dorset, and they'd given him a gift—one of their own, the maiden symbolizing all the women who yearned for his magic. Rose. The moment he'd singled her out and kissed her, he'd felt alive and free, in a way he hadn't felt for years.

His thoughts were interrupted by a tap at the door. "Come," he called absently, expecting Browne, his new steward, to reply.

The tap repeated itself. Kit looked up at the door as he dropped the cloves back in the drawer and closed it. "Come in, Browne," he called more loudly. "You'll not disturb me." Pulling himself to his feet, he strode to the door, rubbing his back and straightening his black leather jerkin. He pulled the door open and stared into the dark passage. No one was there.

Perplexed, he turned back to the room. Come to think of it, that knock hadn't sounded on wood.

Pulling the door shut behind him, he studied the great oriel window on the south wall. Sure enough, a face showed at the glass. And not just any face. It was adorned by two thick braids.

"God's wounds!" He started, realizing who it was. Simultaneously a jolt ripped through his brain and traveled at breathtaking speed to his loins. It spread in the most deli-

cious tendrils of desire, accompanied by a single thought—
she wanted to see him again.

But a second later he hesitated, then cursed. Why would
she come here to his window? During their last encounter,
he'd agreed not to tempt her. Yet here she was, doing the
tempting. She was nothing but trouble, he decided, remembering how she'd refused his ship. By God, he wouldn't be
tempted. He would send her straight home.

Leaping to the window he flipped up the catch and swung
the pane wide. "What in God's name are you doing here,
Rose?" he admonished. "If my steward had been about,
you might have been shot."

A disheveled-looking Rozalinde frowned up at him.
"Such a greeting! I knew you'd be surprised, but in truth,
I had hoped . . ." She tsked with her tongue reprovingly.
"I had hoped at least for politeness, but I suppose you
won't even offer your hand. Ah, well." She shot him a look
of reproach. "I'll do without."

Ignoring his shocked expression, Roz braced both hands
on the window ledge and gave a little hop. She levered
herself off the ground and swung up to sit on the sill. "I
can't help what you think. I decided to come and warn
you," she panted, breathing quickly from her exertion.
"You must hear my news before you send me home."

Kit looked baffled. He *had* thought to send her home.
But now he couldn't, after a statement like that. "All
right," he said grudgingly, "come in. Though I should not
let you. What if you've been seen?"

Rozalinde wasn't listening. Struggling to get her feet over
the sill, her legs twisted in her bunching skirts. She teetered
and started to fall.

"Here, you'll tear something." Without preamble Kit
leaned over and tumbled her into his arms. Lifting her easily, he carried her into the room.

"Stop!" Rozalinde thrashed both arms and legs, outraged
at his presumption. Picking her up like a sack of grain,
indeed! He was always intruding on her affairs when it
wasn't his business. "Put me down at once."

Kit obeyed abruptly. Setting her down with a thud on
her feet, he hurried back to the window and concentrated
on swathing it thoroughly with the heavy drapes.

"Troth," she muttered, rubbing one hand where a thorn

had pricked her. Most likely he was going to be difficult.
Mayhap she shouldn't have come.

Outside, Trenchard shifted his position in the shrubbery
of Lulworth Castle. He had headed for town, then doubled
back. Sure enough, a girl about Rozalinde's height and
weight had climbed the hill to Lulworth Castle. He'd
watched for some time, questioning what he saw.

Now he questioned no longer. The girl at the earl's window had used Rozalinde's favorite oath. Deliberately he
raised his vast bulk to his feet and made his way around
to the castle's back door.

"Well, now, let's have it." Kit turned from his task of
covering the window. "What news is so important you
come climbing in my window at night? Mutilating my best
rosebush in the process, no doubt."

"Blast the rosebush," Roz told him indignantly. "Your
idiot plant wasn't injured. It near ripped me to shreds. Just
look." She held out one arm to show him.

"You're bleeding." Kit's heart stumbled in midbeat at
the sight of blood welling up from a wound. He caught her
by the wrist and pulled back her sleeve. The movement
exposed the inner side of her slender white arm where a
trail of crimson liquid showed. It oozed slowly onto his
hand.

Ruefully, she wrinkled her nose. "That's hardly the
worst. Look what your bush did to my stocks. And they
cost me two shillings apiece."

Right there, standing in the middle of Kit's best Persian
carpet, Roz pulled up her kirtle skirts to reveal her slim
legs. Through her torn, snagged stockings, he could see her
bare flesh.

The sight of it caused his heart to beat with mighty
strokes. Blood rushed to his head. Heat poured through his
veins, riddling his body with wanting. Pressing her down on
a stool, he knelt before her, unable to tear his gaze from
the graceful curves of her slender ankles and calves.

He wet his handkerchief with his tongue. "You must let
me staunch that bleeding," he told her, taking her foot
gently in his hand. He applied the linen firmly against a
wound.

Carefully he cleansed her skin, tucking up her kirtle skirts to expose her legs further. She stared at him helplessly, let him minister to her hurts.

"Poor Rose," he whispered, gently removing her shoe. " 'Tis my fault this happened." Her garter slid off easily, followed by her stock. Cupping her bare instep in one hand, he absorbed the blood that oozed from the gash.

Roz gripped the edge of the stool tightly—the intimacy of his hands was excruciating. The resolve she had brought with her floated away, subsumed by the powerful effect of his touch. "It's not so bad," she protested weakly, thinking she would never deliver her message. "I beg you, leave off."

Grinning up at her, he ran one finger down the slanting plane of her shinbone, then wrapped his thumb and forefinger around her ankle. "Nay, you must permit me one small favor and I will be content."

"What favor is that?" Roz nervously wet her lips with the tip of her tongue.

He didn't answer. Instead, with maddening slowness, he leaned forward and pressed his warm lips to her flesh, just at the place where her calf joined the thigh.

It was a madly sensitive spot, and as he touched it, Rozalinde felt a flash of excitement invade her. How did this man know so much about her? Easily he discovered every vulnerable spot she had. First her worst tickle spot, now this. Unfamiliar feelings roiled through her body, twining themselves insistently around her heart, then spreading lower, setting off that strange tingling deep in her belly. Against her will, her hands reached forth to tangle in his hair. That sweet-smelling, waving hair—she buried her fingers in it. Her head tipped back and an anguished sigh escaped her lips.

"Troth," she whispered, "why do you do this?" She could feel him raise her skirts higher, slide his other hand around her waist outside her clothing as he kissed the smooth flesh of her outer thigh.

"Because you are my flower, Rose. Whenever I see you, I want to touch, to taste, to smell the sweet scent of you, to feel you in my arms. This is meant to be, sweetling. Why don't you try to relax?"

"Nothing is meant to be if I don't want it," she argued,

trying to subjugate her senses. "Your logic is faulty. You must stop."

But he was caressing her legs, making those odd new feelings coil and weave their way through her body. Up and down his fingers traveled, leaving their trail of enchantment, stroking the outside of her legs. He buried his face at her waist. "Do not question passion when it finds you. You must obey its call."

"Nonsense," Roz muttered, getting a better hold on her desire as she realized he might see clear up her skirts. "We have important business." But his face was buried in her bodice, and she could hardly bear to stop him. He was tenderly releasing the first button that closed her smock. "I must tell you," she gasped out, "about the chief alderman. He's been made deputy lieutenant of Dorset."

"So?"

As he applied his lips to the cleft of her breasts, a heat seemed to penetrate. An unbearable urgency gripped her, to do what, she didn't know. But she could feel her nipples harden, straining against her linen smock, and she felt a wild, urgent wish to tear it off.

" 'Tis only that . . ." Roz struggled against the heady sensation caused by his nearness, her thoughts had become a hazy mass of incoherent flame, waving and dancing. " 'Tis only that he wants you caught."

"Not surprising." He stroked her thigh in a long, lazy caress. Not so high as to reach between her legs, but tantalizingly close. "Say my name, sweetheart. Call me Kit. You must always call me Kit."

"Kit," she moaned, closing her eyes. She hoped it would make things easier, but it made them worse. It heightened her awareness of his touch. She snapped them open again. "Why won't you listen? He's got a ship. At least he'll get one if he needs it. He plans to catch you. Don't you see?"

Kit stopped. He sat up straight on the floor and stared at her. "He's got what?"

At last she'd gotten through to him. And with his lips withdrawn, she finally could speak. "He has a ship—that is, one of the Lord Admiral's, but for his work he says. He's to capture the Sea Beggars if they come near our coast. He has many cannon." She shuddered as she said the words.

"How big a ship?" Kit demanded urgently. "How many ton?"

Roz shook her head desperately, her mind growing clearer by the moment. "I didn't hear that part. But you must be careful. You truly must."

"Careful?" Kit laughed recklessly. He felt reckless, having her here alone, kissing her as he had. "You are the one who should be careful, climbing in a man's window at night. Did you ever think," his hands tightened on her waist again, "that you might be compromised? What if I were not a gentleman? What if I took you to my bed?"

"There's no danger of that," she scoffed. "It would never happen unless I wanted it. And I don't."

She bent over for her stocking. As she leaned, one of her braids fell across her shoulder, and for the first time Kit noticed it reached clear to her waist. A wish stabbed through him—a wish to unbind those thick, glossy braids and twine that rich chestnut hair in his hands.

"Besides," she was saying, calmly pulling on the stocking, "I had a task to accomplish tonight and I did it. There's no use worrying about what other people think or want. We can't control things like that."

"You'll get yourself in deep trouble some day, if you think that way," Kit rapped out at her as he stood up. She'd made him as hard as a stone, then didn't worry about consequences. "Listen to your passion for a change. Your thinking leads you wrong."

"There's nothing wrong with the way I think," she told him indignantly, standing up and stepping into her shoe. "Logic told me you needed this information, so I brought it to you. It was the right choice, too, because this man could cause you difficulty, without a doubt. I know what you're up to—"

"You're not to go to Antwerp," Kit interrupted, deflecting the conversation away from the dangerous subject. He didn't dare talk about his piracy. "You can't trade there. Antwerp is held by the Spanish."

Roz stopped in midphrase and looked nonplussed. "Who told you I was going? Did I say that?"

"Never mind who told me." He gave her a stern stare. "You must stay at home. You're not to go."

"I have always traded with my father—" she began.

"But your father will not accompany you, will he?" Kit insisted.

"No, but—"

"But nothing. It's grossly improper for a woman to travel alone. I forbid you to do it. You must remain in West Lulworth."

Roz frowned at him. He could see her lips press tightly together. "And who will see my cargo to the Netherlands? Who will ensure it gets there whole? What about the return goods? You don't understand that our business is at stake. Things will arrive safely if I am along—"

"It's dangerous out there," he said harshly, losing patience. "You could be set upon by Spanish patrols. Worse, you could be stopped by men who would—"

"Nonsense," Rozalinde told him decidedly. "I intend to have a bigger ship this time, one with cannon. No one will dare approach."

"They will if you sail for Antwerp. You'll not make it. You can't go around acting like a man because you're not."

"I'm not acting like a man." Roz stamped her foot, pushed beyond her usual endurance. "I am acting like a logical human being. Whether I am a woman or a man plays no part in it. Why should my actions be 'acting like a man,' just because it's what you'd do. One might say *you* were acting like a woman if you chose something I would do. It's all the same."

"It isn't the same. Women aren't logical. They think of nothing but their clothes or who they're going to wed."

"Well, I don't," Roz snapped at him. "I don't care about clothes except to stay warm and decent. And as for men . . ." She gave him a withering stare, clearly deciding not to utter the insulting thought she'd just had. "I *am* going to Antwerp."

Kit groaned inwardly and looked away. They weren't getting anywhere, arguing like this. She was far too good at it for him to best her. He even had to admit she was right about one thing—she didn't seem to care about clothes. He'd never seen her in anything other than serviceable smocks and kirtles. As for the topic of men, gossip said she'd refused a dozen offers of marriage. "There are the Spanish traders," he began again, trying to be more tactful, "mayhap they'll leave you alone, though they sail armed.

But the Spanish fleet prowls up and down the Channel all the time, looking for skirmishes with the Dutch. The Dutch traders would leave you alone also, your being English, but there are French pirates, if you're unlucky enough to meet up with them. And I'll tell you this—" He paused and cleared his throat. "The Sea Beggars will sink anyone bound for Antwerp. They're vowed to stop all trade with their enemy."

"Yes?" Roz tossed her braids back over her shoulders and gave him a strange look. "Tell me more about their plans."

Kit examined her thoughtfully, trying to decide what to say. Should he explain why she shouldn't go to Antwerp? That if she did, he would be forced to stop her? Yet it wasn't safe to involve her further—she knew too much already. "I've made my livelihood in trade," he began cautiously, "the same as you." He stopped, realizing what he'd said. He'd addressed her as an equal. "And I serve the queen. It gives me access to privileged information."

"Does it? Exactly what?"

He could see blatant curiosity in her eyes. "I fight the Spanish," he said, then stopped again, realizing she unnerved him, made him say too much with only the slightest coaxing. "Never mind the details. 'Tis my task. I don't know why I trust you, but I believe you'll not tell."

She smiled then. So unexpectedly, he almost missed the stool behind him as he sat down. Gripping the seat and centering himself, he watched her pure oval face all alight. She looked overwhelmingly beautiful, with the little tendrils of hair escaping from her braids to curl around her face, those deep brown eyes fringed thickly with glossy lashes. No wonder every man in West Lulworth and nearby had courted her. Courted her and been turned away.

"I shouldn't have told you. 'Tis not safe you should know," he admitted grudgingly.

"My world is a safe place."

"It isn't," he contradicted her forcefully. "Let me help with your business. I can set your troubles straight."

"I'll set them straight myself, thank you."

"Not if you sail for Antwerp, you won't. I have a feeling about that," he hinted darkly, "and 'tis not good."

"A pity," she told him, crossing her arms defiantly. "Because you haven't given me any clear reasons to avoid it. I said I'm bound for Antwerp, so you can be quite sure I am."

Down in the kitchens of Lulworth Castle, things were quiet. All the servants had sought their beds save the cook. When the steward wandered in, the cook poured two flagons of ale, then seated himself. "Sit ye down, Browne." He motioned to the man lounging before the fire. "His lordship'll not need us more. He's up in his cabinet and will stay there, a scratching with his quill. A'times he sleeps there all night."

Heaving a tired sigh, Geoffrey Browne scraped out a stool and sat on it. " 'Tis well," he muttered, swilling a good quaff of the brew. "I'm nigh fit to drop, what with all the riding we did today. We were to every part of the estate, talked to every tenant. His lordship makes a man earn his wage."

"Aye, he does," the cook confirmed. He reached for a bowl warming by the fire. "Here," he said, digging with his fingers into juicy tidbits of meat. "These was left from noon dinner."

Silence reigned in the warm kitchen while the men ate and drank. Firelight shone on the polished copper kettles and savory herbs hanging from the ceiling beams gave off their crisp scent.

"Odd one, his lordship." The cook broke the silence. "But a good 'un to serve. Goes off at the strangest hours and stays away for days. Comes back without a word like he was never gone." He gulped more of his ale. "Not like the old master, but then he's a lying in the churchyard yonder and you never knowed him."

Browne nodded. "I knew the earl long before he was a lord. He gives honest pay for an honest day's toil. I'd just as soon serve him."

"Aye," the cook admitted. "Though he don't give me the same rights in me kitchen as the old master. This one is forever coming down to see what I'm up to and telling me to do it different. The old master wouldn't set foot in the place. But then I'll not be complainin'," he added hastily. " 'Tis easier work now, and that's worth a heap." Lowering his voice, he said confidentially, "The old master was too quick with his rod. And after him, Lord Harry and his wife," he made a face, "she was a devil in petticoats, always with a chiding word. 'Tis a sight better now that she don't rule the roost. I'm glad Lord Kit put his foot down with her."

Browne nodded sympathetically. "I confess I avoid the dowager countess. There's just no pleasing her." He quaffed some more of his ale. "She'll probably wed again soon and move somewhere else."

There was a bump at the kitchen door, then a knock. The cook went to open it, knowing all the servants were in. When he opened the door a crack, it was thrust open forcibly. A huge gentleman shoved his way in.

"What do you want?" cried the cook, jumping back in alarm from the gentleman. He had to be a gentleman—he was dressed like one, in silk long gown and silk knit hose and a good quality hat on his head. "We want no trouble here," he stammered. "Sure an' we do not." He stopped, assessed the man, and suddenly knew him. 'Twas the town's chief alderman. "Your honor," he added, just to be safe.

"No trouble," agreed the man, striding in past the cook and pausing before the hearth to eye Browne. His broad face wore a fierce, determined look, and his shifting eyes were a blazing green. "That you shall not have, if you take me to his lordship and take me fast. I want to see him, so show the way."

"His lordship's abed," insisted the cook, sensing this was trouble if ever he'd seen it. "He's not seein' visitors. Not this time o' night."

"I'm not a visitor." Trenchard pushed his way impatiently past Browne and headed for the passage leading to the front of the house. "If you'll not show me, I'll find my own way."

"Here then, stop. You can't go in there." Browne ran after him, followed directly by the cook. "Can't just go bargin' in on his lordship."

"I'll see him now." Trenchard turned and looked at the servant steadily.

The cook eyed his determined face, the richness of his clothes, and gave in. "This way," he said resignedly, sliding past to lead the way. "He's in his cabinet."

The cook lit candles at the hearth, then led the way up

a stair and down a long passage. The alderman followed closely at his heels, with Browne bringing up the rear. They halted before a door where a light showed. Looking nervously at the man beside him, the cook wondered what the alderman wanted this time of night. Whatever it was, the earl was home and engaged in nothing more exciting than going over his accounts. There was nothing to be learned about the earl's absences at night. Furthermore, none of them at the castle knew a thing about them—only that he went. Lifting his fist, he knocked.

Inside, Kit heard the knock and reacted instantly. He sprang to the hearth.

"Who is it?" Rozalinde felt the blood drain from her face. She'd had no intention of being seen when she made the decision to come here. If someone did, she'd be in terrible trouble. She would lose her reputation—not that she cared about that. But things could go hard on her sisters, and perhaps on the family as a whole. Scandals impeded business, and she couldn't have that. Whirling so swiftly her skirts wrapped around her legs, she headed for the window.

"Not that way." Kit motioned vigorously for her to return. "In here." To the left of the chimney piece he leaned on a carved rosette, one of many that adorned the oak-paneled wall.

Rozalinde stared as a panel slid noiselessly back to reveal a hidden chamber. "A priest's hole," she whispered, "to hide Catholic priests."

"To hide anyone who needs hiding," Kit told her, motioning her in impatiently. "The Howards haven't been Catholic for years. In with you. Why do you wait?"

"You shouldn't share your secrets with me," she said not moving. "I thought you said it was best if I didn't know—"

"You argue more than any woman I've ever met." Kit grasped her by the arm and hustled her toward the chamber. "In with you. And don't give yourself away. I'll tell you when it's safe to come out." Pushing her across the threshold, he reached for the rosette. "I don't know how it happens," his face wore a perplexed look as he gazed down at her, "but it seems you are destined to know all manner of things about me." His hand tightened on her

arm a moment, then he released her and pressed the rosette. The panel glided silently back into place and closed
with a faint click.

It was abysmally black in the chamber, almost as bad as
the cave at Lulworth Creek. Dismayed by her reaction,
Rozalinde lowered herself carefully to the floor, flattening
herself against it for security. She was all alone in the darkness, with nothing to do but listen helplessly and wait.

It was then, crouching in the void where she couldn't
see her hand before her face, that she realized something.
Suddenly her innate fear of the dark, combined with a
growing anxiety, ignited like a bonfire. Reaching down, she
groped desperately, hoping it wasn't true. But it was. Her
stock hung down around her ankle. She'd left her garter
outside.

Chapter 12

Alone in the musty darkness of the priest's hole, Rozalinde listened. The minute the knock had sounded, she'd frozen with fear. Her pulse took off on a mad race as she tried to imagine how anyone could know she was here.

But then she heard his voice and knew. It was George Trenchard. Somehow he had seen her leave the house—seen her and meant to catch her. Oh, he had been angry when she postponed their betrothal. Why hadn't she recognized his firmly suppressed reaction. He was so controlled, so rational, so much like Rozalinde herself she hadn't realized. And now, with this added insult, she might not be able to appease him. Worse yet, what would he do with this knowledge?

Her first thought was that he would refuse to marry her. That might suit her purposes if no one knew why. But he could also use it to *insist* on their marriage. Either way he could ruin their business if he so desired. Roz squeezed her eyes shut and prayed fervently that he would go away.

As she prayed, a small hope flitted through her mind. If he did not find her, he could prove nothing. He might even leave believing he was mistaken—*if* Kit handled things right. Then again, even if he didn't find her, he might be convinced she'd been here and start to gossip.

Never had Rozalinde felt so vulnerable. Here she was, with little more between her and ruin than a single oak panel. It was so thin, that wall, that any second she expected him to detect her, to see through it and shatter her life into a million pieces. Fear coursed through her like a virulent fever, swirling in her brain as she heard him interrogate Kit.

"God-den to you, your lordship. All alone?"

Roz could hear the door to the chamber close and

George's voice, heavy with suggestion. She could imagine his sharp eyes, scrutinizing Kit's cabinet.

Kit answered in frozen tones. "Do you see anyone here?" There was a chilling pause. "Master Alderman, the hour is late for callers. I was about to retire, having completed my work for the night." She could all but see him nod toward his ink and paper, laid out on the table. "Be so good as to state your business so that I may go to my rest." He stifled a yawn.

Trenchard took his time in answering. "You are perhaps unaware of my new appointment. By tomorrow, the entire town will know. I thought you would like to have advance warning."

Roz clasped one hand to her bodice, wishing to still her racing heart. Every muscle in her body quivered with tension. Somehow, Kit must get them through this. If Trenchard did not find her, all could still be well.

"I have been appointed deputy lieutenant by Her Majesty," Trenchard announced. His voice sounded ridiculously pompous to Rozalinde. "You know the duties that will be connected to it." Trenchard's heavy tread sounded on the floorboards, so different from Kit's light one. Roz heard him move around the room, searching for signs of her. The wall trembled as his step shook the floor. If she made even the smallest move, he might hear . . .

Staring intently into the darkness, Roz tried to concentrate on something else, to imagine Kit's face. But an immense well of misery had opened up inside her. Until this week her world had been safe, impenetrable. Now she felt her security threatened. One well-placed slander could greatly damage her father's business. Honest housewives would not buy from a draper if they thought the daughter selling the goods was a whore. Though Roz had never cared much about her reputation, she realized its value. And somehow, Trenchard had discovered she came here.

Something heavy, a book, fell with a slam to the floor. Roz jumped, let out an unconscious gasp. Any second now, she expected George to come over to her wall and bang on it, demanding she come out. In her cramped position on the floor, her every muscle screaming, Roz felt herself break into a cold sweat. She strained to hear. From Kit there was silence. She could imagine him, watching Trenchard with that glacial stare of his.

The door at the far end of the room opened. There was a pregnant pause before it slammed shut. Roz jumped a second time but was able to arrest the gasp before it reached her lips. Her heart had entered her throat, it seemed, and lodged there, blocking her breath. Reaching down to untwist her kirtle skirts, she tried to edge herself backward, away from the sliding panel. Again she felt for her sagging stocking, experienced a streak of fright as she imagined him finding her garter. It was out there somewhere, lying in the room.

"Are you looking for something?" The contempt in Kit's voice was barely veiled. "Sure and you didn't come to tell me the news of your appointment at this time of night."

"Tsk, tsk, don't overset yourself." Trenchard's reply was congenial. "I'm not looking for anything that requires a warrant to search, at least not yet." Roz could hear his voice clearly. He apparently stood before the chimney piece, just beside her panel.

"Then kindly leave me to my rest," Kit said brusquely. "You may call another time."

"Another time, hmm, yes." Roz could hear Trenchard rocking back and forth on the balls of his feet. "What would I find then, I wonder?"

Roz's pulse thundered in her throat. They were only a few feet away from her. Carefully she backed deeper into the hole, wishing she could go out like the light of a candle.

Kit gave a bored sigh. "In truth, Master Trenchard, you hint at this and that, but I have not the least idea of what you refer to. I weary of this discourse. I would bid you good-den."

"Not before I warn you, Wynford." For the first time, Trenchard's voice had an ominous note to it. "You see," he went on, "you have been gone from Lulworth for many years. Things are not what they used to be here—the officials lax and turning a blind eye to the indiscretions of the citizens. I make it my business to know exactly what people are doing. If you understand my meaning."

"I am glad to know you apply yourself conscientiously to your duties."

"I intend to be effective in my position," snapped Trenchard. "And to examine indiscretions at every level of the social strata. The nobility may be privileged, but they have been known to take a tumble or two."

"Meaning?"

"Meaning, I am observant. I already know things about certain individuals in West Lulworth that would interest the Queen's Star Chamber."

"In truth?" drawled Kit. "And what would that be?"

"The Sea Beggars," Trenchard answered. "They've been to West Lulworth in the last sen'night. I intend to see that their visits cease. I intend to see them hang."

"You would need an entire troop to accomplish that."

"I need only ask the Lord Lieutenant of Dorset if I wish one. He's already sent me three men."

"So many? How generous."

Kit was being purposely antagonizing, and Rozalinde's hand itched to slap him. For no good reason he was goading Trenchard, and it frightened her exceedingly. He was guilty of everything Trenchard hinted at. Did Trenchard really know?

"That's not all," snapped Trenchard, clearly enraged by Kit's mockery. "I'll tell you something else. Do not dare to take what is mine. You understand?"

"I do not," Kit told him blandly. "I have nothing of yours. Pray explain."

"Your place has changed in West Lulworth." Trenchard was losing his calm. "You'd best have a care."

"Indeed?"

Rozalinde could hear Trenchard pacing as he circled around Kit. "I have my people everywhere, your lordship." He put an insulting accent on the title. "They see things you might not expect. For instance . . ." He paused tauntingly. "I know you sail away at night and don't return for days. And when you do, there's said to be blood on your shirt."

Rozalinde winced. Blood on his shirt, just as the countess had said. The words sang ominously in her ears.

"You hear correctly, but anyone who makes something unusual of my practice spins an absurd tale," Kit responded crisply. "I sail out because I am engaged in trade. My ships put out from London, or Portsmouth. Ofttimes, I meet them. 'Tis nothing more complex than that. As for the blood, there are injuries among the seamen. Such things cannot be avoided. I do my best to aid them myself."

"I see." Sarcasm ladened Trenchard's voice. "The great Captain Howard, legendary for his skill in trade, not to mention the fortune he has amassed, stooping to aid one of his own seamen. A touching picture, and one I do not believe for an instant. I have a far better explanation for your strange movements at night and your bloodied clothes."

There was an immense stillness, during which Rozalinde struggled to fill her lungs.

"We both know what it is," Trenchard said.

His words hung on the air. Rozalinde had to suppress another terrified gasp.

"When you come down to it," Trenchard continued, "you're no better than the rest of us. Not when you're going after what you want. No, you're not above treason, that I'll warrant. You'll hang just as neatly as the next knave."

"Explain yourself." The bored tone in Kit's voice had vanished. His rasping reply sounded just as dangerous as Trenchard's taunts. Roz wiped her sweaty palms on her kirtle skirts and inched herself back.

"I mean," came Trenchard's reply, "that you're playing a dangerous game and you'll be caught at it, I promise. You think no one knows, but the deputy lieutenant makes such things his business."

"Browne." Kit crossed the room, moving away from Rozalinde, his voice coldly polite. He must have opened the door, for she heard him call Browne again. "Please see this gentleman out. Trenchard, we are finished for tonight. I would have you gone."

Roz backed away farther, her heart racing, her limbs shaking. Trenchard was proving difficult in ways she'd never imagined. The chaos that stampeded through her life looked insignificant compared to Kit's danger. Her problems had seemingly expanded from her small household to include the great earl on the hill. It was so vast a trouble, it threatened to overwhelm her. Somehow Trenchard had learned things about Kit only she knew. Her anxiety escalated. God save us, she thought over and over. This man intended to ruin the earl, and he had the power to do it.

The full extent of Kit's danger came home to her and she backed farther, wanting to escape her involvement in Kit's troubles. Her own were complicated enough. The tiny chamber was musty, but she was grateful for it, for sheltering her with its fearful dark.

Then, as she backed, her feet went out from under her. The floor disappeared. A hole gaped beneath her, and she found herself falling—down, down—into its yawning, terrifying depths.

In Kit's cabinet, the verbal battle continued.

"You threaten me, when you have no basis for it?" Kit kept his voice low, controlled. Trenchard was poised before the door to leave. "If you doubt my fealty to Her Majesty, ask her yourself. If you know her so well."

Trenchard scowled at the jab, put his hand on the rapier that hung at his side. Kit saw his motion and indicated the door. "Sir, I'd ask you to leave my affairs be. I don't expect to be troubled this way again. I'll not countenance your intrusion." But even as Kit kept his expression stony, he churned with discomfort inside. For he had caught a glimpse of Rozalinde's garter lying on the floor. Carefully he manipulated Trenchard, trying to back him away, praying the man would not look down. The garter lay in full sight.

Trenchard smiled, appearing to detect that minute change in Kit's demeanor. His sharp eyes scrutinized the room. He took one deliberate step toward the door but did not pass through it. Outside, Browne and the cook waited, their faces distinctly unfriendly.

"I'll leave when I'm ready and not before. I'll pursue this line of thinking further. You admit to having affairs you would not like inspected." Trenchard clucked his tongue. He seemed to be deliberately baiting, knowing it was not what Kit had meant. "I warrant they're none too savory. Well, well, we shall see. In the meantime, remember the bloody shirt. You can lie awake tonight, guessing who told me. Which of your servants would it be? Hmm? You'd not want to dismiss anyone unfairly, would you? I know you already, you see. So generous with those who serve you, taking up people from the gutter and giving them a place, feeding their families so they'll not starve. Bah!" He scowled. "This town mislikes your charity. You'll reap nothing but trouble for disturbing the natural order of things. They're low because they're born to it. You'll find that out soon enough."

Kit made a threatening sound in his throat.

Trenchard continued. "We shall meet again by and by. I consider it more than generous on my part to warn you. But 'tis as far as my generosity goes. If we meet ship to ship, the law will be on my side."

"Enough." Kit's voice cracked like a cat-o'-nine-tails. "Get out."

"Ah, he angers." Trenchard snickered. "Only a man with a burden of guilt angers when accused." He took a quick step across the threshold at Kit's thunderous expression. "I'll not cross swords with you tonight. Another time, you may be sure. Adieu."

Kit banged the door shut after Trenchard, all but catching the man's heel. Whirling, he contemplated the marble chimney piece furiously, trying to leash the rage that stormed inside. It made him long to whip his rapier from its hanger and charge after the brute.

Lunging forward abruptly, he retrieved Roz's garter and stuffed it in his trunk hose pocket. Then he strode to the wall panel and leaned against the rosette. Damn Trenchard. Damn himself. He should have known Rozalinde might be followed. How could he be so simple as to remain in the room where she'd entered? He hadn't realized the chief alderman wanted Rozalinde so badly, but apparently he did.

The panel slid back slowly. Too slowly for his taste. He wanted to grasp it in both hands and tear it from the wall to get at Rozalinde. She was probably half dead with terror. He expected her in tears.

"Rose?" His voice rang hollowly in the recess. "Sweetling, you can come out."

Silence.

He reached into the darkness, expecting to find her lying in a dead faint, but his hands encountered nothing. Only dusty floorboards warped by time. Rozalinde was gone, and realizing what had happened to her, he swore softly to himself. Bloody hell and damn.

*   *   *

It was not a hole to nowhere. Roz soon discovered that. In fact, she had fallen down a flight of steep, narrow stairs and now lay at the foot. Groping, she strove to rise.

Her heart still pounded excruciatingly as she struggled with her fear of the dark. It rose up from her childhood, unmerciful in its intensity. But now she must rely on this old enemy, the dark, to hide her. Her greater fear was that Trenchard had heard her fall down the stairs.

As she felt in the blackness, trying to get oriented, her hand encountered something hard and cold. A little metal box. Careful not to drop it, for it would make much noise, she picked it up. It seemed to be a tinderbox, for she felt some stonelike shards inside, along with a mound of soft lint. Relief shot through her—she was saved from the dark. Striking the two pieces of flint together, she made a spark. It caught immediately and the lint flared. Grateful for the light, she sought a candle from the box and lit it, then stepped on the lint to extinguish it and looked around.

The passage was ordinary. Its walls were stone. Turning away from Kit's cabinet, she followed it down. Deeper she traveled, probably on a level with the castle cellars, and still she went on. She would do anything to get away from them above, despite who or what she might meet below.

The passage grew damper. She could smell and see moisture collecting on the walls. Moving as quickly as possible without putting out the light, she continued, wanting only to be safe again at home. Home—once it had meant a warm, cherished place to her, but two men had changed it. One wanted to wed her and would stop at nothing to accomplish it. He had a great deal of power and would punish anyone who stood in his way. This man appealed to her but little, yet his strength was undeniable. The other—his attraction was overpowering, she admitted that. But he was involved in political intrigues that were dangerous. Well enough to serve the queen and inspire the poor by masquerading as a Dutch pirate. But in doing so, irony put an English price on his head. She would never be safe with a man like that.

The passage made a turn. There was no branching. Rozalinde discovered she could only go forward, or else back. And she would not go back. As she continued, she stepped on an uneven spot in the floor and almost fell sprawling.

With an effort she managed to save herself and the candle.
But what had tripped her?

Holding the candle aloft, she examined the floor, trying
to see. A stone was clearly missing. But wait. It was something more.

With cautious fingers Roz explored the recess. It looked
too smooth and even to be an accident. Then she felt the
wall above and to the right of the door. Nothing about it
unusual, except . . .

Her fingers encountered a stone extrusion, another bump
in the irregular surface of the wall.

She pushed it hard, felt it give. A door swung open wide.

Her candle illuminated a tiny room. It had no exit other
than the one through which she'd entered. Warily she
checked the door from the inside, to be sure she could get
out later. Then she shut it softly behind her.

She was safe. In this little haven, put here by some unknown benefactor, she could hide a moment, feel a measure of peace. She moved into the room.

A huge four-poster bed dominated the space, hung with
faded red velvet curtains. Silken ropes tied them back to
reveal a snug sleeping place, covered by a silken coverlet.
Against the wall stood a table with two chairs, on it a rushlight. Holding the candle to the rush, Rozalinde lit it.
Within seconds, oil of roses permeated the room with its
scent, excruciatingly sweet.

A carved wooden box also rested on the table. Rozalinde
touched it with one hand, wondering if she should open
it. Mahogany, she thought, examining the wood by double
illumination of both rushlight and candle. A rivulet of tal-
low ran down its side and splashed painfully on her hand.

She peeled off the wax when it hardened, put her sore
hand to her mouth to ease the sting, and looked around.
Something about this room soothed her. It must be the
roses.

The scent swayed Roz's decision. She opened the box.
A letter lay inside, its thick, red seal broken. Like blood,
that seal lay against the paper, a talisman proclaiming
something. It was not her letter but she knew she must
read it. She had to know who had used this room.

The creased paper unfolded beneath her hands as if it

had been read often. "My sweetest love," it began, "my precious Anne . . ."

Guilt overwhelmed her. She should not read it. Putting it down on the table, Roz calmed herself by counting her pulse. Gone was her fear of the priest's hole, her helpless awe. A curiosity overwhelmed her, a desire to know. This room was magic—a lovers' trysting place. And she must understand what it meant.

Hesitantly she stared at the letter without touching it, saw the date. 1568. Five years earlier. She shook her head and moved away, went to the bed. There was an imprint of a head on each of two pillows. Two lovers had lain here, perhaps exchanged vows, undoubtedly known physical passion. On the floor something caught her eye—Roz bent to pick it up. Among scattered, dried rose petals lay a little silver cross hung on a chain. It was entwined with a rose. She held it close to see better. It was exquisitely crafted, the rose perfect in every detail.

She let it fall where she'd found it. Hurrying back to the table, she clutched for the letter, wanting urgently to know how it would end.

Let me write no more of these troubles. With thee, my only wish is to forget these cares. Your touch relieves my sorrow. Your kiss heals my pain. So it has done since I first knew you, when thou we'rt but a little maid. But now, I have lost everything but you. Love is the only thing that lasts, my sweetest, so do not despair. My ship beckons, but I will come again to you. I swear it— though myriad forces plot to prevent me. I treasure you, my jewel, and kiss your beloved face a thousand times. Phillipe

Roz stared at the dark flourish of the signature. The poignant feelings couched in those words overwhelmed her— the tender trust, the bittersweet pain. She let the vellum fall from her fingers, confused by a new desire to escape from this secret place. Quickly she extinguished the rushlight. Then hurrying to the door, Rozalinde touched the spring. Obediently the door swung open. The gaping tunnel greeted her. With impulsive abandon, she cast herself into its dark embrace.

*   *   *

The passage ended at the pirates' creek. Roz had known it would. A secret door, cleverly concealed at the rear of the cave, blocked off the tunnel. Obviously none of the people she'd met the other night knew about it. Pinching out her candle, Roz huddled just inside the entrance to the cave, scanning for the guard Trenchard had said he'd placed.

Leaning her temple against her fingers, she tried to sort out her feelings, which tangled in confused array through her mind. She'd fled from that chamber beneath Lulworth Castle, the emotions it represented frightening her. Yet she struggled to deny her fear. It was nothing, she told herself over and over. She was fine.

It was the dark, that was all. She'd been unnerved by it.

But it was not that. She'd left the safety of the chamber, thrown herself willingly into the darkness to escape something else. That room stood for abiding love—for physical passion between a woman and a man. Vehemently she clutched her fist over her crumpled, now-dirty kirtle skirt and tried to calm herself, to think rationally.

The words of the letter came creeping back into her mind to haunt her, whispering their message. *Love is the only thing that lasts. The only thing that lasts.*

What was it like to feel such passion, such love for a man that spanned time and distance, that brought two people together in spirit even when they were apart because they believed in and trusted each other? She wanted to weep at the thought of it—she who was so unsentimental, so exact. The poignant scent of roses stole into her memory, causing baffled feelings to rise unbidden into her heart.

"Kit," she whispered to herself, marveling that she had spoken to him so intimately, calling him by his first name. Slowly she reached down, touched a wound on her leg that came from his rosebush. The wound no longer pained her. Pain sprang from something else—the memory of his arms around her, the feel of his lips on her throat, the pleasurable tangle of his hair clasped in her hands.

Letting her head list heavily against her knee, she knelt there, watching for the guard. It had begun to rain, and thunder crashed in the distance. A streak of lightning slashed the sky, and she hugged herself, her mind going a thousand different directions, still lost in a tunnel of dark. She was learning many things about herself, not all of them good. Her fear of the dark she had long forgotten, believing it outgrown with her childhood. But here it was again, springing up to torment her, the same way Kit sprang into her life, causing her to question her choices up until now. Before him, she'd lived by logic. A man like Trenchard could have been her savior. He could have helped her business and kept her on the right side of the law.

Right side of the law? The fact that she even considered crossing to the other side appalled her. Had she lost her good sense? Her father, a man so excellent in his judgment, had recommended Trenchard. She should listen to him.

But she hadn't. Instead, she'd gone sneaking out at night, climbing in a man's window to warn him of danger from the very law that was supposed to protect them. What in the bright heavens had possessed her? She had gotten exactly what she deserved from it—she'd been discovered. There was no question she would pay further for that indiscretion.

And yet . . . Rozalinde plucked despairingly at her kirtle skirt, wanting to hide her face in misery. Suddenly she had turned as mad as Bess of Bedlam, for of the two men, the one who awoke the yearning deep inside her was Christopher Howard. Oh, illogical choice. Such thoughts had never tormented her before. But now, on the brink of her twenty-first year, when she should be gaining in wisdom, she was instead regressing. She was thinking like her brother—Jon, the laughing clown, who played the merry fool. She thought just like he did—wanting to reject Trenchard and his reasonable suit. A man from her own class, who wanted nothing more than to settle down and live respectably. Yet she longed instead for an earl who, for all his closeness to the queen, had a secret life that might bring him to death at the hands of the English law.

Then, too, there was her duty. Her most important purpose in life was to serve her family. From her father and mother, love sprang. She didn't fool herself into thinking that, much as Trenchard wanted her, he would cherish her the way they did. And as for Kit, his beguiling kisses were no more than another way of tempting her from her loved ones.

No, she thought, seeing the guard approach and slipping deeper into the cave again, she needed more desperately than ever to guard the heritage of her father. If she married Trenchard, that heritage would merge with his wealth and become unrecognizable. With him she would lose command of her own ventures and have to settle for the rewards he chose, like his grand new house in the middle of Lulworth, or the expensive pew he'd paid for at church. It was no substitute when, to her mind, her father's business represented all his love and affection and guaranteed her freedom and her connection to her family. Those were things so precious, she would protect them with her life.

So thinking, she steeled herself to forget her soft feelings for Kit and strengthened her resolve to reject Trenchard. Concentrating on the guard, she watched him pass by her hiding place and continue up the creek. When the way was clear, she slipped from the cave and hurried through the rain to her home.

Chapter 13

Kit stood before a mirror in his chamber three days later, donning his traveling clothes. Courte Philips lounged on the bed behind him.

"You're off to the queen, then?" Courte tried to banish the wistfulness from his voice. "How much will you tell Her Majesty? About the Beggar King, that is."

"Enough to make her sympathetic to his cause." Kit looked up from struggling with his doublet buttons. "But not a whit more. Why?" He turned back to the mirror and the uncooperative buttons.

"Oh, no reason." Courte traced the intricate pattern on the Ypres coverlet with his finger. "I was just wondering what you would say about the communiqué."

Kit left the mirror and came to stand before Courte. "Curiosity eating you?" He laughed at Courte's obvious discomfort. "No use trying to hide it." His smile was good-natured. "I know you too well."

"You don't have to see right through me," Courte said grouchily. " 'Tis embarrassing at times. And why don't you get a body servant? Your clothes wouldn't take so long."

"I hate servants' fussing." Kit finished the last button and reached for his boots. "As for knowing what you're thinking, if I did you harm, you might complain, but since I don't ..." He reached out to give Courte a friendly cuff on the arm. "You look as miserable as an old cony pelt. What's wrong?"

"Nothing," Courte said sourly. He retrieved his hat and gloves from a chair.

"Why don't you come with me to London. I'll take you to Greenwich, introduce you to the queen."

Courte whipped around to look at Kit. "In truth? Would

I really get to meet Her Majesty? I've not the proper court costume—"

"No matter. I'll buy you one when we reach London: a silk doublet to make the lasses stare and their fingers itch to take it off you." Kit chuckled as he gathered up his packed leather pouches and slung them over his shoulder. "I'll teach you the proper address, then you can help me convince Elizabeth that the Netherlands requires her aid."

"I-I don't know what to tell her," Courte stammered, happiness coursing through him. But he stopped, realizing he would probably be tongue-tied in the presence of the greatest queen in Christendom. "What should I say? I don't know what's in the communiqué."

"You will," Kit promised him, frowning. A shadow crossed his face. "And once you do, you'll be sorry you asked."

A minute later they parted, Kit striding to the stables of Lulworth Castle, Courte setting out on foot, as he had come. Turning toward his small house across town, he headed off in a hurry. He would gather a change of linen and alert the woman who did his cooking when he wasn't at sea. His heart soared with elation at the thought of his journey. London!

Kit saddled his favorite horse and headed toward the draper's establishment. He had one call to make before he left, though he wasn't sure it was wise. But he had decided earlier to stop at Master Cavandish's.

His thoughts seethed as he rode down the main street of West Lulworth. Unfortunately, he was attracting the attention of everyone in town. People saluted him as he passed, men raised their hats or bowed, women dropped curtsies so that their skirt hems dragged in the dirt. It bothered him, but not nearly as much as something he had discovered this morning—he had to see Rozalinde again.

The thought made him uneasy. No woman ever had such an attraction for him that he craved for the sight of her. But it wasn't that, he told himself vehemently. There was nothing behind the call save the need to warn this stubborn wench, once and for all, that she must stay in Lulworth and not go sailing for Antwerp. Christ's wounds, but her life might even be in danger. Certainly her business was. She should stay at home, where no one but this Trenchard fellow would trouble her, though that was bad enough. The man was uncommonly possessive, although if rumor told correctly, he had a right to be. He intended to wed her. Since the visit from the alderman, Kit realized he had best leave her alone.

But he feared for her safety that night, so he followed her through the tunnel, all the way back to her home. There he sat on the hill in the rain for two hours, trying to see in her window, looking for proof she was safe. She'd finally come to close the shutters on the south side of the house. He had seen her clearly, outlined against the light. Only then was he able to go home and sleep.

But not for long. He'd awakened toward dawn, troubled. If the lass sailed to Antwerp, she would sail straight into trouble. The fight between Spain and the Netherlands was serious business, and he was seriously involved. Furthermore, what little she knew was too much. All he needed was for her to get caught in the middle and they would be in a pretty coil. He would have to give her a strong warning. He rode on, trying to think of words she would heed.

As he neared the Cavandish establishment, he debated between the house and the shop. She might be either place. What should he try?

He decided on the house and went straight to the door.

The servant who opened it recognized him at once and sounded like a stammering lackwit, he was so shocked. The master, he tried to explain, was resting but he would summon Madam Cavandish. He then started to rush off to do so, stopped himself just in time.

Kit hid his smile as the footman recalled his training, summoned a boy to lead away his horse, then ushered him into the parlor and offered him food and drink, which Kit politely declined. His face red with excitement, the fellow hurried off to find Madam Cavandish.

The good dame came instantly, looking flustered and babbling nonsense. "Oh, your lordship, we're honored to have you." Her wide skirts swirled around her plump figure as she rushed to arrange her best cushions on a carved chair. "Have a seat," she urged him. "Have a drink of malmsey. Have a sugared rose." She extended a box of the confections toward him. "We made them fresh this morning, my eldest daughter and I."

Kit took a candied rose petal and spoke kindly, trying to soothe her. He seated himself gracefully, refusing to ask for Rozalinde. He waited patiently, knowing she would inevitably appear.

The wait was not tedious. Madam Cavandish bustled off after several minutes, worried about her husband. She'd left him being arrayed, she explained. He'd been at his repose. With a promise to fetch him personally, she dashed out the door in another flurry of skirts.

Rozalinde entered the room a second later. Of course she'd been told the earl had come. She had been teaching Lucina the satin stitch in the solar when the footman came panting in. 'Twas the last thing she'd expected—the earl in their home. How ever would she face him, after the other night? Thoughts of his burning kisses roared hot in her memory and she forced herself to squelch them. Crossing the strings of her starched apron with a yank, she tied them in a severe bow, then took herself downstairs.

Kit had decided he would issue a strict warning, then be on his way. But when Rozalinde came in and shut the door, his heart rose up so joyously, like a flock of seagulls wheeling and turning in the dazzling summer sun, he found himself speechless.

"Why have you come?" she asked him abruptly, putting her back against the door. "My father will be here straight. He is dressing even now."

Life flowed back into Kit's veins. He found himself moving forward, bending to kiss her hand. "What a pleasant greeting." He smiled. "Your manners are so refined."

Rozalinde had the grace to redden. She snatched her hand away.

"I must leave today for London," Kit told her simply, refusing to release her gaze though she'd reclaimed her hand. "I require a word with you first."

"Whatever for?"

But he'd forgotten what for, because her velvet gaze unconsciously claimed his. He felt as if he were drowning.

"You're like to get yourself murdered," she insisted. "You should have a care."

"Murdered?" Her words jarred him out of his enchantment.

"By Trenchard," she said crossly. "Don't you realize how powerful he is? You should after the other night."

"You were the one who seemed to take him lightly," he countered, feeling his blood churn lustfully.

"I won't make that mistake again." She put her hands on her slim hips and regarded him heatedly. "I did not realize it at first, but now I see how it is. I am all but his betrothed, and by calling here, you challenge him. Do you intend to fight a duel?"

"I hardly think he will call me out."

"You are most likely right. He will try more treacherous means to be even with you. Watch what you eat or drink."

"You cannot be serious." Kit was in no mood for a warning from her. "I am not thinking of him. Only of you and me."

"And what can there be between you and me?" she asked indignantly.

He was silent, wondering the same thing.

"Nothing," she told him, letting the word form with cruel precision on her lips. "We are of different classes, as you well know. I have work to do. I pray you excuse me." She turned to go.

"I'll not excuse you." He caught her wrist as she reached for the door handle. "You kiss me one night, then pretend you care nothing for me when we meet again. This must stop. Confess you care."

She turned back to regard him. "Mayhap I do," she admitted, surprising him, "but it means nothing, nor can it ever. The truth is, we should never have met. We each have our duty, which takes us separate ways."

"And your duty lies in getting your father's ship to Antwerp?"

She nodded.

" 'Twill end in nothing but trouble," he warned her, coming to the heart of his visit. "I forbid you to go. If you leave this house, if you set one foot out that door with the intention of sailing to Antwerp, you'll walk straight into danger. I absolutely forbid it. When I return in a two weeks, I expect you to be here."

"Give me one good reason," she challenged, crossing her arms across her chest.

"I'll give you a reason." He frowned, irked by her resistance. "Because I bid you remain at home. I shall come to call when I return, to see you obeyed."

He was furious when it seemed his warning had no effect on her. In fact, it appeared she wasn't even listening. Instead, she stared intently at the door. Putting one finger to her lips, she gestured for him to be silent. He stepped forward, meaning to regain her attention, but she went to the door and gave the handle a sharp pull.

Three small children tumbled into the room. Their guilty faces showed they had their ears to the door.

"Shame on you," Roz admonished, trying to sort out the squirming tangle of arms and legs on the floor. "Listening again. And after you promised not to. I should send you to your chambers straight."

Clearly that was impossible. The three latched on to her and refused to let go, scrambling and wiggling and making such a fuss they could not be ignored. Roz bent over them, trying to get them to hush.

"I was waiting for you, Rozalinde," the boy whined, hanging on her arm. "You promised to tell me a story. I'm tired of waiting. I want my story now."

"No," cried the oldest girl, whom Kit judged to be about six. The child latched on to Roz's other arm with the strength of a joiner's vice. "She's helping me with my sampler. You can have stories another time." With that, she threw herself into her sister's arms and began to bawl. Kit looked away impatiently.

The third child, a girl, remained silent throughout. She hid behind Roz's skirts with only her face visible, observed the earl with wide eyes and sucked her thumb.

"You must stop this noise instantly," Roz told them adamantly. "We have a distinguished visitor. You must remember your manners." She nodded toward the earl and the three faces turned his way. "Come now, Charles. Let us see you make your best bow to the Earl of Wynford. I know you can do it as Father taught you."

"This is unnecessary," Kit began, wanting to be rid of the children. He wanted to be alone with Rozalinde. "The children need not perform for me. Kindly ask them to le—"

"It is most necessary," Rozalinde admonished, shooting him a look of censure. "This is how they learn discipline.

Go ahead, Charles," she urged the child, steering him firmly toward Kit. "The way Father said."

Charles marched forward, seeming not the least intimidated. "Good morrow, your honor." He swept the earl a splendid bow. "I trust your health is excellent? But I suppose I should call you 'your lordship,' " he said, ruining his speech by abandoning his straight posture and pulling at his chin in the most comical manner, like an old man. "Your lordship," he amended. He bowed again, then smugly awaited his praise.

Kit felt Roz looking at him. Clearly she expected him to give an appropriate response. Feeling thoroughly disgruntled, he went down on one knee beside the boy.

"I am pleased to make your acquaintance, Master Cavandish. What have you here?"

Charles beamed with pleasure and pulled out the reed whistle that protruded from the pouch at his waist. "My brother made it for me. Isn't it a rare one?" He blew vigorously on the whistle. It let out a high, thin, shrilling sound. The two little girls covered their ears and began to shriek.

Their noise, Kit thought, was worse than the one made by the whistle. As he stood up, Charles retired to the door, grinning with satisfaction over his whistle. "I suppose," Kit gestured resignedly toward the girls, "they must make bows as well?"

"Girls don't make bows." The expression on Rozalinde's face suggested he was somewhat addlepated. "Kneel down again."

He gave her his most disapproving look. It always got him results, on his ship or with his servants at the castle.

"Do as I say," she ordered, not taking the least notice. Gathering the little girls close, she whispered in their ears.

There was nothing to do but obey. Kit felt ridiculous balanced on one knee, hat in hand. Not even the queen kept him in this position, waiting. At least not this long. He looked up sharply, put on his most frightening frown as the girls approached. He'd never been good with children and he wasn't about to learn how. The oldest one, Lucina, stopped in front of him a foot away.

"He looks cross," the child stated to Rozalinde, speaking over her shoulder. "Are you sure I should?"

"Quite sure, dear."

The girl turned back to regard him, her face solemn. Kit found himself looking into a pair of eyes the rich color of iris, so velvety, they reminded him of her elder sister.... His gaze leaped to Rozalinde and stuck there. He was so busy gaping, he missed Lucina's next move. Stepping forward, she clasped her arms around his neck. He froze in place as he felt her warm lips press against his cheek, just above his beard. The smaller girl followed suit, clasped him with chubby baby arms and assaulted his other cheek with sticky, peppermint-scented lips. Kit felt the blood rise to his face.

He jerked away from the children as Rozalinde burst into an astonishing peal of laughter. Clapping her hands, she called the girls to her and herded them toward the door. "It's all over. You can get up." Her mirth trilled delightedly. The girls giggled behind their hands.

"You can stop being jealous," Rozalinde told Kit, closing the door partway as the girls went into the passage. "You've had your share."

Kit regained his feet and regarded her with exasperation. He didn't even care that he'd made her laugh again. "I was not jealous."

"Of course you were." Rozalinde came back across the room toward him. Her laughter had made her pale cheeks bloom and her brown eyes sparkle. "You were green with envy when they hung on me. Did no one ever kiss you?"

"You are doing everything possible to change the subject." Kit threw her a severe look. "I'm telling you to stay put in West Lulworth or something unpleasant will happen."

All trace of laughter disappeared from Roz's face. "You will find, my lord, that I am not easily frightened."

"Mayhap you should be." He grasped her by one arm and forced her to look at him. "It might serve you best in the end."

A tap sounded at the door. Rozalinde pulled away from him, brushed off her sleeve and straightened her kirtle skirt with an indignant twitch.

Jonathan came into the room. Going straight to the window, he snatched back the drapery to reveal Charles, who grinned at him. "I knew it!" Jon grasped him by the wrist and hauled the lad from his hiding place.

"I must ask your pardon," Jon said to the earl, "for letting the young ones get in the way. My father will be here directly. Out with you," he growled at Charles, nudging him with one foot and jerking his head toward the door. "You, too." He whirled around and lunged, catching the smallest girl who had slipped in and was trying to hide behind Roz's skirts.

"Want Wose," she insisted in her stubborn baby voice as Jon picked her up. She leaned over Jon's shoulder as he went through the door, holding out her arms to Roz.

Kit turned back to Rozalinde, who seemed discomfited by what the child had called her. Then, too, they were alone again, despite the fact that the door stood open.

"At any rate, there's my message," Kit said gruffly, feeling uncomfortable also. "You are not to leave West Lulworth. I hope I've been clear. I shall be forced to do something unpleasant if you do."

"You make yourself clear," she answered, her face resuming its serene expression. "I hear your every word."

"But you don't intend to listen, do you?" He bent over to stare her in the eye. "After your dire warnings to me, I should think you would heed your own advice. Well, I intend to speak to your father. I'll tell him to keep you at home."

She looked back at him and lifted her chin slightly. "Tell him what you wish," she said with her usual maddening composure. "I wouldn't presume to interfere."

Just then her father entered, and the rest of Kit's visit was taken up with the proper formalities and pleasantries, talk of trade and products, and other mundane things.

Kit left twenty minutes later, having issued as strong a warning as he dared. Master Cavandish had only chuckled, agreed he would be sure to guard his "bright jewel," as he lovingly called Rozalinde.

But for Kit that wasn't enough. He felt vastly uneasy about Rozalinde's safety. Now he wondered—would she stay at home while he was gone, or would she not?

The Cavandish grooms brought his horse around. He took his time checking the girth, then mounted. A strange reluctance seized him, making him sorry to be gone. Over his shoulder, he gave the house a last look.

He saw Rozalinde, standing at the window. Quickly he

turned his back on the house, as if caught at something improper. He rode down the gravel drive.

Blast, but it was those Cavandish children. Their presence had unnerved him. And she'd let them interrupt. "This is how they learn discipline," she'd told him. Some discipline! It wasn't the sort he'd grown up with. And because of her insistence, he'd never even had a chance to give her a proper warning. But then if it hadn't been for the children, they might have quarreled, he realized. He had been so exasperated by her stubbornness, he'd wanted to exercise the kind of discipline he *had* grown up with— he'd wanted to give her a thrashing. Now the anger had subsided, and he had his other feeling to contend with— this strange, unsettled feeling deep in the pit of his stomach—the one that had threatened to overwhelm him when the children hugged and kissed him. . . .

He twisted in the saddle, trying to banish the feeling, failing miserably. He'd liked those kisses, despite how foolish he'd felt when he received them. Why on God's green earth, he couldn't fathom, but there was something comforting in the idea of Rozalinde's little sisters liking him. More than that, he'd wanted something today from Rozalinde. And it wasn't that brusque admission of caring she'd given. On the other hand, he couldn't imagine her acting like the other women who'd wanted him—wearing seductive clothing, flirting with him outrageously, even planting themselves in his bed at night. No, that wasn't what he wanted. But by the good lord in heaven, she must concede to something more intimate. The woman knew about his tunnel! She knew about his priest's hole! She knew about his mask and his trips at night. And she had experienced his most intimate desires. He trusted this maid with his life, and he was longing for some word from her—any word at all.

Of course he hadn't gotten it. She'd given him no tender speech like the other women in his life. What if she *did* give it? What then? Would he use and discard her, just like the rest?

He shook his head, realizing that was unacceptable. She was a respectable merchant's daughter. There could be nothing between them. And as he turned his horse toward London, he told himself it was definitely best to leave things as they were.

Chapter 14

Rozalinde left the window after Kit's departure, wanting to laugh and curse at the same time. Troth, but he was domineering, with his orders and warnings. He said she mustn't leave Lulworth. She wasn't to sail on her father's ship. She didn't like him after all, she decided. He expected to control her, and it made him thoroughly dangerous, a man who coaxed one moment, controlled the next.

But then her mouth had to quirk up at the corners. Remembering his face, she leaned against a chair in the passage and burst into another rare laugh. He'd looked so comical, with the girls kissing him. She was wicked to tease him, something she rarely did, but he'd gotten no more than he deserved, being so possessive, wanting her all to himself. She'd had to show him her freedom was not to be trifled with.

Then, she thought soberly, there were his manipulating ways. He was so beguiling, ten minutes by the clock alone with him and he might have her agreeing to anything. She'd been wise not to risk it. Her ploy with the children had been the right choice.

Then again, today was the sixth morning. Any minute now Trenchard would arrive, and she was ready. The encounter with the earl had helped prepare her. She felt strong. She would put him off. Another two days and she would be gone, and then Trenchard couldn't force her to wed. Not until she returned, and by then, their profit would be made and she wouldn't need him.

Stretching languidly, Roz regarded her slippers and rehearsed the words she'd chosen to put off Trenchard. When the bell rang, she stood up calmly. That would be him.

But when Jack opened the door, a tall, thin man entered, covered with dust from the road, his face sunburned. Rozalinde blinked with surprise. The man tendered a sealed letter to Jack, then stood back to wait.

"For the master." Jack brought the missive and laid it in her hand, bowing. "From London, the messenger says."

"Please guide him to the kitchens, Jack," Roz instructed, taking the letter and motioning them to go ahead of her. "Bid Cook give him refreshment. He has come a great distance." She nodded in friendly fashion to the messenger, who looked thoroughly exhausted. "Then you must find my mother. She will pay him."

Roz did not bother to watch them go to the kitchens, as would have been polite. She was eager to read the news from London. Holding the thick letter, she hurried back to the parlor. They needed good news from London, and this would be about their latest ship.

Without closing the parlor door, Rozalinde tore past the seal she knew had been stamped by the chief clerk of the Company of Merchant Adventurers. She scanned the letter quickly. Her expression changed. With a small cry, she dropped the paper, let it flutter to the floor.

Trenchard found her five minutes later, face buried in her hands, shaking with silent sobs. He came into the room without a word, stooped to retrieve the fallen letter, scanned it.

"My poor Rozalinde. I am so sorry."

His hand came to rest on her shoulder.

"My father's company ship," she sobbed. "Lost. We'll never make up the debt. My father's shareholders' money was invested in that ship. Now the whole ship's gone."

"Serious trouble," he agreed, sitting down across from her on a stool and taking her hand in his. "Did it say how?" He reached for the letter again.

"Pirates," Rozalinde said wearily, wiping his eyes. She felt utterly defeated. Here she'd prepared for battle with Trenchard, readied herself with all manner of arguments and witty words to trick him out of his intention to wed her. But this—this was too much.

"Which ones?" When Rozalinde didn't answer, Trenchard referred to the letter again. "What the good year, the Sea Beggars!" He looked up, his face shocked. "This is appalling. Rozalinde, you must let me help you." He stood, raised her to her feet. "You have lost an entire ship, along with your goods to these villains. I must stop these knaves before they undo you further."

"And must I wed with you to have your help?" she asked dejectedly. She hadn't meant to ask so bluntly. But she was too heartbroken to engage in clever argument with him. It was no use anyway. She knew what he wanted.

"I am willing to overlook your one indiscretion," he said softly, massaging her hand in his two large ones. "Provided there are no others."

She shook her head as she stood there, limply submitting to his ministrations. He had seen the garter. But it didn't matter. The earl was no longer worth caring for. Even if it wasn't the Beggar King himself who'd stolen her goods, his men were responsible.

She sighed despondently, noticing how the sun struck Trenchard's broad back through the window. With a twinge, she realized he was wearing his good brocade doublet, the one he'd worn to their revel. His best green, probably for good reason. His next question confirmed her suspicion.

"Are you ready to repair to the church?"

Rozalinde turned toward the door. Her heart pounded painfully in her chest. "You will wish to wed?"

"There is no doubt in my mind that we are meant for each other, my sweet." His voice was soothing. He reached up to caress her cheek. "Could you possibly doubt my sincerity? I wish to care for you, Rozalinde. Come, after we repair to the church, I will send some money to London to hold off your shareholders. They will be most angry when they learn about their investment."

Rozalinde nodded, realizing she had to accept him. Not only did they owe hundreds of pounds to the shareholders of the company, but the one man she'd trusted, the earl, had betrayed her. He'd robbed their ship, probably not even knowing it belonged to her father. Not caring, either. Her instinct had been wrong about him. He'd seemed an honest man who had confided in her his secret. Now she knew he was nothing of the sort. He was a thief. And he wanted her to stay at home—to keep out of his way so he could carry on his ugly business of robbing innocent folk.

And here was Trenchard, who knew she'd slipped out of

the house at night to warn the devil, still willing to accept
her. "You must think poorly of me."

"Nay, sweetheart." He silenced her gently with his hand.
" 'Tis no longer of import."

"I would rather care for my business myself."

"A woman should not have to manage alone. I won't let
that happen to you."

No, he wouldn't, she thought glumly. It hurt her pride
tremendously, but she put her hand in his. "Let me change
my gown," she said, her voice absent of joy. "And call my
mother and Jonathan. Then we may go to church."

The vows were said *de verbis futuro,* which made the
betrothal nonbinding. Rozalinde insisted on that. She had
felt so discouraged when she left the house, she almost
didn't bother. But Jonathan had scowled at her all the way
to church, glared at her with accusing eyes. It made her
think. Could there be some tiny chance she wouldn't have
to wed? Small though the hope was, Rozalinde seized on
it. *Find another way,* Jonathan had said to her. What was
wrong with her? Was she a lackwit, that she couldn't solve
this problem?

Once back from the church, she dismissed the others,
went to her father's cabinet. Trenchard would be her insur-
ance, her last resort if nothing else worked. But even he
couldn't guarantee a solution to her problems. No, someone would have to confront the Sea Beggars, and she would
do it. Her resolve renewed itself. She would go to Antwerp
after all.

The next day she moved up the ship's departure date by
a full week. It meant backbreaking work getting ready, but
she set to it with a vengeance. No arrogant earl or Beggar
King or whoever he was would stop her from supporting
her family. She would do exactly what was required, and if
she encountered him during the voyage, then heaven help
him. She intended to let him know exactly what she thought
of him, and if he dared rob her after that, then Trenchard
could deal with him.

In the days that followed, she concentrated her energy
on the necessary preparations. The many goods to be
traded were bought and delivered to Poole and stowed
safely on the ship she had hired. The ship had to be revic-

tualed and final repairs made. The last crew members were hired and put to work. She pushed everyone relentlessly, from the captain to the cabin boys. She pushed herself hardest of all. And throughout her work, she said not a word about sailing to Antwerp. In outward appearance, she readied the ship only. And everyone, even Trenchard, believed her. Everyone, that is, save Jon.

"What are you doing, Rozalinde?" On the day before the ship's departure, Jon put his cheerful face around the doorway to Roz's chamber and leaned in.

Bent over a trunk, Rozalinde glanced up guiltily. "Just tidying." She hurriedly added a thick book to the pile of things in the trunk and slammed down the lid.

Jon sauntered in and picked up another book from her dressing table, thumbed idly through its pages. "Indeed? Tidying?" He bent over suddenly and grabbed the lid of the trunk, thrust it open and took a good look inside. "I think not," he said, his nonchalance fading as he saw what it held. "I'd like to know what you're up to."

"Nothing," Roz said curtly. She slammed shut the trunk lid, all but catching his hand.

"I think it's more than nothing." He made his voice stern, purposely imitating their father. "I think you're planning something, Rozalinde Cavandish. I'd lay a wager you're going to Antwerp."

Roz backed up against the trunk. "Why would you think a thing like that?"

"I can tell by what you're packing." Jon broke into a smug smile. "You can't fool me, sister mine. I know you better than you think." He stared her in the eye, hands on his hips, daring her to deny it. After a minute she dropped her gaze.

Immediately he felt an urgent desire to banish the frown that appeared on her face. "Don't be afraid I'll tell on you." He reached out, gave her a reassuring pat on the arm. "I promise I won't. I know you're doing it for the best."

Roz didn't seem to believe him. She had tensed all over and gripped her hands into fists. "You'll not tell Father or Trenchard?" she asked stiffly.

He tried again. "Haven't I proved I won't? I didn't tell about the man you were meeting the night of the revel."

"I wasn't meeting—"

"Yes, you were, but I didn't tell. I've helped you in the shop—*and* been reliable. I won't tell about this if you can assure me you've made proper arrangements. Do you have a maid or something?"

Rozalinde's face cleared as he apparently convinced her. He could see her relax her fists. "Yes, yes, I've thought of all the details. I'll engage a maid as soon as possible and no one of consequence will be the wiser. You know I must sail with this cargo, Jon, but everyone fusses so, telling me I'm in terrible danger."

Jonathan grinned. "If there were danger, I would put my wager on *you,* Rozalinde. If you couldn't overpower a man, you'd outsmart him."

Roz gave him a ghost of a smile. "I don't go looking for trouble. I'd rather have a quiet voyage. But if necessary, I'll do what I must."

"For certes," Jon agreed glibly. "I can see you in hand-to-hand combat with a dozen pirates." He gave a mock slash of the sword.

"You're an impudent puppy," she scolded him. "Don't even jest about such a thing. If we do meet pirates, I'll use the cannon before we are boarded. I've made sure we have plenty of powder and shot."

Jon shook his head, once more worried. "Nevertheless, Rozalinde, my prayers will go with you. It's not a journey I would undertake."

"You'll not have to. You're to leave things to me."

"All except one."

Rozalinde stopped and looked at him. "Which one is that?"

"Your departure. You'd best let me arrange it. Otherwise, how do you intend to leave the house? Father will know instantly. And if you board the ship, the captain will know you're there. He's bound to send you home."

Roz shrugged unconcernedly. "I'll manage."

"You'll not. You'll be caught. Especially now that you're betrothed to Trenchard. He watches you like a hawk."

"A lot you know about it." Rozalinde bent to pick up a fallen smock. "The captain won't know I'm there. Nor will Trenchard."

"No!" Jon goggled at her as he realized her intention. "You mean you'll stow away?" He clucked his tongue anxiously. "This sounds risky to me. It was one thing to sail with Father, but to go alone and unprotected? It will not do."

Roz folded the smock and tucked it away. "I chose the captain carefully. He's a respectable family man, with daughters of his own. He'll keep the men in order."

Jon rolled his eyes and snorted. "I pray you are right. If not, you'll have no one to blame but yourself."

"Such encouragement," she said. "Let us talk of something else. How are things in the shop?"

"Superb. Sales have been brisk. The mayor's wife bought new linen for embroidered hangings. She'll have her daughters pricking their fingers for a year hence. I've tidied up, counted all the money, and logged it in the book."

Rozalinde bestowed a radiant smile on her brother. "You have managed well, Jonathan."

Jonathan sighed with contentment. "In that case, might I meet with Margaret? I haven't been with her since the revel." He raised his eyebrows and gave her a wistful look.

"You know better," Roz chided him. "Her father forbids it, and so does ours."

"I know." Jon grew disheartened at the reminder. "But I love her, and you know well enough how that feels."

"I do not." Roz bristled all over. "How should I know?"

Jon shook his finger at her, just the way she always shook hers at him. "Don't think I haven't noticed, your mooning around the house when you're thinking of *him*. And now he comes calling to the house—"

"He did not come calling," Roz lashed out vehemently. "He came to give me a warning and absolutely nothing else."

"A warning is it? Dare I guess about what?" Jon gave her a knowing look. "Proves he does love you. Admit that you love him, too."

Rozalinde flapped her apron at him, shooing him toward the door. "I am weary of the subject, Jon. Run away to Margaret and leave me be."

"You're plenty stubborn, Rozalinde."

"Go on with you. Bring me any news you hear."

Jon paused and looked at her beseechingly. "You will be careful, Rozalinde. I know you're doing this for us." He leaned over and unexpectedly kissed her cheek.

"Get you gone." Roz swatted him with a book, clearly embarrassed at his show of affection. But as he rushed merrily out the door, eager to see Margaret, he caught a last glimpse of her expression. Her eyes were soft with a yearning he'd never seen before—but they changed after a second. She looked disappointed, and though he didn't know why, he felt for her deep inside.

Buoyed by the praise from his sister, Jon hurried all the way to Lulworth Cove where he'd arranged to meet Margaret. Impatiently he scanned the sands for her blond head. She shouldn't be much longer—it was nigh on half past six.

Ah, there she was. He crouched behind a fisherman's overturned boat, ignoring the fact that the grizzled old owner sat on the other side, mending his net. When Margaret was almost upon him, he sprang out and clasped her around the waist.

Margaret had been walking slowly, staring sadly at her worn slippers. But when Jonathan jumped out and caught her, she squealed with pleasure and returned his embrace.

"I was afraid you could not come," he began, pulling her close against him. He caressed her cheek with the palm of his hand. "Is all well, my sweet?"

"All is well, Jonathan," she told him, locking her hands about his neck and putting up her lips to be kissed.

He obeyed her silent command, meeting her welcoming mouth with his own, sliding his hands around her slim body.

"You are a wicked one, Jonathan Cavandish," she teased, breaking loose from his embrace, "always tempting me."

"I'm not. You like it," he teased back, clasping her hand and leading her several paces into the shelter of some tall rocks. There he untied the lace that fastened her one braid and fluffed it out so he could twine his hands in her golden hair. "When I am with you, Margaret, I want so desperately to—to . . . oh, curse it." He groaned and leaned over to kiss her again. "You know what I mean, Margaret. When will the happy day come?"

"The day you are one and twenty," she said boldly back, knowing exactly what he meant. "When you are of age, we can do what we wish and no one shall say us nay. Ohh."

She tipped back her head and breathed in ecstasy. "You are precious to me, Jonathan."

"As you are to me." Jon leaned against the rocks, pulled her hips against his. "Would that I were one and twenty one. I would marry you and bring you back here and bed you."

"Jon!" Margaret laughed delightedly, used to his teasing. "Everyone would see. They would come and watch if you bedded me here."

"Let them," Jon declared, tweaking her nose and making her giggle. "I want everyone to know you belong to me."

Still laughing, Margaret pulled away and began to rebraid her hair. Jon grabbed for the lace as she tied it, attempting to pull it loose again, but Margaret ducked out of his reach. "Tell me about custom, Jonathan," she coaxed. "Are there new silks in the shop?"

"There are." He stood back and gazed at her admiringly. "I unpacked an entire shipment from Genoa last week. We have a saffron yellow that would set off your hair and make your eyes glow." He took her hand and squeezed it. "You have beautiful eyes."

Margaret's smile broadened at his compliment and she blinked her gold-flecked hazel eyes. "You at least appreciate them. Mother calls them unlucky. She is so fearful of late, I cannot think what is wrong with her. Always moaning that I must marry well."

"Does she hate me as much as ever?"

"Nay, she does not hate you. It's only—"

"It's only that she does not wish the squire's daughter to consort with a merchant." Jon picked up a stone, skipped it out over the waves. "But you shall, and more than that." He regarded her solemnly. "Margaret, I have something I wish you to consider. It worries me so much, sometimes it pains me, but I must tell it to you."

"Mayhap 'tis the grippe," Margaret told him saucily.

Jon scowled at her. "'Tis not my meaning and well you know it." Desperately he grasped her wrists and pleaded with her. "Be serious. Let me talk to you."

Margaret scanned his face to gauge his mood. "Speak away, then," she said, growing quiet as she understood his seriousness.

Jon cleaned his throat nervously. "I-I love you, Margaret.

And I want to pledge myself to you." He hesitated, then plunged ahead. "If we do, we'll be legally bound."

Margaret paled visibly. "I do love you, Jonathan. But to pledge ourselves forever when we're only sixteen? What if you changed your mind later. Things are so bad in our family, you might be sorry to join with us. And my mother would be furious if she found out." She shuddered at the thought. "Even your father does not approve. He is too practical to accept us, with my mother always going to the law."

"That does make things hard," Jon agreed glumly. He took her in his arms again, greatly concerned for her. "Tell me everything. How do the latest suits fare?"

"Poorly." Margaret's face took on a remote look. "Mother is so shrewish about them, insisting we bring suit against this person and that. She is never content with what Father has to give her, always thinking to have more. I think Father would not agree, but he's ill and dislikes a quarrel." Margaret's misery showed in her eyes. "Sometimes I believe my mother daft, she imagines herself so much more than the squire's wife. The other day she refused my friend Lucy the door, and her father has been ever good to us, giving us credit in his shop when we couldn't pay him. But, says she," Margaret imitated her mother's high-pitched voice, "Lucy is only the shoemaker's daughter. Can you not do better than she?"

"Tell her nay," insisted Jon angrily, "and more than that, you are going to wed with the merchant's son. I'll not press you, Margaret, but why should we not? We can keep it secret, till we find a proper time to tell. And I'll provide for you. I swear I will."

"Oh, Jonathan. I know not how to answer you. I love you. In truth I do," Margaret went on, giving him a fresh smile of thanks for his vows. "But I feel so frightened. Mother has not been like this before, always worrying. She used to be gay and laughing. But ever since my father's illness, she's glum all the day long."

"Mine, too," Jon assured her. "Now that she's breeding again, she's worse than ever. But come, let us not think on that. Let us savor our time before I have to return to the shop. I shall have to go soon."

"Must you?" Margaret's eyes begged him to stay. "We

haven't been together more than twenty minutes of the clock."

Jon leaned over and let the sweet feel of her body rush through him. "I don't want to, but I've made Rozalinde a promise. If I work hard, she's promised to help me convince Father we should wed. So I must do as she tells me, and I must learn the business, sweet. You do understand? If I'm to claim you, I must do my duty as I should."

"I understand, Jon. Of course you must."

There was silence between them as he put his lips once again to hers.

"Oh, I almost forgot. I've a present for you."

Margaret's face brightened. She tried to hide her eagerness, but she so rarely received gifts. "What is it?"

"You must close your eyes," Jon told her teasingly. " 'Tis a surprise."

Obligingly Margaret lowered her lids, folded her hands primly in her lap.

"Now then, open!"

Margaret let out a cry of delight as she looked at the ivory bobbin Jon placed in her hands. "Jon, 'tis beautiful. I shall use it every day in my lace making."

"I would be happy if you would. I would be even happier if you would leave off the lace making entirely and spend your time with me. You concentrate so much on your handiwork some days, I'm not sure you notice anything around you."

"Jon," Margaret said reproachfully, pouting at him. "I spend as much time with you as I can manage. You mustn't think I forget you just because I'm involved in my work."

"Never mind. Forget I said it." Jon hurried to smooth over his complaint. "Look at your present. I want you to see what I wrote." He turned the bobbin, pointed to an inscription carved in tiny letters on the smooth surface.

Margaret let out a breath of pleasure. " 'My miracle, my Marguerite.' Oh, Jon, is that me?"

Jon put one arm around her shoulders and drew her near. "I wanted to put our names together, like all the men do when they give bobbins to their sweethearts, but I did not dare or your mother might not let you keep it. So I put this instead. I think of you as my daisy, you know. Or as the French say, my Marguerite."

Margaret dimpled as Jon leaned near to brush her lips again.

"I will find a way to see you tomorrow," he continued. "It will be difficult, but I'll manage. Rozalinde is so difficult at times, you know. If anyone else worked as hard as she does, they'd be dead in a fortnight. But she'll grow easier, by and by. You'll see." He nodded with assurance. "There's a secret only I know."

"What?" asked Margaret breathlessly, partly from suspense but more from his kisses. "Or should you not tell?"

"I'll tell if you'll promise to keep it close."

Margaret nodded. "I promise."

"She's in love with the earl. Yes, the one up at the castle," Jon lowered his voice to a dramatic whisper. "And I'll tell you, my sister has never fancied a man. Not that I've seen."

"The earl? God's eyelid!" Margaret gripped his shoulders, her eyes widened. "I heard he called at your house, but I assumed it was to see your father. I never thought she loved him. How can you tell?"

"She badgered me like the very devil at our revel," Jon chuckled as he thought of Roz, "about whether or not he had come. He was invited but didn't show. She disappeared later. After Trenchard got her to agree to their betrothal." He grew sober again. "That part is no jest."

"I agree." Margaret also grew sober. "But really, when Rozalinde left the revel, what makes you think she met with the earl?"

Jon looked pensive. "I just feel it. When the earl came to our house, the expression on her face, the way she acted. I believe she loves him, though knowing Rozalinde, she doesn't realize it herself."

Margaret shook her blond head at the wonder of it. "My word, but things are upside down in Lulworth lately. First this, then the Spanish ship."

"What Spanish ship?" Jon looked surprised. "I've had my head in crates all day. I've not heard a thing."

"Oh, 'tis all the news," Margaret assured him. "A huge ship called the *Gran Grifon* put in at Lulworth Cove, requesting safe harbor because they feared being set upon by pirates. 'Tis so big, it makes me nervous." Margaret shivered and drew her lips together. "At any rate, the mayor granted them asylum and here they be. 'Tis said the admiral is the Marquis DeVega, one of King Philip's favorite officers. He and his men have been put up at Trenchard's, since he's first alderman of the town and has the largest house. Our inns are not befitting a noble. But everyone's so frightened, they think they'll be murdered in their beds. The Spanish sailors are everywhere in the streets. 'Twas hardly safe coming here."

Jon took her hands and gripped them tightly. "You should have sent word and I would have come for you. I'm not so busy in the shop that I'm unconcerned with your welfare. I'll see you safely home." His thoughts returned to the more pressing issue. "You must think upon my proposal," he begged her. "I want nothing more than for us to be pledged."

"I love you, too, Jonathan. I promise I will think on it."

Jon stood and pulled Margaret to her feet, taking her hand in his. "A Spanish ship. My sister in love with an earl." He paused, shook his head slowly in puzzlement. "I cannot think how it all will end."

Chapter 15

Midnight. Rozalinde had been up since early morning, working in the house and shop. Come evening, she'd had to endure a visit with her betrothed, who came to sit with her in the parlor. Thank the good year he couldn't stay long. He had obligations with the visiting Spanish officials. Rozalinde had breathed with relief when he'd gone off again. She'd had no enjoyment from his company, or the kiss he claimed was his due.

Now everyone was abed, and Roz sat before the looking glass in her chamber, studying her reflection. A headache pounded behind her temples. Putting one hand to her brow, she smoothed the furrows caused by her worry and tried to steady herself. Tonight was the night.

The thought propelled her into action. Straightening hastily, she pulled back her loose braids and bundled them into a caul. Then she gathered together a stack of clean linen. She must hurry. It might take some time to stow away aboard *The Chalice*.

Checking outside her door, Roz stopped to listen. The rumble of her father's snores vibrated from the master bedchamber. A dog's bark in the stable yard echoed eerily throughout the silence of the house and surrounding property.

Gazing at the worn floorboards of the passage, Roz thought of the loved ones she was leaving and whispered two prayers. One for her mother—may her babe grow strong and healthy within her. The other for her father— please the Lord that his health should hold until she returned. He'd gotten no worse in the last week, but he was no better, either. Then she prayed for the entire family— her sisters, her brothers, especially Jonathan. It was on his shoulders that much responsibility would fall once she left. She whispered an extra prayer for him.

Finished, she started to turn away, but her gaze caught on something—the place where Angelica had sat as a baby on the top stair, crying for Roz to carry her down. A lump formed in her throat and she took a step backward, then started at the faint movement across the hall.

Calm down, she told herself firmly. It was only her own reflection in the mirror opposite. Meaning to banish her anxious mood, she inspected herself in the familiar glass, but her face beneath her concealing hood seemed pale and frightened. She turned back to her room, the ache of leaving dragging at her heart.

Down the hall, a door handle squeaked. Roz ducked back into her chamber and pulled the door to. It might be her mother, getting up for a drink. The floorboards creaked loudly as someone advanced down the passage. A tap sounded on her door.

Rozalinde froze with alarm. Here she was dressed for traveling. She was sure to be found out.

The door swung slowly inward. Jonathan's head appeared.

He said nothing. Just slipped inside, motioned for her to join him by the window, away from the door. "Are you ready? Shall I take you to the ship?"

Rozalinde's heart melted as she realized he'd come to help her. Never had he been so considerate. Nevertheless, she forced a brisk answer. "I must go alone. But you can help. You can pull up the sheet when I'm gone."

"Pull up the . . ." Jonathan's eyes sprang wide as two shutters opened to the dawn. "You're climbing out the window?" He leaned over the casement to stare at the long drop to the ground. "You've gone to Bedlam if you do that."

"I haven't." Roz pulled on an old pair of gloves determinedly. "Please be ready with the letter to Father. About midmorning tomorrow when I'm well away, you can give it to him. I should be back in a month."

Jon shook his head in disbelief. "My stars, Rozalinde. You and your stubborn will. Use the back door, won't you? I'll lock it again after you go."

"And wake Cook?" Roz shot him a scathing glance.

"You know she sleeps just off the scullery. She would hear me, she sleeps so lightly and guards her precious kitchens so faithfully. No, I'll go by the window. I've done it before."

"You have? When?" Jon followed her to the window and watched with visible consternation as she produced a knotted sheet and tied it to the bedpost.

Roz tugged the sheet sharply to be sure the knot was firm, then payed it slowly out the window. "I did it often in London, when I was younger," she informed him. "No one ever knew. Didn't you wonder why I had so much mending?"

For once Jon was beyond jesting. "God go with you, Rozalinde. I will pray for you. Truly I will."

"You just take care of Mama and Papa." She put out one hand, placing it in Jon's. His hand was slim and graceful, but when he closed it around hers, there was nothing soft about his firm, masculine grip. It felt warm, comforting, and she didn't want to let go.

"I'll do my best," he promised.

Roz squeezed his hand once, then broke away. She mounted the window casement and prepared to descend.

Scarce a minute later she reached solid ground, which felt reassuring beneath her feet. Waving at Jon, she motioned for him to pull up the sheet.

He did so, then watched her dark-cloaked figure until it disappeared into the stable. She emerged several minutes later, leading her mare with hooves muffled in sacking. The two of them took the turn around the corner of the house and disappeared.

Jon waited. After a reasonable interval, he let down the sheet and followed.

The streets of West Lulworth were deserted at this hour. Even the alehouse was closed and dark for the night. Poole lay a number of miles to the south, and it was there Roz headed. Mounted on her mare, she chose the quickest route through the center of town. Someone might see her, but that couldn't be helped. She must hurry or miss the ship's departure. Already she was late.

When she passed George's, she could see the great house blazed with lights. Roz averted her face, not wanting to know anything. Trenchard still entertained the Spanish, who made such trouble in West Lulworth: bothering the girls about town, insisting on special prices from the shop keepers. But at least they took up Trenchard's time and attention, diverting him from her. They'd informed Trenchard that prices for wool in Antwerp had reached a record high.

As for the earl, he was still in London, so she need not think of him. He could not stop her from going to Antwerp, and if he and his Sea Beggars bothered her on the voyage, she would make him pay for it. Putting her mind to the task ahead, she rode stalwartly on.

Someone watched her passage, shrouded in darkness so she did not see. Paul Sutton had stepped outside for a breath of air before directing the serving of supper. He glanced idly at the horse as it reached the town green, then snapped to attention as he recognized Rozalinde. His sharp little eyes followed her. Swiftly he turned and reentered his master's house.

Roz continued toward Poole doggedly. The ride seemed long tonight, and she found herself bent over her mare's neck, hugging the animal's warmth to ward off loneliness. Twice she started at a sound and looked around anxiously. 'Twas nothing most likely—a night bird or animal. Nudging the mare to a trot, she reassured herself that there was naught to fear.

When the Poole quay loomed in view, Rozalinde let out a sigh of relief and slid from the mare. Removing the heavy saddle, she smoothed the animal's back with her hands. "I'm sorry, girl, I forgot your brushes. And I should have brought you some oats." For some unknown reason she tarried with the animal, wrapping her arms around the sleek, warm neck, taking a moment's pause. But she mustn't linger.

After exchanging the mare's bridle for a comfortable halter, Roz tethered her in a little shed beside her father's warehouse. The horse would be found in the morning when the men came to work, and everyone would know where she had gone. But her father must not worry. She would not want that.

At the water's edge, she searched for a boat she could handle. *The Chalice* lay at anchor, halfway out of the calm waters of the bay. Two guards were posted—she had set them herself, assisted by the captain. In her mind's eye she could see them in their positions, one at the stern and one at the bow. Then she pictured the barrel, the one she had left in readiness, midway between the two guards. One empty barrel sitting among the others full of drinking water. She would hide there until the ship was at sea.

Finding a small dinghy, Roz untied the rope. Gathering her skirts, she prepared to step down. Behind her a footfall sounded. Rearing her head, she whirled.

"What do you . . ." She got no farther with her question, for suddenly her head exploded with pain. She staggered forward, almost into the stranger's arms. Desperately she veered away, flashes of adrenaline shooting through her veins, warning her to run. But she couldn't run. Her thoughts grew foggy. Blackness hovered before her eyes.

Roz fought it. She tried to stem the rising tide of pain, the blinding pool of blackness gathering before her. It was too strong for her. Her legs buckled. She sank to her knees.

Rozalinde awoke some time later, feeling as if aeons had passed, more angry than frightened. Moaning softly, she fumbled to sit up, cradling her head. Blasted scoundrel, to hit her so. Opening her eyes, she winced at the pain and tried to make out where she was.

The room was richly furnished. She was lying on a bed curtained with embroidered draperies. A gentleman's suit of clothing and several fashionable hats hung on pegs along one wall. A highly polished cherry table graced the center of the room, the chair pulled out as if someone had recently sat there. A branch of candles gave her plenty of light.

Getting gingerly to her feet, Roz attempted a few steps, testing her strength. Black dots returned to swirl before her eyes and she gripped the bedpost, afraid she might black out again. Slowly, her vision cleared. Making her way to the window, Roz looked out.

What she saw made her blood congeal in her veins. It was the green in the center of Lulworth, and that meant she was in the house of George Trenchard.

Furious, Roz wrenched open the window and leaned out.

Her head ached as if a hammer pounded inside her temples. Clinging to the casement, she stared down. She seemed to be one level up, mayhap even two. The ground looked farther away here than it had from her own window.

Nausea rose in her throat. That bang on the head was making her feel sick. Well, she would just have to bear it, for she could not rest now. Turning away from the window, Rozalinde scoured the room with her gaze, searching for something. She could think of one thing only—to escape.

The door! She crossed to it, carefully this time, trying not to jar her head. Putting her ear firmly to the wood, she listened, hoping there was no one near. Maybe she could creep out without being noticed. It was such a big house.

The voices she heard dashed her hopes. Unashamedly she listened, trying to make out the words. What were they saying? She must know.

"We sail together. I insist on it," came a voice Roz decided must be Trenchard's. The words that followed were lost as he turned away, but she could hear discussion, one voice heavily accented. It was Spanish. The realization made her head throb anew. It must be the Marquis De-Vega, the Spanish admiral. Where were they sailing together? She reached down and tried the door handle. It was locked.

"I swear to you we'll evade them," Trenchard said. "We will sail to Antwerp and then see your message safely to Brussels."

"And what if there is a fleet of them?" DeVega asked. "They travel in a fleet."

"The Sea Beggars?" Trenchard scoffed. "They have little money and scarce any supplies to run their fleet. But if we should spot them, I can summon the queen's navy. As deputy lieutenant, 'tis my right. You are due aid from England, and I shall see that you have it."

" 'Tis well," the other voice growled. "His Majesty expects this communiqué to reach the duke, not like the last one, and so many others in the past year."

"No, no," Trenchard's voice assured. "I'll catch the pirates who have raided your ships. You have my promise. I have learned much about them of late—or rather I should say, of one in particular who is most like giving you trouble."

Roz's eyes widened. They must be talking about the Sea Beggars. Apparently Kit also preyed on the Spanish. Though she should not care, for some reason this news made her want to weep. Pressing her ear tightly to the door, she continued to listen.

"See that you catch the guilty party," the other voice went on dryly. "His Majesty will reward you well if you rid us of these vermin."

"The same price as for my previous services?"

"More," the Spaniard promised. "We hate these Sea Beggars. They cause us uncommon trouble."

"They plague me as well, I assure you," Trenchard answered. "But not for long. I played them a pretty trick the other day. Stole a ship, made off with the goods, and let them take the blame. Ah, but here is my servant. Sutton, be so good as to conduct his lordship to the entertainment below. I will join you shortly. I must check on my wife."

Wife! Stole a ship! Troth! Rozalinde lunged away from the door frantically. Her limbs wanted to rebel against her commands, to freeze with paralysis, but she forced them to move as she searched the room for a place to hide. The many things she'd just heard roiled madly in her brain. She had no time to sort them out.

The door handle rattled, a key was inserted in the lock. But it did not turn.

Hesitantly, Rozalinde tiptoed back to the door, wondering if George had changed his mind. Again she heard voices, and throwing caution to the winds, she pressed her ear to the wood panel. Beyond, she could hear George speaking to another man.

"Damn you, why do you linger? I don't want the footman conducting his lordship. Get to your duties at once."

"Not until you tell me the truth. You never said you were serving King Philip. But you are, aren't you? You let me think you served only the queen."

Trenchard's answer blazed with anger. "You were eavesdropping when I talked to DeVega. That is inexcusable. I'll discharge you."

There was an answering chuckle. "I never did believe your story—that you got all your gold from the queen. She is far too miserly to reward you so lavishly. None of those heaps of coins are from her, are they? You've sold out to the Spanish, telling them everything you know. What did they promise you besides the gold, eh? A position in the new government when they invade England? A title? Whatever it is, I want my share."

Rozalinde expected to hear a refusal from Trenchard, but apparently her betrothed thought better of it. "You shall have your due."

"A title."

"You can't bear a title and well you know it. Get downstairs! There is much work to be done. These guests are only the beginning. They will be asking much of me in preparation for the invasion. I will need more help than yours to satisfy them."

Rozalinde took a shaky step back from the door. The words she'd heard were poison. The Spanish planned to invade England! Everyone knew they wanted to, but to detect an active plot was serious business. For the first time, fear coursed through her.

The other man must have left, because now the key turned in the lock. Roz whirled and froze, her back against the desk, as the metal lock grated and rattled.

Suddenly the air of the room was close beyond bearing. Roz felt she was suffocating. George Trenchard stood in the open doorway, looking taller and more formidable than he ever had before.

Outside, Jonathan Cavandish crouched behind some bushes across the town green, watching Trenchard's big house in anguish. Three men had taken his sister—he'd seen them. For he'd followed her secretly all the way from their home. Now his worst fears were realized. He balled his hands into fists, trying to think what to do.

He knew where she was. Only minutes before, a window on the third floor had opened. A woman's slim figure had leaned out, scanning the ground. It had to be Rozalinde, Jon thought, but what could he do about it? The Spanish, it seemed, were everywhere, lodged in every vacant room of Trenchard's monstrous house. Jon studied the structure in despair. How could he hope to rescue her? He couldn't possibly fight those men! Even with the height he had so recently acquired, he was no match.

Perhaps, he reasoned, he should wait until morning. If

he told their father everything, Master Cavandish could
come and demand Rozalinde back. Even if Trenchard de-
nied her presence, his father could use his authority to
search the house.

But no, Trenchard could force Rozalinde to marry him
by then. Jon discarded the plan and tried frantically to
think of another. His sister could lose her virtue in a minute
flat, and then there would be no drawing back from her
marriage. And he didn't want Trenchard for a brother-in-
law. He had to get her out.

Several paces behind Jonathan, cloaked in the secrecy of
the shadows surrounding the green, Kit Howard glowered
at Trenchard's huge house, then at the boy in front of him,
hiding in the bushes. Fury held him in its grasp, but he
checked it rigidly, cursing his situation, his need for stealth.

All week long he had come nightly from *The Raven*
where it lay anchored several miles to the south. All week
long he had watched Trenchard. The familiar shadows of
the houses now welcomed him, wrapped him in their mysterious depths. He had listened at Trenchard's window, observed his every movement. Then blended back into the
night and disappeared with expert stealth.

No one knew he was in Lulworth. Not a soul. He was
believed to be in London. Otherwise he would free Rozalinde instantly. For it was surely she he'd seen carried into
the house earlier—a wench's skirts trailing as some rough
brute carried her, slung over his shoulder. And wasn't this
her brother, that young whelp Cavandish, hiding in the
bushes, watching the house and fretting?

Kit clenched his fist over his rapier hilt, thinking it would
give him supreme satisfaction to walk up to Trenchard's
door and challenge him. He would enjoy killing him. He
longed to wipe the man's blood from his blade.

But he couldn't risk it. His spying would be found out.
And the Spanish would cease their overt actions so he
could not learn their plans.

They were in league together—Trenchard and the Spanish. Cohorts. His instinct had warned him, bid him investi-
gate further. Now he knew. All the while Trenchard grew
bolder, knowing no one would dare question what he did.
Trenchard, the upright citizen.

Kit shook his head, knowing he was in an awkward position himself, suspected of being the Beggar King. And he shook his head at something else. He'd watched another house regularly this week. Nightly he was drawn to the timbered dwelling of Rozalinde Cavandish, where he hovered like a lost soul, driven by the desperate ache inside.

What madness was this? he asked himself. He had tried at first to name it, then given up. He knew only that he was unable to stop himself, unable to care that he could not, ever since she'd said those three ordinary words.

" 'Tis time to stop this nonsense," he'd told her. "Admit you care." *Mayhap I do.* Those three words, and his world plunged into chaos, driving him to do mad things. But then she'd driven him from the first, hadn't she? Oh, she was not conscious of it, she would deny it if he said so, but from the moment he'd first seen her, from the instant he'd gathered her into his arms and tasted her kiss, he'd found her soul spread forth before him.

Not because she wished to reveal herself. No, it was his fault really. Because he couldn't help reading her thoughts and feelings. It was as if he merged with her, like a lost key fit to its lock, opening the secrets beyond. And though it drove him insane to be so thoroughly connected to someone—he who worshiped his solitude—he found it impossible to resist. He was tied to her by silken bindings, driven by his own desperate urges.

But because of those urges, he was now present when she took her first, ill-fated step into trouble, just as he'd predicted she would. Further, the Lord in His infinite wisdom had sent him the vehicle to bring her out of trouble again. Pulling his hood forward, Kit arranged it to shroud his face. The midnight cloak swung around his ankles as he glided forward on quiet feet.

Jonathan clutched the bushes, thinking dire thoughts, completely at his wit's end. He must help Rozalinde, regardless of his own safety. Releasing his hold on the shrub, he started forward, determined to do something. He was concentrating so hard, he noticed nothing else.

A hand closed around his shirt collar and lifted him from the ground.

Terror rocketed through Jonathan. "Loose me," he yelped, struggling against the huge fist.

"Shhh." The man swept him back into the bushes and whispered to him fiercely. "Do you want to rouse the watch? Quiet. Say your name."

"Cavandish," Jon gulped, trying to see the man. Villains generally stabbed you and took your money. They didn't ask your name. Swiftly he took in the man's black cloak, the way his face was obscured by the depths of his hood.

The man seemed satisfied, for he thrust back his head covering.

"Lord Wynford!" Jon gasped, astonished. "I thought you were in London."

Wynford jerked his head in the direction of Trenchard's house. "We must free your sister, and we must be swift."

"Aye." Jon didn't bother to ask how he knew. "She's in there." He pointed to the window where the woman had appeared. "I saw her just minutes ago."

Wynford unhooked a heavy coil of rope from his belt. "Take this." He handed it to Jonathan. "Here is what you must do."

"Rozalinde, my love, you are feeling better. I am glad." Trenchard moved lithely into the room and closed the door behind him.

Roz stood where she was, fear rooting her to the spot beside the desk. She wanted to accuse him, to fling her rage at him, but she could not do that. If she was to escape, he would require careful handling. "Master Trenchard," she began, forcing the words to her lips. "George. What am I doing here?"

"A better question is, what were you doing on the quay at Poole after midnight?" Trenchard smiled at her congenially. "I asked that myself."

Rozalinde thought desperately. She must convince him to take her home. Mayhap if she made him feel guilty . . . "You are so solicitous of my whereabouts, yet *you* struck me on the head."

"Rozalinde!" Trenchard's eyebrows raised in shock. "I did no such thing. You were discovered in dire trouble and I had you rescued. But still you do not trust me."

"How can I?" Rozalinde ducked behind a chair as he came toward her. "When I am in your bedchamber."

He laughed gently and looked around the room. "This? This is my guest chamber. I merely store a few things here." He nodded toward the clothes on pegs. "You are right about one thing. A slight change of plans. We wed tomorrow. I have decided not to wait."

Roz was seized by panic. "Tomorrow! But I don't wish to wed tomorrow. I have not had a chance to ready my wedding linens. Take me to my father," she ordered, summoning what she could of her dignity. "I wish to go home at once."

"Rozalinde, be reasonable." George approached the chair, put a hand on its arm and leaned toward her. "Surely you can see the difficulty you are in. Does your father know you are out? Does he?" He raised his eyebrows again, questioningly. "So then, if you arrive home in my company in the middle of the night, what will your father think? What will the entire town think? Come, you must allow me to solve this problem for you. Otherwise, you can see how it will end."

Roz shook her head and backed toward the bed. He sounded so reasonable, yet for the first time she realized his true intent. He seemed eminently trustworthy, but he'd followed her to Lulworth Castle. He posed as the loyal alderman of Lulworth, but he betrayed his country. She'd received a letter saying the Sea Beggars stole her cargo, but she'd heard him admit he'd stolen it himself. As he came steadily toward her, she backed away until her calves bumped against the bed. With a twist, she leaped upon it. Her feet sank into the feather mattress, impeding her progress as she headed for the far side. Her movements made her dizzy again. Black dots danced before her eyes as Trenchard approached.

"Yes, I believe we have waited overlong." He began to unbutton his silk brocade doublet.

Her gaze fastened with revulsion on that doublet, his best one again. She hated that deep color of green. It seemed to waver in the candlelight as she stared at it, then at him.

"Let us delay no longer," he crooned, coming closer, unfastening the last button on his doublet. "I have awaited this moment when you would give me your favor."

Roz felt his gaze burning into her. There was a strange glint in his eyes.

"You were, after all, wandering about at night," he said, shrugging out of the doublet and dropping it on the floor. He loosened the collar of his shirt. "You know what can happen to a girl in such circumstances. Fortunately for you, my intentions are completely honorable. The men downstairs think you are already my wife. Tomorrow, I will make it true."

Roz looked around desperately, searching for a weapon. Her gaze lit upon a brass ewer on the stand beside the bed. Leaning down, she grasped it firmly in her fist. Black pinpoints danced distractingly, impeding her vision.

"Rozalinde, my dear, be sensible. I am much stronger than you." Standing with feet spread, he flexed one arm, making the muscles play beneath his shirt. "You cannot think to accomplish anything beyond delay. I intend to show my admiration for you. Tonight."

"Why are you so . . ." She groped urgently for words to distract him, to give her time. "Why are you so set on wedding with me?" She tightened her grip on the brass ewer. "When I have told you I wish some time before we take such a step."

"I want to take care of you, sweetheart. A man should take care of his wife. My father never took care of my mother. He preferred other women. But I won't be like him. You can rely on me."

"What happened to your mother?" Roz queried, realizing she'd hit on a subject he might talk about. Anything to delay him.

Trenchard's face saddened. His sharp eyes glazed over. "She died of a fever. I tried to save her, but my father had taken all the money and left us. We had next to nothing. I could not pay a physician, nor buy proper food or medicine, and I didn't know what to do for her. It was just the two of us, and had been for so long, even before my father was gone."

He bowed his head for a second, leaving Roz a perfect opportunity, but somehow she couldn't hit him. She lowered the ewer onto the bed. "Your mother died? How old were you."

"Eleven."

"Only a little younger than Matthew."

"Aye," he said softly, bringing his gaze back to meet hers. He sank down on the bed and held out one hand to her.

She felt unexpectedly sorry for him. His past had been ugly, and apparently he had profound feelings for her. But she couldn't bring herself to feel anything in return. Before she'd felt nothing. Now she felt loathing strangely mixed with pity. He'd done things that couldn't be excused, committed crimes against her and his country, all to soothe his pain from his past. Yet had he done none of these things that she considered wrong, marriage to him would still have been a daily trial, as she chafed under the restrictions he would place on her while he "cared for her." Her spirit groped for guidance. She must somehow bring this man to justice. The words he had spoken earlier, even though she heard them while eavesdropping, set her free to do what she must.

A pistol shot vibrated in the night.

Shouts broke out downstairs. Trenchard threw up his head to listen, and Rozalinde went completely still.

"Master Trenchard, come quickly." Someone pounded up the stairs and banged on the door. "Lord DeVega has been shot."

Trenchard leaped to his feet. "Damn!" He looked back at her, where she'd sunk down on the bed. "I'll return anon. Do not move." He went out and slammed the door behind him. She could hear him turn the key in the lock. "Alert the watch." His shout floated back to her as he clattered down the stair.

Hatred suddenly flared in every fiber of her being. He was dangerous, a criminal trying to trick her. The realization made her even more determined to escape.

Troth, Rozalinde thought, drawing herself carefully into a sitting position and burying her head in her hands. Her head was throbbing like a great kettledrum. But that pistol shot was a gift from God. She must make use of it.

Dragging herself to her feet, Roz staggered forward several steps. Once again the motion made blackness froth and foam before her eyes. Clutching the chair before the cherry table, Roz bent over and willed herself not to faint. Her gaze came to rest on Trenchard's doublet.

A carved wooden pomander had rolled from his pocket. Men and women alike carried them. It was undoubtedly filled with scent.

Scooping it up, Roz put it to her nostrils, praying it contained something pungent that would clear her head. She inhaled the sharp scent of cedar and felt better.

"Hst, Rozalinde. Are you there?"

No, she wasn't better, Rozalinde thought morosely. For now she was hearing things. Was it something in this pomander? She held up the bauble in her hand and squinted at it.

"Rozalinde! Grab the rope. Do you hear me?"

Sudden hope pierced her. She turned toward the sound of the voice. It seemed to come from the huge, ostentatious chimney piece. Could it be . . . ?

The hearth was cold. Thrusting the pomander into her kirtle pocket, Roz raced for it and without hesitating, bent over and thrust her head inside. The flue was big and dirty, but there was no fire in the hearth downstairs, for she smelled no smoke. It would easily accommodate a woman her size.

Something brushed her face, dangling from above. It was the rope. "Jonathan?" she called softly. "Is that you?"

"Aye, sister. Tie the rope around your waist."

She did so, not stopping to ask questions. At her tug, he began to haul her up slowly, while Roz helped with hands and feet.

"By heaven, I'm glad to see you." Roz emerged into the open and breathed deeply after the suffocating closeness of the flue. She reached out her arms to Jon, who helped her down from the tall chimney stack.

"Aye, well, we must be away. Come," he whispered, clasping her arm as he balanced precariously on the sharp pitch of the roof where the two sides joined. "We must go to that tree." Letting go of her, Jonathan began walking steadily across the point of the roof, balancing precisely, putting one foot before the other. He'd always had perfect balance—it seemed to go with the juggling and the tumbling he so loved.

Roz swallowed with great difficulty, finding a sudden lump lodged in her throat as she watched him move along the dangerous path. The tree looked far away. "I don't know if I can make it, Jon." She could hear her own voice tremble. She took a grip on herself before continuing. "The roof is so steep."

"Sit down," he told her over his shoulder, "and slide yourself across."

" 'Twill take forever," she muttered, more to herself as he drew farther away. And what hour was it? She must get to *The Chalice* before it left port. Troth, she thought dismally, Kit's words ringing in her memory. *If you set one foot out of your door for Antwerp, you'll walk straight into trouble.* Gingerly she placed one foot on the pointed pitch of the roof, extended both arms for balance, and took her first step.

It proved to be the longest walk of her life. Each placement of her foot seemed to take her nowhere, her journey endless. She had to count something, to steady her nerves. People she loved rose up in her mind. With fierce concentration, she began.

One, for Angelica, always into trouble. But that reminded her of Kit and his warning. She thrust him from her mind.

Two for Lucina, always hugging her so desperately. Right in front of the earl, too, who'd clearly been shocked. Oh, she had been wicked that day, to do what she'd done—to make the girls kiss him. He'd been so angry. But the thought of that led to thoughts of his embraces, and her face flamed red. Oh, why did she keep thinking of him? It was too confusing. For days she'd thought he'd stolen her cargo. Then she learned it was Trenchard. So how should she feel about the earl, now that she knew? She took another step and pushed him from her mind.

Three, for Charles, with his whines and his smiles. *That* didn't remind her of the earl—troth, there he was again. She took two steps in rapid succession without even counting. She would never make it.

Despite the coolness of the night, beads of sweat gathered at her hairline. One trickled down her forehead, dripped into her right eye. She batted her eyelid futilely, trying to clear her vision.

Four for Jonathan. Oh, thank the good Lord for Jonathan. Five ... six ... seven ... eight ... nine ... She stepped slowly and deliberately, relying on the numbers, trying to keep her mind blank to everything except their soothing formations.

Down below there were shouts in the town green. She could hear footsteps, people running. Intent on her own business, she continued to count with each step.

Ten . . . eleven . . . twelve . . . The commotion below died away, but images of Kit returned to torment her. Scraps and snippets swirling in her memory—Kit in the black velvet mask, bending to kiss her mouth; the rich scent of cloves and his wonderfully musky pomade; Kit in the stormy black cape, standing alone on the Spanish ship, entrusting her with his secrets. His handsome face had looked down at her, passion burning in his eyes as he warned her to remain at home. The thoughts were joy and agony, all leading to her present trouble. She was just where he'd predicted she would be, and it was her own fault. But it was too late—she could not change her mind about going to Antwerp. Scarcely daring to breathe, she inched her way along.

"You can do it, Rozalinde. Just a little farther." Jon had reached the tree long ago. Now he encouraged her in a loud whisper. "You're almost here."

She dared raise her eyes from the roof, seeking his reassurance. As she did so, one foot slipped.

Down she fell, grasping at anything to stop herself. One of her hands hooked on the roof's pitch and hung there, her heart pounding with deafening loudness, her breath rasping wildly in her throat.

Kit winced sharply as a stone pierced his shoulder. The instant he'd aimed his pistol through Trenchard's window, then fired a ball straight into Lord DeVega, this fellow had leaped out and pursued him. He ran like the wind, the devil. And now he was gaining on him, coming closer and throwing stones, though Lord knew how he stooped to get them.

Redoubling his speed, Kit dodged around a house and changed direction, heading south. He must get to *The Raven.* Some way farther on he stopped, leaned against the wall of a house and listened, filling his lungs with searing breaths of air. Had his pursuer realized the trick? Was he followed?

The sound of footsteps echoed in the quiet town, not running now, but moving steadily, pausing every so often to determine which way the unknown assailant had gone.

Blast! Kit set off, used the trick again, circling around several houses and traveling north. At this rate he would take hours to reach *The Raven*. Not that it mattered. His diversion had done its work—created chaos in Trenchard's house. He hoped it was long enough for Jon to help Rozalinde escape, because he couldn't help her now.

From above Jonathan saw the commotion, the people coming and going, and whispered a thanksgiving. No one had heard his sister fall. No one looked up. Turning resolutely, he crossed the roof to where she hung by one hand. "Steady, now, Rozalinde." Lowering himself carefully, he sat with one leg straddling each side of the roof. "I'll have you up in a thrice." Grasping her arm, he braced himself and pulled.

When he had her sitting before him, skirts bunched around her waist, legs on each side of the roof, she collapsed. He put both arms around her to give her support.

"Pull yourself together, Rozalinde. My stars." Jon had never thought to say such a thing to his sister. 'Twas she who'd always said it to him.

"I feel dizzy." She clung to him fiercely. "They hit me on the head. It pains me so, I couldn't keep my balance."

Jon held her tighter. "I know. I saw them."

"You followed me, didn't you?"

She didn't ask, she stated the fact, and he thought she was going to chastise him, but she didn't. "Thank you," she whispered after a moment, "I'll never doubt you again. I'll trust you with anything. The house, the shop."

"Don't thank me yet," he said gruffly, elated by her gratitude. "We still must get down."

"And you must get me to the ship."

"You're still going?"

"I am."

"But, Rozalinde, you've been hit on the head. You just said you can scarce keep your balance, that your head pains you. You should come home, go back to bed."

"I must go with the ship, Jon. Things will not be better

with the business if I remain at home. They'll only grow worse."

Jon gave her a last pat on the back, realizing she was determined, then began the slow process of turning himself around. "All right, Rozalinde. Just as you say."

"I think I can climb the tree if you'll get me to it."

Jon nodded resignedly. "Hold on while we slide back. That way you won't fall."

They got down safely, slipping into the shadows at the back of the house. The tree's height had let them see and avoid the watch, several of Trenchard's servants, and two Spaniards who stood out front, waiting to see if the mysterious attacker was caught. Jon's horse was tethered a few streets away. The beast whickered when they drew near.

"Up you go, Rozalinde." Jon boosted her into the saddle, then prepared to swing up behind her.

"What hour is it?" Roz whispered, holding the horse steady for him to mount. "The ship will leave at dawn. I'm not too late?"

" 'Tis well after three, but never fear. I'll see you on that ship." Jon took the reins and nudged the horse into motion, feeling a faint twinge of guilt for concealing Kit's part. Nonetheless, his lordship had ordered it thus. "I'm not much good with numbers. Not like you. But I can manage this," he assured her.

It was hours later, just before dawn, when a tired Kit arrived at Poole. At the risk of being seen, he approached the quay cautiously, then concealed himself in a shed. From there he scanned the harbor, looking for *The Chalice*. He'd meant to catch up with Jonathan and Rozalinde, to take Rozalinde and force her, if necessary, to accompany him on *The Raven*. Since she was so intent on going to Antwerp, why not go with him? Either way she would be missing from her home, so it didn't make much difference. He would give in to those urges that drove him. That was his plan.

He hadn't counted on that fellow from Trenchard's household reacting with such insistence. Lord, but that underling could run! For over an hour they'd played cat and mouse in the dark streets of West Lulworth. But Kit had the advantage. He'd grown up in this town, and the place had changed little over the years. How well he'd known the obscure hiding places, how often he'd used them to hide from his father, who would storm down from the castle and search for hours before catching him and dragging him home for a beating. Those hiding places had served Kit well tonight. The barn loft behind the shoemaker's house, the huge box where the alemaker stored his wood. They'd allowed him to outwit the fellow, then make his escape.

Scanning the bay rapidly, Kit searched for *The Chalice,* but failed to see it immediately. Thinking he must have forgotten where it lay anchored, he changed his position and looked again. Intently he studied the water, seeing the fishing boats, the usual small hulks at anchor. A vast displeasure deepened in his mind. There was no mistaking it. *The Chalice* had left port.

PART TWO

The Sea

Chapter 16

Two days later, Kit scanned the horizon, looking for Rozalinde's ship. Devilish puzzling, he told himself as he stood at the rail of the *Swiftsure,* his hair and cape ruffled by the brisk breeze. He had sailed from the coast of Dorset to this point just north of the Straits of Dover. By rights he should have encountered *The Chalice.* But he'd seen not a trace of the English ship.

Now he approached his expected rendezvous with Phillipe. Just ahead, the dozen or more ships of the Beggar Fleet arranged themselves to guard the passage to Antwerp. From the *Swiftsure* he could see *The Hope* sitting in the position of authority. Feeling a driving need to be on board that vessel, he issued orders to move ahead.

"Christopher, *m'n vriend,* I am most pleased to see thee."

Entering the captain's cabin, Kit found himself enveloped by Phillipe's massive embrace, then guided to the best chair. The welcome sound of Phillipe's deep-toned voice accosted him.

"I am relieved to see you yet whole, with your dangerous work, *mijn vriend.*"

Pulling off his heavy gloves, Kit sat, let his gaze linger on Phillipe as the man stoked the brazier with fresh coal, then seated himself opposite. Something radiant seeped into Kit, taking him by surprise. Warmth. Fingers of it spread through him, and it was not just heat from the brazier after the chill of the afternoon wind.

At the count's command, a cabin boy entered bearing two hot platters of food. The odor of hot chicken in pungent sauce tantalized Kit's nostrils. When it was served and the boy had withdrawn, Kit fell to, ravenous with an appetite he hadn't known in days. As he ate, he found himself pouring out the details of his secret movements in West Lulworth—how the Spanish had requested safe harbor in the town, his discovery of Trenchard's collusion with them. All of it dropped from his lips like a confession. "The Spanish ship is on its way here with the next communiqué. This Marquis DeVega is to deliver it to the Duke of Alva at Antwerp. All we need do is wait. They will sail right into our hands."

"Well done." Phillipe offered Kit another helping from the platter of roast capon. His mouth widened in a smile of congratulation. "I beg you, eat."

Kit lifted his knife again with relish. "You cannot imagine how good this tastes. I have not supped properly in over a sen-night."

"*Sakkerloot!*" Phillipe muttered in a chastening tone. He refilled Kit's flagon of wine, ignoring his own trencher of food. " 'Tis ill for your health, this moving about at night, going without rest and proper food, it wears on your strength. But your discovery is an important one. Now we know this Trenchard is in league with our enemy and a traitor to England. The Spanish must be moving forward with their plan for an invasion. What does your queen say?"

"The same thing she always says. Destroy him but keep her name out of it. She is a hard mistress, Her Grace. I would rather arrest him in the queen's name."

"You cannot, of course." Phillipe ran his hand through his thick gray hair distractedly. "If your countrymen knew a traitor lived in their midst, held a trusted position appointed by the Crown, they would lose faith. They would begin to suspect one another, would quarrel among themselves. Division within a country is lethal. You must rid Lulworth of this man without giving away his secret. Mayhap at the same time we can put a stop to the invasion."

"A tall order." Kit speared a piece of meat with his knife and downed it. "I would speak of it later. Let's to my news for you. You've not even asked."

Phillipe nodded, and Kit wondered how he could be so calm. In his place, Kit would have demanded the information. It must be his age, he decided, studying the lines reaming Phillipe's face, the dignity of the chiseled grooves around the eyes and mouth. It made Kit aware of the blood in his own veins, blood that was too hot, too impatient. "Her Majesty wishes to aid you," Kit told him, then stopped, realizing he had to tell the unpleasant part first. "Unfortunately, she cannot do it openly."

Phillipe's expression remained unruffled. " 'Tis not unusual. Our allies often resort to subterfuge."

"I am sorry," Kit breathed, feeling vastly uncomfortable, "but we cannot afford open war at this time. Spain would crush us. Our navy is still small—"

"No apology is necessary. I accept God's will."

Pangs of remorse throbbed through Kit. He had let his friend down. "But wait ... There is also good news. Although the queen does not wish to drain her treasury, she will borrow money from her nobles. I have the funds needed to recruit men and outfit more ships. You tell me there are many people who want to leave the part of your country ruled by the Spanish—we'll simply put them to work for the Prince of Orange."

"I thank you."

Kit's heart sank. Phillipe was not responding as he'd hoped. He probed his mind for some other way to help. "You need a safe port for the fleet—a place to make repairs and take on water. I could arrange it for you, somewhere along the Dorset coast."

"I will not go there." Phillipe shook his head firmly. "I told you before."

" 'Twould be a place well concealed. I know many excellent harbors. I could bring supplies—"

"That is scarce the difficulty." Phillipe's gaze shifted away. "I did not tell you previously but ... there was once a woman in Dorset ... She is now dead ..."

Words froze in Kit's throat. He tried to swallow and found he could not. "I understand," he said, trying to fight the painful, powerful feelings, that surged within him whenever he thought of Rozalinde. "These feelings for this woman—you wish to forget them. They bring nothing but pain. Entanglements are best avoided before they take root." He stopped, wondering how Phillipe would answer. When he looked up, the older man was staring at him.

"Do you really believe that?"

"Why should I not?"

Phillipe scrapped back his chair and stood. He regarded Kit steadily, arms crossed before his chest, expression inscrutable. "You have much to tell me, Christopher. I would like to know where you got such ideas. Are those your father's words?"

"Of course not." Kit bit out the retort. "I am master of my own thoughts and feelings. It's only that once I left home, I swore never to be tied to persons or places. Such emotions are ultimately meaningless. I merely thought you felt the same. Why should you visit a place that reminds you of pain?"

Phillipe shook his head. "That is not why I refuse to visit Dorset. I love the woman I mentioned."

The statement caught Kit off guard. He looked up, incredulous.

"Why does this surprise you? Our love gave us strength. At times, it was all I had." Phillipe's eyelids closed and a great calm seemed to suffuse his person. When he opened them again, he fixed his gaze on Kit. "You cannot call that meaningless—something that gives your life purpose."

Kit didn't hear him. His thoughts were still riveted on Phillipe's first revelation—this was a man he respected, yet he said he *loved*. No matter that the woman was dead. Kit winced inwardly as an unexpected gush of pain surfaced inside him. Unable to move, he stared at his mentor.

"You do not believe me, do you?" Phillipe sat down again and drew his chair close to Kit's. "Listen, then, and let me tell you. When I was young, I met with a maid. She was traveling in the train of the English ambassador to the Netherlands. As his only daughter, she was well guarded, greatly revered, but I encountered her often at the court of Emperor Charles in Brussels. I danced with her, dined with her, rode out with her, though always in company. It made no difference. In the presence of others or alone, I had eyes only for her. We fell in love.

"When I learned she was betrothed to another man, I was beside myself. I promised to challenge him to a duel, to kill him any way I could. My father forbade me. He locked me in my chamber, telling me I would not cause a scandal or wreak diplomatic ruin on relations between our countries. I knew I was indiscreet. I realized my impetuous nature, but I could not control it. My father, being a wise man, took precautions to do it for me. He keep me under lock and key, well guarded until such a time as the spell would pass.

"I was underage. What could I do? As I sat in my lonely chamber, I had much time for thinking, and I realized killing the betrothed would solve nothing. My lady was a great heiress and her father was set upon marrying her to an English noble. Still, I endeavored to send her a message, to tell her my love was true. She received that message. I knew that much for certes, because her father found it. He raised a great scandal about it before taking her away to England where he made sure she wed the titled man he'd chosen. Meanwhile, I was wed to the girl of *my* father's choosing. Eventually, when I had a son of my own and many duties to fulfill, I thought my first love was at an end.

"I was wrong. Much later when I visited England on government business, without expecting it, I saw her. We were older then—she was five and twenty; I nine and twenty. And because we had both known married life and all it entailed, we succumbed to temptation and became lovers. It was only once. The shock of seeing each other after so many years, the ecstasy of knowing I still loved her and she, me, swept us away.

"The next day she left for her husband's country home in Dorset, determined not to give way to temptation again. She was a woman who believed in honor, though she had little else in her life.

"It was then that I began to visit her secretly at her home along the Dorset coast. She refused to engage in lovemaking with me, but I saw her often and we talked of many things, until the deep hours of the night. There was a secret room in her husband's castle where we met. My heart wept for her because her husband was a cold man. Oh, he treated her properly, in a manner befitting a countess, but he gave her nothing ... no emotion, no love, because he was empty inside and had nothing to offer. And then there were his expectations for the children. They did not agree on the subject. It caused much dissent between them and misery on her part."

Kit leaned forward in his chair, gripping its arms, enthralled. "My life was much the same. My father was a cold man, unable to love my mother or any of us. He insisted we children be raised according to strict ..." He stopped, speechless as a flare of realization sparked to life.

Phillipe nodded. "The woman I loved was your mother. She was my fair rose of Dorset, the love the legends say I sought, though you may not have heard them. And to me, she was simply *mijn geliefde* Anne."

The blood drained from Kit's face. He stared down at his hands, saw them like things detached, the knuckles white where they closed around the arms of the chair. "Then she ... you ..." No coherent words came, but one hand jerked to his temple. He slumped his back. "I cannot believe it." He shook his head painfully. "How could she? She betrayed him. She must have—"

"No!" Phillipe roared at him, leaping to his feet. "You think to blame her, to put her at fault. Yet she was not responsible for your father's cold nature, his unfeeling behavior. She might have been untrue to him, but only because she was driven to it. For five years we met secretly, yet I never touched her after that time in London. She would not permit it. Only later did she change her mind. I'll never know why, but five years after London she agreed to love me with her body as well as her heart." Phillipe paused, shook his head in a gesture of despair. "But it would never have happened at all, our meetings and loving, if your father had been kind to Anne. Dèspite his coldness she spent years doing her duty, trying to please him by bearing him children. And she refused to leave him, though I begged her to come away with me. I ask you, Christopher, what did he give her? What did he give you? Love? Affection?"

"No, certainly not that, I ..." Kit stopped, longing to banish the unspeakable roar of pain pounding in his ears. He shut his eyes, wanting to forget his mother sitting at the table across from his father, her thin figure frail, yet proud and unbending. Her fading beauty came back to him, the softness that sometimes lit up her eyes when they rested on him. The storm lessened in his head.

"There were months between our meetings," Phillipe told him, his voice strained, "days and hours she spent serving the family name of Howard, doing her part as wife and countess because she believed in honor. But for me there was no other woman in my life save Anne. My own wife had died in childbirth years earlier. Yet Anne would not go so far as to leave your father. She bore him two sons— and two daughters. Yes," he nodded as he saw Kit wince, "I know about your infant sisters, the first one before your birth, the other after. Both died, and your father did not offer a word of consolation to your mother. He believed girl children were useless and better off dead. Anne thought their loss was her own punishment, because she could not love her husband. Only a woman of her nature would believe such a thing. But tell me, Christopher, tell me what your mother received in return for her suffering. You were there. What did you see?"

A vision of his mother crystallized in Kit's memory for an instant. At first she was young and beautiful, but then the image faded, and he saw her ill and strained, lying in the huge poster bed in her chamber. He'd slipped in to look at her, been told by the maid that his mother had lost a child, that she was very ill, might die. The memory receded and suddenly he felt a hundred years old.

He shrugged wearily. "I concede I am wrong to blame her for events beyond her control. But I can't think why she didn't try to escape from my father. I did. I took the first chance I got to leave. And there was no secret room in our castle," he added. "A secret passage, yes, but no room."

Phillipe gazed at him, an expression almost of reproach in his eyes. "I met her often in a concealed room deep beneath the castle. Your father did not know of it, so why should you?"

"It was my father's castle. He would have known."

"Not if *his* father before him didn't wish it. Apparently your grandfather didn't consider your father worthy of the secret during his lifetime. Or mayhap he was hiding something himself. Whatever the reason, after his death, your grandmother told Anne."

Kit shook his head and frowned, unable to grasp all this information. "She never told me about it. Not that she had a chance. I saw little of her as I grew older. She finally died of the smallpox only a year before my father." He looked up, studied the older man's face. "You knew that, didn't you?"

Phillipe nodded slowly. "Many people survive the smallpox, but Anne did not. I believe she was worn out by the heartache of being wed to such a man. No, it is too painful to think on. I prefer to remember her whole and happy, as she was in my arms, each time we met."

"I considered her weak."

"Weak?"

Kit heard the barely controlled rage seething in Phillipe's voice. It was the Beggar King who towered over him now, fists clenched at his sides. His eyes, which had previously softened as he spoke of love, grew cold and hard. "You covet the power of the Beggar King's mask," Phillipe's voice was dangerously low, "and dare to call another weak? You, who want the mask for all the wrong reasons? You think to sail away blissfully, to avoid commitment. But you cannot escape emotion by hiding behind a mask. Loneliness follows. It will pursue you like the hounds of hell, snarling and growing uglier each year. I know this for truth. I see it in your eyes."

His expression was angry, and Kit stiffened against it, flinging back his own anger in return. "I hide behind nothing. I did not even want the mask, if you recall. You were the one who insisted I take it. It was your choice."

The fury in Phillipe's eyes dwindled. The older man passed one hand across his face and looked away. "I did not mean to be harsh." He bent over the brazier, extending his palms to the heat. "I was overwrought. Forgive me. But you must heed my warning." He turned his head sharply to address Kit. "You like this role of the Beggar King too well. You imagine his life to be carefree and joyous, but it will leave you empty, just like your father and your brother. Eventually, you must give it up."

Kit scarcely heard his last words. He was busy struggling with a new thought that had sprung into his head. "Tell me," he whispered, reaching to touch the count's sleeve. The heavy black fabric felt firm and tangible in his hand. "Tell me, am I your son?"

"As I said, we made love only once before your birth, your mother and I. Often I wondered myself, but you were born eight months later. The timing was wrong. Anne told me you were not mine. Yet there is a certain resemblance."

Kit's gaze jerked to the small looking glass that hung on the wall of the cabin. He rose and went to stand before it, gazing into its murky pool of light. His own reflection stared back at him, looking strangely haunted. He turned back and studied Phillipe, making the comparison.

"We will never know for certain if what we share is the tie of blood." Phillipe's expression was speculative. "But what does it matter? The important thing is to know yourself. Just now you are searching for your grail and I urge you to continue. You will eventually find it. But I predict you will know true freedom only when you believe in the kind of love I shared with your mother."

Kit gripped the back of a chair, many thoughts warring behind his furrowed brow. Desperately he strove to grasp these new ideas, to reconcile their meaning with the torment of his past. "I must think upon it," he said at last, his breath coming harsh and labored. Leaning over the chair, he rested his head momentarily against one hand, struggling to find words. "I thank you for telling me the truth."

Phillipe's answering smile was full of healing.

Kit cleared his throat, groping to cover his unaccustomed awkwardness. "Of course I can appreciate the natural affection between comrades. I can accept that and still be free."

"But I expect much in return." Phillipe's voice had a warning note to it. "I expect your confidence, your trust, and your guardianship of my role as the Beggar King."

"All that I give gladly. I would give it without your asking."

"There! Do you see?" Phillipe's mouth curved in a smile of triumph. "Love is thus. Between two men. Between a man and a woman. Such gifts are no burden because despite the sacrifice, they are given gladly."

But still Kit felt unsettled. He turned away and stared unseeing at the looking glass, fighting off the phantoms of his past. *Loving a woman means having things demanded of you,* a needling voice told him. *Things you do not wish to give. Love means forfeiting what is most important to you for things that are trivial and stupid.*

Kit's thoughts floundered as though in rough water. He had always had these thoughts, but now, in Phillipe's presence, he suddenly felt a violent urge to toss them away. Were they his father's words? He couldn't remember. But

his father was dead, and this man who stood before him—
so vibrant, so full of heart—made him feel secure and cared
for. They were feelings he'd never had from his father.

"Come, let us pray for guidance." Phillipe indicated a
silver cross hanging on the wall. "We have work before us,
capturing the next communiqué. We must be ready when
the Spanish ship comes."

Slowly, Kit moved to obey, still shaken by his turmoil.
They knelt, their high leather boots creaking. Phillipe
crossed himself. Kit buried his face in one hand, his elbow
propped against his knee.

A distant boom shook the air.

They both surged to their feet. The cabin boy burst in
without knocking. " 'Tis cannon fire," he shrilled excitedly.
"Lookout spied two ships."

"Spanish?" the count barked, catching up his cloak and
striding for the door.

Kit followed, the cabin boy hurrying at his heels.

"Don't know for certs, me lord," the boy answered.
"Might be."

They raced out into the afternoon light. From the stern
deck, Kit surveyed the scene. He clenched his teeth and
scowled at what he saw. At least a league away, so distant
he could scarce make it out, a big galleon pursued a smaller
ship. Kit pulled out his spyglass, scanned the high-charged
vessel. He could make out the Spanish cross, etched in
blood red on the pristine white sails of the big ship. His
pulse began its familiar throb of anticipation. His hand fell
to his rapier hilt, massaging it as his rage grew.

"I shall go after our communiqué," he said to Phillipe,
who had come to stand beside him at the rail. "You may
take the other ship, if you please. She must contain something of great value, else they would not bother chasing
her. She looks English, from the shape of her hull." He
squinted through the glass again. It was then his mouth
went dry. His heart bucked violently in his chest. "Damn,"
he breathed harshly, clenching his fist over his rapier hilt.

He should have expected this, he told himself. He should
never let himself be caught off guard. But he'd been concentrating on the Spanish. Now events in West Lulworth
returned to haunt him. For he recognized that ship, as it

plowed through the water toward him. It was *The Chalice,* and Rozalinde would be on board.

Raging memory swept in to claim his thoughts, forcing him to relive the moment at Lulworth Cove—how Rozalinde's lips had parted eagerly beneath his, returning his desire, how she had bestowed that heavenly smile when he entrusted her with his secret, the pulse-stopping sound of her last words, ringing in his ears—*Mayhap I do care, but we should never have met.* The hell with her denial. He would not stand for it anymore.

"Aye. I intend to take her," Phillipe said, not noticing Kit's tumult of feelings. "I could not permit it to sail to Antwerp, if that is where 'tis bound. I cannot let any ship trade there. And since the Spanish want her, I want her as well."

Turning to his fleet captains who were huddled on the stern deck, waiting, Phillipe flung out the details of their attack. "Battle formation," he shouted. "Clear all decks. Ready the cannon, but only fire if I give the word. We will frighten this English ship, make it surrender. The *Swiftsure* will take on the Spaniard."

Men ran in all directions to their stations. Sails were unfurled and the fleet adjusted its position.

Kit banished all thoughts of Rozalinde. He would think about her later. Right now he had a battle to fight. With a quick command he sent two younger sailors running to lower a skiff.

"I'm for the *Swiftsure,*" he told Phillipe tersely, holding out his hand. "I wish you success."

"And you." Phillipe gripped Kit's hand, then dropped it to crush Kit in his embrace. "Go with God."

Chapter 17

On board *The Chalice,* Rozalinde paced her cabin, debating what to do. Up and down she walked, agitation filling her.

From the bunk she crossed the narrow room. Just before the table and chair, she turned and started back. Every few minutes she nervously checked the porthole. *The Chalice* had achieved full speed. It skimmed over the water like a bird, but it wasn't fast enough.

Troth, she whispered to herself, tugging at one of her loose braids while her thoughts leaped with turmoil. She must do something. Someone must. A Spanish ship followed them. She'd seen it herself from the stern deck when she'd gone for her daily stroll. There it was—a mere speck in the distance at first, but following relentlessly. Now it bore down on them with terrifying speed.

The Chalice, of course, could do no more than lumber. Its heavy cargo slowed them. Roz's heart contracted as she remembered the way the hull of the Spanish ship sliced the water in a razor-sharp furrow. She remembered something else too—the name painted on the hull. Dimly she had made it out through the captain's spyglass. The ship was called the *Gran Grifon. Trenchard,* she thought, squeezing her braid tightly in her sweating palm.

A sudden ungodly explosion shattered the afternoon, followed by a thud that shook *The Chalice* from stem to stern. Heavenly Father, they were being fired upon!

Catching up her cloak, Roz made a decision. Whirling the garment around her shoulders, she crossed the cabin and took up three items laid out neatly on the table. The short measuring rule and plumb lines went easily into her pocket. The third item she tucked under her arm, then arranged her cloak to conceal it. With a rush she made for the door.

A brisk wind tugged at Roz's skirts as she stepped outside. Scanning the sky, she noted the clouds gathering to the south. Well, that meant nothing. It was usually cloudy over the English Channel. Hurrying along the deck to the helm, she found the captain and tried to get his attention.

"You *must* fire the stern guns!" she cried, trying to make herself heard above the commotion of men who arrived for orders and dashed off again. "The Spanish are attacking. Since they draw nearer, let us bring down their masts."

Captain Wellham looked over his shoulder distractedly. Seeing who it was, he turned away, yelling more orders at his men. From the moment he'd discovered this lass on his ship, he'd tried to convince her to go home. He'd even put in at Dover, which delayed them several hours while he pleaded and bargained with her. He'd begged her earnestly to accept an escort back to Lulworth, but she'd have none of it. No, she was bound for Antwerp, and she would not be put off. She'd offered him many gold pieces to take her to Antwerp, and, in the end, it was far too rich a prize for him to refuse.

Lord have mercy, he thought glumly. He should have dumped her in Dover harbor. Now a Spanish ship was chasing them, firing its cannon, and the maid dared to leave her cabin. Was she mad? If the Spaniard didn't sink them, it would probably kill all the men and take her captive, but she didn't seem to care. She was tough as tanner's leather, this master's daughter. And admittedly she knew a thing or two about sailing—she'd already proved that. But he couldn't stop now for discussion. There was too much to do.

"Captain, do you hear me?" Rozalinde demanded, then turned away in despair, realizing her words were lost in the confusion. He was too busy trying to speed the ship to listen to her pleas, but someone had to direct the firing of the stern cannon since their side guns were of no use.

Roz hurried back along the ship's midwaist, ignoring the looks she received from the seamen. Grasping a ring on the hatch, she wrenched it up and all but fell down the ladder as another explosion sounded and the ship lurched. The ugly sound of splintering wood filled her ears.

Another direct hit, she thought blackly, righting herself and hurrying on to the gunner's deck at the stern of the ship. She made her way virtually unnoticed to the first gunner's port where several men tended the cannon.

"You there, pull back your culverin. Tilt it thus so I can measure. We're going to take down the Spaniard's mast."

The crew of the gun gaped at her in astonishment. Everyone on ship knew who she was—half of them had been hired at Poole by Mistress Cavandish. Since she paid their wages, they usually responded promptly to her orders. But until now, her orders had pertained strictly to care of their cargo. Now she was ordering them into battle. Dead silence reigned on the gunner's deck.

"Aye, by God," one man yelled finally, "look how they gain on us. Let's fight 'em." He leaped to do her bidding, and another one followed. The three men hastened to roll the cannon back on its four wheels from the gun port.

Roz ran her hands appreciatively over the eleven-foot brass barrel of the two-ton culverin, assessing its power. What a beauty it was. But there was no time to waste. Swiftly she went to work, dangling the plumb lines and measuring with the rule the muzzle of the great gun, then repeating the process at the breech.

"What are you doing, mistress?" One of the gunners stared at her, fascinated.

"Getting to know this gun." Roz ran rapid calculations in her head. "I've never worked with it before. I need to estimate how far it will shoot." She put away the rule and plumb lines and pulled out her other instrument.

"Lord 'a mercy, what be that?"

The men stared while Rozalinde adjusted the right-angle metal measure at one end of the gun. " 'Tis a gunner's quadrant," she said absently, calculating quickly. She squinted through the open port at their target. "Tilt the gun on its swivel," she instructed. "I want it aimed higher. Thus." She showed them what she meant. "Then push it through the port and prepare to fire."

The three men angled the big brass gun and pushed in the locking pin, responding to her prompts with alacrity.

"Now then, is the powder dry?" Roz rapped out. "The ball rammed? Good. Prepare the slow match."

The Spanish ship drew closer by the moment. She could

see men on the ship behind them, see their gunmen as they prepared again to fire. "Get ready," she ordered tersely, studying the motion of both ships and the swell of the waves. "Touch the match to the powder . . . now!"

The gunman put the lit match to the tiny pan on top of the powder chamber.

A blaze of fire and smoke leapt before them. The English cannon boomed with deafening magnitude. Roz dodged out of the way as the brass gun recoiled and its rope restraints caught. The smell of burning sulfur assaulted her nostrils.

"Direct hit on the main topgallant!" she cried. "I think we got the mast." Elation filled her as she thrust her face out the gun port so she could see. "Reload," she urged the crew, bringing her head back in. "I want you to start taking out their guns, one by one."

"Mistress Cavandish, get below!" Captain Wellham appeared, distressed beyond measure. He took Rozalinde by the arm. "You cannot be here, mistress. 'Tis dangerous. What would your father say?"

"But we've struck their main mast," Roz argued with him, waving her gunner's quadrant at the Spaniard. "We'll take down the whole thing. We'll blow away their main braces—"

The simultaneous boom of multiple cannon shot rang out. "Captain!" A crewman approached at a run, as if pursued by fiends. "Ships a league off, sir. A whole fleet of 'em and coming fast."

Roz and the captain stared at each other, then raced for the upper deck. Every hand appeared topside with them, their eyes trained to the south. An entire fleet of ships could be seen just ahead.

"What nation?" one voice cried.

"Not French," shouted another.

Rozalinde scrunched up her face, trying to discern their flag. It was impossible this was happening, but even so she knew who it was. " 'Tis the Beggar Fleet," she cried, unable to contain her exhilaration. "Look at the shape of their hulls. They are Dutch ships. The Sea Beggars have come to our aid!"

The captain looked skeptical, but Rozalinde paid him no heed. Thank you, Kit, she breathed silently to herself. Thank you with all my heart.

Already one of the fleet's ships had cut away from the others and approached at great speed to challenge the Spaniard. Roz ran to the stern deck to see their pursuer fall back. Coward, she thought, as the Spanish ship adjusted its sails and began to retreat before the insistent cannon fire of its challenger. She could see Trenchard standing with the Spanish captain on the forecastle deck. Gritting her teeth, she turned away. George never risked anything if he could run away in time. Clearly he would retreat once he was outnumbered.

Casting a last, bitter glance at the *Gran Grifon,* she looked toward the Dutch fleet. She would concentrate on greeting the Sea Beggars and give proper thanks to the Beggar King.

"They are sure to liberate us," she told the captain jubilantly. "We will be permitted to sail on."

She let the captain lead her back to the helm, where he and his first mate could keep her safe. They'd insisted on this since the voyage began. But now she was too relieved to mind their hovering.

"Are you sure 'tis safe?" asked the captain, viewing the fleet with trepidation as it drew near, leaving the two ships behind to battle. "There's so many of them. They might loot us. I hear the Sea Beggars always lack for food."

"They would not do such a thing," Rozalinde assured him. "The Beggar King would not permit it. I know it of a certain. They'll let us sail on to Antwerp. Let us find the flagship and give the Beggar King our thanks."

It appeared there was no need for them to do so. The flagship approached. It came within hailing distance and a man in a black cloak stepped to the forecastle.

"In the name of the Prince of Orange, what port do you seek?"

"We thank you for your aid," Rozalinde shouted back, ignoring the captain's attempt to answer. "We are for Antwerp. Again, our most hearty thanks."

"Hold," cried the black-cloaked figure. "I claim your ship. You may not sail on."

Rozalinde leaned over the rail, unable to believe she'd heard right. "What?" she blazed at him. "We've a schedule to keep. We're due in port tomorrow. You'll not hold us back."

"I shall," shouted the Beggar King menacingly. "I command you to join our fleet or I shall take down your mainmast." Even as he spoke, the Dutch ship drew nearer. Roz could see men at the cannons through the gun ports. Others stood ready with grappling hooks, lining the rails.

"What do you want?" she raged at the Beggar King. "I said we are bound for Antwerp and it's the truth. We're honest tradespeople, why should you stop us?"

The Beggar King confronted her across the rail. "I forbid you to trade at Antwerp. And I warn you, do not attempt to fight us. Our number is too great."

"I'll not listen to you." Rozalinde gestured adamantly for the captain. "Adjust the sails, Captain. We're moving on."

"No! You shall not."

Roz shot the Beggar King her most challenging stare. As she did so, he sprang forward and grasped a rope tied to the yard. Before Roz could guess what he meant to do, he swung across to land with a thud on her deck. With deliberate stride, he planted himself before her and pushed back his enveloping hood.

Rozalinde gasped with horror as she stared at the determined, craggy features of a man fully fifty years old.

She let out a shriek, startled beyond comprehension. "Who are you?" she cried, taking a step backward.

"I am known as the Beggar King." The powerful giant came after her, locked both massive arms around her body. Before she could protest, he hurried her across the deck, boosted her up on the rail and, climbing up beside her, swept her tightly against his imposing chest. Grasping his rope, he swung them both across to his ship.

For one giddy moment Rozalinde thought she was falling. There was nothing beneath her feet, wind whistled in her ears, and her stomach lurched drunkenly. With hysteria threatening, she clutched the man with all her might. They landed with a jolt on the other side. Gratefully she felt solid deck beneath her feet. Within a second, she resumed her rage.

"Loose me, you villain!" Vigorously she pushed away from the beast who'd captured her, unwilling to admit she'd clung to him unashamedly a bare second ago. "How dare you accost me, you knave, you . . . you pirate." She summoned all her scorn. "I thought the Beggar King and his Sea Beggars had come to our aid. But instead I find you want prisoners. I suppose you'll want to plunder my goods, but you'll not have them. I won't let you take them."

"I can see we have much to discuss."

The Beggar King scowled back at her, and for a second Rozalinde faltered. He was tall and forbidding, his stern features reflected his determination, and his steely gray hair bespoke his age. How could she hope to best him?

Abruptly he turned away. "Back to your duties," he thundered at the crew gathered around, staring openly at her. "This lady is under my protection."

Grasping her elbow, he propelled her forcefully toward the stern, his mouth drawn into a grim, tight line.

Rozalinde fought him. "Where are you taking me? I must return to my ship." She wrestled with him unrestrainedly, losing all decorum, but he was too strong for her. His powerful hands held her tightly as he hauled her along.

"You cannot return to your ship. The situation is too dangerous. You will stay with me."

"Send for my trunk," cried Rozalinde. "I must have my trunk."

The Beggar King's face became a mask of wrath, hovering above her. "The lady's trunk," he instructed a gaping seaman. "Get it and make all haste, before our ships part. God's precious will," he cursed, resuming his progress along the deck with Roz still struggling. "A prisoner and she wants her trunk. You are fortunate to have your life, mistress. You must accept your fate." Jerking open the door of the stern cabin with a vicious wrench, he pulled her inside.

"I'll not be anyone's prisoner," stormed Rozalinde. "I'll kill you if you think to ravish me. I'll kill myself."

The Beggar King slammed the door shut behind them and banged a heavy bar into place. "I have no intention of ravishing you. Stop these dramatics."

He leaned against the door, and for the first time Roz noticed he was breathing heavily. Her struggle had cost him some effort—mayhap if she tried again . . .

But he waited only long enough to see her trunk delivered. Then he left, locking the door firmly behind.

*   *   *

It seemed like hours before anyone remembered her. Roz was tired, hungry, and more furious than ever when a man finally entered, a crass old fellow who spoke only Dutch, and motioned for her to leave the cabin. Outside it had begun to rain. The Beggar King joined them on deck, huge and forbidding as before, and indicated she must follow him into a skiff. The waves tossed and churned, threatening to swamp their tiny boat as they made their way to another ship. Through the downpour, Rozalinde looked at the hull and realized it looked English. It was much too big to be Dutch.

"On board, mistress," the Beggar King ordered, motioning to the rope ladder hanging down the side. Drenched through to the skin, Roz searched for some avenue of escape; anything would do. She wanted away from this tyrant.

Nothing but choppy water met her eye. With a huff of defeat, she turned to the ladder. Given no choice, she began to climb.

Rozalinde's long skirts impeded her, twined around her legs, making a damned nuisance of themselves. Once on deck, the Beggar King took command again, propelling her into a dim little cabin. Perhaps she could reason with him, she thought, seeing him close the door behind them. She was preparing a new verbal assault when she sensed danger behind her. Whirling, she squinted in the lantern light. The sight of the man standing there caused her fury to return.

"I should have guessed you were behind this, Christopher Howard." Haughtily she raised her chin. " 'Tis a shallow ruse, pretending you were the Beggar King. Now I know the truth."

Kit ignored the venom in her voice. He turned instead to the Beggar King.

"Delivered, as requested, Christopher." The Beggar King indicated Rozalinde with a nod. "And mind you, she's had enough shocks for one day. I did not handle her gently, getting her there. She is most upset."

"I am no such thing," Roz insisted, her temper blazing. "If I am anything, 'tis disgusted, I am—"

"She would have known eventually," Kit replied, as if Roz were not there. "And now mayhap you should leave us. You see, this lady has defied my instructions," he threw a calculating glance at her over his shoulder, "and on that subject, I have something rather strong to say."

The Beggar King gave Kit a wry grin and turned to go. It was clear he wanted no part of the quarrel. As he opened the door, two seamen arrived. "Ah, here is the lady's trunk."

Rozalinde thought she detected a slight hint of sarcasm. When the two men were done, the Beggar King sent them out ahead of him, then saluted Kit and Roz and left.

"I am the one who has a great deal to say to *you*, Christopher Howard," Roz stormed when the door closed again. "Just because you're an earl doesn't give you the right to take my ship. You haven't the right to give me orders in the first place. Orders, indeed! I'll see you tried in the Admiralty Court. I'll not stand for this." Roz ran around to plant herself in front of Kit but still he ignored her. It filled her with wrath to be dragged here in an unseemly fashion and deposited like a prize before him. And then to be treated like an imbecile, as if she had no rights. Balling her hands into fists, she prepared to unleash a string of unsavory oaths at him.

"Do you not even thank me for rescuing you from that Spaniard?" Kit put his hands on his hips. "The devil got away, you know. Turned tail and ran just as I was getting within cannon range."

Roz called him a name that was thoroughly unladylike.

Kit gave her a steady look. "Mayhap I shouldn't have bothered rescuing you in West Lulworth. I told you to stay put, but you would not—"

"What do you mean, in West Lulworth?" Roz demanded hotly. "You were no where near."

"Wasn't I? Who do you think shot the admiral? It was much trouble, too."

Roz stared at him, overwhelmed by fury. He had rescued her in Lulworth, but made her think it was her brother. "Why you disgusting, boorish . . ." she spluttered with indignation, "pretending to be the Beggar King, then tricking me into thinking my brother—"

"On second thought," Kit headed for the door, "I would rather confront the Spanish than your temper. I will leave you till it cools. Mayhap we can talk when you're done with your tantrum. I never saw a woman in such a passion."

"I'm not in a passion. I'm logically, reasonably angry with you. You've—"

"Logical? Ha!" Kit threw back his head in that irritating way of his and barked with laughter. "A part of you may be logical, Rozalinde Cavandish, but you've more passion in your little finger than most people have in their entire bodies. It's one of the things I like about you." He unbarred the door. "Just the same, I'll wait until later. Even I can get too much of passion."

"I'm not passionate. I'm not!" Rozalinde ran after him, threw herself before him and tried to make him listen.

He moved her firmly out of the way, gave her a stare she found shockingly lewd. "Aren't you?" His voice was low and silky, like the glide of smooth fabric against skin. "When I return, we'll see."

He went out. The door swung shut. Rozalinde was left alone to seethe and wait.

"You see, they follow us. I told you they would." Satisfied that the *Swiftsure* pursued them, George Trenchard moved away from the rail of the *Gran Grifon*. "Tell your men to lure them farther north. When we're well away from the Beggar Fleet, we'll take them on."

Lord Francisco DeVega remained at the rail, frowning at the English ship. He nursed his left arm, which was tied up in a white sling. "I am not certain this is wise. The weather is changing." He cast a glance at the sky, indicating the gathering black clouds that had accumulated in the last hour to the south.

Trenchard scoffed and straightened his new green doublet. "A little cloudy weather and you give up. And after His Majesty assured me you were his most seasoned commander."

"A seasoned commander knows it is foolish to head into open water when a storm threatens," DeVega snapped. "We should seek safe harbor."

"Do you want this communiqué or no," Trenchard snapped back at him. "His Majesty expects it to be delivered to the Duke of Alva. I should think you would be eager to carry out his instructions."

"And I should think you would be more careful with such an important item. Leaving it in the room with that female—your weakness for her has put us in a difficult position. I will be sure King Philip knows how the problem came about."

Trenchard cast a baleful glance at the Spaniard. "The fact is, the girl's involvement will prove to our advantage. She wishes to go to Antwerp. We have only to capture this ship, put the men to the sword, and take her on to her destination. She will consider me her savior and allow me to serve as her escort while she unwittingly carries the communiqué straight to the duke. In the process, we will capture this English pirate who plagues your shipping and do away with him. We can best them easily with our superior size and cannon. It will serve both our ends."

"And her ship, *The Chalice*?"

"The Sea Beggars took it. They are pirates and she will have to believe the evidence of her eyes."

"And how do you explain our bombarding her ship?" DeVega queried, quirking one of his thick, dark brows at Trenchard.

"That is accomplished with ease," Trenchard answered, straightening his doublet. "I spoke to her father after she left West Lulworth. He knew she had gone—she left a letter. With his permission, I followed to see to her safety. We signaled her ship numerous times, indicating we required speech with the captain. Not only was there no answer, but the ship increased its speed and began to fire at us. You would agree it was my duty to do what was required to rescue her."

"Very smooth," admitted DeVega, moving forward to instruct his men. "No wonder His Majesty agrees to work with you. Very well, we move north. Weather or no, I want that communiqué."

Ten cables off, Kit and Phillipe watched the Spaniard maneuver. Kit indicated the blackening sky. "How bad do you think it will be when the storm breaks?"

Phillipe studied the cloud formation for several minutes before answering. "It could be intense," he said finally. "But it also seems far enough away to risk it. We might have an hour or more."

Kit grimaced. "The timing is not to my liking. We should

not follow the Spaniard, but clearly that is what they wish.
If we're to have the communiqué . . ."

The Spanish ship shifted its sails and headed in a north-
erly direction as they spoke.

Phillipe studied their adversary again, then the black
clouds piled in a tall, ominous stack to the south.

"The devil with it," he said finally. "Let us follow. The
cowards will not fight as long as we remain here, near my
fleet. We will take the chance."

"Aye," Kit agreed. "We can ride out any storm that
strikes. But we'll not have another chance at this
communiqué."

"How much food and water do you have," Phillipe
asked, "in case we are blown off course."

"Enough for several days," Kit assured him. "You don't
mind leaving your ship?"

"I mind." Phillipe took one last glance at *The Hope,*
nestled among the other ships of the Beggar Fleet. "But I
mind more letting you follow this treacherous ship on your
own. The Spanish fight viciously."

Kit grinned at him, then strode off to give orders to
move north.

Huddled in the bunk of the main cabin, Rozalinde listened as the storm rose. Wind roared. Every timber of the
ship groaned. As she waited, her fury rose also. She was
furious with Kit for bringing her here, and furious she could
not see what was taking place.

At first the ship moved rapidly, obviously chasing the
Spanish. Then it seemed to slow. Outside she could hear
rain batter the deck above her head. Then she heard the
dull roar of cannon fire. *Not this ship,* she prayed, *don't let
us sink. Please.*

The vessel lurched and she gripped the bunk where she
sat and whimpered. Locked in belowdecks, she couldn't
help defeat Trenchard. It made her feel helpless, a feeling
she detested. To her shame, she began to weep.

That made her angrier still. Brushing away the tears, she
groped her way across the heaving floor. One porthole
stood on each side of the cabin. She looked out the portside
one first.

Cannon boomed again, making the floor quiver. They

would be the stern guns, a level or two below her. Several more boomed from the gun decks below and behind her. But she saw nothing on this side. The Spanish must be to their lee.

Weaving and swaying, she hurried to the other porthole.

Just as she put her nose to the glass, lightning lit up the darkened sky, illuminating the ship opposite. Its name stood out clearly on its hull—the *Gran Grifon,* looking just as she had when pursuing *The Chalice,* just as she had in Lulworth Cove. With one important difference. Now her great guns blazed. Balling her fists, Roz prayed Kit would sink it. Lord, he must, else they were all dead.

The wind screamed like the Furies. The ship lurched. Roz heard an ugly cracking, the splintering of timbers. Lord in heaven, one of their masts? Struck by lightning or cannon? She couldn't tell, for the storm chose that moment to hit with full force.

Grasping a desk that was bolted to the floor, Roz held on for dear life as the ship rocked to port side. Thunder rolled in the sky and rain rattled like stones against every surface of the ship. As she watched through the porthole, Roz saw the *Gran Grifon* disappear into the storm.

The cabin door burst open. Kit entered, followed by a driving sheet of rain and a whirl of wind. He banged the door shut and stood, water sluicing off his cloak and hat. A puddle formed around his feet.

Roz scowled at him. With his expression every bit as grim as hers, he slowly let his eyes travel up and down her form, lingering on her waist, then stopping deliberately at her bosom.

A shudder racked Rozalinde as she realized her gown was in shambles. Her hair hung lopsided, and she had lost her forepart, which completely exposed her neck and the swell of her breasts. Her kirtle skirt was rent in two places, and what that exposed she was afraid to know. What she did know was that Kit's eyes had a monstrous look in them that could mean only one thing. Slowly his handsome mouth curved in a grin.

Chapter 18

"**W**orm," Rozalinde cursed Kit irately, backing away. "You have the audacity to betray my trust. You knew I planned to sail with my father's ship, but you have no respect for an honest trader's endeavors. No, you must come cavorting after me and take my ship. I'm disgusted by you. I would like to spit upon you. I truly should." She stamped her foot, fury gripping her. "I will never trust you. Never, never again."

Kit said nothing. He stalked toward her, still wearing that maddening grin.

"What are you doing? What do you want?" Roz lunged away from him and squeezed around the small table. It was only a moderate-size cabin; his muscular form dominated it. And he was pursuing her relentlessly. Troth, she gasped silently, pressing herself against the wall. A tingle of panic raced down her spine. What did he intend to do?

"Don't touch me," she cried, putting up both hands as he towered over her. A flutter rose in her throat, threatened to choke off her breath. Bracing both arms against him, she pushed, but she only encountered the hard muscles of his chest, which loomed so close.

"Oh, what do you want of me!" she wailed abysmally, shrinking against the wall.

"You have disobeyed me, Rozalinde." Kit found himself breathing heavily as he leaned over her, overcome by a rising sensation he could not name. "I told you to stay at home in West Lulworth, but you insisted on putting yourself in peril. Think what could have happened to you if Trenchard had prevailed. For once your perfect logic has failed you."

"Trenchard did not prevail," Rozalinde insisted, feeling his powerful hands close over her shoulders. The now familiar excitement surged in her belly, excitement only he could arouse. "If not for you, I would be safely in Antwerp by now. Take me back to my ship," she pleaded. "You can still let me sail on."

"Too late, sweetling." He chuckled deep in his throat, knowing he'd planned to have her like this ever since he'd missed her ship at West Lulworth. "I intend to teach you two lessons tonight—one about obeying me when I tell you, the other about your passion. You think you don't have any, but I intend to prove otherwise. The lesson begins like this."

His lips descended, came to rest just above her bodice, arousing an uncontrollable thrill that swept through Rozalinde. Why did he make her want to touch him so badly? His hands unfastened her hair, letting it fall around her shoulders. Then he twined his hands in it and put his lips against her throat.

Rozalinde twisted against him, feeling his thighs pressed to hers, feeling his manhood outlined beneath his trunk hose. It made her tense inside with some undefined need. The sound of the storm had risen to full intensity outside, and also within her. The wind shrilled and the ship careened out of control. Suddenly she was out of control with it, torn by a storm of wanting. As it overwhelmed her, she gave in to it, burying her own face in his hair that was stiff and salty with sea spray. Lacing her arms around his neck, she arched her back and let her response pour forth. Oh, how desperately she wanted him.

With a groan Kit tore at her kirtle bodice, scattering half the buttons on the floor. Engaging her lips with his own, he kissed her fiercely, with an urgency he wouldn't define. Her mouth was tender and yielding and he found himself demanding, wanting more from her. When she responded instinctively, gripping his shoulders, he kissed her harder. "Tonight," he breathed heavily against her cheek, "you will throw aside your logic, stop letting it rule you. Show me your true self, Rozalinde." Gathering her yielding form in his arms, he carried her to the cabin bunk. "Tell me you love me, Rozalinde. Give your passion to me."

"Why?" Roz moved on the bunk, trying to make room so their bodies weren't touching. "Why do you do this, when you know I cannot resist?"

"You love me willingly, or you would not feel passion for me. That part of you *is* logical, Rozalinde. Say you love me. Say it." Kit knelt over her, his legs splayed on either side of her thighs, his hands burning her shoulders.

"I do not love—"

"You do. You are a free woman. Your heart is free to love where it will. And you have chosen to love me."

"No, please. I only love—"

"—yourself? No, you are not a selfish woman. Admit you love me. We are bound together, and the path we travel is one. I am your other self, whether you wish it or no."

"I don't know what you mean." Roz tossed with confusion. "I don't."

"You do. You love me, and because you love me, you long for my touch."

She could feel him undressing her, removing her busk, unlacing her kirtle skirts. Though she shut her eyes tightly, she could feel the strength of his gaze feasting on her body. The expression on his face, when she dared look, made her shiver. In his eyes she saw a man famished, starving for her. Never had she felt herself the focus of such appetite, and it filled her with fascination. He deftly removed her garments one by one.

"From me and me alone," he whispered, "you like it well. I told you some day I would acquaint you with certain facts. This is one of them. Come, admit the truth."

"Heaven help me, I do ... want you." Roz moaned, unable to escape those eyes, the way they devoured her. Suddenly he shed his doublet, ripping it over his head with lightning swiftness, following it with his shirt. The sight of his muscle-taut chest, so near, filled her with trepidation. His huge biceps tensed and flexed as his fingers explored her body, stroking and rubbing.

"Ah, perfection," he murmured as he touched her everywhere, amazed by her beauty. His gaze was drawn to her high firm breasts, and he reached to fill his hands with their bounty, to stroke the full nipples surrounded by darker areolae. Her responding gasp made his body tighten with excitement. "I shall make you soar with pleasure," he muttered, concentrating on moving his thumbs rhythmically on her nipples. "You will want to say the words."

Rozalinde gasped as his fingers massaged and smoothed with skilled care, finding new places of secret pleasure she had not even known existed. "Please, Kit," she cried, closing her eyes against the rising feelings he kindled. "Do not do this. Do not make my body betray me."

"It does not betray you. It reveals your true self. You have a wild, passionate nature."

"No! I am careful and meticulous. I live by reason."

"I can free you, Rose. Put aside your logic and let yourself feel."

Deliberately Kit placed his hands on her, watched with satisfaction as she unconsciously clenched her thighs together and squeezed spasmodically. He was succeeding in reaching her body. Now if only he could reach her mind. If he could force her to admit her feelings verbally, she might let her body rule.

But to convince her she had feelings, he must control his own. And that was becoming damnably difficult. Gazing down at her face, he observed the rapid flutter of her breath, saw the quick leap of a vein in her throat, and recognized his own arousal. He was not known for his self-control. He'd told her so at Lulworth Cove. Unquestionably he had aroused her. Why should they not couple? That had been his plan.

Slowly he trailed his fingers along her shoulder, tracing the rounded curves, the fragile sweep of her collarbone. Her quiver of response overwhelmed him with alien feeling of his own—the familiar lust was different from what he had experienced with other women.

Shifting position, he gazed into her eyes, soft brown eyes awed at his sexual power. And he admitted he knew what was different. She was a pure woman, respectable and virgin. Unlike the other women he had possessed, this woman's entire financial and social future hung in the balance, ready to be swayed by his slightest move. Recognition of her vulnerability mingled with his awakening desire and emerged as a new desire—the desire to protect her. Her future must be his responsibility. Making this decision to control himself, despite the effort it cost him, he bent down, smoothed away a tumult of silken hair from her face and kissed her ripe, alluring mouth.

"You have beautiful shoulders," he murmured, letting

himself down by her side, pressing himself against her softness. "Have you ever looked?"

"No," she whispered. "I couldn't do that."

"You can, Rose. Let me be your mirror. Look into my eyes."

Roz looked. Before, she hadn't dared face him. She had turned her eyes away while his hands demanded her, cupping her breasts, stroking and beguiling her body. Urgently she had tried to deny her feelings. but now he insisted she admit them. His thumbs, circling gently, teased her breasts with rhythmic motion while he insistently studied her face.

"Look at me, Rose. What do you feel?"

His hunger frightened her. Looking into the mirror of his eyes, she believed she would be overpowered by the strength of his personality. Valiantly she fought her instinctual response to him—the desire to return his touch, to explore his magnificent body the way she had begun to that night at the cove. The rush of terror and excitement deep in her belly made her give a small cry, cover her face with her hands, but he took them down and held her tightly. Once more she looked into his eyes. His breath had quickened, sounding harsh in his throat. His nostrils flared rapidly each time he exhaled.

"What do you feel, Rose? Answer."

"I burn inside."

"What else?"

His hands taunted her willpower, glided low, molding her hipbones, rounding over her abdomen. Her eyelids flew wider than ever as his fingers tangled in the hair between her legs.

"Yes, Rose, even there." He chuckled at her reaction. "I want to touch you everywhere. Know everything about you."

"Everywhere?" she cried, watching his eyes, seeing his insatiable hunger. He would consume her utterly. She clutched again at her willpower, forced herself to proceed calmly. "I don't think this is a good idea. I think you'd probably better stop."

Kit's hands never faltered. "You *think* I should stop. But that's your problem, Rozalinde—you think too much. Let your feelings decide and you'll realize I'm right. I'm helping you experience desire for the first time in your life." He laughed, exhilarated by his power over her. His own excitement heightened as he watched her react to him. It rushed inside him to fever pitch, making him feel alive, vibrant. His plan was cemented. He would prove he could control himself by postponing their lovemaking. Tonight, he would teach her about sexual fulfillment and take great pleasure in doing so.

He rubbed and fondled her luscious breasts, her curving shoulders and tiny waist, her flaring hips. Her flesh was like satin, only much better—alive and glowing. His hands reached for her slim, white thighs, so tender, so inviting. With a gentle touch he parted her legs. "Let me pleasure you, Rozalinde. Give me your trust."

"Oh, troth. I don't want to feel this," Roz moaned. "I truly don't."

His fingers made a liar of her. They came to rest on a spot between her legs and rotated, creating a ripple of heat inside her, a burning, magic fire. She could feel a wetness against her thighs as his other hand reached for her bare breasts. Carefully, like an experienced craftsman, he stroked the fire inside her.

It was beyond her ability to do anything by purpose now. Her skin tingled as he touched her all over: her breasts, between her legs, especially between her legs. The rising sensations he created in her body took over, and she reached out to steady herself by his shoulders and gripped him tightly. On and on he went, his hands speaking magic between her legs, imparting exquisite pleasure that took her to greater and greater heights. Arching her back, she helped him, unable to restrain herself. Soon he was bent over her, putting his lips to her breasts, laving them with his tongue, his breath scorching her skin until she thought she could stand no more of this raw exhilaration, these surges of pure ... what was it?

The fire gave her its answer. What she had felt until now was nothing in comparison. Flame ignited with savage intensity, carrying her to a dizzying altitude so that she was borne aloft by it, swept by its pulsating power.

"Say the words," he urged her. "You know what I want you to say."

"I love you," she cried, as she soared into release. Still he did not stop. On and on he led her, drawing her through a fiery storm of feeling, the seconds stretching out one after another before he gently began to lead her down. And throughout, his touch sent his message, making it pulse insistently to her brain—she loved him, this man, above all others. . . .

She lay in his arms afterward. He bent over her, soothed her cheeks with kisses, whispered words she could not decipher while she twined her hands about his neck and brought his face near so she might taste his lips. For no reason she could comprehend, she gazed at him and smiled.

In the semidark of the tossing cabin, he saw it and thought it well won, that smile. Of course, he thought, shifting his position to hold her more comfortably, he still hadn't reprimanded her for disobeying him and putting herself in danger. With one hand he smoothed her thick tangles of hair, which had loosened while he pleasured her, untwisting from her neat braids. He longed to protect her, and he had no intention of letting her out of his sight.

He was puzzled, though, at how pleased he had felt to win her smile, at his ecstasy in hearing those three words *I love you*. As she said them, he had found himself moved so profoundly, he couldn't understand it. Holding her close against him, marveling at her sweetness, he puzzled over why they meant so much.

It seemed they lay together forever, she sated and languid, reveling in his arms; he triumphant, caressing the magical textures of her face and hair. For the first time he let himself admit he was jealous that George Trenchard had been betrothed to her. Though he knew she didn't love the alderman, he still craved reassurance. He wanted the satisfaction of hearing exactly how she would reject Trenchard from her life.

"I need to know something," he whispered against her hair, trying to hide his anxiety by asking indirectly. "Why did the Spanish pursue you? What was their chief reason?" He bent to trace the curve of her ear with his tongue.

He expected her answer to focus on Trenchard. Instead, Rozalinde's smile faded. She sat up and pushed him away, struggled to pull up her smock. "I see," she said icily, jerking at her trailing laces. "This all had a purpose. No, don't touch me." She rose as he reached for her and began to dress.

Kit sat up, too, astonished at her reaction and immediately indignant. He sought reassurance and she gave him none. "If you refer to the lovemaking," he answered just as coldly, "it was your own requirements that invited me. You have been greatly in need of a man to liberate your passion. The Spanish have an entirely separate business."

"Of course," she said, frost hanging from her words. "And it was my own need that required me to say 'I love you.' You wanted it for no other reason, for my gratification."

"You were glad to tell the truth."

"I wasn't." Rozalinde snatched up her bodice and put it on.

"I believe you are. A woman needs a man. It's the way of the world."

"Then we live in different worlds, your lordship." Roz drew her cloak about her disdainfully. "I still believe we should never have met. You give me physical sensations, but they mean nothing. I want more from a man. Something you can't give."

Kit's mouth compressed into a tight, angry line. He fetched a wet cloth from the ewer stand and tossed it to her. "You might wish to freshen yourself."

She threw it back at him. It hit him in the chest and fell limply on the floor. "Don't remind me of what just passed between us. I should not have let you touch me, but I forgot. You're a man, determined to impose your will."

"A woman's lot is to wed and bow to the will of her man, as you will learn to do."

"A woman's lot is to be a partner, as I am to my father. He trusts me. He has every confidence in my skill and ability. There's no need for me to bow to him or anyone. But you! You want information and you coax it out of me in unorthodox ways and expect me not to mind. You toss around orders and expect me to obey."

"You would have obeyed if you'd understood how dangerous it is to sail to Antwerp, but you chose to learn the hard way. You should have listened to me." His face hardened. "That brings us back to the original question, doesn't it? Why did you leave West Lulworth when I instructed you to stay home?"

Rozalinde tossed her loose hair over her shoulder and

donned a scornful expression. "You clearly do not understand, though I should think you would. *You*'ve been in
shipping."

Kit ground his teeth. "I have indeed. So I think you
should listen to me. I have more experience. If only you
had been there, to Antwerp—"

"I have," Roz retorted brusquely.

"How long ago? Two years? Things were different then."

"And what was the difference, your lordship?" Rozalinde unleashed her most biting sarcasm. "Go ahead, I'm
listening. Perhaps you should enlighten me. And I refuse
to apologize for the fact that I don't believe in blind faith."
Crossing her arms tightly, she regarded him.

Roz felt sure Kit would explode at her words. He
looked furious.

"By all that's holy, woman, you make me want to commit
violence." He seized a chair, with a mighty blow sent it
smashing across the table. The table jumped and the chair
shattered into a million pieces. "I'm trying to tell you we're
fighting Spain," he bellowed, planting his feet in the midst
of the rubble, "we're fighting in every way possible without
risking open war. Here I work day and night with the Beggar Fleet, trying to free the Netherlands, and you want to
trade with the enemy. You want to trade with Spain." He
stopped where he was, his chest heaving.

Roz let her crossed arms drop and stared at him. "Say
that again."

"Spain is our enemy, and I work as an undercover agent
for Her Majesty, aiding the Beggar Fleet and the Prince of
Orange." Kit's voice had returned to its normal level. "I
haven't told anyone. I shouldn't have told you."

But Rozalinde, in her turn, was furious. With a shriek,
she launched herself across the cabin and began to pummel
him. "Christopher Howard, you horrible, horrible person!
Why didn't you tell me? I thought Antwerp was neutral.
That's what everyone said."

"Neutral!" Kit cried, catching her by the arms to stop
her flailing. "It might have been once, but not anymore.
Not since two months ago when King Philip levied the tax
calling for every tenth penny earned by the people to be
his; not since he brought the Inquisition to the Netherlands.
Did you hear nothing of that?"

"No." Roz's arms stopped flailing. She stood still, tears pooling in her eyes.

"You didn't hear what the Duke of Alva has done to the people? Last month he strung up twelve well-known merchants, left them kicking and dying in front of their wives and children, just to make an example because they refused to pay that damned tax." He reached out to wipe away one of her tears as it trickled down her cheek.

"I heard nothing. Only that it was not our war, and trade should continue as usual...." She stopped, clapped both hands to her mouth as realization hit her. "My news came mainly from Trenchard. Whenever a trade ship put in at West Lulworth, he told me about it. In fact, the captains were required to report to Alderman Trenchard before unloading. All my father's captains did."

Kit grimaced and let go of her. "Trenchard was suppressing the truth in West Lulworth. Any news you received was biased, slanted to suit his needs."

Rozalinde bowed her head. "I believed everything he said." Her voice had sunk to a whisper.

Kit put one arm around her shoulders. "You must not blame yourself, Rose. He deliberately set out to deceive you, and I must say he was clever. I didn't suspect him either, not until he came to Lulworth Castle that night. Even then I never guessed he was deceiving you."

"No, no, it's more than that." Roz wrung her hands. "Don't you see. It was all my fault. I wanted to believe everything was well in Antwerp so we could continue to trade there, to get the splendid prices my father customarily did. It seemed the only way I could keep the business afloat. I did not seek information elsewhere because Trenchard told me what I wanted to hear." She sank down on the bunk, buried her face in the blanket, and began to cry in earnest.

"Do not take it so hard." Kit sat down beside her and rested one hand on her hair. "We all underestimated Trenchard. He seemed honest, seemed to be doing his duty. His official work made his meetings with the Spanish natural. It took me a long time to become suspicious. And in an isolated town like West Lulworth, he had everyone in his power." Kit unfolded a blanket from the foot of the bunk and wrapped it around her. "The truth of the situation is ugly. Even now the Duke of Alva plots with King Philip to assassinate the Prince of Orange so the rebellion in the Netherlands will die. The Spanish ship that followed you— *that* ship carried the latest communiqué from Philip. We learned through the queen's intelligence network how these messages are concealed. Each time they send one, we intercept the ship and steal the communiqué. We are desperate to have this one. We know Spain plans to send an agent to kill the prince, but we do not know when or where."

Roz sat up in the bunk. Her tears had stuffed her head unbearably. She could scarce breathe. Fumbling in her skirt, she searched until she retrieved the little carved pomander. Putting it to her nose, she breathed in its scent.

Kit eyed her strangely. "Is that made of Spanish cedar? Where did you get it?"

"Trenchard gave it to me," Roz said, drawing in another deep breath of the fragrance. "That is, he didn't exactly give it to me, he—"

"Let me see." Without a word of apology Kit snatched the pomander from her hands.

Roz stared at him in astonishment.

"This is it!" he crowed victoriously, clutching the pomander and leaping to his feet. With a flourish he pulled out the stopper and fished a slip of paper with two fingers from the recesses of the bauble.

"This is *what*?" Rozalinde thrust aside the blanket and staggered from the bunk, clutching at his arm. "Do you mean to say *I* had the communiqué, that I carried it all this time? What does it say?"

"God's dignity!" Kit banged the pomander down on the table. "It's not in the usual code. Phillipe!" he bellowed, striding to the door and flinging it wide. "Phillipe, they've changed the code again."

The Beggar King appeared a second later, as poised as if nothing unusual had happened. "The communiqué? Wonderful!" Grasping the paper, he spread it flat on the table. "Let us employ patience. We have deciphered them all before."

"Aye, and we will again. But it takes time." Kit dropped despondently into a chair. "I had hoped we would know immediately. We could lay more sensible plans. Now we must delay."

"It matters naught, just now, what our plans are," the Beggar King told him, his voice laced with irony. "The storm controls us. These winds will blow us God knows where."

Rozalinde watched the Beggar King and fury reared inside her. *This* was the man who had confiscated her vessel. Slipping from the bunk, she planted herself at his elbow. "I want my ship," she challenged, crossing both arms and jutting out her chin. "I want your promise that I shall have it back."

She must have taken him by surprise, because something flickered in his eyes when he looked at her. But only for the briefest second. Then he straightened from the table, drew to his full height, and also folded his arms across his chest. "What is that you say?"

Roz gulped. He was so tall, she had to tilt her head back to look him in the eye. His massive height was unnerving. He was even taller than Kit. Things in the room shrank by comparison—table, chairs became minuscule as he towered over her.

She forced herself to meet his gaze disdainfully. He would have her feel guilty, like a child caught in a prank, but she would not. Defiantly, she met his smoldering gaze, taking in the long gray locks, the craggy features, the solid, imposing stance of this aging king. "I want my ship."

"You desire a reckoning?" he growled, leveling a hard look at the English maid. So this was Christopher's love, though the lad would not admit it. He studied her from head to toe, scowling his blackest, wearing the outward demeanor of the fearsome pirate. Let her be frightened. She deserved it, giving him such a difficult time over her ship. Let her quake inside. Let her beg.

Navigating the ship's motion, which had subsided to a rhythmic roll punctuated by occasional thrusts and lurches, Phillipe frowned at her. Ah, but she was a beauty. He could see the perfect oval of her face, illuminated erratically by the dim light of the ship's lantern as it swung on a peg. She did not seem intimidated either, as she should be by rights. "You'll not have that ship," he told her slowly, "until I approve the port to which you sail."

"Orders again." To Rozalinde, those few words, the dominating voice, curled around her like the lash of a whip, demanding her subjugation. She flung up her head defiantly, fixing him with a tight, stony stare. "I tire of orders from men." Her tone was scathing. "I don't even know who you are."

Frowning, he studied her, taking in the way her eyes assessed him, the way she stood her ground. He must not be fooled. She was capable of many things, this woman. Kit had chosen her, so she *would* be a formidable adversary. She would be both bold and intelligent. Suddenly he had to turn away—to hide his smile. He knew exactly what he would do.

Disappointment streaked through Roz as he left her, finished with his scrutiny. He swayed across the room on those agile cat's feet and beckoned to Christopher.

"Offer the lady some comforts. We are all tired, and she is most likely cold."

She *was* cold, Roz thought, shifting her feet and feeling water squish in her shoes. Her gown was damp from her earlier exposure to the storm, but she had not noticed her discomfort. It took the Beggar King to call it to her attention. Unaccountably she found herself wanting to go over and put her freezing hands in his pockets. He was probably as warm as he was big and she longed to snuggle beneath that warm cloak with him, as she had with her father when she was small and they took winter walks in London. She was so cold now, she longed to . . .

Troth, she swore at herself, interrupting her ridiculous fantasy. She had no reason to like him. She must tread warily, if she was to get her ship back.

A coffer lid banged. Roz jumped. She had been so intent on the Beggar King, she hadn't noticed Kit. Now he crossed the cabin and led her to the bunk, spread a heavy wool blanket over her and tucked it around her waist. It was far warmer than the light cotton blanket he'd given her earlier.

"Excellent," the Beggar King praised. "Now then, food."

Kit took down bread and cheese from a shelf. "We have nothing hot, Rozalinde. The storm prevents our making a fire."

Hunger growled in Roz's stomach. She snatched the bread Kit offered and bit into it, not even pausing to think why the Beggar King was being kind. She devoured the cheese in rapid bites. It was dinner since she'd last eaten, and that was long ago.

Kit passed her a pewter flagon of water and she drank thirstily, watching them both over the metal rim as they moved around the cabin. Briefly she let herself long for creature comforts: some clean, dry clothes, a hot drink, a bed heated by a warming pan.

"Now then." The Beggar King recrossed the cabin and planted himself before her, where she sat tucked up in the bunk. "I think it best you understand exactly who you're dealing with. I am Phillipe de Montmorency-Nivelle, the Count of Hoorne at your service. Admiral of the Prince of Orange's Navy and bearer of his letters of marque."

Roz looked at him askance, shocked that he would reveal his identity so readily. "I am pleased to make your acquaintance," she said stiffly, good breeding answering before her anger could.

The count laughed vibrantly. "No, Mistress Rozalinde, on the contrary. You are not pleased to make my acquaintance. You would rather scratch out my eyes, and you are most justified in that wish. I interrupted your work, and you are furious with me. You want your ship back, though since neither of us have it at the moment, 'tis a moot point. And you would like to be alone with Christopher, and for me to mind my own business." He took a mammoth step, closing the space between them. Leaning over, he cupped her chin in one great hand. "I shall not mind my own business just yet," he informed her, his powerful voice mirroring the startling intensity that poured from his eyes. "You are far too intelligent for me to leave your fascinating mind untested. I can learn much from you. And I intend to do just that."

"I'll not tell you anything," Roz jerked away, breaking their contact, "unless I wish. You don't frighten me. And I cannot see why you reveal your secret identity, unless it is some sort of trick."

"I tell you because Christopher has trusted you," Phillipe said simply. "I assure you, he seldom makes a wrong judgment about such things."

Rozalinde fixed him with an incredulous look. Blast this devil, he was as beguiling as Kit. She should think of him as her enemy. Yet he began by disarming her totally—by being thoroughly, unnecessarily honest with her. What was she to do? There was no fighting such a man.

She did the only thing possible. She relaxed. The stiffness went out of her body. She let the wariness retreat from her eyes. "I suppose I should return your trust. It seems that Kit does."

"That would be an admirable start."

The count smiled at her, and the fearsome mask disappearèd. A vital, animated man took his place, and Rozalinde found herself startled again, as his eyes warmly caressed her.

It was pleasant to watch them, the two tall men moving around the cabin, so similar in stature. This Phillipe—something about his name struck her, but she could not think what it was. Her mind probed, turning the name over and over, examining with obsessive insistence.

Phillipe. A common name. But referring to someone specific . . .

He approached the bunk and bent over to offer Roz a pair of dry woolen socks, which she accepted graciously. As he leaned forward a small silver cross on a chain slipped from his shirt and dangled before her eyes.

Roz's gaze fastened on it. She saw it was exquisitely crafted, entwined with a single blooming rose.

Insight burst upon her. That cross! It matched the one in the room under Lulworth Castle. Her mind raced urgently, making the logical connections—this must be Anne's lover, the man who'd written the letter she'd found in that secret room.

With dawning fascination Roz watched the count look for more clothing, search the coffer and pull out folded linen. If this was the same Phillipe, then who was Anne? Not the present dowager countess. Her name was Mary, and she was the wrong age for this man. A vague recollection surfaced—Roz had visited Lulworth Castle with her father over a year ago. There had been some reference made to the former countess, now dead. Lady Anne. That had to be it! "You say you are the Count of Hoorne," Roz blurted out, "but were you not—"

"—beheaded?" Phillipe finished for her, mercifully mistaking what she had been about to say. "Aye, so 'twas said." He brought a clean linen shirt and placed it on her lap. "But you see I am very much alive. Hence the birth of the Beggar King. Among my men, I am Count Phillipe and nothing more. When I go raiding, I become a masked noble. A romantic figure, but in reality, a man of necessity."

"I see." Rozalinde put down her empty flagon, stifled her urge to question him further. There was no need. Kit's mother had loved this man. She knew it for a fact. Furtively she studied him, comparing him to Kit, wondering why this was important. Yet they were similar in build and in posture. Even the way they carried their heads was similar, high and proud.

Phillipe, in his turn, conducted his own assessment, seeing how Rozalinde's eyelids listed heavily and Kit's shoulders drooped. They were all of them exhausted, and yet there was still information to gain. "Come, my dear," he said gently, seating himself on a stool near Rozalinde and drawing close. "You must tell me how that Spanish ship came to pursue you. I must know all."

Roz groaned inwardly. Once again business encroached on worldly things. She must respond to the call of logic.

Love is the only thing that lasts. The words of the letter intruded on her consciousness, making her shiver. A giddy joy swept through her body before she crushed it ruthlessly, setting aside thoughts of herself in favor of the business at hand.

She described the plain, hard facts. First, of how she'd been struck on the head, then of how she'd found herself in Trenchard's house, unsure of whether he rescued or abducted her. Next, of how she had escaped by way of his chimney with her brother's help and stowed away on her father's ship. "I didn't think Trenchard would go to so much trouble as to follow," she concluded. "I truly did not. But now I know he is involved with King Philip of Spain." She grimaced bitterly. "And 'tis my guess he has been for some time."

"So this is how you came by the pomander." Phillipe nodded. "Now I understand. Clearly Trenchard and his Spanish friends do not know the contents of the message. They must get it back at all costs and deliver it to their Duke of Alva. But we now have it and will decipher it, if we can manage this new code."

Even as he spoke, Kit sat drawn up to the table, bent over the coded message. The storm had subsided such that he might sit quietly. He had been hard at work the entire time Rozalinde and Phillipe talked. On a separate piece of paper he scribbled different keys, trying out one after another.

Roz couldn't see the paper, not from where she sat. Now curiosity rose inside her, hard and insistent. She slipped off the bunk and crept forward.

The paper was covered with numbers. Rows of them, scripted precisely. "Strange," she murmured, leaning forward to trace a figure with one hand. " 'Tis not a code substituting numbers for letters of the alphabet." She shook her head at what Kit was doing, frowned over the paper as she often did when encountering a challenging problem. "What were the other codes?" she demanded without moving her eyes. "Were they easier than this?"

"Aye, they were," Kit answered gruffly, still working. "It took us some time to guess them, but they were fairly logical in the end. This looks to be more difficult."

Rozalinde refocused her thoughts, released all other ideas and let herself drift, entering the meditative trance that claimed her mind whenever she studied numbers. Without conscious effort, patterns arranged themselves, etched their stark quantities against the clear backdrop of her mind. With joy, she gave in to their power. . . .

Phillipe watched her, his eyes narrowed to two speculative slits. Christopher, he could see, paid no heed to the girl. He was too busy working with the numbers himself. It was not good, he decided, to let the girl do this work tonight. Her face, for all its beauty, looked pinched and tired. She had been through much. And it was eerie, the way she lost herself so thoroughly in a set of numbers scrawled on a sheet.

Making his decision, he scooped up the paper and thrust it into his doublet.

Roz looked up, startled. "Why did you do that? Oh." She relaxed suddenly and sent him a smile of understanding. "It will take us days to decipher, won't it?"

"Exactly, mistress. Rozalinde," he corrected himself, nodding with fatherly solicitude. "I have much experience with these codes, and each new one is more devilish than

the last. I want the meaning, but we have time enough for
that. Just now, you would benefit more from sleep. We all
would," he admonished, tapping his foot as he regarded
Kit, who looked indignant. " 'Tis late. When the light
comes, when this storm blows itself out, we must get our
bearings and return to the Netherlands. You, my dear, shall
have this cabin for the duration of your stay on board. I
see there is a bit of water left in the ewer if you care to
wash. Tomorrow, when the ship is steady, I will see you
have hot water. Bar the door when we are gone.
Christopher."

He gestured imperiously. Kit got up reluctantly, as if
wanting to prolong his stay. But he did as instructed. The
two of them withdrew, leaving Rozalinde alone.

Rozalinde obediently washed herself, removed her wet
garments, and hung them over a chair to dry. After drawing
on the huge linen shirt and warm stocks given her, she
clambered into the bunk and sank with a sigh into the
feather mattress. Pulling the blankets to her chin, she stared
restlessly into the darkness.

Chapter 19

Rozalinde wanted to sleep. Every fiber of her body ached, begging her to rest, to lose herself in the comforting blankness of slumber.

But her mind disdained respite. Her thoughts sped forward, examining what she'd learned from Count Phillipe, appraising her earlier time alone with Kit. Analytically, dispassionately, she reviewed them.

And came to one conclusion. Kit spoke truly. She loved him.

Troth, she thought, stuffing her clenched fist against her mouth to stop the sobs that welled up from deep within. It could not be. It was impossible that she, so cautious, so careful with her heart, should succumb to love. So long she had guarded against it, throwing up her strongest barrier, her inflexible will. But all the things she felt were indisputable.

Raging passion that ruled her body and her mind whenever she was with him.

Searing release when his hands brought her to fulfillment.

And unbearable torment, knowing she was his.

No! She rose up in the bed, the scream tearing at her throat while she fought free of the bedcovers, the ones he had wrapped around her. No and no again!

She must not love him, for love meant marriage, and marriage meant the end of everything she treasured in life. She would have to give up her place of authority in her household and take a place of subjugation in his, to forgo any dealings with business and relegate herself to mindless childbearing and pain. Look at her mother and her grandmother before her. Wives were nothing but chattel, forbidden to think or express their thoughts. But her father—*he* acknowledged her gifts, encouraged her love of numbers, exposed her to the most brilliant mathematical men in England, France, and the Netherlands. He was an exception to the rule.

Her legs now free of the blankets, Roz forced herself back to calmness, sinking down on the bed and letting her thoughts race back to her last journey to the Netherlands, long before this Spanish trouble had erupted, to a time when her father's health was good and they lived happily in London.

Her mouth curved into a specter of a smile as she remembered those love-filled days. Her father had been a fine figure of a man, the most knowledgeable, the most honored gentleman in the Company of Merchant Adventurers. And she had been at his side, sharing his triumphs, so proud and full of the excitement of life.

She'd been only ten when her father first took her along on his travels. Her mother had come, too, on a journey to France, leaving behind the little ones in the care of their devoted nurse. It was then Roz had discovered navigation. Long ago she'd been entranced by numbers. On this journey she'd learned of the astrolabe, the new cross staff, the compass, and the wind rose.

By twelve she was sneaking out her window at night to learn from her father's navigator. This lasted only a short time, though, because when her father caught her, he didn't whip her, as perhaps he should have. Instead, he chided himself and employed an instructor for Rozalinde. By fifteen she knew everything the man could teach her. On every voyage she accompanied her father and practiced her skills, letting him indulge her desires. But it was valuable work she performed, calculating the ship's latitude, working with the ship's pilot, and perfecting her ability to read the sun and stars.

There was one fateful trip to the Netherlands she would never forget. She had a new rutter, which described all the landmarks along the Netherlands coast. It was as she worked from that book, talking to the ship's pilot, that she learned of Gerard Mercator, a Flemish man.

"Please, Papa," she had begged, "arrange for me to meet him. They say he is a mapmaker and a skilled mathematician—that he knows the formation of many lands and bodies of water. I must hear his theories. Say you will." He had smiled indulgently and caressed her hair—her strong, loving papa. "I should not," he told her, pushing back his own graying hair as he weighed his decision. "What would your mama say, if I let you go among so many men?"

"'Twill be only you and he," Roz wheedled, hanging on his arm and reaching on tiptoe to kiss his cheek. "Perhaps one other if you must find someone to introduce you. Say you will."

He'd given in to Roz's cozening. He loved her too well to deny her anything. And she ... she adored him, in part because he reveled in opening her mind to the wide world of the intellect, in seeing her grow and gain knowledge. And he let her display her skill before any man.

Late into the night she'd sat at her father's side while Mercator talked, filling sheet after sheet of paper with calculations and sketches to demonstrate his theories. The host of the inn where they dined brought candles by the score to illuminate their work, and Roz stared, fascinated, lost in the numbers, only coming back to earth to barrage Mercator with questions, insisting on knowing everything, often taking up a pen to illustrate certain ideas herself.

It would be goodbye to all that if she wed. All that she held dear would disappear, like sea mist evaporating before the hot morning sun. Worse still, her father was dying. Bending her head until it submerged beneath the blankets, Roz wept, releasing the hot tears along with the pain.

But when her tears were spent, when she lay with her head on the pillow, once again calm, logic returned, soaring into her soul and repossessing her mind.

She would not wed with Christopher Howard, as he'd hinted. Not even if her father died, which he would not, she swore fiercely. She would redouble her efforts when she returned, arranging for her mother to be completely free to nurse him, sending for the best physicians to restore his health. And when she was one and twenty, she would be his partner. She would let no one deny her legal rights. As a woman of age, she could own property, hold money in her own name, do almost anything she liked. When she was one and twenty....

Rozalinde sat bolt upright in the bunk, a sudden thought striking her. What day was it? Since leaving West Lulworth, she'd lost track of time. Urgently her brain scrambled to count the days. Today must be the twentieth of September.

Three days! In three days she would be one and twenty. Legally she would have rights!

Letting herself drift back down on the pillow, she cherished the thought, relishing its comfort. She need not rely on a man to handle her affairs. Jonathan could belong to the drapers' guild, which would keep things proper. But she would continue to run her father's business, just as she did now.

And she would not succumb to love, even if she felt it.

So resolved, Roz settled herself in the bunk and prepared herself for sleep, alone with the swinging lantern, the creaking sounds of the ship, and the lash of wind and wave.

Pale pearl of morning. Cocoon-like curve of dreams. Somewhere just beyond the edge of sleep, Kit hovered. She was there again, that silken, provocative siren. She haunted him nightly, offering the thing he wanted. Usually she tempted and taunted. When he reached, she would fade. A dream, cracked and broken, oft repeated and old. Tonight he didn't want her—a woman who didn't exist.

But this time something was different. He drew breath, held it—the moment infinite and silent, and he, afraid to hope.

For the first time, he saw her distinctly: her face of infinite sweetness, her eyes all alight. Earth, air, fire, and water—elements combined and crumbled to nothing before her glory. Parting the ether where angels tread, she came to him. Even the stars were muted, shining around her. Beauty's overmatch, this time he knew her. Tonight he was sure.

Shedding her garments, she revealed more of her secrets. The plain kirtle skirt she always wore fell to the floor with a whisper. The kirtle bodice, simple to the point of severity, dropped from her fingers to join it. Next she removed her busk and tossed it away. Pulling down her smock, she revealed her ivory shoulders, which gleamed a scintillating white in the sultry dawn.

The need in Kit intensified. He wanted her with all his being, not just with his body. Where previously a stone resided in his chest, an awakening, throbbing heart now took root. Yet she was a woman of scruples, and he, a man of transient fires, burning in the night. For her he would fling the waters, douse the flame. Anything, to have her. Slim, tapering waist, flaring hips and thighs, she provided constancy against his mutability—they were opposites hung together in eternity, preparing to merge.

Still his desire escalated. He was ruled by the stars and the stars were heathen. His pent-up need spilled over. His fingers met the bare shoulders that so bewitched him. Her breasts were like blossoms, demanding his lips. Bending over, he savored their fragrance, letting her purity invade him. *I love you.* For the first time in his dreams, he heard the living words fall from her lips. Her eyes spoke her heart's constancy, plainly for him to read. She was a woman of honor. If he took her, he must return her feeling. And that he desired above all things. Parting her legs, he prepared to give himself up to the holy ecstasy of her warmth.

The dream changed abruptly; a nightmare loomed with gaping maw. He fought it, tried to hold on to the first dream, but the nightmare closed in on him, negating all else.

He was very small—no more than five. Across the chamber stood his mother, fair as the rose, dressed in shining garments. She held a gaily wrapped present—something for him . . . something forbidden by his father.

She set the top spinning. The marvelous colors swirled dizzily in his head, along with her laughter. It was his natal day. God, how he loved her, so full of light and pleasure—things alien to his father. As Kit watched the whirling top, his entire being quivered with fear.

Pressing her finger to her lips, she shook her head, bidding him keep the secret. He must not laugh out loud, he must not tell . . .

It happened like evil magic—the Earl of Wynford stepped into the room. Silent. Ominous. Ordered the toy away. His knuckles showed white where they gripped the hated cane. It tapped against his shoe, deafening in the room.

"No," Kit cried. Brave in the midst of innocence. "It's my top. From Mama." He tried to run to her, crying piteously.

His father caught him in his uncompromising grasp. One

slice of the hated stick smashed the top against the wall.
The cane raised again and stung his shoulders. Words
rained with blows—words he didn't understand . . . fastened
inside his consciousness, fused with his pain. *Instant obedience . . . fear of God . . . frivolous nonsense.*

His mother stood watching. Tears poured down her
cheeks, onto her gown, spotting it. She did not dare save
him. She, too, was guilty. Words delivered to her in rapid
fire, hard as blows. *Useless female . . . shirking duty.*

The hold on Kit's collar tightened and he felt himself
choking, unable to escape his hate for his father, for the
things he demanded—discipline, lessons, perfect self-control. His need for those other things from his mother—
forbidden things like laughter, games, spontaneous affection—burned inside him too strongly, making him
weak. . . .

Gasping for air, he fell to his knees before his father,
clutching his throat. His mother was gone. There was nothing but this stern man and the hated discipline.

After that, there was the journey. Five days on horse-
back, traveling with his brother and father to Oxford. Too
many lessons for a boy of five, of six, of seven. Too young
to be at school with only an older brother and a tutor.
Wanting his mother. She was gone when he returned to
West Lulworth. Looking everywhere for her. Empty inside
when he heard she had been sent away, too far for him to
follow, far to the north . . .

"No!" Kit struggled to regain his senses beneath someone's hand.

"Christopher." The hand shook him again. "Wake up."

Phillipe's face hung above him as Kit came fully awake.
He struggled to sit. With relief, he remembered. He was in
a common seaman's hammock, slung on the gunner's deck.
Sunlight streamed through a gun port, focusing on his face.
Squinting, he rolled out of the hammock to gain his feet.
"This is unseemly. Why did you not wake me earlier?"

"You needed rest. I instructed your men to leave you."
Phillipe's voice soothed, like unguent meeting a hot, fiery
wound. Concern radiated from him. "Tell me, Christopher.
Tell me about the dream."

Kit squeezed his eyes shut, wanting to escape. But the
nightmare part of the dream enveloped his consciousness.

His throat burned raw with bile, just as it had when his father clenched him in his hard grasp. "When I was very young, I . . ." He groped for words, found them, let them spill forth. "My mother brought me a present. It was my natal day; I was only five. I loved toys, games I could play with my mother, but my father considered them weakness. My mother was incompetent and frivolous for teaching me to like them. He believed in strict discipline for children; believed she was unfit to teach us proper fear of God. I was foolish enough to demand the right to keep the toy that day, to refuse his orders and say what I wanted instead—to play instead of study lessons, to be with someone who enjoyed life and cared about me. . . ."

The image of his mother flared like a light in his memory. Kit could see her clearly, her smile as she played some meaningless game with him, her laugh the time he bested her at shuttlecock. He could feel her hand as she steadied him before throwing a quoit at the target, the sound of her voice as she said his name.

Another hand was suddenly reassuring on his shoulder. Kit fought the impulse to turn toward it. Standing stark still, he opened his eyes to encounter the blue eyes of his friend. "My disobedience was the last straw, it seems. My father sent me to Oxford with my brother, who had just reached the proper age. I always thought it my fault, for defying him. Later he brought me back to West Lulworth, but my mother wasn't there. He sent her on various trips to his other properties to refurbish the houses and carry out useless tasks. Now I know he purposely removed her influence. He would control his children's rearing, with uncaring servants to do his will. Later, I heard she was at Lulworth when I wasn't. When I was older, we were even there at the same time. Occasionally I tried to remember how I had once felt for her, but I'd lost it. It was better that way, believe me. The worst was over after that."

Phillipe grimaced. With a curious, detached satisfaction, Kit observed the pain gather in his friend's face. "Ugly, isn't it." He turned away, letting Phillipe's hand slide from his shoulder. He stowed the hammock in a sea chest, giving it a vicious shove in with the others. "You should have woken me earlier. I'd not be a slugabed on my own ship."

"No one said you were."

"There is always someone to think badly of you."

"Yourself?"

Kit gave him a savage look before striding off toward the ladder to the upper deck.

"I have already broken my fast," Phillipe said, climbing the ladder behind him, his emotion now carefully masked. "There's hot food at the helm. Not anything special, but it's the best the cook could manage. We can take a bearing when you've eaten. I'll talk to you anon."

Kit ate on deck, all the while looking for Rozalinde to emerge from the captain's cabin and feeling irritated that she did not. The events of last night troubled him with obstinate persistence—chased by this morning's painful dream. Gulping a bowl of hot porridge, he looked out over the calm waters and reviewed that ghostly memory. Where had it hidden, buried in his brain for all these years beyond conscious thought? It was so painful, he could hardly bear to think of it. Yet it had nestled there patiently, waiting to be rediscovered. The talk with Phillipe last night had triggered it in his mind, and his encounter with Rozalinde had released both the good dream and the nightmare from his heart.

He flinched at the thought of the first dream. It was a false one, because never again could he give his heart freely to a woman, as he had to his mother. Never. It invited agony. How he had trusted her, adored her. But overnight she disappeared from his life. As easily as if she were an object, with no will of her own.

Far away at Oxford, he'd cried himself to sleep at night, hating his father, hating her, too ...

The suffering reclaimed him as he remembered his father's words—from the time he was old enough to understand them: *You have an excess of passion, Christopher Howard. I shall teach you to curb it.*

Over and over his father punished him, to drive that excess of passion from his body. For shirking his lessons, Kit was locked in his room; for riding without permission or riding too far from the castle, bread and water for a day. When Kit grew older, he discovered wenching. Nightly he sought the tenderness of a woman's arms. Somehow his father always knew—he brought out the hated cane. Kit limped for days after those beatings, unable to sit, unable to lie on his back.

By the time she was allowed to remain at West Lulworth when he did, his mother was more shade than woman, flitting about her duties. He remembered little about her from that period of his life, his adolescence. Finally, he had escaped.

The thought of freedom brought renewed images of Rozalinde to him, the vision of her sweet face caught in the excruciating pleasure of release. He had given her that freedom, that release from her bondage. And he had taken nothing for himself. He had curbed his passion, proved he could do it while arousing hers.

Kit smashed his fist against the rail where he stood, staring blindly out to sea. His father was wrong. He could control his passion if he wished. But most of his life he hadn't. He'd spent it recklessly and deliberately, every night with a different woman. One after another, always seeking the new challenge, following their beckoning fingers, and still the ache in his body refused to forsake him.

Kit leaned against the rail and let his eyes wander over the water. Now it had been a year since he'd had a woman. An entire year. Even when this bewitching siren of a maid came within his reach—a woman he would gladly bed—he curbed his passion. He granted her the ecstasy instead.

Just thinking about Rozalinde awakened a flash of lust deep inside. Once again he scanned the deck, cursing her slowness in rising. He needed to see her, to study the look in her eye. When he'd set out to rescue her in West Lulworth, he'd meant to abduct her himself, to learn exactly how she felt—whether she loved him or no.

Damn and damn again. He struck all thoughts of her viciously from his mind. The others who had loved him, who had said they did, had been a nuisance. Trouble of the worst sort, hanging on him, dependent, demanding things he did not want to give. The last thing he should do was make some maid love him, since he didn't care a farthing for her.

Groaning inwardly, he returned to the helm, cast his empty bowl in with the other dirty ones and headed for the main mast. Lithely he scaled the ratlines to the lookout, where the man on duty stopped whistling and came to attention, snatching off his cap. Kit nodded to him briefly and turned away. Looking out over the lonely waves, he tried to recapture his solitude, to determine where they were.

Not a shred of land was in sight. The sky, so dark and tumultuous last night, was a clear, innocent blue this morning. The sun shone brilliantly. What clouds there were rode high. The water lapped the ship tamely, as if asking pardon. It never meant to betray them, as it had last night.

Last night. Other thoughts emerged. Rozalinde, always Rozalinde. Kit ran his fingers through his hair, wanting to avoid those thoughts, concentrating instead on his appearance, removing the tangles and bringing his hair into some kind of order. He would need a comb later, and he would like to wash ... and damn. Here he was improving his appearance for her. He gave up trying to forget her. Down below, he spotted Phillipe and clambered down to take a turn with him around the deck.

"I have no navigator, you know. I lost him last week to ship fever," Kit began, inclining his head toward the man who hovered at the helm, holding an astrolabe by a rope threaded through its suspension ring. The fellow was trying to line up the sighting vanes so the sun shown along them properly.

Several men busily swabbed the deck nearby. Phillipe turned and led Kit away, farther down to the quarterdeck where they would not be overheard.

"Hadn't replaced him when we got caught in that storm," Kit went on. "Damnable thing to happen."

Phillipe offered his condolences. "If you're worried about the calculations, I'll do them, though I suppose you can yourself."

"Aye, but I'd appreciate your consultation. In the meantime, I am letting Wrightman try his hand with the astrolabe. He knows only the rudiments, but I promised to let him have a go at it."

They both stopped. Rozalinde stood at the port bow, arrayed in her dry kirtle and wrapped in Kit's cloak. Her hair hung in two long plaits down her back and the freshening breeze stirred little tendrils of hair around her face. She looked very young, leaning against the rail, staring out to sea. Kit left Phillipe without a word and went to her.

"Good morrow, my Rozalinde." He barely restrained his hand from seeking her hair.

"Good morrow. And I am not *yours*."

"Are you sure?"

"No." She sent him a brief, scathing glance over her shoulder. "But do not jump to conclusions. I never act on things if I am unsure."

Kit sighed deeply and stepped closer. Still, he did not touch her. He stood at her shoulder and looked out over the water, so near he knew his breath warmed the back of her head. He could see her shoulders move slightly with each breath she took. Her back remained stubbornly toward him.

"You make the logical choice, as usual." Kit picked up one of her plaits and tickled his palm with its brushlike end. "I suppose you wish to belong to no one."

She twisted her head to confront him. "That's the first true thing you've said since this voyage began."

He thought of his mother—her beauty shining from across the room. Everything she stood for, forbidden by his father—love, tenderness, given in proper mixture with passion. Wanting them desperately, he breathed out evenly, drew in breath deeply, steadying himself. "I might say others like it if you would but give me a chance."

"Such as, my lord?" Her eyes, as always, challenged him.

He raised his hands in exasperation, dropping her plait. "A truce between us, Rozalinde. Let us have no more quarrels. We have worked out our differences—"

"Only with regard to my ship and sailing to Antwerp, my lord."

He sent her a reproachful look. "I did ask you to call me Kit."

Her gaze shifted uneasily away from him, ranging back over the sea. "Where are we . . . Kit?"

"I don't know."

"You don't!" She swung back to face him. "Hasn't the pilot been taking the readings? Hasn't he been doing his calculations? He must have some idea."

Kit was tempted to take a step backward to escape her protests. "These things take time, Rozalinde."

Roz sniffed as if she did not believe him and twitched the cloak straight on her shoulders.

He offered his arm. "You should break your fast. Allow me to escort you."

Rozalinde took it stiffly. "Very well. But let me be clear about one thing. I would have you remember that I am presently at your mercy."

"Are you? I had the impression you were never at anyone's mercy."

"That is not what I mean. I am presently dependent upon your hospitality. I expect you not to take advantage of that fact, sir. You have already gone too far."

He walked her to the helm where hot porridge awaited, valiantly suppressing a smile. "I promise to try."

But, he added to himself, he would probably, unfortunately, fail.

When Kit joined Phillipe a short while later, Wrightman busied himself over the chart book, a stub of pencil in hand.

"Is he any closer to a reading?" Kit said in a low voice to Phillipe, avoiding catching his seaman's eye.

Phillipe shook his head furtively. "I think you'd best ... Good morrow, Mistress Cavandish." He rallied gallantly as Rozalinde came down the deck to join them. "Have you dined?"

"You might call it that, Phillipe."

Kit was surprised to see her expression change. She smiled brilliantly as she came abreast to Phillipe and looked up into his eyes. Kit's blood roiled with irritation at the intimate glance they exchanged. Some understanding appeared to exist between them, and he did not know what it was.

He turned his back on their idle chatter. He could hear Rozalinde quiz Phillipe on the weather, their location, everything to do with shipping.

The men who passed up and down the decks about their business stole glances at her, clearly discomfited by a woman on board. He knew them well enough to realize there'd been grumblings. He'd heard last night as he went to sleep on the gunner's deck. The *Swiftsure* was no pleasure ship, and his crew was not accustomed to carrying lady passengers.

Kit watched through half-veiled eyes, three men swabbing the deck nearby. Whenever one of them turned to plunge his mop into the bucket, he would throw a black look in Rozalinde's direction. She had left Phillipe by now and strolled over to where Wrightman struggled with his calculations. Kit regretted the absence of Courte Philips at the helm with him—he'd left him behind on *The Raven*. Now the man steering cast a gloomy gaze at Rozalinde. It did not bode well. Determinedly Kit turned his back on them and mentally began his plans.

"*That* is incorrect." A voice pierced his reverie. "You are determining direction entirely wrong. It should be thus."

He whirled to see Rozalinde step up to Wrightman and snatch something from his hand.

He knew it was a compass box. Taking the painted box in hand, she set it to float in the large basin of water standing on the navigator's table.

"There." Wrightman pointed his stocky finger, indicating the pointer affixed to the lid. "'Tis north."

Rozalinde shook her head vigorously, without a word to break her concentration. Taking the lodestone in one hand, she raised the basin and passed the stone carefully underneath. "This will correct your bearing, from the celestial pole to the magnetic pole."

Wrightman stared at her. The men swabbing the deck stopped their work. Other members of the crew drew near, their expressions disapproving.

"Now your needle will read accurately." Rozalinde put down the basin and handed back the lodestone. "This would never happen if you had a Flemish compass."

"There is nothing wrong with my compass," began Wrightman.

"It's prettily executed but inaccurate. Haven't you wondered why it was always just a little off the meridian?" Rozalinde peered down at his paperwork. "You've ruined all your reckonings without the correction. They'll have to be done again."

"Now see here." Wrightman's ire flared and he glanced around at his fellow crewmen for support. "I don't need no woman to tell me my job. I—"

Kit took that moment to stride deliberately into the crowd. "What is this all about?" His voice was curt.

"This fellow," Roz spoke up promptly, "is taking a reading. But he does it all wrong. I am trying to show him the correct way, but he won't listen." She glared at the seaman, who pulled his forelock and looked stubbornly at the deck.

"How should it be done?" Kit asked.

"You know well enough how it should be done." Rozalinde caught up the lodestone again. "First you float the compass box in the basin and let the needle stabilize. Then you pass the lodestone across the bottom, like this." She demonstrated, scrapping the magnetized stone slowly across the bottom of the basin. The needle adjusted itself slightly. "That corrects your variation." She displayed the proper action again. "Otherwise you get the wrong reading. He's also been using the astrolabe incorrectly. I saw you," she said to the seaman, her voice accusing. "You were lining up the alidade wrong." Roz caught up the astrolabe and suspended it from its cord. "First you turn it so the sun shines squarely from above. You rotate the alidade until the sunlight passes through the pinnule of the upper vane." She demonstrated, turning the long hand of the astrolabe, lining it up so the sunlight exactly pierced the pinnule of the upper arm and fell on the pinnule of the lower arm. "Then you take a reading. With his information, he's charted our position thus." Roz stabbed at a place on the map unrolled across the table. "But if that's the case, and we follow his directions, I guarantee we'll end up in Norway. We might anyway, the way the wind is blowing." She stopped speaking, held up her hand to feel the breeze.

Kit stared entranced. From the second she'd begun to talk, to handle the navigational tools, he'd been captivated. She had said she could do it, use an astrolabe and compass. He'd supposed it was true. But seeing it was different. He wanted her to do it again.

But the men were drawing closer. He frowned mightily. Blast her, she was both amazing and a nuisance, and she put him in a tremendous quandary. She publicly challenged the navigator so that he must make a choice—either uphold Wrightman and thereby insult her, or take her side and alienate his men. He glanced around, realizing they were in a foul mood. They didn't like the storm last night, and now it was hard to tell when they could take on food and water. Abruptly he decided in their favor. To a captain, his crew came first.

"Mistress, I must think upon the matter. Come to my

cabin. I'll examine your calculations and let you know what I decide." He took Rozalinde firmly by the arm.

"Troth!" She tried to shake him off. "Do you mean you require further proof?"

He pulled her close. "My dear," he hissed, speaking very low, "these men are not accustomed to women. They would as soon dump you over the side as let you insult one of their own."

Rozalinde glanced around her. The angry expressions on the men's faces registered with her for the first time. "Oh." She took his arm with unexpected swiftness.

"I knew you would make the logical choice," he said grimly, sweeping her off to his cabin. "You always do."

The interior of the cabin was dark after the brilliant light of morning. Once inside, Rozalinde blinked and stood still.

"I'll not have you behaving this way on my ship, Rozalinde." Kit slammed the door behind them, making the darkness even more intense. "Our situation is fragile. These men can't handle a quarrel." He went to the table and rolled out a map. "You're not to talk like that again before them. Not for any reason."

She ignored him, groping her way to the porthole and standing in its ray of light.

"Do you hear me?"

"I hear you, Kit." She swept over to her trunk and searched her pockets for the key. "I hear you well enough. You always make sure I do."

"There you go, just like a woman." He gestured vehemently at the trunk, thinking the spell was broken. It had been his imagination—she couldn't navigate. Furthermore, he was exasperated by her attitude this morning. She'd said she loved him last night, but this morning she didn't act it. "I see you have to have your trinkets and baubles to console you the minute things become unpleasant," he sneered.

"Trinkets, indeed." Rozalinde's answer was curt. "You think you're so clever, so powerful, but there are certain things even you fail to observe." She produced her key at last.

Kit spoke through clenched teeth. "And what might those certain things be?"

"First of all, that *I* am the best qualified individual on this ship to help you." She inserted the key into the lock and tried to turn it. It seemed to be stuck, because she frowned, then got down on her knees to struggle with it. "You won't learn your location from that bungler you have up on deck. He's incompetent."

"That's beside the point. I decide who does the navigating. I'm the captain."

"If you rely on him, *you're* incompetent."

Kit's eyesight wavered as his choler rose, hissing its way through his brain. "Don't be so quick to criticize," he said curtly. "With training equal to his, you could probably do no better."

"But my training is far above his, and I *can* do better." The key turned at last, and Rozalinde threw open the lid. She removed her astrolabe. "I can do better and I shall."

Kit's gaze snapped to the astrolabe. It wasn't at all what he'd expected to see emerge from the trunk, and it changed his mood abruptly. He took one step toward her. "God in heaven, what's that?"

Rozalinde pursed her lips and tossed him a scornful glance. She put the astrolabe aside and drew out something else.

Kit closed the distance between them swiftly. "A rutter!" He caught the little book from her hands and opened its cover, thumbed through its pages reverently. "A beauty, too. Look at this." He stopped at a page, gazed at it. "This is the coast off Haarlem and Brederode. A perfect rendering." He turned the page, thoroughly surprised at these treasures her trunk contained. "And here is the Zuider Zee."

Rozalinde raised her chin and regarded him victoriously. "And you thought I brought gowns with me. Or trinkets." She sniffed contemptuously. "If that was the case, why did I agree to sleep in your shirt? And why am I still wearing this?" She gestured to her wrinkled kirtle.

Kit gave her a sharp look, but she kept her expression innocent of all accusation. He returned to studying the rutter.

Someone rapped at the door. Phillipe came in.

"Look at this, Phillipe. Such a pilot's book." Kit passed the book to him.

"Please be seated." Rozalinde indicated the best chair for Phillipe, but he was studying the rutter now and failed to move. Roz took his arm and coaxed. "I wish to get started," she murmured, pulling him gently. "Not tomorrow, not in a fortnight. Now."

Phillipe sat where she indicated, his eyes still fastened to the page before him. "This is truly wonderful," he said. "Where did you get it, Kit?"

Kit didn't hear him. He was bent over the trunk, examining another book.

"I brought it," Roz answered briskly. "In my trunk. The one you thought was full of gewgaws." Neither man appeared to hear her. "I also brought a two-headed gargoyle."

No reply.

"Troth! I thought so." Roz walked over and snatched the book away from Kit.

He looked around at her with irritation. "Can't you see I was reading?"

"I want your attention. Where is the bungler? I expect him as well."

"Now just one second." Kit rose to his feet reluctantly. "For what purpose do you want the navigator? I said I would think on who should do the navigating and I shall, but I have not yet decided."

Rozalinde regarded him sagely. "Looking for an excuse to put me off? Never mind, I shall convince you. I'll show all three of you my skill. You, Phillipe, and the bungler. I'll have him down to join us at once."

Kit returned her look indignantly. "Again you order my crew. I'll not have it."

Rozalinde marched to the door. "Nonsense. The bungler shall come and bring his instruments, and by the time I get done with him, he'll realize his errors." She flung the door wide and shouted. A cabin boy came immediately, looking shocked. "Send for the fellow who is serving as navigator," she ordered crisply. "Tell him to bring his instruments and maps. The captain expects him."

Kit waited until she closed the door again. "Whatever you do, you're not to humiliate Wrightman."

Rozalinde laughed delightedly. "So that's his name, Wrightman. Thank you for telling me. I intend to do nothing more than enlighten all of you. Just as you instructed. You seemed to require further proof of my accuracy. You shall have it. You need do nothing yourselves."

"I'll grant you can do calculations." Kit looked her over, feeling again that strange feeling—he wanted to see her hold the astrolabe, scribble the calculations on paper with pen. "You say you were trained to navigate, but that was under normal circumstances, when you left a port and headed straight to your destination. Are you sure you can deal with the present lack of information? Perhaps I should handle it."

"Christopher Howard!" Roz shrieked, going over to confront him, hands on hips. "Don't you dare try to cozen me. I *shall* show you the accuracy of my calculations, whether you wish to see them or no. And the Lord of Hoorne shall serve as judge." She turned to Phillipe, gave him a winning smile. "What say you? If I convince you I'm right, shall Lord Wynford agree to sail by my directions?"

Phillipe was clearly having difficulty keeping a straight face. "I believe we should give the lady a fair chance," he said. "There is certainly no harm in it."

Kit looked skeptical. "There may be harm, though not the kind you think."

Wrightman appeared some several minutes later, clutching a rolled-up map in one hand, his astrolabe in the other.

Rozalinde guided him to a stool, not giving him a chance to speak. Taking up Kit's rapier, she went to the map tacked to the wall. Awkwardly, because it was so long, she drew it from its hanger.

"What are you doing?" Kit started up. "That's my best rapier—"

With sword in hand, she faced him. He stopped. While they all looked on, she deliberately used it to point to a spot on the map. "If I may have your full attention, messieurs, I will begin with an explanation of the determination of latitude."

Chapter 20

Rozalinde talked for an hour. In the beginning, Kit told himself it would be mildly entertaining to hear her stumble through the material. Women couldn't navigate. This would be make-believe.

But within seconds, as she held up her astrolabe and discussed the setting of its arm and use of the sighting vanes to capture the light of the sun, he saw she knew her business. The realization was followed by a rush of exhilaration.

Kit puzzled over this feeling while she left the cabin to take readings. Once again it occurred to him that in many ways she was like a man. Her logic, her direct manner of address, her way of saying what she thought and not what was proper—all were traits of a man, yet she was not a man. He didn't feel in the least about her the way he did about Courte or Ned Ruske or even Phillipe.

Rozalinde returned from above deck and fell to work on the figures, immersing herself in the numbers. The three men were forgotten as they sat in silence behind her. But Kit's awareness of her heightened. No, he thought wryly as his loins tightened with the familiar excitement, her slender figure moved him in different ways. Her plain, wrinkled kirtle, so unfashionable and mussed from its days of hard wear at sea, draped stiffly around her slender hips. The fine bones of her face, the fragile movement of her hands over the paper, contrasted strongly with her confidence as she harnessed the power of the numbers. His excitement escalated, became a fierce, incoherent longing.

Why? he questioned, his thoughts blurring as feeling overcame deliberation. The many women he had taken over the years, they had hungered to possess *him,* not the other way around. He had needed them only to ease the urge in his loins.

Now he sat transfixed, watching Rozalinde work. She kept up a constant dialogue as she sketched and calculated, explaining what she did in an undertone, almost to herself. Every few minutes she would stop, straighten her back and stand perfectly still, as if listening. Her eyes glazed as they fixed on the wall before her. Just when he thought she was permanently immobilized, she would bend swiftly over her work again, some new insight into the problem rushing from her lips.

Kit shook his head, marveling. Each step she took in the familiar process of finding their position and plotting a course struck him like the unfolding of a secret only the two of them knew. The haven-finding art was his special love, always had been. And now, to see a female loving it . . . obsession struggled to life within his breast, born of a fierce desire—to possess, to have this entrancing oddity for his own. . . .

"If we are here, in the North Sea," she said, pointing to the map, unaware of his emotional tumult, "as I believe we are, then the prevailing winds will be from the north by northeast." She searched through her chart book, opened it to a page and held up the book so they could see a wind rose showing the north and north by east winds.

Kit grew still inside. He had a sudden vision of himself as a boy, sitting in Lulworth Castle's stillroom, turning the pages of his mother's great herbal. He could almost smell the heavy scent of rose water the maids had been distilling from flowers in the garden, but it was not those roses he remembered.

The image of the little English poppy surfaced in his memory—the wild wind rose. It bloomed all through the meadows of West Lulworth in August. No cultivated, spoiled beauty, but an apothecary medicinal used to ease inflammation of the eyes, to cure wounds. It was capable even of expelling deadly poison from the body. A powerful flower, its image took root in his thoughts.

"If we wish to return to our original point of departure," Rozalinde went on, "we will need to sail by this course." She took up the pencil and sketched a curved line from the North Sea down to the coast of the Netherlands. "However, I expect we'll need to travel east first." She pointed to the coast of Jutland. "No doubt we will require fresh water.

Well, my lords? Sir?" She turned to the men, for the first time acknowledging their presence. "I have calculated a course that will return us to the location we held before the storm broke. Do you have any other instructions for me?"

"Mistress Rozalinde, I salute you." Phillipe had been silent throughout the last hour. Now he gave Kit a brief, searching glance, then stood to take Rozalinde's hand. "Your skill with ciphering equals that of any mathematician. Or any geographer. My congratulations." He met her gaze with his own as he brought her fingertips to his lips. When he was through, he moved to the map, still holding her hand. "I do have instructions for you. I wish you to plot a course for this location." He tapped a place on the map. "Two weeks hence, I promised to meet the rest of my fleet here. Given the distance, we should be able to arrive early, even if we stop to take on water."

Roz frowned at the map, studying the location he indicated. "But that is the head of the Zuider Zee. I thought you wished to go to Antwerp."

"Antwerp is held by the Spanish. We cannot land there or take on supplies. Our base is at Enckhuysen, here." He pointed to the map. "And to make the destination more appealing, the Prince of Orange will rendezvous with us. We see him so seldom, it gives the men courage. Now then, I will speak to the helmsman and set the ship's course for the day. Come, sir." Phillipe gestured to Wrightman. "We will put Mistress Rozalinde's calculations to work." He moved toward the door, instinctively acting on Kit's desires.

Kit sent him a mute look of thanks. It was all he could manage, because his thoughts were whirling. That curved line Rozalinde had drawn—it astonished him.

He stood as the others left the cabin, crossed to her side. Here was a woman who knew as much about navigation as he did—a woman who treasured an old pilot's rutter more than gowns or fripperies, whose happiest moments were spent scribbling calculations for the correction of latitude, who knew that the shortest distance between two points on the flat map was not a straight line. Her slight figure warmed to his eyes. He wanted nothing more than to take her in his arms, to caress her face and whisper his surprise at the many treasures she revealed. "You know about the Mercator projection," he said softly.

Rozalinde looked at him crossly. "Of course I do. You needn't be so astonished. Now give me your answer. Am I to be navigator of your ship?" She was tired after all her discussion and calculations. It was time for her reward.

But he was paying no heed to her question. A mass of unruly tendrils had sprung loose from her severe braids, and he put out one hand to smooth them. They flattened temporarily beneath his fingers, then sprang back in defiance of his taming.

"Don't try to cozen me, Christopher." Roz retreated a step, wanting to escape that intense expression in his face. "I've kept my side of the bargain."

He leaned down to brush his cheek against hers. His arms stole around her waist.

"You said you would decide whether I should be navigator," she insisted, wishing her heart would remain slow and steady when he touched her. Instead, it insisted on stepping up its pace, on rushing ahead with breathtaking furor. "My calculations are sound. You can't say no."

Reluctantly Kit dragged his thoughts back to her statement, saw the anxiety mirrored in her eyes. "It means so much to you?" He remembered when something had once meant so much to him—the image of his mother glimmered painfully in his memory. Instinctively he hardened his heart against it. "No, Wrightman must be the navigator."

"Christopher!" Her single word spoke her agony. "We'll end up in Finland." Her features crinkled and he wondered if she would cry, but she didn't. A furious expression replaced the previous one and crept over her face.

"You misunderstand me." He was sure of his decision and wanted to finish the matter. "Wrightman must act as navigator, but you shall be his tutor. You will be the knowledge behind his actions. Outwardly, the men will see him at the helm taking readings, and they will be satisfied. It's for the best, Rozalinde. For both you and the men. I won't be crossed in this."

"You don't trust me." Her voice was bleak.

He went to the table, began putting away the charts and books with impatient hands. "Rozalinde, be reasonable. You have a great gift. It will do you good to share it with another."

"I don't want to teach." She stuck out her lip rebelliously. "And Wrightman is not my choice of pupil. He has a wooden head, like this table." She struck the table with her fist, making the books jump. The pencil rolled to the edge and fell.

Kit sent her a quelling look. "Be fair, Rozalinde. Do you know he is stupid?"

"He did the calculations wrong."

"Because no one had taught him the correct way. I had only begun his introduction to the rudiments. He comes from peasant stock and has had no formal tutoring. He has nowhere near the years of experience you have. Give him—"

"I can't give him experience. I can only teach the mundane facts."

"Navigation is not mundane facts. Don't teach him as if it were." Kit leaned across the table and again caressed her hair. "Teach him the magic," he whispered, his voice low and tender.

Rozalinde started away from the turbulence his touch aroused. "Navigation is just numbers. Nothing more."

"It's not," he growled, his eyes fastened on the swelling outline beneath her smock and bodice. His hand extended, came to cup one breast. "No more than a kiss is just mouths meeting."

"Oh, troth," Roz wailed, dismay filling her as she strained away from the imprint of his hand. He was going to control her, and the quickest way to do that was to touch her. When he did, she could never resist. No matter how urgent the subject on her mind, the instant he started, everything else fell away. Snatching up a book from the table, she clutched it to her breast, wrapped her arms around it like a barricade.

"Come, sweetheart." Kit circled the table after her. His arms captured, swept her away from reality and into that magical world he created.

She wilted. It was not what she meant to do, but his effect on her was overpowering. Against her will, she uncoiled her arms from around the book. It slid to the floor between them and landed with a bump on the floor as she stretched out her arms to capture his heat.

The kiss *was* more than just mouths meeting. The tender warmth of his lips searched hers, questing, asking the eternal question. She clung to him, letting her hands love the feel of his solid torso, the splendid muscles of his sides and back. As she moved her hands against him, let them slide lower to caress his narrow waist and abdomen, she could feel those muscles, vital and quivering in response to her touch, followed by an instinctual tightening of his hands.

"Do you agree?" he queried, leaning forward to stop her exploration. Capturing her hands, he trailed his lips across her cheek, nuzzled her ear. "You will teach Wrightman?"

"I-I agree to nothing," she stammered, fighting a little jolt of pleasure that shot through her.

"You're not angry?"

"I-I—yes, I am," she insisted as he caught her earlobe in his teeth and worried it until her legs weakened, threatened to collapse. She shivered. "You use unfair tactics."

He pulled her closer. One of his hands splayed low across her back, bringing her hips to mold against his. She could feel distinctly through his trunk hose the outline of his passion. Why did she always yield to him? This was not in her best interest.

Her throat tightened with sudden fear. She would be completely at his mercy if he had his way, and she couldn't bear that. Looking up, she prepared to tell him, but her gaze fastened on his throat, where she could see his life's blood pulsing. The smell of fresh salt spray rose from his clothes, his skin, and she was engulfed by a dizzying rush of sensations.

He caught one of her plaits and pulled off the bit of yarn binding it. Cascades of silk flew free. He captured the other plait.

"What are you doing?" She struggled, tried to catch the second braid from his hand. "I spent an hour combing out the tangles. Stop!"

But already he had it loosened. Her hair fell around her shoulders, thick as a veil. He scooped her into his arms.

"Christopher!" she cried, hitting him with her fists, kicking her legs ineffectively. She knew it was no use.

He put her down on the soft feather mattress of the bunk and bent over her. "Let me pleasure you, Rozalinde." He tugged off his boots and kicked them away, stood unbuttoning his doublet.

She stared up at him, her eyes wide, waiting, while tingles of wanting exploded in her belly like cannon fire.

He stripped off the doublet with one clean movement, pulling it over his head. Roz had a brief vision of flexing muscles beneath his linen shirt, then he slid onto the bunk and stretched his lean, hard body at her side.

The tingles grew, became waves of flame that licked her insides lasciviously. Rozalinde tried to roll away but found herself trapped against the wall. Kit caught her hands, pinned them against the bunk and sought her mouth.

Skillful. Oh, he was so skillful. Roz thrashed beneath him while he plundered her mouth with his own. Gently he probed, seeking her tongue, the taste of him infinitely sweet. His invasion made white hot heat kindle in her body. She felt dampness gather between her thighs. Soon her will-power would evaporate. Through a haze of excitement, she heard his answering groan.

"Oh, Kit." She turned her head weakly, needing to escape him, if only for a second. "I don't agree to your demands, no matter how much I agree to ... to what you do to me."

"My wind rose—" His hands moved across her breasts, coaxing, teasing. "You must learn to love your passion—to understand your other side."

"I don't have one."

"Admit it," he insisted. "What you feel each time I kiss you is your passionate side. You were made for loving, made to feel like this." His hand reached.

Rozalinde gazed, awestruck, as his fingers came down on her right breast. He stroked his way to its peak, let his fingers coax the hardened tip through the fabric, rolling, manipulating. Violent shivers ran through her.

"Come with me, Rozalinde. Enter the dream."

"I-I cannot. I'm not a dreamer. I never have been."

"You can be. Try. Take a deep breath."

To her own surprise, she giggled. "You don't dream by breathing deeply." She shifted in his arms, suddenly feeling comfortable, as if she belonged there. "That is quite the opposite to dreaming, or so I've been told."

Kit balanced himself on one elbow so he could look at her and felt his mood change. She was tense as a bowsprit sail and thoroughly likely to tear if he made love to her—

emotionally, physically. She was totally unready to receive him. Yet he felt a driving need to prepare her as soon as possible, so that he might indulge his rising lust. Last night he had restrained himself, but he wouldn't wait forever. He would work on relaxing her first. "You know nothing about the subject," he chided playfully, meaning to distract them both. He tapped her shoulder with one finger. "Close your eyes and I shall teach you. You have nothing better to do."

Rozalinde hesitated. It was true, there was nothing more urgent demanding her attention. Her calculations were done, at least for the time being. Phillipe would set the ship's course for the day. And although she was not pleased with Kit's plans for her to teach Wrightman, he was unwilling to discuss it further. For the first time in months, she was literally without responsibilities. Forcing herself to lean back against the pillows, she closed her eyes. "What do you want me to do?"

"First of all, I want you to relax. We can't get anywhere if you're not. You have to promise to try."

"I am trying," Rozalinde snapped at him, piqued by his criticism. "What do you think I'm doing? I'm relaxing."

"I shall begin, then."

Kit didn't touch her. Not as she thought he would. He began speaking softly.

"I want you to imagine something . . . something you love."

"A ship," she said immediately.

"All right, then. Let it be a ship."

She closed her eyes reluctantly. Her body was tense with anxiety. If only she could relax, the way Kit obviously did.

"You are on a ship," his voice murmured in her ear, leading her. "Not as big as this one. A small ship, just the size for you to sail alone, with a single sail. You are drifting on calm, warm waters, in the midst of a pure blue sea."

"A warm sea?" Roz's eyes flew open. "That seems contradictory. There's no such thing around here."

"Imagine it's the Mediterranean," Kit soothed, drawing his broad palm over her eyes, forcing her to close them again. "Don't question everything. This is not your usual world, where you must understand everything and order it. This is your fantasy. I'm going to take you on a journey. Listen and let yourself feel."

"Oh, all right." Roz grudgingly resettled herself. She did not know why she listened to him, but perhaps there was no harm. And it did feel comfortable, lying here so close to him, without her passion threatening to sweep her away.

"Now then. Again. Imagine you are floating on water. Your ship is light and quick and responds to your commands easily. You feel completely in control and as weightless and buoyant as the ship you sail."

"Is it a square-rigged ship," interrupted Rozalinde, "or a Dutch rig?"

"It doesn't matter," Kit told her. "What matters is that you are floating calmly, and you have never felt happier. The sun shines down on you. The water looks so pleasant, such a deep clear blue."

Roz relaxed. A feeling of lightness wrapped around her. She felt a deep calm invade her soul.

"Now you are going to breathe deeply, fill your lungs with the calming air."

Obediently Roz breathed and was surprised at how it brought with it a wave of relaxation. The muscles in her arms and back softened. The old air rushed from her lungs, making her eager for the next calming breath. It was strangely like her experience had been in the cave by Lulworth Creek. Her thoughts began to drift.

Kit's voice droned in the background. Comfort enfolded her—so soothing. Roz found herself slipping away, to a realm somewhere between sleeping and waking. The only thing real was the vast comfort holding her, and the sound of Kit's voice.

"You have sailed the ship around the entire bay. Now you will explore the land. The boat obeys you and runs up into the shallows as you turn it."

Rozalinde leaned over the side of her boat, could see the sandy bottom through the clear waters. Raising her head, she sniffed the clean, earthy smell of land, so reassuring after the sharp tang of the sea. Easily she hopped over the side and swished through the warm water to dry ground.

"Before you is the gentle rise of a grass-covered hill." Kit's voice led her onward. "The sun is shining and you decide to sit in the warm, sweet grass, to think awhile. You can see little white flowers growing in the grass. Touch them, Rozalinde. Reach out."

"Umm." She lay completely still, immersed in the dream. She was sitting beside Kit on the hill, wind ruffling her hair. The sweet scents and sounds of August hung heavily on the air—newly mown hay drying in the sun, the drone of bees gathering nectar. Kit plucked one of the flowers and put it in her hands.

"It's the wind rose, Rozalinde." Kit's voice shimmered through the haze of the dream. "The wild poppy. You are like the wind rose. From your wild side, you take your true strength."

"How do you know?" Rozalinde's lips formed the question, moving with the barest trace of sound.

"Let yourself feel, Rozalinde."

She opened her eyes and held out her arms. "Show me."

"Are you sure you wish me to?"

"Oh, yes. I want you, Kit."

Her love surged inside her, sending tingles of anticipation through her limbs as he moved to obey her. She reached to help him untie and unbutton her clothing. Her kirtle, so many times wet and dried, dropped to the floor, followed by her bodice and busk. Away with her logic, away with her cerebral ponderings. She discarded them without shame as he removed her garters and stockings, sent them to join her other garments. Reverently he removed her smock.

She felt her body was lovely. His eyes told her it was. Raising his arms, he pulled off his shirt, let her take it from him and toss it away. His trunk hose and netherstocks followed. He was every bit as magnificent without his clothes as with them. No, more so without them, Roz decided, trying to be objective. As he rejoined her on the bunk, she reached eagerly to explore him. With careful concentration she touched his bare chest, allowing her hands to experience the smoothness of his rippling pectorals, to curve along the muscles of his sides, narrowing to the taut strength of his waist and stomach. Fascinated, she stared down at his massive manhood thrusting upward from a mound of dark, curling hair. She had never seen a man naked and sexually inflamed. Her right hand moved lower, closed around the thick shaft. Amazing, but his flesh was smooth and velvety here, the tip especially. She rubbed it experimentally, then let her fingers encircle. Now she could feel the hardness that held it erect. In a state of wonder, she stared and touched, letting her hand slide down, noticing as she did so that Kit's breath had grown rapid, rough.

With a growl, he attacked her, captured her wrist and jerked her hand away. "Keep your teasing, tantalizing little hand to yourself, Rose. Unless you want everything to end this instant. Is that what you want?"

"Would it end? Why?"

Her surprised, innocent expression irritated him. "You'll understand later." Pulling her close with urgent arms, Kit reached for a small pouch under his pillow. Damn her, he was in control here. He would sway each of her senses— touch and taste, scent and sight. And he, not she, would decide when he would spill his seed and when he would not. Opening the pouch, he sprinkled a brown trail of spice across her breasts, bent to lick it away.

For an instant Roz was surprised again, then dared to let the pleasure enthrall her. The feel of his hands smoothing the flesh of her stomach was firm and comforting, the thrill of his tongue came to tantalize her nipples. Waves of heady pleasure surged through her skin.

When he sought her mouth, she was overwhelmed by the rich taste of his tongue, girded with clove. The crisp odor burrowed deeply into her mind and lodged there. Cherished, these feelings he aroused within her.

He sprinkled the trail of spice lower. She could feel his heart throbbing where his chest leaned against her side. Slowly he licked the cloves from her belly, the texture of his tongue rough and dazzling against her flesh. The trail ended just below her naval, yet lower he traveled. Shifting his position, he took her thighs gently in both hands and parted them. Dropping down, he sought the source of all her dreams. Finding it with his tongue, he made her soar.

"Kit," she cried, momentarily shocked at the intimacy of their act. She had not known a man could pleasure a woman thus. But his tongue was more sensitive than his fingers had been the night before, and infinitely more clever at awakening the bud. In fact, it was more than awakened. As his slick tongue glided and teased, she felt the rising heat of the fire within her. "Please . . ." Her hands reached for him, pulled him into her embrace so that they lay skin to skin, his length cradled against hers.

Without fear, she parted her legs and looked into his

eyes. They were full of that same intense appetite she had witnessed last night, but now she wanted it. She wanted to believe he needed her desperately. Reassured, she nodded, closed her eyes and let herself go.

Kit saw that blind trust burning in her eyes before she lowered her fluttering lids, and he hesitated. Oh, he had done everything to prepare her, but did she know for what? Beyond agreeing to the act of love, would she agree to become his wife and therefore his chattel, as was necessary and proper. Well he knew her opinion of such status. But there was no going back. He had put their fate in the hands of Dame Fortune long ago, when he first brought her aboard the *Swiftsure*. Now his control crumbled, and he eased himself into position over her.

Urgency mounted within him. To have her, to possess this beauty and make it his—he wanted the love she exuded so deeply it throbbed like a wound within him. Eagerly he sought the place between her legs, which made her moan and tighten her grip on his shoulders. The sweetness of her touch unnerved him, even as the tight membrane that formed her maidenhead resisted. It reminded him of everything about her that resisted his wooing and drove him frantic with need. With impatient fingers he kneaded the flesh of her breasts, her hardened nipples, raised himself up to feast his eyes on this lovely possession. Her hair, loose and tangled on the pillow, made him want to loosen his feelings. Her skin, white and soft beneath his fingers, gleamed as pure and urgent as a prayer.

He pressed harder between her legs, demanding entrance. She moved beneath him and moaned low in her throat, which made him swell and grow harder, if that was possible. He was so swollen with lust he thought he would burst with it. Desperately he wanted to be inside her, to pierce her so deeply he would find her rich core, that secret she hid. Straining to control his violent desire, he pressed against her until, with a shock, he fell forward, entering her tight, hot depths.

Rozalinde shuddered as she felt the pain. Squeezing her eyelids shut, she held on as if she were drowning in the midst of this storm. It wasn't her maidenhead tearing, it was her restraint giving way. All her life she had ruled this secret side of her nature. Temptation to indulge in physical passion had been unknown to her. Now, as Kit moved slowly within her, a light flared inside her that was utterly primeval. She gave in to it, letting her hands rove where they would—to clutch his back, his shoulders, to feel the taut muscles from his neck to waist.

He groaned deeply at her touch, a response that delighted her. It urged her to further daring. Her fingers strayed to his hard, rounded buttocks, his tight, straining thighs, exploring the foreign regions of his maleness. And all the while that vision of light and heat mounted, growing within her as he filled her with his shaft. She trembled in the grasp of excitement, thrills of it tingling through her limbs and deep in her vitals. She was almost there—where she had been the other night, that first night on the *Swiftsure*.

"Rozalinde." Kit whispered her name, pressed his lips against her throat. She felt his teeth nipping, the tiny pain awaking her body until it was alert and quivering. "Rozalinde," his voice rasped, "hold me tight."

She squeezed spasmodically, holding him as tightly as her womanly muscles permitted, and he gave a hoarse cry, seemed to grow and swell within her. His response fueled her own, pushing her excitement to fever pitch. With a shudder, she gave in to it and entered the fire.

Fulfillment swirled her into its giddy grasp. Abruptly she arched her back and cried out, the beauty of it encircling her. She would never escape from it, never want to, this blaze of fervent feeling—each step in the flame with Kit burned her clean—the healing, cleansing fire. Exultation coursed through her body, making her feel free and wild. This was the enchantment Kit had promised her—this, his treasured gift.

When at last the beauty began to dim, the throbbing pleasure between her legs subsided, she stepped from the experience feeling renewed. With a small sigh of contentment, she opened her eyes. Kit was still buried deeply inside her and holding her in his arms, a grave expression on his face. And something deep in his eyes. She wasn't quite sure what it was, but it touched a chord of sorrow within her.

"I love you," she whispered, stroking his cheek. "And you love me in return. You will say it, won't you?"

The words were wrong. She knew the minute they were spoken, yet she couldn't help it. His lovemaking had given her the freedom not just to feel, but to say what lay in her heart. His expression grew remote. He withdrew from her, pulled away and left the bunk.

"Christopher?" Fear rose within Roz as he deserted her. Sitting up, she drew her knees to her chin and wrapped her arms around her legs for protection. "Why should I be the one to confess my love but you do not?"

"I've never loved anyone." His voice floated back over his shoulder as he stood examining the map as if he'd never seen it before.

"But you cheat me," she tried to argue reasonably. "You withhold something you need to share."

His silence hurt her. He paced to the porthole with restless feet, interest in the map gone. On his way back, he paused to confront her. "I would have your answer, Rozalinde. I would know that you agree to teach Wrightman."

Roz regarded him in dismay. Their intimacy should have brought them closer, but clearly it had not. A pained look lingered in his eyes. Now here was his demand. Had it been his goal all along—the sole intent of his lovemaking?

She unfolded herself from the bunk and padded to his side, her bare feet rasped by the roughness of the floorboards. "Please be reasonable, Kit. I'm not one of your men, to order about. If you would only share yourself with me, you would see the difference." She could tell he was intensely aware of her nakedness. Reaching out, she touched his arm.

He pulled away as if scorched, and she searched his face, trying to understand. He averted his eyes, reached for his clothes and began to dress.

"You refuse to answer," he said as he pulled on the last boot and caught up his cloak.

"I don't see why I should answer such a question, asked at such a moment. Why are you angry?"

"You," he said tersely. "You make me angry. So sweet and seductive, yet you expect to have your own way. Regardless of what is right."

"I don't," she cried, wounded by the barb he flung at her. "You're the one who wants your way with me. And you are so moody, I can't predict what you'll do from one minute to the next. First you seduce me, then you order me around."

"I wasn't seducing you. I was trying to help you."

"You did help me. You helped me see I love you. But instead of returning the feeling, you make me pay an ugly price for offering it. Maybe I don't love you after all. Maybe I was being maudlin and stupid."

"Stop it, Rozalinde." Kit drew himself up straight and glowered at her from across the cabin. "I'll not ask again for your consent. You will let Wrightman navigate and that's an order. If you want any involvement in this at all, you will tutor him as I've instructed. Otherwise, you are to have nothing to do with running this ship. I will confiscate your tools and maps to prevent it. Is that understood?" And before she could answer, before she could do more than gasp in shock, he headed for the door. "It's damnably close in here. I'm going out for air."

He left, slamming the door viciously behind him.

Rozalinde sat down heavily in a chair, holding her astrolabe in one hand. Without bothering to dress, she pressed the other hand to her cheek while the tears gathered in her eyes.

Kit left his cabin and flung himself up the ratlines, one after another, seeking the highest point of the ship. Damn Rose and damn her again. He was so angry with her. When he finally arrived at the lookout's perch on the main mast, he was still disgusted. The man assigned to duty was there as usual. Blast, but he couldn't be alone anywhere on his own ship. That was the way of things at sea, but just now he wanted to be solitary. There was only one place to find that in the middle of the day, and that was somewhere out of the sun.

With a sigh Kit headed back down. Making for the bread room where they keep foodstuffs, he examined their rations. Might as well do something useful while he puzzled. Entering the dim, windowless cabin, he steeled himself against the usual smells of dampness and mold. It smelled like that despite the fact that they stored food in this upper cabin. A ship was no more than a floating body of decay, which the crew must work at frantically until the next port could be reached.

As he sorted through the few remaining bags and kegs, Kit let the complicated feelings aroused by Rozalinde twist and turn through his mind. He'd wanted to liberate her passion, set her free to trust her own emotions. 'Twas his own idea and one he'd enjoyed thoroughly the first time he'd done it. This second time was different. When he'd finally made love to her, when he'd seen her face change to one of radiant joy, he'd felt pained beyond imagining. Caged. That's how he felt—caged like the pigeons they kept for fresh meat on long voyages.

Anger swirled through his thoughts, lacing with his desire, leaving him defenseless and defensive. She could feel love *and* passion. The two feelings could coexist within the same person. But not in him. No, he could only feel passion. Never love. It was a bitter, ugly realization. Heightened by the fact that he had made her whole, taught her to be a complete person, while he remained an emotional cripple.

Violently Kit heaved a sack of meal to one side, slamming it against the floorboards in retaliation. He wasn't happy about anything he discovered here—with regard to himself or the foodstuffs. They were both bad news. Turning on his heel, he went to do what he would about each of them.

Eventually Rozalinde dressed and left the cabin. She couldn't sit there forever, despite the fact that Kit preferred she stay below. But it was well past time for supper and no one had come to offer her any. She was hungry, and her stomach growled irritably. Dressed in her usual serviceable kirtle, wrapped in her own cloak for a change, she walked along the deck, looking for Kit or Phillipe.

Neither one was visible, and she finally had to ask. She found them both in the bread room, discussing the food stores. As she approached, Kit gave her a dark look.

"Mistress Rozalinde." Phillipe came to greet her, eminently correct, his expression betraying no hidden conflict. Rozalinde found it a relief to talk to him.

Kit refused to look up. "Take her out," he growled to Phillipe as he continued counting sacks with two crew members.

Phillipe took her arm firmly and led her away.

"What is it?" Rozalinde asked anxiously as they came out into the sunlight. The men seemed sullen and tense to her. Phillipe drew her to the rail, away from everyone else.

"The food stores. We're short. Much of it was destroyed in our brief battle with the Spanish and the storm. It wouldn't be so bad, to be a little short on rations, but we're short on water, too. With thirty men who must work hard to keep the ship running and on course, such a thing can be disastrous."

At his words, Rozalinde grew edgy and looked around her. The men were gathering down near the quarterdeck. Kit emerged from the bread room and went among them, mounted the ladder and waved them to silence. He began to speak.

It was a routine address as far as Rozalinde could tell. He called them his good and trusted company. He commended their ability and their loyalty. But when he paused, she sensed the men shifted uneasily, anticipating the coming bad news.

"The storm took us by surprise," Kit continued. "We could not fight the wind. It was the correct choice to run before it. Now we are heading for the nearest shore to take on water and food before we return to the Netherlands, so you need have no fear. It will delay us only slightly. Our navigator," he gestured to indicate Wrightman, who stood among the others, "knows his business. We are certain of our position and direction. You must bear with a little shortening in rations for now. It will be made up when we reach port. There will be triple pay for everyone once we've landed in the Netherlands and I've had a chance to visit my bankers."

A pleased rumble swept through the men.

"Until then," Kit continued, "each of you will have porridge, a ration of salt meat daily, and bread."

A universal groan sounded. For a working man, this was far too little. Comments could be heard rising from the crowd.

"We'll be starved."

"I can't last."

One man shouted, "How long till we reach port, Captain?"

"We will reach the coast of Jutland sometime tomorrow," Kit answered. "Until then, all duties will be lightened. We'll do the bare minimum necessary. Ah, and there are the lemons. I have not forgotten them—you will each have a whole lemon today and a half the day after."

"What about water?" one man called out. "How much's left?"

"I estimate four gills per day per person."

An agitated sound rose from the crowd. It was too little.

"Only for today and part of tomorrow. Come, be of good cheer. I will take the same with you," Kit promised. "No more, no less. And we will rendezvous with the navy of the Netherlands two weeks hence. Keep thinking of the triple pay. All of us have seen far worse hardship than this."

There was grumbling, and it was more than idle complaint. A discussion seemed to be going on, as far as Roz could tell. Then Ruske stepped forward as spokesman.

"We will bear with you, Captain," he said, bowing slightly to Kit and gesturing to the others. "But what of her." His thumb stabbed the air in Rozalinde's direction. "A woman aboard is bad luck. She's brought us to this."

As Rozalinde watched, Kit nodded, acknowledging the statement. Fury swept through her, and she took a step forward. Phillipe's hand on her shoulder arrested her. She looked back at him and saw his warning shake of the head. To a man, all eyes were trained on her and a quiet settled over the ship. For the first time Rozalinde was aware of being a lone female among men whose feelings about her presence had honed to an intense hostility.

Kit broke the tension. With a loud laugh he slapped Ruske on the shoulder. "Believe me, our situation right now is due entirely to those Spanish whoresons. It was their ship that lured us into the North Sea during storm weather. But I have good news for you. We will be revenged on them for that indignity. We will join them in battle, I promise you. The *Gran Grifon* will not evade us twice." He warmed to his topic, and the men let him capture their attention. He had a way of cajoling the crowd that drew them inexorably. Putting his hand on his rapier, he nodded confidently to them. "The woman, you may forget. Since she is to be my wife and countess, she will obey me implicitly. She will keep to my cabin, come out only for occasional exercise around the deck. Treat her as if she weren't there."

Rozalinde stiffened with horror at his words. Scanning the men for a reaction, she saw none. They seemed unsurprised to hear this news—that she would wed with their captain. As usual, he was manipulating them, and though it was to protect her, she could not believe what she'd just heard. She fastened her gaze accusingly on Kit, but he purposely avoided her. He and the men were engaged in that bizarre male ritual she had often observed but never understood, the self-congratulatory goodwill, the hail-fellow-well-met.

She still seethed with anger when she saw Wrightman at the helm later. Her supper had been scant—a small piece of salt meat, not even boiled to make it tolerable, a swallow of water. Her stomach was empty, and now she must pretend to admire the view while checking Wrightman's readings. She was barely civil to him, though he tried hard to please her. Clearly he craved her approval since she had proved to him and the others her skill and knowledge. But she would show him no mercy. She would work him hard and make him suffer the lack of praise. He was a man; he must do without.

By the time she returned to Kit's cabin, darkness had overtaken the ship and she overflowed with choler. Though the hour was not late, every man who wasn't on duty had retired early to conserve his energy. Moving up and down the tiny space, she let down her pinned braids so they hung over her shoulders. And she cursed Kit.

"Troth," she muttered, pouring some water in the basin and trying to wash her face while the ship rolled. It was salt water and most unpleasant to wash with, but they couldn't use scarce drinking water. As she scrubbed her face, she bemoaned her fate. Why had she ever left Lulworth? She had tried to see her cargo safely to market and *he* stopped her. She tried to save the ship and all the crew, but *he* stopped her. And where was her cargo? Where was the shipment of wool she should be selling, for some kind of profit, right now? She paused at the reminder, cloth and soap forgotten in her hands. "I should be doing my duty," she said out loud. "My family needs me."

Tears stung her eyes at the thought. Her father's wan

face came back to her, pale as the linen pillows coverings.
Presumably he would not worry about her. He would have
read her letter. Fervently she prayed he would believe she
was safe, not fret over her and hurt his health. She had
considered that possibility before leaving and weighed it
against the need to gain immediate profit to pay their credi-
tors. In her letter she had assured her father all would
be well.

Her thoughts stimulated her anger. This was Kit's fault.
She would have been at Antwerp by now otherwise, and
... Brokenly she discarded her anger, realizing her logic
was flawed. She'd been wrong about Antwerp from the
first, falling for misinformation. Her mistake shamed her
deeply. Yet the truth was that Kit was a manipulator. Look
how cleverly he'd handled his men over the food issue.
Look how he manipulated her—telling her the truth only
when he felt ready, not when she needed most to know,
before she left West Lulworth. The men now thought him
their savior, and to her, he was ...

What? Lover? Husband? She said the words out loud,
her own sarcasm twisting her mouth into a grimace. What
false words they were. Once again Roz's thoughts raced,
taking her back to the afternoon when Kit had freed her
body, her mind, her passion. Yet all the time he'd been
after something—to make her his possession. Next he
would insist she obey him. Oh, she had noted well how
those two things hung together in his words and his
thoughts—marriage and obedience. Damn his eyes, didn't
he understand she didn't want to be his countess. She just
wanted to be herself.

Done with her washing, Roz poured a little wine in the
cup on the stand and drank it. She'd rather drink water,
but now they were rationing. The wine was sour and she
immediately choked on it. Spluttering with rage, she
slammed the cup back on the stand and bent over double,
choking and hacking. "I hate him." The words fell from
her lips as she coughed and tears sprang to her eyes. "I
wish he would drop me at the nearest port and I would
never have to see him again."

"That seems an ungrateful attitude to me, after all I've
done for you."

The coldness of the voice behind her made Rozalinde

jump. She whirled, clutching a towel she'd caught up to her chest. "There's nothing wrong with my attitude, as I've told you before. And if you were so eager to do something for me, you might have asked me first."

"Asked you what?" He closed the door of the cabin, went to sit on a chair and began to pull off his high black boots.

"My God, you don't know?" Rozalinde came over to stand before him, her fists clenched against her thighs. Her rage swelled inside her brain until she thought her head would burst with it. "You don't even know the question, let alone why you should ask it."

Kit had already shrugged his way out of his doublet and hung it on the pegs. He stood without answering her and stripped off his shirt.

Roz stared at him. "W-what are you doing?" she stammered uncertainly, backing away and fumbling at her throat for the laces to her smock. Finding them, she pulled them tightly together. "You're taking off your clothes."

"Most observant, mistress. I am getting undressed for bed. I've had enough of the gunner's deck. I'm staying here tonight."

"No." Roz backed over to the porthole, realizing vaguely that she'd begun to shake all over. She knew what his actions meant. "You can't sleep here."

He still didn't answer, only continued to remove his clothes. It was one thing to see him without doublet and shirt. But when he removed his stocks and cannions and began to undo the points and laces on his trunk hose, she bolted for the door.

"I'll sleep on the gunner's deck," she cried, groping for the handle but unable to find it in her blind panic. The sun had sunk beyond the western horizon in the last few minutes, and the light had dimmed in the cabin until she could scarcely see.

"You'll sleep in this bunk and no where else," Kit told her sternly, coming up from behind and capturing both her arms.

"I can't stay here," she wept, desperate now to escape him. "I won't."

"You must. There's no where else for you."

She felt trapped. "How could you tell the men ..." she choked out, "what you did ... earlier. It's a lie."

Kit's hot breath quickened on the back of her neck. "That you are to be my countess?"

"I won't do it!"

She struggled against him, but his fingers tightened on her arms.

"Let me go," she cried. "You're hurting me."

His grip loosened, but his voice was tense. "Can you honestly say you don't want to be my countess?"

"I don't want to be the person you think you want."

"I'm offering you something most women would kill for and you scorn it."

"You didn't offer. You demanded I take it."

He erupted in fury at that. He pulled her to him, handling her body as easily as if she were a doll. "You will take everything I offer. You'll not resist me any longer, Rozalinde. I've had as much of this as I can stand."

His face was contorted into a mask of rage and she flinched before him. "You would be sorry an' you wed with me," she cried as he pulled her across the cabin. "We would fight every day of our lives, exactly as we're doing now."

"In that case we will be no worse off than now."

With one smooth motion, he swept her off her feet and into his arms. It happened so quickly, it left her dizzy and disoriented. By the time he landed her in the bunk, the room seemed to swirl with motion. She could only stare at him as he continued the job of undressing.

"Christopher," she began uncertainly, scooting to the wall side of the bunk and eyeing him warily. "You will wear something to sleep in, at least for decency's sake?"

"I don't intend to sleep." He removed his trunk hose and tossed them aside.

Her gaze was drawn to the strength of his body, his stomach rippled with muscle. "I won't submit quietly to your dominance," she managed to falter, realizing her voice quivered with fear. "I would rather die." His answering smile seemed cold and heartless to Roz.

"Well, it's too bad, you are stuck with me. Necessity dictates that we wed. I won't be blamed for ruining your reputation. I'll make an honest woman of you whether you like it or no."

"You don't have to," she railed at him. "You could help me find a female companion once we reach the Low Countries. I can return to Lulworth and no one will know."

"They would guess. Your business would be injured. Your sisters would be ostracized by polite society."

She knew he was right, but she couldn't accept it. Her mind searched for escape, lunging desperately from one thought to another. "You can't really want me," she pleaded. "You said you've never loved anyone."

"I'm under an obligation to wed with you."

"I'll wager you never felt such an obligation before. Why now?"

"Though you may not believe it, Rozalinde Cavandish, you are not the only one who believes in honor and duty. I, too, believe in them."

"Honor and duty," she cried, crushing herself against the wall. "This is honor and duty?"

"Yes." His lips parted in a grin that showed his white, even teeth. Coming over to the bunk, he stood before her, his body bared of garments.

He looked glorious, Rozalinde thought, unable to tear her gaze away from him. Like one of the Greek gods she'd read about in her father's books. His skin seemed to gleam in the candlelight, and her gaze was riveted to the juncture of his thighs. His arousal stood out thick and large from his body, and she stared at it in fascination, just as she had earlier. Only now it was worse, because she knew how it felt to have that fascinating appendage give her pleasure. "Heaven save me from honor and duty," she whispered, forcing herself to avert her eyes, afraid he would see how much she wanted him. "Heaven save us both."

Of course he saw it. She could hide nothing from him.

"Look at me, my Rozalinde," he commanded. His silken voice cajoled. "I like it when you look at me. Don't play coy."

"I must not look," she answered thickly, her throat suddenly drier than it had been all day, lack of water or no. "We'll both be lost."

"And what will we lose?"

His question wove a confusing web of thoughts through

her mind. What would she lose, indeed, besides her freedom, her independence—things that he cherished for himself but never considered necessary for her. "You don't understand," she said heavily, trying to avoid his compelling blue eyes.

"I understand better than you think. Look at me, my Rozalinde."

Slowly she let her gaze return to meet his.

"That's better. Now we shall begin."

His voice mesmerized her, and as always, she gave in to it.

Slowly she rose to her knees on the bunk. He motioned her out, and she came to stand before him.

"First your kirtle skirts," he commanded, his voice rough from his uneven breathing. "Then your garters and stocks."

Blindly she followed his orders, removing each item, casting it away, not knowing where it fell. When she was wearing nothing save her smock, she gave him an entreating look. "Must I?" She could hear her voice quiver.

In answer, he stepped forward, grasped the white linen at the hemline and whisked the skirt over her head. With a swish, the fabric flew through the air like a bird and settled on the floor behind them with a sigh.

Rozalinde sighed also. Kit's arms were still outstretched from tossing away the smock. She stepped into them, as naturally as if he'd bid her come to him.

"You're making a mistake," she said, tilting back her head to look into his sea-blue eyes. "I'm a lowly merchant's daughter."

It was not the sort of conversation Kit was used to having with a woman. Her statement was not the least self-serving, and Kit found himself appreciating her honesty. For that, she deserved an honest answer, and he didn't hesitate in giving it. "I was never meant to be earl, Rozalinde. I was a lowly, second son, the stuff that gentry families are made of. I am no better than you in any way." He forced himself to calm his anger and loosened the grip of his hands on her shoulders. Those shoulders were white and perfect, just like in his dream.

"I'm a terrible shrew," she was saying earnestly.

His hands crept lower to revel in her flawless breasts. "As if I didn't know." His voice grew husky as he traced the thrust of those orbs, saw her shudder with pleasure as he drew the flat of his palm across the tips of her pale pink nipples. First one, then the other, he stroked them, relishing the way her eyes glazed with enjoyment, the way the muscles in her jaw quivered as she clenched her teeth. Despite this, she spoke again.

"Would you not prefer to wed a woman you can love, Christopher? You don't have to do this. You need not."

Suddenly he'd had enough conversation. He was enflamed with need for her, unable to wait. His hands devoured the slimness of her waist, traced the flare of her hips. Moving lower, he cupped the firm muscles of her buttocks, reveling in her answering touch.

"There's no going back," he whispered, scooping her up and laying her on the bunk. Quickly he took his position, his body hovering above hers. "Love is irrelevant when we share a passion like ours."

"Is passion enough?"

Again her words deserved an answer, but this time he couldn't give it. His desire had risen unbearably. Having tasted her sweetness before, he would wait no longer. Once again the passion in his life was out of control, and he hated himself for it. But it couldn't be helped. She belonged to him.

Eagerly he parted her legs, searched with his fingers for the source of her pleasure. Finding it, he grinned with triumph as she closed her eyes and let out her breath in a gasp. He could feel that she was slick, ready for him. Swiftly he removed his finger, lowered himself between her legs. "'Tis too soon after your first time, but I will try not to hurt you." He let his weight descend, and with care, he penetrated her.

The heat of her core was so intense, he felt himself seized by an agonizing excitement. The old anger surged along with it as he recognized his lack of control. No, he would be in control, he would go slowly and pleasure both of them. Suddenly it was difficult to breathe, and he fought for air, turning his head away and drawing air into his lungs, calming himself. His heart pounded crazily, and he restrained himself, resisting the desire to ram himself blindly into her depths.

When he was quite sure he was in control again, he

turned back to rain her forehead and cheeks with kisses. Cautiously he began to move within her, but seconds later he again lost his composure. Trying to check his speed, he pulled out. It was agony to leave her. He thrust deeply.

She let out a small whimper.

"There now, my flower. It will hurt a bit this second time, but if you are patient, I will help you forget the soreness."

God in heaven, he was the one who needed patience. The incredible sweetness of her, the fluttering of her heart whispering in the vein at her neck, threatened to overwhelm him. He wanted to unleash his passion, to dive into her body like a mindless animal. He wanted to ride her with one thrust after another until he lost himself in completion. But he would not. Control, he urged himself sternly. He would keep control.

She moved unexpectedly beneath him, spreading her legs wider to take more of him. Without warning, he found himself besieged by emotion. As she rose to meet him, unconsciously twisting her hips to work him deeper, he probed her softness, searching for something. Her hands on his shoulders clutched so tightly, he could feel her fingernails make little crescent dents in his skin, hear the delicious moans she made deep in her throat.

It drove him to a frenzy of wanting, and suddenly he was hungry for everything she could give him. "Say you love me," he rasped eagerly, straining against her. He needed to hear those words.

But she only twisted beneath him. Raising his upper body, he braced himself with his hands so he could watch her face. Her brown eyes met his, full of love and deep with promises. If only he could believe in that emotion again. He moved faster inside her, the friction of his strokes making bursts of feeling cannon through his body. In response she cried out in pleasure, tossed her head back against the pillows, her glorious crown of hair spread around her like a halo. She had to say those words.

It made him feel guilty, his wanting. How badly he required her to say she loved him. Yet could she deny it? Each move of his body was met by hers. She wanted him, despite her words to the contrary. Deliberately he placed one hand between them, seeking the place between her thighs with his fingertips.

At his touch, Rozalinde thought she would take leave of her senses. Like the rare fireworks she had once seen, startling explosions of sensation surged to her brain, making her dizzy with pleasure. Shifting her legs experimentally, she sought more of him, eager for each drop of liquid flame he poured into her. Kit's answering groan, the famished look in his eyes, fueled her excitement. She could give him excruciating pleasure. New bursts of pleasure swept through her as Kit's fingertips rotated between her legs, and she found herself rising to unbelievable heights. Pulling away his hand, she clutched his torso against her, wanting only the slick heat of him deep inside her, the pumping of his hips as he delivered one exquisite torment after another. He controlled her utterly, and willingly she let him. It was an unsolved mystery she could not fathom, only submit while her body burned. Fiery flames teased at her core, whispering dark images in her thoughts. Kit commanded her body, Kit released her passion. With one hand he took. With the other he set her free. She would follow him willingly, if only he would do this to her forever.

"This is madness," she heard herself sob in his ear, sure she would melt from the heat he aroused within her.

"No," he growled back, determined to hear what he wanted. "Tell me what it really is."

"It's love," she cried, "I love you, Christopher Howard. I don't want to, but I can't help it. Ohhhh. . . ." With a cry she clasped her arms around him and buried her face in his shoulder. Deep inside her a deluge broke loose. A storm of delicious convulsions swept through her, whirling her away to the heights of rapture. Acutely she was aware of Kit straining against her, his reaction as her muscles clenched and convulsed around him.

Feeling Roz's body tighten in fulfillment, Kit rushed to follow. With a last stroke, he arched to a climax, his body shaken by a succession of trembling spasms. Buoyed inexplicably by her words, he poured forth his passion, wanting it to go on indefinitely.

In the aftermath, he leaned on his elbow and watched her sleep. He had forced the confession from her, and would do so again. Over and over she would say the words. Willing or unwilling, she loved him. And willing or unwilling, he found she was something he required, just as he required air to live.

Chapter 21

Their third morning at sea dawned brisk and sunny. The wind blew steadily from the northwest, pushing the ship through the lapping waves. Rozalinde sat in the charthouse, her gaze fastened to the shaft of sunlight slanting through the wide windows, striking the map before her on the table. She was ruminating. This morning, she felt less confused. At least it had been settled last night—she would wed with Kit. Reluctantly, perhaps, but she would do it.

Not that she was giving in, she told herself adamantly, smoothing the page before her, tracing the path she expected to take, over to Denmark and down along the coast to Germany, then to the Netherlands. But some things were inevitable. This was one of them.

She accepted it. But not him—not the way he was. Domineering, arrogant and irritating. He was all these things in every part of life, especially in bed.

She felt herself blush as she thought of bed. Last night had changed something within her. At last Kit had made love to her and not retreated after. She had known the satisfaction of lying in his arms until they both fell asleep. True, he'd been an arrogant knave about their lovemaking, insisting on controlling her every feeling as well as his own. Deliberately he'd given her pleasure, then sought his, not for an instant letting down his guard or losing himself in her love.

No, he didn't trust her, because he'd never trusted anyone, not growing up with a father like his. But she could teach him. Though it might take time, she was sure she could.

Why she felt so confident of this, she wasn't certain. It wasn't sensible to believe she could change him. But such a feeling suffused her this morning, made her feel glowing

and radiant inside. The only way she could describe it was to liken it to a picture she'd once seen by an Italian artist whose name she couldn't remember. She'd been with her father, having dinner with one of his acquaintances in Amsterdam. The name of the burgher also escaped her memory, but he'd been rich and his house well appointed. His wife and three daughters had taken her to see this picture— a madonna and child. A mere sketch with charcoal. Yet she could see the glow of the holy figures, feel their radiant love. How ridiculous to think she and Kit were the least bit like them. Yet she felt a deep reverence for last night— reverence for what she and Kit shared.

"Is this correct, mistress? I have tallied the numbers as you directed."

Rozalinde jerked out of her reverie, surprised to find Wrightman seated across from her. He'd been sitting there all along, but she'd forgotten him. Kit had insisted she give him lessons each day. Today she must direct him in calculating how far they'd sailed during the night, then show him how to determine their present position and correct their course for the day. More importantly, they must determine how soon they would make landfall.

She was still furious with Kit for making her tutor Wrightman. She could do the calculations more quickly and efficiently herself, but Kit had decided otherwise.

Wrightman pushed the paper across the table toward her, an anxious expression on his face. He was in awe of her, she realized. He hadn't seemed so initially, but once she'd proven her skill, once Kit had decreed she would be his tutor, he'd changed considerably.

With a nod, she took the paper and scanned the figures he'd written in his clumsy handwriting.

"This is not right." She frowned at the numbers. Couldn't the idiot see he'd added wrong? All he need do was figure distance traveled, determined each morning from the numbers on the helmsman's slate. Each day Wrightman made a similar error.

A stricken look crossed Wrightman's face.

Once she would have scowled at him, slapped the paper down and ordered him to find the mistake. Now, for some reason, her heart softened. "There now, 'tis not so bad. You are trying so hard, you make an error each time. Let me show you." Turning the paper back to face him, she patiently pointed out his problem and bade him try again.

Kit, listening from beyond the half-open cabin door, grinned and moved on about his business. His plan was proceeding admirably. Wrightman was a good pupil; Rozalinde, a competent tutor. *If* she kept her temper in check. It was good for her to teach another. Instinctively he knew it, having found great comfort in sharing his own knowledge with Courte and others like him. Once she gave Wrightman a chance, she would see the rewards to be had from sharing her gift. For it was a gift she had—no doubt about that. The lass ate, drank, and dreamed numbers. He'd heard her last night, mumbling in her sleep, reciting the most recent distances from the helmsman's slate.

Swinging down a ladder, he went to check their water supply. It was dangerously low, and he was concerned about when they would see land.

An hour later Rozalinde finished with Wrightman, having worked him to the point of mental exhaustion. Dismissing him, she went on deck for air. Lord, but she was thirsty. It was Phillipe's turn as helmsman—that she knew. Since their sailing, Kit and Phillipe each took one watch a day at the helm. The rest of the time it was manned by Kit's officers. After a brisk walk around the deck, she made her way to the helm.

"Good morrow, Mistress Rozalinde. I trust you are well."

Phillipe was always proper with her. For that, and for many other reasons, she gave him her smile in return. "I would be better," she said, "if I had something to drink."

"We all would." He ran his tongue over his own dry lips. "I find it better to think and speak of other things. How go your lessons with the young seaman?"

Roz pulled a face that reminded her of Jon as she did it. "He's actually not too bad with the logic," she admitted grudgingly. "But he's had so little experience. Holding the pencil straight sometimes seems too great an expectation. And he knows next to nothing about calculations. I have to tell him every little thing."

Phillipe cast her a sympathetic glance. "'Tis a hard task, to be the lesson giver, *m'n lieveling*. Almost as hard as

learning the task yourself the first time over. Sometimes
you search in vain for the proper way to convey your meaning. And even then, when you have tried your honest best,
the pupil still comes up lacking. I have had my share of
such discouraging encounters. It can wear you out as much
as a day of physical labor. But it also has its rewards. You
will know them when you see the look of respect in your
pupil's eyes."

Roz nodded, thinking he was right. Phillipe, it seemed,
understood her—unlike Kit, who chastened her for her
quick temper, her bad attitude about her pupil. It made
her chafe when he did it, and she turned her temper on
him. What pleasant diversion to speak of the subject with
Phillipe, who soothed her about the difficulties and offered
encouragement.

"Do you miss your ship?" she asked, changing the subject. "You are a captain in your own right. Nay, an admiral
of your prince's fleet."

Phillipe shrugged. "We must school ourselves to accept
the things life hands us."

Rozalinde shivered involuntarily. "I find that difficult."

"Then you are not alone. What do you find difficult to
accept?"

Rozalinde paused, a deep sense of guilt consuming her.
"Being a wife," she whispered, desperately wanting that
guilt to leave her.

"Why?" he asked gently. "Kit loves you."

She turned to stare at him. He seemed younger this
morning, carefree. He'd put away his black cloak and mask,
and without them, in his white linen shirt, black trunkhose
and netherstocks, his white hair curling crisply around his
shoulders, he seemed familiar and comfortable to her.
"You're saying that to console me—and to protect him.
Don't. He doesn't know how to love, and he can't change."

"Life changes people."

"As it has changed you?" She saw him search his pocket
for something. The heady odor of cloves drifted to her.
Drawn irresistibly by the scent, she stepped near, touched
his cheek gently, drinking in the aroma she associated with
lovemaking. "I am sorry."

"Why are you sorry?" He turned to look into her face,
surprise lighting his eyes.

They were wonderful eyes—a clear blue, inviting her confidences. "I'm sorry for all the things your life should have been...."

"I have much that makes my life worth living. For one thing, my prince needs me."

"I wish I could be so accepting. I wish I could be like you." Her eyes honored him.

"And I ... I wish I were thirty years younger."

The longing in his voice took her off guard, making tears leap to her eyes. Despite his courage, Phillipe was a man in mourning. And only she knew why, because of his beloved Anne. Her tears multiplied, and one spilled over, rolled down her cheek. He put out his hand to catch it—the drop falling on the glove he always wore at the helm to handle the heavy whipstaff. The stain spread, forming a dark blot on the leather as another tear joined it. This man had the power to move her deeply with few words. Wrapping his arm around the upright post that guided the ship, Phillipe drew off the glove and wiped her eyes gently with his handkerchief. First the right, then the left.

"Why cannot Christopher be like you?" she said softly. "Like father, like son." She saw him start.

"Why do you say that?"

"I found the secret chamber beneath Lulworth Castle. I-I saw your letter to Anne. It's still there, you know. Along with the cross twined by the rose." She waited, wondering if he would be angry at her intrusion. But his eyes reflected only sorrow.

"Anne told me Christopher was Henry's son."

"She didn't want you to feel responsible for what happened to Kit." Roz put her hand on his arm. "She knew you would have no legal right to him, no access. And she knew her husband. Tell me about him—Kit's adopted father."

The watch ended just then. The bosun blew his whistle. Phillipe turned the hourglass. A few minutes later the first mate arrived to take the helm. Rozalinde watched while Phillipe transferred information from the traverse board to the helmsman's slate and removed the pegs from the board.

"Come." Duties finished, he gestured to her, led her up to the forecastle deck where they leaned against the rail and watched the waves.

He talked in a low voice to her for some time, telling her many things—what he had learned about Henry Howard, Earl of Wynford, his growing love for Anne, the years they spent apart, their brief times together that made their lives bearable.

"There was only one time when it might have been possible for Kit to be conceived. Many years after our first meeting, I came from the Netherlands to the court of Elizabeth, and there I saw her, my sweet Anne, so long after her father had torn us apart."

His blue eyes were distant and Roz felt it only natural to slide her one arm around his shoulders. She wanted to ease his pain, to remind him that those days were now long past. But she sensed they were never so distant for him. That each day, his pain, as well as his love, lived fresh and vivid in his soul.

"We had thought never to meet again, Anne and I. It was the shock, I think, of seeing each other. We both went a little mad. We made love that night, in the garden. It was the only time. After, she felt guilty—though I cannot think why. She had already borne her husband an heir." A shadow crossed Phillipe's face. "I wondered if Kit was my son, but Anne told me he was not. She would have known.

"Yet whether he was or no, I should have forced them both to come away with me. Henry had an obsession with duty, and an attitude about raising children that was strict to the extreme. That, along with his rigid will, I believe made him dangerous. Yet he never went so far to the extreme that he could be accused of real violence. It might have been easier if he had. No, his worst fault was his lack of feeling. And for that alone, Anne could not justify leaving him. She said our lives would be chaos if she did, that Henry would destroy any hope for a relationship between us, either approved or disapproved by society. Henry was capable of everything she feared. Yet it was hard to hear that I was powerless against him. And now—now I believe, from what Christopher told me, that Henry separated him from Anne when he was very young. Mayhap no more than five. A child needs his mother." He bent his head, looking at the water with tormented eyes. "Instead, I let myself believe what Anne told me—that Christopher did well enough. But now I know why she finally agreed to see me again, why she at last consented to our being lovers. It was around that time that Henry took Kit away ..." His voice choked slightly. "We began to meet in the secret chamber beneath Lulworth Castle that only Anne knew. I enjoyed her company and went away thinking all was well. I cannot forgive myself."

Rozalinde tightened her hand on his shoulder and leaned against him, wanting to block the pain she saw in his eyes. She scarcely came to the top of those shoulders, she was so small compared to his height and breadth, yet she offered the comfort. Her throat had a lump in it, her eyes blurred with tears. "You believed what you had to believe in order to survive."

"I took the coward's way out."

"No coward could have borne what you did."

Kit watched them, standing at the rail together, Phillipe and Rozalinde, and felt a rising anger. He couldn't make out what they were saying, but he heard Rozalinde's tone of voice, saw her sympathetic gesture. She never talked to him in that way. Nor did she offer him comfort. She admitted she loved him, yet was brusk and angry about it. He turned away, filled with choler.

It was because they were all thirsty, he told himself. There was a restlessness among the crew. He took himself off to see to his duties—anything to avoid the sight of Rozalinde lavishing her attention on Phillipe. She hadn't been sweet like that with him when they awoke that morning. True, when she'd first opened her eyes, she had smiled at him a lazy, sated smile. But he'd gone and called her his countess. He'd meant it as an endearment, but of course she didn't like it. She had thrown him an angry look, then left the cabin and refused to speak to him again. She made him furious. He hadn't given her orders or been domineering—he had called her what would have pleased most women. So he had been domineering later, when he perceived she had not begun her daily lesson with Wrightman.

He had chided her thoroughly. She'd called him a tyrant and left the cabin in a fury. But she'd deserved the chiding, for shirking the work he'd assigned. He was captain on this ship and he expected everyone to obey him. Everyone. Without question.

An hour later, he saw her up on the poop deck, pretending to take the air but furtively watching Wrightman, who was reading the compass and fussing with the astrolabe. Determinedly he concealed himself and continued to observe her.

Rozalinde *was* watching Wrightman, and chafing unbearably while she did it. It was painful as a nettle sting, she thought with exasperation, to watch him holding the astrolabe wrong. If he didn't straighten it, he would get a false reading when he "shot" the sun. She *was* trying to be patient with him, despite what it cost her . . . and despite what Kit said—that she had no patience worth mentioning.

Looking away at last—if she watched him anymore, she would do something rash, like shout at him or give him a well-deserved cuff—she struggled to pretend she enjoyed the scenery. Absently, she took a nibble from a chunk of ship's biscuit, what was left of her midday meal. It was so hard she could scarcely get her teeth into it, and so dry, she had to hold each bite in her mouth for some time before it would soften and slide down her throat.

She was so involved with her covert observations, it took her several minutes to hear the crewmen nearby. They were talking quietly among themselves, but eventually their words pierced her consciousness.

"We'll never see land. We'll die of thirst."

"Or starve. This never happened before on board with the earl. It's her, I say. She's brought us bad fortune."

They were talking about her, Roz realized. It was positively embarrassing to be the object of their talk. What did they expect her to do? Jump off the ship so they could be free of her?

Boldly she turned and walked over to them. The faces of the three men registered their shock as she addressed them. "You must have faith in Wrightman." She swallowed her pride. "He is a very good navigator. He knows what he's doing. His lordship, your captain, has checked his calculations to be sure they are correct. You must trust him. Has he ever led you astray?"

They shook their heads, astonished that she addressed their concern squarely.

"You must be of good faith," Roz went on, determined

to cheer them. "We will see landfall by tonight, he says.
I'm sure he's right."

Actually Wrightman had said nothing of the kind. Rozalinde had just determined it that morning herself. She had
calculated their latitude, plotted their position based on the
distance covered that night, and counted the hours before
they made land.

The men said nothing in response. One of them eyed the
piece of biscuit in Rozalinde's hand. His eyes were bleary
and resentful, and Rozalinde could see the sallow look they
all had, along with the slight puckering of the skin that
meant too little water. She looked down at the biscuit, then
held it out to the man. "Here. Take it. I don't have to
work, as you do."

He snatched it without hesitation and turned away to eat
it before anyone could comment. Later, he sent her a ghost
of a black-toothed smile from where he worked, adjusting
the rigging on a sail.

Her own stomach rumbled emptily, but she was glad
she'd given it. If only they could catch some fish, but they
had no nets, and they moved too fast through the water to
fish with hook and line. They must sacrifice food for speed
just now, and food could not help them once the water ran
out. She was heading for her cabin to lie down when she
noticed something odd about one of the younkers, as the
youngest crew were called. His duty was with those who
took turns endlessly swabbing the deck to keep the boards
expanded and tight. As he stood among the others, Roz
saw that he swayed dangerously on his feet. Suddenly he
keeled over in a faint, hitting the deck with an ugly thud.

Rozalinde froze where she was as men calmly went to
his aid. The ship's physician was called, but there was nothing he could do for the boy. Not enough water, the man
pronounced, knowing the lad had had the last of his daily
ration after mending broken rigging high on the mainmast.
The boy was younger than she, Roz realized, looking at
him from a distance. Perhaps a year older than Jonathan.
Seventeen and about to die for lack of water. It wasn't to
be borne.

The others pulled him into the shade of the forecastle
and left him there.

Whirling purposefully, Roz hurried belowdecks to where

the water supply was kept. The old man who guarded the precious casks stood when she appeared. Catching up the large tin measure they used, she held it out to him. "I want my ration," she said. "The rest I am due for today."

"All, mistress?" The man gaped at her. "Now then, you don't want to do that. 'Tis early yet, and you've already had a quarter. Take another quarter," he coaxed, beginning to fill the cup. "You'll have the rest for later on."

"I want my ration and I want it now," she insisted, wondering at herself.

The man gave it to her reluctantly. Carefully she carried the precious liquid up on deck to the fainting boy.

He was conscious when she got there, lying listlessly on his side.

"Can you sit?" She went down on her knees beside him. "Let me help you." Her arm encircled his shoulders and she raised him. When he'd fainted, she had been far away and judged him to be about Jon's size. Up close, she found him larger than she had expected. Clearly he would need all her water to be restored.

She brought the cup to his lips.

The boy didn't question. Only drank gratefully.

"Not too much at one time," Roz warned, taking the cup away but continuing to support his shoulders. "You don't want to bring it back up right away. That would be a waste. This cupful is yours, so take your time."

She spent an hour at his side, coaxing the water down him, watching it take effect. His eyes lost their glazed look. She tested the skin of his forearm, pinching it gently between thumb and forefinger, watching for it to spring back to show he'd had enough. Satisfied at last with his condition, she took him to the forecastle and had an older man put him to bed.

"See that he rests," she admonished before heading for Kit's cabin. If she could escape in sleep, she would forget her own thirst, though that seemed unlikely. Here she had the rest of the afternoon and evening before her, with nothing to drink until midnight.

It was a lowering thought. She stretched out on the bunk and dozed off, resolved to bear it. Much later she awoke as the latch rattled and someone came in. Stubbornly, she kept her face turned to the wall.

"My countess?"

She wouldn't move. She wouldn't answer him. He was lording his victory over her. Moreover, he didn't love her, and she was unwilling to settle for anything less.

"Rose?"

His hand came to rest on her hip. He stood directly behind her, apparently, for she could feel his palm move slowly along her side.

"Umm." The sigh broke from her involuntarily, though she refused to turn his way.

"Ah, she answers to that. I am getting somewhere. So she would rather be my flower than my countess."

"The lesser of two evils," Roz replied testily.

"I see."

His hand retreated from where it seared her hip. She heard him cross the room, peel off his doublet and toss it across a chair.

Rozalinde closed her eyes and drifted. The image of water formed before her eyes. The vast body of Lulworth Creek tempted her senses. Looking the way it had that night, a few short months ago. The Spanish galleon floated on it, the magic of the Beggar King enticed her. Oh, that water. She wanted to leap into the delicious depths of that creek now, gulp mouthfuls of it to wet her parched throat. She could almost hear the sound of falling water, its rich, cooling trickle refreshing her. Her body cried out for water, she was so thirsty. . . .

Rozalinde jerked to a sitting position as she realized the sound of water was real. "What is that? I . . ."

A moan escaped her. Kit bent over the table, squeezing a half lemon into a cup that, by the sound of it, held water. Putting down the lemon, he came to her side.

"Drink." He sank on the bunk and pressed the cool metal to her lips.

She drank gratefully, watching him over the rim of the cup, her hand wrapped over his as the delicious water tinged with lemon delighted her throat. Not all of it though. She would not drink all. This was his day's water ration he gave her.

Partway through, she forced the cup from her mouth and pushed it back toward him.

"Your turn," she whispered, then watched him take the

cup. He drank from the same spot she had, his lips full and enticing against the metal as he swallowed the last drop and put the cup down.

"I saw what you did. You have my deepest respect."

She brought her lips to his in answer. They met like a rush of dreams, fulfilling her expectations. His mouth felt warm and tender, making something deep within her belly stir. Lifting her hands to his shoulders, she felt the magnificent swell of muscles. Eagerly her fingers sought his arms, his back, exploring.

"You gave me your last water," she began.

"I would share everything I have with you."

It was a small admission compared to the one she wanted. Yet it showed his generous nature. Besides, he had promised her passion, not love.

He pressed her back onto the bunk, then left her side for an instant. The other half of the lemon looked small and shriveled. Several black spots scattered across its rind. But the flesh, when he turned it toward her, looked firm and yellow. He held the fruit suspended above her lips.

"Open."

She obeyed. The juice of the lemon dripped into her mouth like liquid gold, its tang so sharp it was blinding. The room, Kit, his touch, seemed to grow radiant and vibrate as the lemon shocked her senses. Still, Kit wouldn't stop. He urged her to take more.

"It will wet your throat," he insisted, laughing when she shuddered and pursed her lips. With a chuckle, he dripped some of the lemon into the cleft between her breasts, just above her bodice. In a leisurely manner he bent over and let his tongue lave away the juice. "Great heaven," he groaned between probes of his tongue. "You are a maid of contrasts. Sweet and sour."

The core of Rozalinde's being quaked violently at his touch. A tension infused her limbs. Her breath came more quickly. "You are the one of contrasts. You give me relief and torment at the same time." She shuddered again as he pulled her smock away from her skin and let his eyes feast on her bare flesh.

Watching her face intently, he reached inside her smock. His warm hand caused a havoc of wanting to course through her.

Her body shuddered again, as if he'd given her more lemon. Grinning ruthlessly, he began to unfasten her bodice. Their garments melted away, as magically as snow in springtime. With the juice of the lemon he anointed each part of her body, let his tongue stroke it away. A small drop on her neck. His lips kissed it away. More of the lemon's treasure beside her ear. His teeth caught her earlobe and tugged until she trembled.

"What are you doing to me?" she whispered.

"Guarding you against scurvy," he teased, holding out the lemon.

She watched as he crushed the fruit between strong fingers, then she looked into his face, her gaze questioning. Drawing back, he returned her stare, the power in his gaze snaring hers. He'd held her in his spell since the beginning, in the shop. Even as he captured her mind, his hands reached for her body. The liquid from the lemon felt cool on the sensitive tips of her breasts before the heat of his mouth seized her. Her vulnerability flared and she thought for a minute she would lose control. That was it—he made her vulnerable, each time he did this. His mouth drew strongly at her flesh, and she cried out, not knowing what words she spoke. He moved to the other breast, anointing the tip, then covering it with his mouth and drawing until she felt a throbbing between her legs and cried out again.

Moving lower still, he let a drop from the lemon fall just above the curls that covered the juncture of her thighs. The faintly rough texture of his tongue rasped against her bare skin. She could see he was ready. Lost in a dangerous rapture, she reached for him. He groaned as her hand closed.

The sound wrung a similar confession from her. "Please, Christopher," she pleaded, caught in the throes of her desire. That she should desire him—it astonished her.

He laughed, an opulent sound to her ears, parted her legs and thrust himself between them. In no time at all they soared to fulfillment. He understood the needs of her body.

When it was over, he sat back, and she followed him, refusing to let their intimacy end. "Why wouldn't you love me that first time?" she asked, settling against his chest and arranging his arms around her middle.

"My intent was to *give*—not to take for myself."

She twisted her head and searched his sea-blue eyes. "I don't understand. Why?"

"I've always had an excess of passion. I needed to control it."

"You?" She pushed away and turned to examine him, hands resting on her thighs. "You may have passion, but most of the time you behave in the most dispassionate, self-contained manner I've ever seen."

"Only in the last year," he said moodily, looking away.

"But don't you see?" Roz went on, determined to say what was on her mind. "You're too controlling. You control yourself far too much and you insist on controlling others as well. Their feelings, their actions, your own. It's positively—"

"Just one minute," he interrupted abruptly. "What exactly do you mean by that—I'm too controlling?" His gaze snapped to meet hers. A curious, agonized expression hovered in his eyes.

"Just what I said," Roz continued carefully, suddenly sure of what she said. "You don't want to be like your father. But you are, at least in some ways. Your father was obsessed with controlling others. And such an obsession is a type of passion all its own. Think about it," she urged. "You'll see I'm right."

Kit squeezed his eyes closed. At Rozalinde's bidding, pictures appeared in his mind—scenes of his father controlling him, controlling others. It *had been* a passion to him. The earl had centered his entire life around control. And Kit was his father's son. . . . The thought was a disturbing, confusing one—to imagine his cold, unfeeling father having a passion for something, an obsession that eventually destroyed people around him. . . .

Kit got up from the bunk, sat down heavily at the table and leaned on his forearms, staring at nothing.

"It's an ugly irony." Rozalinde's voice came from behind him. "But it's true, that a person could fix his entire life's passion on depriving others of pleasant feelings. I believe he—"

She stopped speaking as Kit turned suddenly, crossed the distance between them in a single bound and crushed her against his chest.

"By God, but you have the right of it." He gripped her as if his life depended on it.

"Yes," she breathed, trying to wiggle free so her nose wasn't squashed against his left nipple. "It makes our passion reasonable in comparison." Her lungs emptied and filled rapidly, making her feel breathless and giddy all over again, despite her earlier fulfillment. Looking down, she saw it was the same with him.

"I promise to wed you as soon as we reach port." His voice cracked on the last word.

"Yes, yes, you said that before." She pulled free of his crushing embrace and moved to where she could kiss him.

Without further words, he took her. But it was as if he meted out his passion in precise, methodical portions. He entered her carefully, sliding his entire length into her, making her gasp with pleasure at the feel of him, it was still so new. His measured motions, for all that he controlled them, sent her mind spinning into oblivion, until all she knew was the surge of feeling as he buried himself within her, then withdrew, only to return with renewed intensity. But it wasn't enough. It was too reserved.

Rozalinde exhaled deeply as he immersed himself once more and buried himself with a slowness that made her want to scream with frustration. Heaven above, how could he do this? His mind acknowledged his sorrow, but his body, his heart, did not. Unconsciously he still repressed that passion his father condemned him for having, that his father had himself, in a different form. With a groan, she realized she hadn't reached him yet.

The thought ebbed abruptly. She hadn't imagined it possible for her to be aroused again so soon. But she was. Troth, but she felt like the powder in a cannon, teased with the slow match until the final moment when the blazing instrument would thrust to her center and she would burst into flame. Her breath came in short bursts and she felt sweat beading at her hairline. But Kit—his chest and back were cool and dry to the touch. He wasn't even panting.

It made her so angry, she thrust her hips against his, grinding, seeking to pleasure him as he pleasured her. Instinctively she lifted her legs, twined them around his. She felt his answering shudder.

"No!" He raised himself on his elbows to look at her

and cradled her cheek with one hand. "I am in command of myself. There is no release until I permit it."

"Then permit it," she cried, struggling to create that penetrating friction between them. "Don't hold back from me. If passion is what you have for me, I want all of it. Stop controlling."

He stopped instantly and stared at her strangely. "You want me to be uncontrollable, like an animal?"

"Yes," she almost shrieked, thrusting herself against him, taking him deeply within her so that he groaned involuntarily. "But you're not like an animal. I want you desperately. I want you to want me, too."

"I do want you," he said, mystified. "I couldn't be doing this if I did not."

He grinned at her and moved his hips, making her writhe with excitement at the way he impaled her.

"Then show me," she insisted, reaching up to maul his shoulder with her teeth. "Show me how much."

A ripple of darkness descended over his features. "Just this once, then."

She smiled at that and prepared herself. But she couldn't have been ready for what happened next.

He began slowly. But within seconds he had caught the contagious thrill of her excitement. He began to pump against her, setting a rhythm of furious intensity.

Roz moved eagerly in response. With one arm she encircled his neck, pressed her face against his neck and urged him on. Just as she thought she would be overcome by the unbearable torrent of flame he aroused, she felt him swell inside her. Exulted by the feeling, her desire flung itself to meet his. With that, they erupted in a mutual storm of fulfillment, his body surging against hers, the power of it building. Together, they crested the waves and reached their pinnacle.

Roz was so exhausted, she slept after. She hadn't meant to slip into unconsciousness, but with Kit's arms around her, sunk in that glorious feather bed, she was gone in an instant. A rosy haze of pleasure surrounded her, and for the first since the voyage began, she felt a curious peace. Her last thought as she gazed at Kit, then let her lids close, was that tonight was a beginning. . . . She fell asleep with a smile of satisfaction on her lips.

Kit let her sleep, gazing down at her face. The frown she wore so often was far away, her expression sweetened by repose. It was better she should sleep, he thought, drawing away from her stealthily so she would not wake. There was practically nothing for supper. With a small nod, he dressed and went on deck to check the helm.

Sometime later, Rozalinde awoke, alone in the cabin. It was dark, and she wondered what time it was. Groping her way out of the bunk, she felt for her clothes in the dark. Then she remembered. The power of their lovemaking returned to her, and she felt herself blushing in the darkness. "Troth," she said aloud, pulling on her smock and tying it at the neck. She was all but married to the man, why blush.

As she fumbled with her bodice buttons, she shook her head, wondering at this pleasure in the midst of the many troubles she must contend with. Perhaps life's pleasures always came that way, amid difficulty. She must take comfort from them, because violence lay in her future. She knew it of a certain. Trenchard would have his day.

The buttons of her bodice refused to go in their proper places, so she cast it aside. There would be only the watch awake. She would go in smock and kirtle skirt. Feeling in the dark for her astrolabe, she grasped it and left the safety of the cabin.

Kit was dozing. He had turned the hourglass earlier, then settled down in the shelter of the helm, eyes half closed, watching Ruske guide the ship. Some time after midnight, he let himself drift off—and found himself no longer on the *Swiftsure*. No, it was another ship he sailed tonight— the *Elizabeth Bonadventure*. He was fifteen again, fresh out of Oxford. In fact, he'd run away from the servants his father set on him, for he'd won a large wager in cards that night, and having money for the first time in his life, he headed for Bristol.

The ship's master he approached hadn't believed his story—that he was an orphan without parents. But no one would care if Kit went to sea. For a small fee to compensate for his inexperience, the master took him, warning Kit that life at sea would be hard. Especially for a pampered young gentleman. From the start, Kit strove to prove him wrong. Because he knew the truth—no one could set stiffer rules than his father, or inflict punishment more rigorously for breaking them. In point of fact, the captain of the ship seemed tame to Kit in comparison, for all he had to do was what he was bid, and that was to work until he dropped each day. It was easy compared to the confining rules made by his father, the worst of which applied to the concept of pleasure. Whatever he did in life, he was not to admit pleasure, not to show the signs of pleasure—no laughing, no singing, no jesting, no embracing. Such things were signs of emotional weakness and were driven away by beatings. With his captain, Kit was never beaten unless he failed in his duty. And that never happened but once. Knowing the requirements, Kit was scrupulously careful after that, doing his work thoroughly and with goodwill.

Once accepted by the crew, each task was a joy to Kit. His sense of humor surfaced, and because there was always a rollicking song on his lips and a jest to be shared with a shipmate, he became well liked. The comraderie he experienced on board ship deepened, the men became friends and family—friends to toil with, friends to visit the ale-houses and taverns with, where they spent their few shillings and tumbled the prettiest wenches. To Kit, this was freedom. More than that, Kit's stint aboard merchant trad-ers taught him that trade was his destiny. Then one day, when he'd returned to port, on impulse he'd sent a letter to his quiet, ghost of a mother. She was the only being in his life who might care about his disappearance, and he felt a burning desire to share his joy with some living person. He told her everything in that letter, that he was happier than he'd ever been. But he didn't disclose his location. No, his father would be looking for him. For two years he'd moved from ship to ship, finding good captains to crew with, learning the trade. Every other month, he would write to his mother, never letting her write back, but telling her he was well.

At eighteen, he met Courte Philips during a voyage to the Netherlands. The two became fast comrades, and when they once again reached England, he wrote to his mother, giving his friend's address. And lo and behold, along with her reply expressing thanksgiving for his safety and ap-proval at his happiness, she'd sent money—a good deal of it. From his maternal grandmother's will she'd told him.

With it, Kit had bought his first ship, lying about his age to make it legal. He'd named the pinnace *The Raven*.

After that, life treated him well by his standards. Taking Courte with him, he'd made money from his first cargo. But on his next voyage, pirates struck—French pirates off the coast of France. Damn if they would ruin his freedom or take his ship away. Kit fought them like a man crazed. All the hatred he'd felt for his father poured into that battle. He'd fired his culverins, let fly his cannon, and the French had backed off, afraid of this English madman who fought like a devil. Kit had flourished after that. Not that pirates didn't attack again—they always attacked merchantmen. But he bested them, until that time off the coast of Spain with men who weren't pirates. Spanish officials accused *him* of being the pirate, of robbing others. He'd been stupid to trade with Spain. Some did it, but many suffered at their hands when they were in Spanish waters or Spanish territory. They'd killed all his men, taken his cargo. Half dreaming, half waking, Kit ground his teeth together until they grated. He hated the Spanish. Hated them.

Even so, he had returned with his ship intact, bought another cargo, sailed to a different country and continued to amass money. Women drifted in and out of his life. He discovered he could have any female he wanted, just by beckoning with one finger. They came willingly to his bed—tavern maids, ladies' maids. Then he tried the ladies themselves and found them just as willing. Married women were the best—they were eager for his muscular young body, experienced beyond his wildest dreams, and the children he begot, if any, were quietly absorbed into families.

Kit's career advanced further when one year he met Lord Howard of Effingham, his distant kinsman, at Dover. As Lord Admiral of England, Effingham had many connections. Kit arranged to do him several favors. For example, transporting English troops for free with his regular merchant cargos earned him the admiral's appreciation. In return, Kit received an invitation to meet the queen. It had been a heady experience, kneeling at the feet of Elizabeth, seeing her admiration for his handsome figure. By then, he was more than one and twenty; his father couldn't touch him. And the queen thought well of his exploits and invited

him to pay his respects each time he was in London. He'd
done so, taking care to bring her clever or valuable gifts at
each visit, knowing she was both a statesman and a woman,
with an eye for value as well as a woman's vanity.

It was shortly after that and the Spanish ordeal when his
mother had died. Her letters, which he'd received every
month like clockwork, stopped coming. At first he gave it
no thought. He had his own troubles recouping his losses
from the Spanish voyage. Finally, he'd run into his brother
at Whitehall where the queen held court, deigned to speak
to him, ask the damned viscount how did their mother.
Dead, he'd been told. From smallpox.

He'd put it quickly from his mind. He didn't want to
think about his past, so he immersed himself in other
matters.

His mother had floated out of his life as quietly as she
had lived. She was dead and no one missed her. At the
time, he hadn't mourned her. But now he felt a deep sorrow, although for what, he couldn't fathom. He'd loved her
when he was three, four, five, and had probably needed
her. But afterward, he'd done without her.

The wind shifted slightly. Kit felt it in his sleep and
stirred, coming awake where he sat, propped against the
wall behind the helm. Opening his eyes groggily, he
blinked, focused on the upper forecastle deck ahead and
above him.

She was there, moving in the wind.

Kit's eyelids snapped open. He sat up, pulled himself
hastily to his feet. Patches of mist floated across the ship,
and a hazy figure in white fluttered on the forecastle deck.
It couldn't be ... Kit started to his feet, then stopped.

Her long hair played about her face, teased by the wind.
Shifting his position, he tried to see her better, squinting
through the haze. She faced him, but didn't seem to see
him. Her chin was lifted as she gazed heavenward.

She held out her arms to the sky, as if making a supplica-
tion to the stars. He wanted to run to her. A flood of
feelings deluged him—like in the dream he'd recounted to
Phillipe. Somewhere inside him the love he'd once had
broke a small hole in the dam that held it prisoner. A
violent gush of it burst forth, taking him by surprise, just
as the dream of his five-year-old past had surprised him. It

stormed through him, upsetting his equilibrium. Pain swept over him. He saw his mother sitting on a bench in the gardens of Lulworth Castle, holding a lap full of roses. A child of three or less, he giggled and teased her, pulled more roses from their canes and tossed them into her skirts until a thorn pricked him and his finger bled. He cried, but his mother threw away the roses, gathered him into her arms in their place so she could kiss away his pain.

The mist thickened. Ten paces ahead and up the stairs, she stood. He need only climb to the forecastle deck to reach her. Surely he could do it. But his body felt heavy, immobile. Painstakingly he put one foot before the other, wanting to go to her, yet afraid. What would he say when he got there? *"Why did you desert me? I needed you. But you did as my father ordered, without protest."*

She lowered her arms. In the shifting fog she stared at him, frozen in place, her white garment fluttering against her arms, her slender body.

He could take no more. The gush of love was too painful. He must rebuild the dam. With a cry he lunged away from the steps, cast himself against the rail, almost going over in his agony. Closing his eyes, he clung to the rail and tried to make his mind go blank, the way he'd learned to do whenever his father disciplined him. Always before he had willed the memories away, shut them out. They would recede, leaving desolation in their wake.

But not tonight. Tonight he couldn't forget them. The anguish washed over him again and again, the loss of his mother. Love, hate, he didn't know which he felt anymore. The memories were agony and he longed to escape their power.

A warm hand closed on his forearm. He looked down.

He started when he saw it was Rozalinde. What was she doing up? She never came out at night, so he couldn't think why ... She had her heavy brass astrolabe tucked securely under one arm. Other than that, she wore her smock and kirtle skirt without the bodice; her feet were bare. The white sleeves of her smock fluttered in the breeze and floating wisps of hair played around her angelic face. Shocked, his gaze darted to the empty forecastle deck above them, then back to her.

"The sky is clear in patches," she said, her voice calm

and rational. She pointed to the deck above. "I got a good sighting of the pole star. According to my calculations, we'll see land soon."

Kit turned away and leaned heavily against the rail. It must have been Rozalinde he'd seen. Not his mother's ghost. He was being ridiculous and fanciful.

Without warning he whirled on her, gathered her in his arms, astrolabe and all. "Come back to bed," he bid her hoarsely.

He carried her to his cabin and laid her on the bunk. Taking the astrolabe from her, he placed it on the table, then stripped off his clothes. She had risen to sit on the bunk, and he motioned to her. "Now yours."

She rose to stand before him, slim and proud. Like in his dream, her kirtle whispered to the floor. Her smock slid down to expose her white shoulders, her full, shapely breasts gleaming ivory in the half dark. Lower the smock went, and lower still, baring the sensuous tuck of her waist, the firm swell of hips and buttocks, her long, slim legs.

But it was not like the dream. This woman was real, comforting. He gathered her to him so he could feel the firm globes of her breasts pressing against his chest. Cupping her buttocks, one in each hand, he reveled in the feel of her, the profound sweetness. He wanted to pleasure her, give her excitement and release she'd never before known, with a man or with any other pastime or person in her life. Yet what he'd shown her in lovemaking heretofore failed to fulfill his intentions. What would?

Intently he contemplated the question, all the while enjoying the allure of her body. With his lips he showered her neck and lips with kisses. He filled his hands with the richness of her ample breasts. By heaven, but the feelings she gave him when he held her in his arms—he was the mightiest man on earth.

But that was it, wasn't it! She wanted power. The power to be who she was, what she was, without changing. Instinctively he realized what she would like.

"Come, sweet," he panted, his knowledge raising his excitement to fever pitch. Seating himself on a stool against the wall, he drew her toward him, indicated she must straddle him, one leg on each side. "Let me show you how to love me."

Her eyes widened, and he looked into their velvet depths. He had apparently shocked her, for she didn't move.

"'Tis your fondest desire and well you know it," he teased, softening his voice to a caress. "You wish to control me, and in some things you shall."

"I don't believe you," she whispered, standing stark still before him. "You want a subservient woman."

Kit threw back his head and roared at that. "You, subservient? If you obey me, it's only because you decide my orders are acceptable and what you would do anyway. Admit it, Rozalinde. If you must settle for a master, I'm a damned reasonable one."

"You're not. You're as likely to do your own choosing as not."

"Then don't trust me."

"I didn't say I don't trust you."

"You didn't have to. You don't trust me." He was silent, letting his words sink in. "You were right when you decided *I* don't trust you. But you are no more trusting yourself. Now I'm offering you control in our lovemaking. Take it, Rozalinde."

She seemed determined to do as he bid her. For she set her jaw firmly and straddled him where he sat on the stool. Grasping his shoulders with both hands, she lowered herself slowly. The ecstasy of her body assaulted him as she guided him toward the place. His body pierced her, then entered her tight, wet depths.

"Troth," she murmured, throwing back her head so that her hair hung down her back, tickling his knees. The motion bared her throat, and he leaned forward to kiss the cool, ivory column of flesh.

Placing his hands around her waist, he rocked back and forth, maneuvering their bodies, making his passion flare unbearably.

"Oh, troth," she murmured again. "Don't stop."

He stopped instantly. "You must decide how it will be. Fast or slow. Gentle or hard."

"And what if I'm too gentle to suit you? Or too slow? You'll change things to suit yourself."

Their eyes met. For the first time he recognized her vulnerability, her fear of being dominated, running through

her thoughts as deep as the sea. It surprised him—why had
he not noticed before? Surely that was what made her testy
with him, resistant to his orders and insistent on her rights.

But he would show her. With a disarming shrug, he invited her. "'Tis your decision, Rozalinde. Enjoy me any
way you like."

Her expression of distrust didn't change. But she did
begin to move against him. Experimentally, at first. Then
more surely. She began by testing the different motions she
might make, rising slowly, then letting herself fall back into
his lap. After about the fourth time, he moaned, closed his
eyes, and leaned back against the wall. It was heaven.
"Might I use my hands?" he asked, determined to give her
all power.

"Permission granted," she rasped roughly.

Her breath, he noticed, came in tight, short gasps. She
moved against him more quickly. Languidly he reached out
and gathered a handful of her lush left breast. With his
thumb he smoothed the rosy peak. He could feel her entire
sheath, her thighs, quiver with pleasure. He reached for the
other peak.

Her speed increased. He didn't think he could last much
longer, yet he wanted to be there as long as she needed
him.

"Tell me when, sweetheart," he panted as she rode him
more wildly. "I'll do my best."

"Oh!" She grasped his shoulders so tightly, he started.

Then she gave a savage scream of pleasure and dug her
nails into his arms. At her signal, he released his pent-up
passion and thrust upward. Their mutual groans of fulfillment rent the air. With one last cry she collapsed against
his chest.

They sat there for some time in the afterglow of their
lovemaking. Rozalinde huddled against his chest. Gently he
smoothed her face and hair, pleased with the result of his
decision. If this didn't convince her, nothing would.

"We're near land," she whispered. With one finger she
traced the line between his beard and his shaven cheek.
"I'm quite sure."

"How do you know?" He smoothed her hair, marveling,
as he often did, that the curls sprang back beneath his hand.

"Mmm, I love your arms, your shoulders." Her fingers glided over his upper arms.

"Don't change the subject. How do you know we're near land."

"I can smell it."

An hour later, Kit sat up with a start from where they slept in his bunk.

"Land, ho."

The distinctive voice of the lookout drifted to him through the cabin door. And with a smile of pride on his lips, he looked down on the sleeping Rozalinde.

Chapter 22

Rozalinde was more relaxed after that night. And to Kit's way of thinking, it was a blessing she was. Their following days of bad luck put him in the foulest temper ever.

Mounting the steps to the forecastle deck the next day, Kit propped a booted foot on the lowest rung of the rail, leaned against the top rail, and prayed for a place to land. But no, fortune wouldn't oblige him. The coastline of this godforsaken country was made up of nothing but wide, barren sand flats. They had sailed steadily south for hours, and no where could they approach shore. The expanses of sand were backed by dunes. Beyond, he glimpsed an occasional lagoon or marsh flat. There was probably fresh water there, lurking among the sea grass, but they couldn't get to it. All along the shore, sand shifted into dangerous bars, creating treacherous traps for a ship with a hull as deep as a galleon's. With each passing minute, he felt the fuse on his temper grow shorter, and his ship's company, down to the last man, shared his state of mind.

The low-hanging sky was the color of dull, unpolished pewter. Pushing back an irritating lock of hair that the wind kept blowing into his left eye, Kit watched Wrightman who stood on the channel-wailes and dropped the hand lead line into the water, hauled it up to read the little tags of red and blue cloth or leather to determine the depth. They had found a landing place earlier, but the inhabitants living in the small village didn't like foreigners. Especially those who arrived in a galleon equipped for battle. Their small landing party had been filling their casks at a spring when they were driven off by a gang of men with pitchforks and guns. Kit wanted no trouble, so they had sailed on. They'd gotten little water for their trouble. Thoroughly irritated and frustrated, Kit left the deck and sought his cabin.

Rozalinde greeted him as he entered and pushed a cup into his hands.

"What's this?" He stared morosely at the contents.

"Drink," she insisted, pressing it toward his lips. "I know you didn't have any of the water brought back. I saved you some of mine. How many others went without?"

He didn't tell her nearly a dozen, and the rest had scarcely a swallow. He drained the cup and banged it on the table.

"For once you don't argue?". She went back to her books and charts, settling herself comfortably before them at the table.

"Where are we?" Kit changed the subject, leaning over her shoulder while he loosened his shirt collar.

Rozalinde closed her book with a snap. "We have a good way to go if we expect to find a stream or river."

"We are near one thing we want." Kit went to stand by the bunk, stripped off his doublet and shirt, then loosened his trunk hose. Within minutes he stood naked before her. Sinking into the soft feather mattress, he held out one hand.

"Come to bed," he coaxed.

Later, as she lay languidly in his arms, drowsing, she counted the black hairs in his arm where it lay, drawn tightly across her waist. His hair was so dark, his flesh also a shade darker than her own. She wondered which of them their first child would favor, then caught herself.

"Talk to me," she whispered, moving in his arms to see his face. "I require distraction."

"A topic for the lady," Kit answered. "What shall it be?"

Roz blanched and looked away, unable to speak. His words reminded her of Trenchard.

Puzzled by her response, Kit gave her a pained stare. "Why don't you talk to Phillipe? Mayhap he can please you."

"Not likely," she countered, rubbing her hips against his. It was too tempting, with both of them naked.

"Caterwauling wench." He bent to kiss her.

"Varlet," she whispered as his lips dropped lower, searching for her ear beneath the riot of her hair.

"Ah, I know your trouble." Kit roused himself after a few minutes and left the bunk. "You're hungry. It makes you shrewish."

"I'm not shrewish." Roz flopped onto her back and crossed her arms over her chest.

He went to his seaman's chest and rummaged for something.

"What are you looking for?" Roz sat up in the bunk. "Don't let it be another lemon."

"It's not a lemon." Laughing, Kit came back to the bed. "I've just the thing for such a moment as this. Saved it for you."

It was a disgustingly stale hunk of biscuit. Roz took it without thanks and ground away at it with her teeth until a chunk crumbled into her mouth. "It'll take me all day to eat this."

"Good. 'Twill keep your mouth engaged."

"If mine is engaged," she said between gnawings, "you talk. Tell me about your mother."

"There's not much to tell." Kit's tone was dismissive. "She was timid and self-effacing. Did whatever my father told her. When I went away to sea, I eventually wrote to her. I don't know why. I didn't really care about her by then. It was out of respect for the memory, I suppose, for how I once felt."

Roz chewed thoughtfully. "Does it make any difference, realizing how you once felt?"

"Hardly." Kit withdrew his arms from around Rozalinde and crossed them behind his head.

She liked looking at the broad, muscled planes of his shoulders, the way they sloped down to his chest. It gave her gooseflesh all over. Hastily she hid the reaction by flopping over on her stomach, resting her chin on folded hands. "Tell me something about her. What did she look like?"

Kit seemed vexed by her question. "She was small and thin," he snapped, brushing a fly away from his face and closing his eyes.

"Like me?"

"Not like you." Kit opened his eyes and gave her a short examination. "She was smaller, and her manner was differ-ent. Her coloring was perhaps the same." He eyed Rozalinde with a wary eye, seeming to compare. "Her hair was brown. I got my dark hair from my father, along with a lot of other traits I don't like."

"Her eyes?" Roz went on, determined to ignore his negative comments. "Do you have your mother's eyes?"

"Her eyes were ... I forget the color."

He said it so quickly, Rozalinde knew he was lying. "Never mind," she soothed. "Tell me something you did together. Tell me something she said."

"I don't remember anything she said."

He closed his eyes tightly, a stubborn look on his face. Rozalinde let him sit there. Be that way, she thought silently, willing him to remember. She wouldn't interfere.

A second later, Kit's face relaxed slightly, his mouth curled up at the corners the slightest bit.

"I do remember climbing the cherry tree in the kitchen garden," he said, his voice low and tentative. "I was probably less than three."

Rozalinde stuffed her wadded smock against her lips to hide her smile of triumph. There *were* good memories. She'd felt sure he had some.

"I'd seen the kitchen boys climb it all week long to pick cherries for tarts and jam," Kit went on, eyes still closed. "I was mad with impatience, waiting for my mother to propose one of our rare walks outside so I could try it." He frowned a moment. "She had to wait until my father was away, you understand, though I didn't realize it at the time. And I wasn't allowed to go alone. At any rate, when I finally got to the tree, I was dismayed to find I was too short to reach the lower branches. My mother lifted me up to them, laughing as I remember, at my wish to climb. I probably would have fallen on my head if she hadn't kept hold of me, but she did. She kept a firm grip on my middle and refused to let me go higher. I recall howling something fierce when she made me come down."

Kit fell silent and Roz studied him anxiously. All signs of his smile had disappeared, and she wondered if she dare prompt him. It might destroy his concentration and bring him out of the memory. She sat very still, trying not to distract him.

Finally he opened his eyes and gazed at Rozalinde. "There, I remembered something. Satisfied?"

Roz pursed her lips, realizing the memory was deserting him. "How did you feel?"

"Then or now?" he asked harshly.

"Then."

"I don't remember. But I did sense my mother was always nervous, afraid of something. Later, when I was older, I thought back on it and realized we were never together in my father's presence. In fact, if I was with her and a servant announced his return, she would send me off with one of the maids. She was afraid of being caught coddling me. That wasn't permitted. She was to treat me impersonally, to give mundane orders for my care to the servants and then ignore me, like everyone else does their children."

"Where was your brother?"

He shrugged. "I don't remember much about him, except that he usually got me into trouble when he deigned to come around." He grimaced. "When I was six or seven, I often went to bed with a black eye from him and a sore backside from my father or the tutor he kept for us."

"Doesn't it help to remember how much she loved you?"

"No." His voice was sharp as he rose from his chair and caught up his shirt. "She gave up too easily, let my father make the decisions of how to raise me. No matter where the thoughts start, I always end by remembering that."

"But look at the man who made her do it. How could she fight him? He was her husband."

Kit looked at her, clearly stung. "You take her part? She couldn't overcome her husband's will to care for her child the way she thought best."

"No, she couldn't. Not if he sent her away." Roz bit her lip and waited, wondering if he would see the logic of her statement.

Kit stood. Looking away, he pulled his doublet on over his shirt, donned his boots, and went out without another word.

Rozalinde turned back to her books. It seemed hopeless to overcome his animosity. He might have loved his mother, but that love had been killed by a circumstance that hurt him as badly as a betrayal. It pained him so deeply, he had forced his entire past from his mind. He didn't remember much of anything about his youth, and what he did remember was devoid of feeling. She washed her hands of him, at least for now. Burying her nose in her books, she sought solace. He didn't remember how he felt, but she, Rozalinde, hurt for him. A young boy, all alone, in the care of a harsh father, with no warm thoughts or feelings to call his own.

Kit hunted with his men the next day. While he stalked his prey on the shores of Jutland, Roz worked. Seating herself at the wide desk in Kit's cabin, she arranged before her the silver ink pot, the sand caster, and several fresh quills taken from her trunk. The sheet of paper lay smooth and blank before her, bidding her begin. Trying to forget a throbbing headache that tormented her, she prepared to start.

What would it be today? Not location. She'd figured their position so many times even she tired of it. Once she had determined their latitude, it was child's play to chart their course every inch of the way down the coast of Jutland, on to Germany and the Netherlands. She must make another selection. Something to soothe away care.

The instant she lifted the tiniest corner of her thoughts, the ugly images of her worries escaped from the place where she'd locked them. They bombarded her consciousness. With a moan she rubbed her aching temple, then shoved them back. She must not acknowledge them. Tidal calculations were the answer. Pulling the white sheet closer, she dipped her quill.

For several minutes there was no sound in the cabin except the usual noises of timber and rigging and the rasp of quill tip crossing paper. Since they were headed for Enckhuysen, she would figure for the bay there. With bold strokes she prepared the table, then began filling it with numbers, guided by her almanac. It was September now. From her pen flowed a neat list of the days and their corresponding figures. Neap tide. Ebb tide. Tidal intervals. Water rising and falling, dictated by shifts of the moon. On the twenty-second, which was also her birthday, came the day of spring tide—the highest tide of the lunar month. A time of equinox, when days and nights drew out in equal measure, light and dark, half and half. So orderly, the progression of days, the law of tides. Why couldn't her life now be measured and orderly, like it once had been? In her father's London house, her days had been reassuringly systematic, devoid of trouble. Now, despite the deceptive calm on board the *Swiftsure,* her future threatened.

Irritated with her own volatility, she returned to her work. Volume of their ship's hull came next, along with how deeply it rode in the water. Yet concentrate as she would, the numbers failed to deliver their usual soothing dose of mental numbness.

Ceasing her work, Roz stared at the little compass box to her right. Like most compasses, it was topped with a wind rose, the flower to which Kit likened her. Was he right about her nature? Did it matter if he was?

Automatically she named the rhumbs of the wind showing on the compass rose, just as she always did, starting at the twelve o'clock position and moving clockwise: Tramontana, Greco, Levante, Syroco, Ostro, Garbino, Ponente, Maestro. Two of these winds would blow them to the Netherlands. How long would it take? One more day, two at most? When their voyage ended, no more could she indulge in an idealistic dream of love and healing. Reality yanked firmly at her sleeve, bidding her to admit its sordid truth.

And the truth was, love could make little difference in her life. Here on board the *Swiftsure,* she thought she loved Kit. But back in the everyday world, it would disappear.

Rozalinde let her gaze travel to the map pinned to the wall. She tapped the quill against her cheek, trying to understand her own apprehension. For one thing, she was a realist, wedded to responsibility. And her responsibility loomed pressing and definite before her in the form of her family—her parents, her younger brothers and sisters—people who had meant everything to her for as long as she could remember. They wouldn't survive without her care— not that she had a distorted idea of her own importance. They wouldn't perish without her, but they could suffer considerably if ruin overtook their finances. She must prevent that.

Balanced against it, on the other side of the scale, was Christopher Howard—Earl of Wynford and lord of her heart. But that was all nonsense. Here, at sea, cut off from reality, it was one thing to play at love when their daily activities were dictated by the need to pursue the necessities of life—food and drink and the correct course at sea.

If Kit was dictatorial about those things, it could be justified as necessary for their survival, or so she had told herself. Even then she chaffed as she obeyed his orders.

Once back in England, she knew what would happen. She would again feel the urge of duty, of all the things she considered important and pressing in life, and Kit would interfere. He would tear her in two by requiring she serve him first—his needy insistence that she proclaim her love for him proved it. Whether he would be controlling about the business itself was difficult to know. He might wish to run it, to merge it with his own business endeavors, or he might not. Without question he would object to her going off daily on her own, devoting her time to shop and warehouse decisions. A husband was supposed to be the center of a wife's world, she thought dismally. And suppose she had children? He would expect her to stay at home and tend the nursery. Her siblings had never been a drain on her energy because neither her father nor her mother had ever dreamed of tying her to them. The thought of losing her freedom for such a reason was excruciating.

No, it was impossible. She needed her independence. In fact, upon her return to West Lulworth, she would need to set out for London immediately, to meet with the company shareholders and undo the harm caused by Trenchard in stealing their cargo. West Lulworth had never been more than a temporary resting place for her family while her father's health improved. A Merchant Adventurer needed to be in London, at the center of commerce.

The very thought of Trenchard made her writhe with anguished impotence. Since the night of the storm, she had purposely pushed him from her memory until she would be in a position to take action against him. Now that time was near at hand. She would have to deal with his many betrayals.

With a whack she threw the quill on the table and began to work her hand, meaning to relax the writer's cramp from the last hour of scribbling. But the hand clenched and squeezed like a claw, reminding her of the anxiety pent up inside her. It looked exactly like her stomach felt.

With a groan she covered her face, wanting to deny it all.

It isn't fair, she thought rebelliously, immediately realizing the childishness of such an idea. The world wasn't a fair place. Many times had her father reminded her of that fact. But he softened it with his loving admonition to treasure her family, to remember that people she loved and who loved her in return would give her truth and fairness. Other people felt no compunction to provide such things.

But that was the crux of the trouble. If Kit couldn't love her, if all he felt for her was passing fancy or physical passion, they would eventually land in a situation where he would fail to grant her truth and fairness, simply because a man who didn't love would not feel obliged to consider her needs and desires. There was no guarantee she could teach him to love as deeply as she herself was capable.

Given all these facts, could she really wed with him? It seemed pure madness.

Pushing back her chair with a nerve-grating scrape, Roz abandoned her work. She was sorely in need of someone to talk to. Opening the door, she went in search of Phillipe.

While Rozalinde wrestled with these dilemmas, the man she feared most stood outside the presence chamber of Fernando Alvarez de Toledo, Governor of the Netherlands and Duke of Alva. George Trenchard straightened his best green doublet, then glanced at his grave companion. "Is there always such rain in Antwerp?"

"Always," replied Francisco DeVega tersely. He pulled repeatedly on the blue ribbon hanging down his chest that dangled the medal of the Order of the Golden Fleece. "'Tis generally worse in spring, when everything floods. I prefer Seville with its sun and citrus fruits."

Trenchard did not bother to reply. He practiced his speech to the Duke of Alva again, running through the long version he'd prepared, then the short version, then answering the questions he anticipated. Idly he glanced around the chamber, barely seeing the gilding on the plaster garlands above his head, the carved, polished wood ornamenting the walls, doors, and windows of the Hotel de Ville, where the duke resided when in Antwerp. The guard on duty at the duke's door coughed, shuffled his feet and shifted his pikestaff.

"Are you certain that messenger was trustworthy?" DeVega's voice cut irritatingly into Trenchard's meditations. "I don't like to think—"

"The good fellow will undoubtedly go to his grave carrying our secret," Trenchard replied, not bothering to turn around. He'd never said anything truer, he finished silently to himself.

There was a moment of quiet in the lavish room, during which the sound of the guard's cough resounded.

"Will you ask the duke for a recommendation to His Majesty King Philip?" DeVega interrupted again.

Trenchard swung around angrily, having been in the midst of another rehearsal of his speech. "You have that backward. The question is, will the duke heed His Majesty's recommendation? I should think he would."

"Then you'll sail with me on the *Gran Grifon* when we rejoin the rest of the navy?"

Trenchard snorted, deliberately failing to display appreciation for the invitation. "You need me for assurance. To save your hide again if need be."

"I just want—"

The door leading to the duke's presence chamber swung open. Two men in rich burgher's garments exited. The guard saluted them, then stepped forward to announce Trenchard and DeVega.

Introductions made, Trenchard arranged himself before the duke and waited expectantly. He disliked standing at attention beside this underling. Yet he must do it to gain access. Here resided the seat of all authority belonging to the King of Spain in the Netherlands. The hardened Spanish duke looked just as Trenchard had imagined—aging figure regal, lavish garments befitting a duke, the king's trusted appointee and a ruthless military commander. His many brilliant victories in the field attested to his power. And he was slowly, gradually defeating the plodding Netherlands burghers who understood nothing but the making and selling of ordinary goods and the continual need to drain their land so it would not be claimed by the sea. George noted the gray hair of wisdom at the duke's temples, the quick, penetrating movement of his eyes as they entered, eyes that were alert, assessing. He was aware of everything about them. Now if only the duke would bid him speak.

With impatience, Trenchard watched the duke turn back to study the papers before him, taking his time, making them wait. Finally he raised his gaze back to them. His praise was brief.

"DeVega, you delivered His Majesty's latest communiqué. Well done. It has been translated." He sifted through the stacks of papers, withdrew a thick sheaf covered with close writing.

DeVega bowed slightly and said nothing.

Trenchard fidgeted, wanting to nudge the admiral with his right foot. *Say something, fool,* he thought grimly. *Silence does not aid the man seeking advancement.*

"We are pleased the message via sea arrived safely," Alva continued. "But I am told the simultaneous messenger sent by land did not make his destination." The duke fixed his penetrating gaze on DeVega. "His body was found last night at Ghent, in the back room of a tavern. He had been drinking and wenching, a fatal combination. His message was not on his person, nor was it with his belongings in his inn room. We must assume he was robbed by our enemies, who may now learn our plans."

DeVega stared, expressionless, and said nothing.

Trenchard thought with satisfaction of a certain well-placed dagger. "Begging the pardon of Your Grace," he ventured, feeling emboldened by his successful treachery. He took a risk, speaking impromptu when the duke hadn't addressed him. The duke's gaze snapped to him instantly. "Anyone having the fortune to secure the message would be unable to translate it." He knew this for certes, for he'd tried himself. "They would never learn King Philip's intentions."

"You are the Englishman His Majesty spoke of?" The duke's tone was neutral, noncommittal.

"Aye, Your Grace, I am he. And prepared to make myself useful." Trenchard gave his most graceful bow. "As I have done previously. His most sovereign Majesty has been most pleased with my contributions. And I, with his tokens of appreciation."

The duke studied him with a deliberate eye, then turned back to the translated communiqué. "We determine that the time is ripe for confrontation with our unruly subjects in the Netherlands. Ships, troops, and supplies are all in readiness, awaiting the order. My network tells me the Prince of Orange moves north toward his stronghold cities

in Holland and Zealand. The Gueux de Mer, his disorga-
nized rabble of a navy, will unquestionably sail down the
Zuider Zee in the coming weeks to meet him. His Majesty
bids us seize the moment—we will move forward with our
plans." His gaze roved back to peruse Trenchard, studying
each line and curve of his face, penetrating his thoughts.
"His Majesty specifies that he sends us special support. You
offer what?"

The muscle in Trenchard's eyebrow jerked. The duke
acknowledged his potential worth as well as challenged,
both at once. "As I assume His Majesty mentioned me
in the communiqué, I am happy to say I possess special
information about the composition of the Sea Beggars navy
as well as details about their one English supporter." He
spoke clearly, concisely, in his best accented Spanish. He
could thankfully speak it better than he read it.

Alva seemed to consider this for a moment. "We will
permit you to sail with Lord DeVega on the *Gran Grifon.*
Tomorrow there will be a meeting with our chief naval
commander, Count von Bossu. Be there, both of you." He
dismissed them, turning back to his papers, as if they were
gone already.

Trenchard backed out of the presence chamber, bowing,
pleased with the outcome of the interview. He hadn't been
able to give his speech, but the result was still favorable.
Maximilian de Hennin, Count von Bossu, was a Dutch loy-
alist supporter of the Spanish king and chief commander
of the combined Spanish-Netherlands fleet in Dutch waters.
Bossu would call on him for his information and include
him in plans for the battle. He, Trenchard, would be part
of a surprise, fatal attack on the Sea Beggars. And he felt
confident the Spanish would win.

Back off the coast of Jutland, Rozalinde found Phillipe
shortly after leaving her cabin. He was on the quarterdeck,
skinning a rabbit. Kit's hunting party had bagged several
with bow and arrow and delivered them to the ship. Then
they had gone out again, meaning to stock the ship's larder.
Two or three rabbits were nothing to feed twenty hungry
men. . . . And one hungry woman, Rozalinde thought, stopping several yards off to watch the way Phillipe's strong
hands deftly handled the blade. Rozalinde recognized the

knife as one that usually hung in Kit's cabin, in a sheath on the wall. The metal flashed silver in the sun as he worked, peeling back the soft hide to expose the inner core of flesh.

"Come here, Rozalinde, and talk to me."

Phillipe's deep voice startled her. Apparently he knew she was there, though she'd come up quietly behind him, treading gently on the stair.

Feigning a nonchalance she didn't feel, Roz circled around him, careful her shadow didn't block his work. Squatting down on her haunches, she settled herself. His face hovered over his work in concentration, the craggy features set in relief by the rays of the sun. She watched his bushy eyebrows knit together as he scrapped the cony.

"You are chaffing, *m'n dochter*?" He sent her a brief, sideways glance.

"No. Er, that is . . . yes," she admitted, feeling miserable. "I don't want to go back."

He stopped the skinning to scan her, then returned to the rabbit. After a few more minutes, he separated the pelt from the rest, in one clean piece. "If we could dry it properly," he said, placing the brown fur on the deck and smoothing it, "I could have it made into a muff to warm your hands in winter. You would look *heel bekoorlijk* carrying it. It would match your brown hair and eyes."

A ghost of a smile haunted Rozalinde's mouth.

Phillipe glanced up again, his blue eyes assessing her before he refocused on the cony and began to cut its carcass into pieces. "You are worried," he stated. "I don't blame you. You have more than your share of troubles. But you must lay your plans and move ahead. Brooding doesn't help."

Roz shook her head dismally. "I used to do just as I pleased. But now . . . now . . ." She couldn't bring herself to put words to her thoughts.

Phillipe summed up for her swiftly. "Life will change when you wed."

"Yes," Roz acknowledged. "That's it exactly."

Phillipe's knife bit deeply into the rabbit's flesh, severing legs from body, quartering the parts. Rozalinde felt a raw clutching in her belly and bile rose in her throat. She couldn't face being married. The prospect made her ill.

Phillipe seemed to sense something of the kind, for he finished with the rabbit and, setting aside his knife, wiped his hands thoroughly on a rag. Drawing Rozalinde to her feet, he encircled her shoulders with one broad arm.

"Rozalinde, you will never know unless you take the risk. You must take the step fortune dictates. Otherwise you will wonder for the rest of your life about what might have been. And love is a precious thing—*uiterst kostbaar.*"

Roz rubbed her cheek against his shirtfront. It felt comforting in his arms, just the way it did when her father held her. "But marriage does not necessarily mean love," she said sadly, toying with one of his mother-of-pearl shirt buttons. "Sometimes it means the man is the master; the woman, his property. It could be unbearably . . . restrictive," she said finally, unwilling to explain her fears more fully.

"In truth?" Phillipe looked skeptical. "Is that how life was with your father? Restrictive?"

"Of course not," Rozalinde said decisively. "My father and I work together. We have discussions. If we must make a decision and I have information, I share it with him. He shares any he has with me. He often tells me the history of a particular person or transaction so I will understand it better. We consider various options. Then we decide."

"We?"

"Yes, we," Roz said, feeling slightly impatient. "I don't work alone. We work together. Even if he's not there, I have him in my thoughts every moment, in everything I do. I consider how he would act or how he would think about a particular difficulty." She tapped the side of her head. "I imagine I hear his voice, discussing the problem. I know what he would think."

"In truth?"

Rozalinde leaned back against Phillipe's arm so she could look into his eyes. "You don't mean to imply things might be that way between Kit and me? They can't be, you know. He's too controlling. When he tells me to do something, I'm to jump. If I don't, he chides me."

"When did he chide you last?"

"Just the other morning, about working with Wrightman. The fellow is dull as a post, but Kit has it in his mind that it must be this way. 'You both gain immeasurably by engaging in this activity.' " She mimicked the haughty tone Kit had used when he instructed her. "'Tis a great jest, really, but it doesn't matter what I think," she went on in her own voice. "I'm to do what I'm told. If I didn't, I would end up in the hold with the bilge water and the rats."

At that, Phillipe threw back his head and laughed. He looked and sounded so much like Kit, Roz pulled away from him. "I mislike your answer," she muttered, crossing her arms and turning away. "It's of no help."

"I am sorry, *m'n rozekleur*." Phillipe obligingly turned his laugh into a cough, then stopped it altogether. "I do not mean to offend you. But does this Wrightman learn nothing?"

"Oh, he learns." Roz retreated to the side of the ship and stood, clenching and unclenching her fingers on the top rail. "Though I have to beat it into him with a vengeance. He may be a dull post but even wood takes an impression if pounded long enough."

For a second Phillipe looked as if he were going to laugh again. Roz turned away to examine the shore. "I've never liked teaching," she went on, picking out points of the landscape as she spoke, thinking she saw a movement by the faraway trees. Perhaps the hunters were returning. "I'm too impatient. Numbers make perfect sense to me, but most people consider them a mystery. People fear things they don't understand."

"You have the right of it. People fear the Beggar King, because he is a mystery."

Phillipe's voice floated to her from behind but she refused to turn so she could see him. "They love him, too," she insisted, sounding petulant to herself but refusing to regret it.

Phillipe chuckled low in his throat. "Those with a clear conscience love him. Those with evil deeds to their credit fear him because he's known to champion the rights of the weak against the powerful who abuse their strength."

"I wish I could do that."

"But you do." Phillipe leaned on the rail beside her. "You help Wrightman."

The blood rose to Rozalinde's face. "I hadn't thought of it that way. You mean he'll have a worthwhile occupation if he keeps at it. Before, he was a common seaman with no special skill."

"Ah, so he is learning."

Roz nodded her head with some embarrassment, lowering her gaze to the deck.

"Do not be troubled, *m'n vriendin.*" Phillipe's massive hand wrapped around Roz's where it lay on the rail, his touch warming. "We learn our worth and that of others through experience. But let me tell you. Wrightman is a changed lad since you began tutoring him. He works at his numbers all day, even when he is not with you."

Roz ducked her head, discomfited by this revelation.

"You didn't know, did you?" Phillipe smiled at her. "You also did not realize that he strives desperately to please you. Your approval means more to him than did his captain's, and that's saying a good deal. But then Wrightman is not a slow lad. He recognizes genius when he sees it and considers himself fortunate to study under you."

Roz felt herself blushing furiously. "I have no such thing."

"Do you not?"

She turned back to him. "Whatever I have, it has gotten me in a great deal of trouble."

"It will get you out again."

"But I shall have to wed with Christopher, in which case I won't be able to use it. I would refuse him—"

"—but you have already given him your promise," Phillipe finished for her. "I know. He told me. But think, my dear, what would you have without him?"

Roz wrinkled her forehead. "Independence."

"You have that already," he said gently. "You carry it here," he tapped his own chest, "in your heart."

Rozalinde looked at him, frowning in her effort to understand. His words made sense when they discussed it, yet when she found herself alone with Kit, reason fled.

The lookout in the fighting top yelled out a joyful greeting. Looking down on shore, Roz saw the hunters returning. The younger ones cavorted and capered. A fresh deer swung on a heavy branch, slung between two men. Fresh venison for supper tonight. The saliva rushed to Roz's mouth and she swayed on her feet for an instant, feeling faint at the thought of the rich food after their meager fare.

The meat was delicious, just as Rozalinde anticipated. The cook set to work at once, and everyone devoured their fill of food for the first time in a handful of days. All that afternoon, men sat, reclined, some even slept, scattered over the decks of the ship.

Now it was early evening and Rozalinde sat on the quarterdeck, having consumed two huge trenchers of stew until she thought her stomach would rupture. Everyone drank their fill as well, and though they had no wine, good cheer reigned. With a sigh of contentment, Roz gazed out over the heads of the men, realizing that for the first time there was no hostility from them. For their various reasons, because of things she'd done and things she hadn't done, they had changed their minds about her. She was no longer bad luck.

That was a relief, she thought, as she smiled at Tom, the young man with whom she'd shared her water. Jock, the old fellow who had eaten her bread, raised one hand to salute as he passed a bucket of water with a dipper among the men. Even Ruske acknowledged her from his perpetual post at the helm, sending her a friendly smile over the heads of the others.

She continued her silent inventory, involuntarily seeking Kit among the men. He was up on the forecastle deck, mingling with them. As she watched, he turned, seeming to sense her looking at him. Their gazes meet across the distance.

He made his way to her slowly, taking his time, chatting with this man and that, assuring himself of their comfort. At last he mounted the steps to the quarterdeck and paused where she sat, with her meager skirts spread, a cup at her side.

"Mistress Rozalinde, would you grant me the favor of walking out with me?" He knelt on the deck in mock gallantry, put one hand to his heart. His other hand captured hers and he bent over it. His lips made a warm imprint on her flesh, and a quick shiver ran through her as he drew her to her feet.

"I should like to walk with you," she answered, "but we cannot walk *out*. There is no *out* where we can walk."

"There is," he said in her ear, leaning close. "Allow me to show you. This way."

He led her to where the longboat waited, riding the waves in the leeward shadow of the *Swiftsure*. Gently he helped her down the rope ladder and into the boat. After seeing her safely to the prow, he seated himself and began to row.

"Where are we going?" Roz twisted around to watch their forward progress.

"You need not know everything," Kit chided as he turned the boat north.

Rozalinde settled back to watch Kit. The oars moved in his powerful hands, first cutting graceful arcs in the dark water, then rising to pass through the air, leaving a shimmering half circle of drops on each side of the boat.

Roz sucked in her breath and held it. She felt acutely aware of him, sitting so near, only a few feet away. With his back to her, she could satisfy her wish to observe him— the way his fingers, well shaped and strong, closed over the oar grips, the beautiful tensing and bunching of his arm and shoulder muscles beneath his shirt as he leaned into a stroke. He had rolled his shirtsleeves to the elbow, baring his darkly haired forearms. Those muscles rippled, too, as he worked them. A giddy feeling swam in her stomach, as if she'd taken a dangerous draught of intoxicating liquor. His masculinity whispered ominous words in the growing dusk, words that frightened and thrilled simultaneously.

He didn't stop until they reached a small stream. At first she didn't see it, its entrance was so hidden by water weeds. Kit forced the prow of the boat through the clogged path until they entered the clear expanse of the estuary. Here the stream widened as salt water changed to fresh. A full moon had risen. It shone on the broad stretch of water, turning everything to fine, shivering silver. Vegetation on the shore was drenched with light.

The boat's hull ground against sand as they approached the bank. Kit leaped over the side of the craft and drew it ashore.

Wordless, he held out his hand for hers.

Her feet met with sand. She watched him secure the boat, then turned away. The shore, so barren during the day, had become a landscape of magic by night. Night animals and insects crept through the lush deciduous growth. The contrast of moonlight and black shadowed forest lured her, and she strayed along the stream bank, taking in the welcome sights and sounds of land. Sitting on a log, she drew off her shoes and stocks so she might enjoy the grainy touch of sand against her bare feet. A clump of marsh grass rose in silhouette against the pale sand. Something on wings, a night bird or perhaps a bat, flapped across the moonlit sky. After too many days at sea, she inhaled the rich smell of moist land.

A splash sounded behind her. She whirled, wary. Darkness closed around her and for a second she was frightened, alone. Anxiously she sought Kit, her protection. He was knee deep in the water, and by the grace of heaven, he was entirely without clothing.

Rozalinde stifled a cry as she stared at his body, sleek and muscled like that of Neptune rising from the sea. The spirit of the water god seemed to possess him, making her want to commit rash acts. Greedily she drank in the sight of him, just as she'd drunk her first water some hours ago. His form spoke of magic—the proud set of his head supported by wide, strong shoulders, the tapering, muscled torso, the juncture of his thighs where his masculinity lay at rest.

"Come here," he called softly. His hand moved through the water, causing ripples to flow toward her. She watched the sweeping rings widen, one after another emanating from his hand until they broke against the sleeping shore.

The water felt cold and fresh to her skin as she waded in, let it lap over her feet. The moon shone overhead, and slowly she shed her clothes, gazing down at herself pensively, avoiding eye contact with Christopher. Wadding her garments together in her kirtle skirt, she flung the bundle so it landed on the shore, then turned to face him. There was no going back. Loosing both braids, she tossed them over her shoulders and took the plunge.

The rush of cold liquid shocked her senses, made her skin tingle. She burst through the surface, laughing and spluttering. "Thank the good heavens for water. I'll never take it for granted again," she cried, splashing great handfuls of it in silvery arcs toward the moon.

Kit came up behind her, his shadow dark on the surface of the stream. "I've seen men die for lack of water."

"Where?" Roz stepped back to find him unexpectedly close. Her body brushed his.

Paying no heed, he sedately lowered himself into the water. Unlike her brash assault on the water, he took it slowly, in no hurry to wet himself.

"The Mediterranean," he said, his voice dismissive, as if he would not speak of it further. Stretching out his body, he floated, as easily as if born to it. "Can you swim, Rozalinde?"

"No. Can you?"

"Aye, I can. You should learn, you know. Sailing so much. How is it your father failed to teach you?"

"It wasn't seemly," she said, gesturing the idea away with one hand. "Where would we have done it? Down on the Thames, near Whitehall? Near London Bridge, so everyone could watch? No, he never taught me, though I know he could swim himself. I remember his talking about it, swimming with his brother when he was young."

"Come here," Kit ordered. He rose out of the water, dripping.

For once it seemed natural to obey him. Roz came and stood before him. She was borne up by some exuberant emotion, something she couldn't name that burned within her—an aching wish to give him the joy he'd never known. His life was made of searing loss and sorrow. Putting her hands in his, she beseeched whatever gods ruled the night on that isolated stretch of Jutland for the miracle of change.

As Kit's fingers closed around Rozalinde's, his gaze took in her beauty, the way the light of the moon gilded her skin, turning it to purest ivory. His pulse quickened. He wanted to possess her, to make her his in every sense of the word. He knew she was but a woman, bound to betray him. But at that moment he didn't care. He wanted her with a fierceness that defied caution. He could only pray that when the pain came, it would be brief.

That thought of pain forestalled the kiss he had been tempted to give her. No, he would teach her to swim first. It would give him such pleasure that no betrayal on her part could steal away, either now or later. Guiding her arms, he showed her the strokes.

"Like this with your hands." He demonstrated how to push the water away with cupped fingers. "Like this with your legs." He stood on one foot, lifted his opposite leg high out of the water to show her, making her giggle at the froglike motion. "You try. Each separately at first."

Rozalinde experimented with the motions, splashing in the shallow water. She began to get the idea of it. First arms, then legs, then both together. In water that came barely to her waist she managed to lift her feet off the sandy stream bed and swim a dozen feet to Kit. He caught her and pressed her tightly against his chest, and she could feel his need, urgent against her thighs.

She laughed, wriggled out of his grasp, her skin slick with water. Gaining her feet, she backed away from him, smiling in a way that reminded her of the night at Lulworth Cove.

He came after her, strides firm and unwavering. "Come here, Rozalinde."

"You come to me," she teased, retreating steadily, her back to the shore, her face to him.

He followed relentlessly.

Rozalinde was in deep water, backing toward an overhanging bank, when she bumped her leg. An old tree lay half in the water, thick with water weeds, captured debris, and rotting vegetation. Its branches probably extended under water, which explained what she'd bumped.

But the water felt strangely thick and slimy here. Roz recoiled at the texture, took a step away. But it was too late. Something sleeping in the mud awoke.

A massive weight collided with Roz's body. She screamed and staggered backward as her footing gave way. Panic struck as she felt herself falling, water closing over her head.

This descent was different from her earlier, exhilarating plunge in the water. This time she felt the water's death grip as it invaded her unprepared air passages. A searing pain slashed into the calf of her right leg.

Frenzied, she fought both water and attacker, made contact with a thin, snaking body. Then Kit was beside her, thrashing in the water, working to protect her. Fear for his safety tore through her, as painful as the wound in her leg.

A second later she found her footing, broke through the surface of the water, coughing and choking. Whatever her attacker might be, Kit fought it. She could hear water churning nearby while she struggled for breath. If only the thing would stop. Staggering from the wound to her leg, she flung herself away from the log, still coughing water from her throat and nostrils. The liquid miracle had become a curse, threatening to choke off her breath.

Kit stood more than a boat's length away with dagger drawn. He plunged it again and again into the water. Her eyes widened with horror as she made out the form of some sea creature, trailing clouds of blood in the water as it swam away.

Her breath came in a jagged sob.

Each gasp of air drawn into her raw throat and nasal passages burned, white hot like the tear in her leg. Then Kit was gathering her into his arms, carrying her from the water.

"Troth," she whispered as he put her down and checked her over. "I hate the dark."

"Eel," he said shortly, his breath coming in shallow rasps. "Grown large and daring, living were there are no men. It wanted you to feed on. Sweet heaven, it's torn your leg."

She moaned when he touched the spot.

"I must bind it. I'll use my shirt."

"Don't!" She sat up, though the movement made her dizzy. "Don't ruin your shirt. My leg is fine," she insisted, sinking back again.

"It's not," he scolded. "Sit still and let me bind it. Enough of your stubborn arguments." The shirt tore with a raw, crackling sound.

He was gentle as he bound her leg. But Rozalinde chafed under his ministrations. She hated being cared for, being at someone else's mercy. In the Cavandish household she was the one who gave the care. When he finished, she pulled herself to her feet and reached for her smock.

"Let me dress you."

"I can do it myself, Kit!"

He got to the smock first, though, and if she wanted it, she would have to wrestle him for it. Which was beneath her dignity. "I prefer to dress myself," she insisted. "I hate being coddled."

He looked at her strangely. "Is that what I'm doing? Coddling you?"

He held out the smock and she snatched it, pulled it over her head while he watched. He didn't say a word as she stepped into her one petticoat, arranged her kirtle skirt, and buttoned her bodice. Gathering up her shoes and stocks, she headed for the boat.

At the water's edge, he started to hold out his hand, then lowered it to his side. "Am I permitted to help you into the boat?"

She swayed her way to the bow without his aid and sat down.

Giving her a last moody glance, he pushed the craft off from shore and hopped in. "When we return to the ship, you're to wash that leg and bind it with fresh linen. I have some in my trunk. My shirt is none too clean after hunting today. Then I'd see you eat once more and straight to bed."

His words, his mood, made Roz's fears well up. They threatened to suffocate her like the dark water.

Without looking over his shoulder, Kit rowed them back to the *Swiftsure*.

Chapter 23

Roz had trouble falling asleep that night. She finally drifted off, but woke later, tears streaming down her cheeks from a bad dream.

Dark. The interminable dark from her childhood had rushed over her. Shifting waters closed over her head. Suffocating, she had struggled for breath.

"No!" she cried, sitting up so suddenly she struck her head on the top of the bunk. Her leg throbbed dimly and, realizing where she was, she leaned against the wall of the bunk and sobbed brokenly. She was safe from the eel, but she was not out of danger. It followed her relentlessly in many forms.

One of them lay beside her on the bed.

Kit shifted as he came out of sleep and turned toward her. One hand sought her on the pillow. When he did not find her, he sat up.

"What's wrong?" He groped for her groggily, still half asleep. "Does your leg pain you?"

"No." She huddled against the wall, letting the familiar creak of the moving vessel soothe her. Then she remembered. Kit had ordered the anchor hoisted when they returned to the ship that evening. The sails were unfurled and they moved south. It was all her fault their sojourn was ended. They hadn't even finished stocking the ship with food.

"Lie down. You must rest if you're to heal." Kit's hands swept the bunk, searching for her.

He didn't reproach her, she thought guiltily. He was capable of kindness, it seemed. He did not remind her of how she'd ruined their stop for provisions, of how stupid she was, blundering into an eel's lying place. She'd only meant to tease Kit. But foolishness did such things to you. It got you in trouble. It always had Jonathan. It certainly did her sisters, Angelica and Lucina. But Kit's kindness didn't help now. It twined confusingly with her fears, augmenting them. She didn't want to belong to a man. She slid away from him farther, toward the foot of the bed.

"Rozalinde, come back and lie down. You have no reason to resist me except your own irascible temper."

He was angry now. She'd made him angry. They would argue, and she couldn't bear it. "I am perfectly well," she snapped, trying to keep her voice from trembling as she crouched against the far wall. "You can go back to sleep."

His fist hit the wall. "Damn you, Rozalinde, you make me furious. Whenever I offer you help or comfort, things most women would be glad of, you act as if I'm trying to poison you." He struck the wall again, venting his ire. "I'm tired of it! Do you hear?"

His voice rose to a shout, and she cringed against the wall, knowing she shouldn't provoke him. But the dream hovered within her, enveloping her in its horrifying embrace. She stumbled up on shaky legs, moved across the cabin, as far away from him as possible.

The blackness of the cabin's interior increased around Rozalinde. Each gasp for air brought her nothing. The dark, Kit—they merged synonymously in her thoughts, both threatening to overwhelm her. She didn't want to be possessed. "If you're tired of it, then leave me alone," she lashed out at him. "You always want what you want, when you want it, and nothing I want matters. For once would you leave me be?"

"I can't," he raged back at her. "God knows I would like to. I swore I wanted no woman in my life, at least none beyond casual alliances in bed."

"And that's exactly how you treat me," she cried, stricken by his revelation. "When you require stimulation, you come to me. When you're done, off you go, forgetting me along with the rest of the women you've had."

Roz drew a long, shaky breath after her speech. She'd accused him of something terrible, something she didn't even realize she believed. But if Kit didn't love her, wasn't that all she meant to him? She was no more than a physical pleasure, which was passing and temporal.

He seemed to be mulling over her last statement, for his

silence was oppressive. At last he cleared his throat. "You are perhaps justified in accusing me, because I have said I am not capable of loving you the way you would like. Yet that does not mean you are just like the other women I've had, and I admit there were many since you seem to know all about my past. But I swear to you, I have considered you different from them. I am willing to make you my wife, and none of them—"

"Oh, I'm supposed to be gratified that you didn't want them. Just because you finally deign to wed with the woman you bed, I'm to be eternally grateful. I'd be better off a spinster. It was my plan. My life was complete without a man."

Just as she'd expected, his answering anger lashed back at her. "Then why did you agree to wed with me?"

"Would you let me disagree?"

"No," he ground out through clenched teeth, "I wouldn't. Because *she* left me. Don't you understand? I won't let you go."

His words had a stunning effect. Roz went still all over. She hadn't realized it. Not consciously, at least. But now that he said it aloud, it made perfect sense. Her own fear wilted as she took in the vastness of his pain. It was far deeper than hers. She struggled only to remain free, to retain her independence in the face of being swallowed up by another. But Kit, she realized, had been a prisoner for years, condemned to a loveless life. "I won't leave you," she said. The words sounded silly to her ears, but she meant them. As she crossed the room in the dark, she bumped against the desk, bruising her thigh. By the time she fumbled her way to the bunk, she couldn't find him.

"You will." His voice wafted to her out of the blackness of the cabin. It was like a raw wound. "Mayhap not physically. But eventually, this love you claim to feel will evaporate. It's quite clear from the way we quarrel. One day you'll withdraw it and it will be done."

Roz searched with both hands. Damn it, where was he? "I gave you my promise."

"Such a promise means nothing. I most assuredly wouldn't hold you to it. When you are done loving me, it won't matter. But I won't let you go."

She couldn't find him. The darkness was complete and

she felt for him blindly. Then she realized he'd moved to the opposite end of the bunk, sat in her previous position, huddled against the wall. "I've given you my heart," she whispered.

He laughed harshly. "Empty words. They mean less than your promise."

"No." Tears started to her eyes. She extended her hands to him, seeking but not finding. "You don't believe that. Tell me you don't."

Seizing her suddenly out of the darkness, he crushed her tightly against his chest. They clung to each other for a long time, rocking to and fro, both suffering the pain of unshed tears.

Roz stirred first. Hesitantly, she cupped his face in her hands and kissed his cheek.

Kit responded before he could stop. He'd sworn to harden his heart against this woman. He didn't want the sorrow she would bring, but he couldn't help it. The lure of her body, the warmth of her spirit, the aching need he had for this abstract concept she called her love—all of them drew him undeniably. His fingertips feathered against her flesh, seeking her breasts. "It doesn't matter what I believe," he lied, weaving a pattern of kisses through her hair. Feeling her heart quicken beneath his hand, he dropped his kisses to her neck. Someday, when she stopped loving him, he would have no choice but to bear the pain.

Rozalinde tensed for only a second at his onslaught on her senses. Then she relaxed. For all her fear, it was nothing compared to his. She had feared the way he released her passion, because each time he did it, he claimed another part of her. Eventually, she had believed he would own her entirely, robbing her of the very freedom he offered to give.

Yet it was nothing compared to his fear. She knew what love was—had experienced its nurturing tenderness from her mother, knew its proud guidance and support from her father. But Kit did not. His pain sprang from the fact that he hungered desperately for something he believed ultimately didn't exist.

Their lips met, and she kissed him fiercely, arching her body against his with an urgency that was frightening. She would let him release her passion, let it fly free like a bird.

Their desire progressed rapidly. Within minutes Kit was

parting her legs, feeling that she was wet and ready for him. He'd told himself to go slowly with her, but his own need was too great. Tonight he'd almost lost her. He'd seen her go down in the water, dragged by an unseen assailant, and his heart had threatened to break from his chest, he'd been so shaken with fear. He wouldn't lose her to an animal or an accident. No, she might some day destroy his faith in her, but until then, he would possess her utterly.

And as he buried his length in her, he heard her answering moan, followed by the words of love she whispered. And though he knew they were meaningless, he craved them more than anything else he could name.

At dawn the next day, the shores of Germany appeared to those on board the *Swiftsure.* By late afternoon they were within sight of the outlying islands of the Netherlands archipelago. Phillipe flew his admiral's flag from the top mast, and the *Swiftsure* was readily admitted to the north port town of Enckhuysen located at the head of the Zuider Zee. There, gathered at the quay, was the entire fleet of the Sea Beggars. Rozalinde spotted *The Chalice* anchored among them and longed to go straight to her ship.

She was soon disappointed in this desire. In his maddening way, Kit issued strict orders for her to stay on board the *Swiftsure* while he went ashore. She was to prepare for her wedding. Without waiting for her argument, he disembarked with Phillipe.

As she watched the two men disappear among the throng crowding the busy Dutch quay, Roz felt depressed and disillusioned. Here was proof that Kit insisted on the role of master. Her decision to wed, made in the midst of an idyllic journey, now seemed a miscalculated answer to a confusing equation—try as she would, the answer still came up wrong. *No,* should have been her answer. Instead, she had said *yes.*

Standing before Kit's tiny looking glass, Rozalinde inspected herself critically, wondering how she was supposed to prepare for this wedding. Her hair trailed limply over her shoulders, her linen smock had turned a nondescript shade of gray from its repeated encounters with salt water and soap. She would look a fright for this occasion she decided, wrinkling her nose at her appearance. Worse, she had no special gown to wear.

Troth, she thought rebelliously, quitting the mirror and going to gaze morosely out the porthole. She was not vain, but even she desired a garment to do her wedding credit. And a bath first, so the gown would not be sullied. Oh, for her own ornamented tub at home, replete with delicious steam as Margery poured hot water before the fire in her chamber. And the fragrance of sweet lavender soap, made fresh in her stillroom. The comforting scents and sounds of home teased her, making tears leap to her eyes as she thought of her father.

A knock sounded at the door. At her bidding, Tom entered—the young man to whom she had given her water during the voyage. A bucket swung from each hand. Water sloshed on the floor as he crossed the cabin and set them down. Two other crewmen followed bearing a brass hip bath. Roz eyed them with surprise.

"Master ordered it," Tom explained, noting her expression. He emptied first one bucket, then the other, into the bath, followed by an abrupt about-face and a retreat for refills. The other men lit the brazier, and soon it burned merrily, dispelling the room's moisture. Much as she resented the "orders," Roz watched with anticipation as Tom and the other men brought bucket after bucket to fill the bath. It would feel heavenly to wash.

"'Tis steaming hot, Tom," she remarked when he announced his last trip. She plunged one finger into the water, pulled it out again. "Would you boil me to soup?"

Tom's cheeks turned the color of a fall russet apple. "Nay, mistress, I mean your ladyship." He stumbled and stammered, embarrassed at his confusion over how to address her. "Cook said to make it hot. I was just followin' orders."

"So you were," Roz said more gently, wanting to put him at ease. "I only made a jest. Is it not allowed, for me to jest with you?"

"Oh, aye." A new flush crept over Tom's face, darker than the last. "'Tis honored, I am. I-I think most well of your ladyship. I mean ... we all do."

Roz found her own color rising. "Did your captain instruct you to pay compliments to his wife?"

Tom regarded her with genuine astonishment at the suggestion. "Begging your pardon, but he didn't never. We would give you your due as his wife, no matter what we thought. But we like you for yourself, an' it please you."

Roz's expression must have flustered him, for he strove immediately to apologize.

"Begging your pardon, your ladyship ... I mean, mistress." He shuffled his roughly shod feet on the floor. "I shouldn't have said so, but 'tis the truth of it. When you gave your water to me, and your bread to Jock, 'twasn't necessary. But you did it just the same."

He meant every word. Roz saw that he did, and she relaxed, feeling gratified. "You don't want to dump me overboard anymore?"

"Oh, no!"

The young fellow's eyes grew so round and horrified, Roz had to fold her lips in a solemn line to contain her laughter. She had no wish to lose this new friendship, so she thanked him and sent him on his way.

He paused at the door.

Roz had placed one of Kit's shirts on the bed—something clean to wear after her bath. But it was stiff and unpleasant to the touch from many washings in salt water. And the lad still lingered at the door. "What is it?" she asked, smoothing the shirt's wrinkles.

"Might we, that is, the crew would like ..."

"Out with it," chided Roz. "What would the crew like?"

"We'd like to give you a revel," he declared impulsively. "We've been paid."

He patted his pocket lovingly and Roz realized the triple pay received that morning burned to be spent.

"When you're wed, come back to the *Swiftsure*," he pleaded. "We'll have some victuals for you and his lordship."

"Why, Tom." Roz went closer and stared up into his earnest face. "Did they send you to ask?"

His color heightened once again, which answered her question.

"Then we'll come," she promised. "And you may all visit the church with us if you wish."

"Oh, yes, mistress." He bobbed his head eagerly. "We shall."

So Rozalinde went to church that afternoon, not attended by her brothers and sisters and her parents, as she'd always imagined her wedding would be. Nor was she given away by her father, as she'd dreamed. Instead, her family consisted of thirty brawny ship's men, and she was given in marriage by the Count of Hoorne.

As she walked down the aisle of the tiny Dutch church, clean and freshly scented from her bath, laced into a new silk gown of azure blue with sleeves of primrose yellow that Kit had unexpectedly, gratifyingly, bought her, she gazed into the face of her intended and felt her heart swell.

She had buried herself in logic for so long, emotion felt for a man had frightened her. So she had cast it out of her life, choosing instead to immerse herself in the love of parents and siblings. Her days had been calm and orderly. Given the rewards of work and family, she'd not missed being wed. She had convinced herself she didn't need it, and no man had tempted her from her stance.

Christopher Howard had changed all that. For the first time, she found herself drawn to a man—passionately, illogically, irrevocably. Her generous heart, taught to love by loving parents, had gone out to him joyously. Here was a kindred spirit—a mind that worshiped at the same intellectual altars as hers, a spirit that cherished freedom.

But there the resemblance ended. Where Rozalinde's heart had been opened by nurturing, Kit's had been closed by fear. Where she had been taught to reach out to others, Kit had learned withdrawal as the only protection from pain. The emotions passed to him by his father had been hurt and rage. His life's tutor was sorrow; whereas Rozalinde had looked up to a father who taught her self-respect through his unconditional love.

Could she change what Kit was and what he felt? There was no reason to think so. Yet she did think it.

The swelling tones of the organ vibrated in the tiny church. Roz placed her hand on Phillipe's arm and they began the long walk down the aisle. He wore a new doublet for the occasion. Clearly the men had gone on a shopping foray, outfitting both themselves and her. The warmth of his body emanated through the stiff black silk of his sleeve, and she sought his gaze as they walked, looked into his blue eyes, gratefully received his reassurance that she did the right thing.

They drew closer, and for the first time Roz dared search

the gathered figures before the altar for Kit. He stood beside a man in gray, whom she recognized as Courte Philips, the captain who had called on her in West Lulworth to offer *The Raven*. So, she realized, the fellow had worked for Kit from the start. A spark of irritation jumped inside her, then subsided as she recognized Kit's attempt to protect her on her voyage, Kit's wish to buy all her damaged lace. Her heart was too preoccupied to linger over old grievances. It contracted and expanded, pumping a multitude of emotions through her body, some of them joyous, many of them fearful.

She and Phillipe passed the last pew and stopped at the altar. Before Rozalinde the priest waited. Kit stood a few feet away.

By rights he should have come forward to meet her, but he stood as lifeless as a block of stone dug from Portland quarry near Lulworth. Roz loosed Phillipe's arm and went to him. It might always be her fate to put aside her pride and reach out to him. She risked her entire future, yet she did it willingly. Catching Kit's hand, she placed her palm trustingly in his.

A spasm crossed his face. Alarm filled her at the sight of his fear. But it vanished as quickly as it appeared. Kit again assumed the controlled mask he showed the world instead of emotion. Turning, he led her to their expected position before the priest.

The priest prayed. The brief vows were said. The last words of the rite melted away into echoes in the church, and the crew of the *Swiftsure* gave a great huzzah as Kit guided the new countess of Wynford the way she had come up the aisle of the old church.

As they approached the door, a man stepped out of the shadows. He looked to be in his early forties, tall, auburn-haired, blue-eyed, his dashing handsomeness not the least faded by his age. Stepping forward to tower over Roz, he took her free hand and bent over it in a courtly kiss.

By then Phillipe had spied him and hurried forward to fall on one knee before his prince. Roz felt a great wave of awe mixed with gratitude as she realized her humble marriage ceremony had been attended by William of Nassau, Prince of Orange. It was easy to understand how the man inspired fidelity in his people. The vibrant eyes radiated a warmth Roz sensed as he gazed at her. Then he smiled, and she felt the charisma emanate from him.

"Your Highness, I am honored." She dropped him her deepest curtsy while Kit bowed and the prince raised Phillipe to his feet.

"The honor is mine."

His gaze admired her in a courtly manner, traveling rapidly over the low-cut neck of Roz's gown, lingering on the tight lacing of her waist. Roz blushed hotly, returning his smile. "Will Your Highness honor us by coming to the *Swiftsure* for a wedding revel? We have only meager hospitality to offer, but what we have is yours."

The prince sketched a bow and inclined his regal head. "I would be pleased to join you tonight for pleasure. Tomorrow," he nodded to Phillipe, "we must get down to business."

Roz stepped forward boldly. "You will allow us to aid you? We shall expect to do all we can after the devoted assistance given us by the Count of Hoorne."

Again his eyes assessed her, and Rozalinde felt herself gripped by the intense personality of the man. She was overjoyed when he nodded, accepting her offer. When the time came to fight the Spanish, she would refuse to be left behind.

Back on the *Swiftsure,* night swooped down on them in a rush, overwhelming in its beauty. A slice of moon rose in the inky black sky that hung, full of glittering stars, over the vast bay of the Zuider Zee. Kit's men set off fireworks as part of the promised revel, their flaming lights dazzling against the curtain of night. They ate and drank for hours by the light of wax tapers, toasting one another, Dame Fortune, and God in His goodness for bringing them safely home.

When Roz's heart was too full to speak, Kit hoisted her in his arms and carried her to his cabin, where they made love slowly, deliberately, giving each other such pleasure as neither had imagined possible. After, Roz fell into an exhausted slumber, worn out by this intense culmination of their voyage. *The Chalice,* her revenge against Trenchard, would wait until later. Her sleep was deep and utterly without dreams.

Toward dawn she came awake suddenly, wondering

where she was. In the pale light of morning, she remembered, and felt for the gold ring on her right hand. It encircled her second finger, solid and heavy. She was wed.

The clutch of doubt tore at her. She pushed it away. She would not succumb to it. It was a thing of the past.

Rising quietly from the bunk so she would not waken Kit, she pulled on a silk night robe Kit had bought her. Its amber ripples slid over her bare skin, making her feel bewitched and bewitching. In a pensive mood, she sat herself down at Kit's desk and pulled the Spanish communiqué toward her.

The numbers entered her thoughts, turned about in pleasant arabesques, weaving and twining with other thoughts. Soon the other thoughts dissipated and she entered the numbers totally. Bent over the paper, she traced them with her finger. They made no sense. Yet they did. There was no pattern present, and yet if something had no pattern, there would be another key to its meaning. Her gaze lingered over the groups—sets of three and sets of four. A one, a six, a one. A two, an eight, a one. A three, a three, a four, a two.

She let her mind drift, open to suggestion. Mayhap if she prayed, God would show her the answer. The thought made her remember Phillipe, the Latin words he spoke when she'd heard him at prayer one night. How strange that he must pray in Latin while she prayed in English. Yet God heard them both. She knew he had prayed for the same thing as she, and behold, they had arrived safely at the Netherlands.

And then there were the Spanish, who also prayed in Latin, the same as Phillipe. This wicked Duke of Alva, for example. They probably even used the same Bible. Yet the two had little or nothing in common. It proved that sharing a religion did not cause people to understand one another.

Suddenly Rozalinde gripped her quill so tightly it snapped between her fingers. That was it! Latin. Prayers. She must see Phillipe. Leaping to her feet, she began to dress.

A scant half hour later she was back. She'd found Phillipe easily, thank the good heavens for her fortune. He'd returned to *The Hope,* as she knew he would. He and the prince were sitting up late, talking. They looked up in sur-

prise as she entered their cabin, escorted by the man on
watch. Though Phillipe had thought her mad, he had willingly given her his Latin Bible for her prayers, as she requested. He then insisted she be escorted back to her ship.

Now she trimmed a candle wick and lit it, set the flaring
light in its holder beside the open book. Placing the communiqué before her, she searched the book for the first
number. With one finger poised on the column, she began
to write.

"Rozalinde, 'tis not yet dawn."

Kit felt a vast irritation as he stirred and opened his eyes.
Rozalinde sat at the desk, working. She was always working. "What are you doing?" he grumbled. "You can't have
slept more than four hours."

"Nothing," came the terse answer. Her head didn't come
up. She didn't stop.

So be it. If he wanted to know what she was doing, he
would have to get up. He would chide her a bit and cozen
her back to bed.

The predawn air was chill to Kit's skin after the warmth
of the blankets. He shivered involuntarily and reached for
his shirt and trunk hose. After pulling them on, he groped
for his stocks on the floor. His shirt released the odor of
perfume that he'd brought Rozalinde earlier. It smelled of
new spring roses, the scent his mother had worn.

In a dim little Dutch apothecary's shop, he'd found it.
At first he'd turned away, wanting to avoid it. Choose an-
other, he'd told himself. The apothecary had many scents.
It need not be that one.

But he'd been drawn to it, until finally he relented. He'd
been born of that woman and all his feelings had died because of her. He would think of her as he wed with another
woman, to remind himself of the vulnerability of the heart.

When he'd returned to the *Swiftsure,* ladened with gifts
for his intended, he'd found Rozalinde nude and tempting
in the hot tub of water. Uncorking the little bottle, he had
rubbed its sweet contents all over her swelling curves. Her
hair was wet and tangled from washing, and he combed it
out for her, scenting it with the perfume. He'd never ren-
dered such service to a woman, and as he did it for the
first time, he realized he liked it—enjoyed the feel of her
hair drying in his hands.

Now, in the darkness of early morning, he smelled the scent of roses and remembered his intimacy with Rozalinde. Pausing behind her chair, he leaned over her shoulder and kissed her cheek.

She looked up and pointed wordlessly to the book.

"Latin," he murmured, glancing down. "Where did you get that ..." He stared more intently at the book, then at her writing. "You've done it! You've broken the code. Rozalinde!"

With a whoop he wheeled about, pulled up a stool and reached for her pen. "It will go more quickly if I write while you read the letters. The Spanish are eternally pompous, even with their secrets. They'll go on for pages. I pray you," he said, gesturing with the quill. "Begin." It was then he noticed she was grinning at him.

"You agree to take *my* dictation?"

"It means nothing," he growled at her in mock anger. "I concede nothing to you."

She arranged the Bible and communiqué side by side, in meticulous order. "Not even my genius?"

He grinned back at her. "You *are* a genius. But you're also an irrepressible saucebox. Begin."

Rozalinde read off a set of numbers, then searched for the place in the book—the chapter, verse, and word. She read off the word's first letter. The pen scratched in Kit's hand. He stopped to dip it in the ink pot and Rozalinde paused, continued. She read another set of numbers, matched them with the indicated section of the Bible, found the correct letters. Slowly, an intelligible message unfolded beneath Kit's hand.

"By heaven!" He stood up abruptly, knocking over the stool. "It says the Spanish intend to attack us two days hence. They intend to take the Beggar Fleet by surprise, conquer it, and assassinate the Prince of Orange."

"No!" Rozalinde strained to see Kit's writing. "Why didn't you say so sooner. We must finish the letter. There will be important details."

Fighting his impatience, Kit righted the stool. They labored painstakingly until the letter was finished. Just as the sun slipped over the horizon, Kit sent a messenger to Phillipe and the Prince of Orange, telling them the news and setting the hour that day for a council of war.

The council was held on board *The Hope*. Rozalinde refused to be left out. She sat in a corner and listened to the men, the captains from each ship of the Beggar Fleet, Phillipe, Kit, as they hammered out the details of their strategy. The mayor of Enckhuysen joined them, along with the captain of the garrison. All that day they pored over maps, sent messengers into town to amass supplies and weapons, assembled men to stand at the ready on land and men to fight at sea.

Rozalinde fell into bed at noon and slept for several hours, the dreamless sleep of exhaustion. When she got up, she retrieved her tide charts of Enckhuysen, read them over, then went out to check their accuracy on the bay itself. By night, she was exhausted, having spent all afternoon on the water in a small boat, rowed by Tom from the *Swiftsure*. She had checked depths over and over with a lead line, rowing up and down the city's shores. She measured, she memorized landmarks. That night she slept soundly. There was going to be a battle, a surprise attack the Spanish hoped to spring on them. But because of her efforts, the Dutch would be ready and waiting. And despite Kit's orders to the contrary, despite their raging argument on the subject, she intended to be there.

Chapter 24

On the fifteenth of October, just as the communiqué stated, the Spanish fleet was sighted. It sailed en mass down the mouth of the Zuider Zee, proudly displaying the Spanish cross on each sail, set upon conquest.

Huddled at the windows of the *Swiftsure*'s charthouse, Rozalinde waited and watched. Suddenly the sound of cannon fire split the golden calm of the afternoon. Roz shot to her feet and craned her neck to see.

Sun reflected off the blue waters of the Zuider Zee, blinding her with its brilliance. It was deceptive, that cheerful light. Because all around her ranged the ships of the Sea Beggars, armed and ready for battle. She swallowed hard and sat down again. The shot must have been a warning. Enemy ships were not yet in range, though all ships flew the red signal banners meaning they were about to attack.

Roz shifted on the cushions, pounded one fist against her open palm to still her agitation. The waiting hung like a sentence of death over her. She shouldn't even be here— if Kit knew, he'd send her back to Enckhuysen. But she had defied his orders, stowed away in her instrument trunk. There was a reason for its exact dimensions, made to accommodate her body in a comfortable position. But when she finally emerged from the confines of the trunk, she was rewarded only with the sight now displayed before her.

The fleet of the Sea Beggars sat wedged at the head of the Zuider Zee, ships crowded bow to stern in battle formation. To lee and port rose the forest of masts belonging to twenty-two Dutch caravels, the sum total vessels of fighting consequence. To the back of the wedge floated numerous smaller pinnaces, each with a cannon or two, and behind them the miscellany of smaller boats that would scavenge when the time came.

Rising from the window, Roz went to the door, pushed it open a crack. On both sides she observed the ships, crowded with men and boys who strained to see their attackers.

At the entry of the bay, where the land to the east and west narrowed to a slim bottleneck, Roz knew Dutch soldiers crowded the shores. They would aid their rebel navy if the opportunity arose. Any Spanish ship that came within wading distance would find brutal treatment at the hands of these men. To their backs stood men, women, and children of the city, ready to aid them. They were a fierce, devoted people, these Dutch, ready to fight for their town and their freedom.

Having heard the battle plans last night, Roz knew the *Swiftsure* sat toward the front of the formation, just behind *The Hope,* which took the flagship position. But she couldn't see it from her vantage point. Tension squirmed and twisted in her belly as Roz doubted her decision to stay on board. Kit had warned her.

"I'm your wife now. I'll go with you."

He'd bristled at that. "You're my wife. You'll obey me."

"The devil."

"You might see him if you persist in this madness."

"I'm looking at him now." She eyed him furiously.

He burst out laughing.

Ruefully she'd put aside her anger and laughed, too. Kit often ruined her arguments by laughing. "You might just as well let me have my way," she told him firmly. "You know I'll stow away else."

He'd eyed her appraisingly. "You have a propensity for such things."

"Do I have a propensity for anything else?" she teased, encircling his waist with both arms, rubbing her cheek against his chest. She felt sleek and contented, like a well-fed cat. Never had she known marriage would bring out such feelings. He was entirely, splendidly her own, this man. Well, not quite.

Now Roz pushed a sagging braid behind one ear and peered through the door crack, remembering their last lovemaking before the battle. No, it was bad fortune to call it their last. Their most recent, she corrected herself. As she studied what she could see of the Spanish battle formation, she thought of Kit's reserved expression afterward. Must she always endure his mystifying changes of mood?

The wind blew in a steady gust from due west. The lead ships would be within range any minute. Fear ground in the pit of her stomach as she observed the *Gran Grifon*; she felt certain Trenchard was on board. He would be eager to taste the spoils of war should the Spanish prove triumphant. Unconsciously she clenched her kirtle skirt, her thoughts swirling.

Suddenly, the ordnance of the Spanish flagship thundered. The attack began. Rozalinde scrambled back into the charthouse and pulled the door closed, praying for their victory.

The sound erupted in the quiet Dutch afternoon, echoing into the surrounding low lands. Black smoke wafted through the crystal clear air behind the charthouse. Roz chaffed her hands one against the other. This was unbearable. She couldn't see a thing!

She felt the *Swiftsure* change direction. Kit would be on the forecastle deck. At his signal, Ruske had shifted the tiller.

Mentally Roz reviewed the battle plans. The first rank ships in the Dutch vanguard would cut into the Spanish wedge and break it up, clearing the way for the second rank Dutch ships to surround individual victims, grapple and board them. The Spanish galleons lumbered in the water—heavier, bigger, with many more guns. The question was, could the Dutch break their ranks?

Hurrying back to the windows, Roz pressed her nose against the leeward glass. The Dutch ship beside them had dropped back. The *Swiftsure* surged forward, her timbers shaking beneath Roz's feet with each blast of gunpowder. At the same time Roz felt the vibration of the masts. The wind was changing! Closing her eyes, Roz tried to judge its direction. If only she were outside, she would know what to do. Rigging clanked as the sails were adjusted. The *Swiftsure* made its bid. She could feel it move.

Slipping to the door, Roz opened it a crack. To their lee, the *Gran Grifon* towered, majestic with its four top-heavy masts and high-charged decks. The ship moved sluggishly, struggling to maneuver her guns into a better position. The *Swiftsure* circled to her left, nimble in the water. Oh, let them draw the *Gran Grifon* after them, Roz prayed, hanging on to the door latch with all her might.

The *Swiftsure* kept up a constant barrage of volleys, moving east by north. To their portside, Roz could see the other Spanish ships interspersed with Dutch ships. Their tactic was working. The Spanish wedge was breaking up.

As the *Swiftsure* moved toward shore, Roz lost sight of the *Gran Grifon*. Was it following? Unable to stand the suspense, she slipped from the charthouse. Stooping low, she made a mad dash for the quarterdeck. Reaching it, she huddled against the protective partition of the ship's side. Around her the shouts of the men rose as they worked frantically.

A Spanish cannon barked. A thirty-two-pound ball roared through the air above their heads, missing the low-riding English ship entirely. Don't let them strike the masts, Rozalinde prayed fervently from her crouched position. If only she could stand up to see.

One peek over the side stilled her questions. The *Swiftsure* was headed for shore just north of the city, followed at several cables' lengths by the *Gran Grifon*. Even now Kit was bringing the *Swiftsure* about. They would lay to the seaward, waiting for the Spaniard, then double back and pass, shooting as they went. She could see the men of the *Swiftsure* as they gathered in the topsails to slow the ship.

Roz peeked again, realized she was demented to be here in the midst of cannon fire. The *Swiftsure* crew hadn't suffered any hits yet, but they would. It was inevitable. She could hear the screams of wounded men from a distance as she watched the crew of the *Gran Grifon* adjust their sails in answer. The return brought the two ships precariously close. So close, Roz could see the faces of the Spaniards on board the *Gran Grifon*. As the space between them closed, Rozalinde's gaze lit upon Trenchard, standing on the quarterdeck surrounded by Spanish officers in uniforms and half armor. Her heart plummeted as their eyes met across the water and Roz felt determination emanate from him. With maddening calm, Trenchard held out his hand to her. He beckoned. *It's not too late,* Roz could almost hear him saying in his calm, logical voice. *Come, Rozalinde. We were meant to be.*

With a cry of agony, she ducked behind the ship's protective side. She could not, would not think of him or what he wanted. Gathering her wits about her, she scurried for the opposite side of the *Swiftsure,* just as their cannon spoke from the lee. The upward roll of the waves lifted the *Swiftsure* high in the air. She let loose with her culverins and demi-culverins.

Deadly wooden splinters flew on board the *Gran Grifon* as masts shattered and rigging tore. The lower shrouds ripped away on the forward mast and the towering column wavered unsteadily. On the downward roll, the *Swiftsure* let loose with her heavier cannon, hitting the *Gran Grifon* broadside. Now they were close enough that the *Gran Grifon* could fire back. A heavy roll of Spanish cannonade rent the air. Roz turned just in time to see a group of men on the *Swiftsure* disappear in smoke. Their screams were cut mercifully short.

Roz clapped her hands to her face, horrified. Bile rose in her throat, threatening to choke her. This was the end they came to, men she cared for. The rubble of their bodies stained the deck in sickening reality. Tears stung her eyes and rolled down her face as the acrid odor of smoke prickled her nostrils. Roz sucked in her breath and tried to think clearly. How could men experience this hell they called war and not question its necessity? Even she had not doubted it until now. Nay, she had wanted to be here, to help Kit. Groping to keep her sanity, she turned to the one thing left her—her task, her reason for being here. Taking a grip on her emotions, she gaged their distance from the shore, then headed for the channel-wailes where the pilot often stood.

They had passed the Spanish ship to her lee. Now they circled to her portside, ready to draw her toward shore. The heavy galleon followed. Easing herself cautiously over the rail on the side away from the Spanish, Rozalinde took her place on the narrow ledge. She groped for the lead line and dropped the weight over the side.

The water depth was dropping rapidly. Expertly Roz scanned the surface, shutting out the ugly sounds of war around her. Her mind dove swift and deep, remembering the shifting sands of the coast. There would be a sandbar just ahead. They must swing away.

Frantically she waved to catch the attention of a man nearby, then shouted the reading to him. He stared at her in surprise, then leaped to set up the relay. The leadsman was in the sounding station. The ship must respond.

In response to Roz's reading, the ship veered to the lee. They headed for deeper water. Roz breathed a sigh of relief and dropped the lead again.

This time the depth dropped. They could edge back toward the shore. Loudly she called the reading. The man on the deck nodded and relayed the information to Kit, who was out of her sight at the helm. Behind them Trenchard's ship came on steadily. Roz sucked in her breath and held it as she dropped the lead again, then emptied her lungs as she checked the colored tags. If only they could draw the *Gran Grifon* shoreward. . . .

Down went the sounding lead. Up it came. The tags showed depth holding steady. Sand stuck to the wax on the lead indicated what she hoped for. Swiftly Rozalinde assessed the ship behind them, trying to estimate the volume of her hull. She calculated the tidal depth in her head, her many hours spent poring over tidal charts fueling her decision. She said a brief prayer of thanks that she had checked them meticulously the day before and memorized the landmarks. Knowing the exact flood point of the tide told her how deep the water would be this time of day. She knew the *Swiftsure* was the lighter ship and could easily navigate in this water. But the *Gran Grifon* sat deeper. By Roz's calculations, it would be her undoing.

She called out to the relay once more, sending the *Swiftsure* even closer to shore, luring the other ship onward. The *Gran Grifon* came on relentlessly, gaining on them. The ordnance of the Spanish ship thundered. One front-placed cannon was positioned to strike the *Swiftsure*. A huge ball whizzed toward them.

Roz almost shrieked as a ball flew by her platform, within feet of hitting her. Another struck their stern with a sickening explosion of wood. Another volley and Rozalinde heard the cry of a wounded man. She clamped her eyes shut, realizing it was someone she knew. Damn the Spanish and damn George Trenchard. He would cripple their ship, kill their men, then grapple and board.

Determinedly she opened her eyes and concentrated on the water. She lowered the lead, took the reading, called it to the relay to pass on. Straight sailing ahead. The sea bottom was rich in sand. The bar she memorized yesterday lay just ahead.

Roz gripped the lead line and held on as the *Swiftsure* reached the sandbar and began to cross. Around her the sounds of battle shattered the day. Screams of wounded men and crashing of cannon rocked the harbor. The water was littered with debris from ships—broken masts and rigging, barrels and other goods fallen overboard.

Staring down into the churning water, she imagined the bar beneath them as they crossed. She counted the seconds, pleading with God for speed.

Tensely she turned to watch the *Gran Grifon* follow. The other ship was so close she could see George Trenchard on the quarterdeck, sheltering his massive body behind the mast. Even at this distance his eyes focused on her, and she clung hard to the wales, her body shaking uncontrollably. He would have her within minutes if her calculations were wrong. A sob escaped her throat as she cast her gaze away and clutched desperately to the rigging stretched against the side of the ship.

The hull of the *Swiftsure* rasped a warning against the sandy bottom. Roz saw the relay look at her inquiringly, waiting for her to order them to the lee. But her calculations were not wrong and she shook her head, trusting her knowledge. The complete layout of the ocean floor unrolled in her memory. She could see every sandbar and shoal of this bay in her mind. Holding her breath, she waited for the inevitable.

The cannon of the *Gran Grifon* thundered again, bombarding their ship. Trenchard's mouth creased in an ugly smile. Triumph shone in his eyes.

It was then the *Gran Grifon* faltered in her course. Roz squinted, trying to be sure. The distance between the two ships widened.

Roz let out a whoop of triumph. "Run aground!" she cried to the relay, whose face lit up with understanding as he looked where she pointed. Quickly he turned to deliver

the message to his captain while Roz collapsed on her platform, weak with relief. "We've done it," she choked out to
Kit when he appeared a second later. She found herself
ecstatic, multiple emotions streaking through her. "Look."

Kit hesitated, one arm reaching to help her over the side
of the ship.

Men swarmed on the deck of the *Gran Grifon*, throwing
things overboard in an effort to lighten her. But to no avail.
The huge ship ground to a complete halt.

"We did it!" Roz cried as Kit turned back to her, looking harassed.

"Get over this side. The battle's not done." He grasped
her arm roughly. "I've ordered the ship to come about. We
must take up our position to her lee so none can escape
before the men on shore capture her. Our anchor will go
down in a minute. I want you safely in my cabin by then.
They'll bombard us with cannon for as long as they can."

Roz resisted his grasp. "I don't want to stay in the cabin.
I want to stay here and watch."

"You'll do no such thing. You'll come in . . ." He froze,
his face molded into wary lines.

Roz stopped her protest. Turning around, she followed
the direction of his gaze. As she looked, Trenchard and the
other men of the *Gran Grifon* launched a longboat that
was piled with open barrels. An instant after it touched the
water, Trenchard stepped to the side of his ship and flourished a lighted torch in one hand. He gave a mocking bow,
then with a swift movement tossed the torch into the lowered boat. The blazing torch came to rest crosswise, across
the top of two barrels.

A man dangling from a rope against the side of the *Gran
Grifon* gave the longboat a mighty shove. It coursed swiftly
with the tide toward the *Swiftsure*.

The barrels were undoubtedly full of tar and pitch, for
they burst into flame. A whoosh of hot air seared the
afternoon.

"Fireboat!"

The cry went up from the *Swiftsure*. Horrified, Roz
stared at the approaching craft. Within seconds it had become a blazing funeral pyre, the steady shore breeze blowing its flames straight for the *Swiftsure*.

With a leap Roz vaulted back over the side onto the

ship's deck, stumbling against Kit in her haste. He clutched her hand and together they sprinted for the stern as the fireboat crossed the short distance between them, sparks dancing on the wind. Its flames licked the air, yearning for the *Swiftsure*'s dry timber and canvas.

Reaching his cabin, Kit opened the door and thrust Rozalinde inside. Without further discussion he slammed the door and was gone. Roz heard him join the men, give them orders to slip their cable. It would take them interminable minutes to accomplish the task that would set the ship free and allow them to flee the fire.

At the leeward porthole, Roz pressed her face against the glass. The fireship drew nearer as she watched. Even within the cabin she could smell the sharp odor of tar burning. The *Swiftsure* was lost. Turning, she fled for the door.

As she wrenched it open, she heard the ugly crackle of flame devouring canvas. From the doorway, she saw the sky above her head blaze. The wind whipped the sail into a solid sheet of flame.

The heat made her shrink back. She must get to a longboat. There were two on the *Swiftsure,* more than adequate to carry all on board to safety. She could see one being lowered from each side of the ship's waist. Casting a last glance toward the burning sail, she hurried for the portside boat.

"Quick, my lady." Tom motioned to her frantically, grasped her arm without ceremony as she reached for him. All around the remaining men jumped over the side into the water to escape the spreading flame. They could climb into the boat later. The heat bore down on them, and without looking Roz knew all the sails burned. But she couldn't jump overboard. She would drown from the dead weight of her wet skirts. As quickly as possible, she hoisted up her skirts and climbed over the side.

She was the last one to quit the ship. Only Tom remained on board, and as the right topgallant broke away from the mainmast and crashed to the deck behind them, he gave a bellow of fear and leapt over the side, hitting the water with a smack.

"Hurry!" he shouted to her after bobbing to the surface. From her rope ladder against the side of the ship, Roz looked down at him, then back toward the waist of the ship.

Kit moved from the helm toward her. Only now that the others were safe would he quit the ship.

"Christopher," she screamed at him, clutching the side of the ship and bracing her feet to keep from slipping. "Hurry!"

His head came up. Even at that distance, she could see the agony in his eyes—he was losing the *Swiftsure*. But his life was more important. She scrambled with both feet, trying to hoist herself over the side. He must escape.

As he crossed the expanse toward her, a mass of rigging broke away from the mainmast, came crashing down in a hail of burning debris. Kit lunged to escape. It looked as if he was clear. A burning spar appeared out of nowhere, caught him squarely across the shoulders. He stumbled and went down.

A scream tore through the afternoon. As Rozalinde catapulted over the side of the ship onto the deck, she realized it was her own cry of anguish. The burning spar had rolled clear of Kit and come to rest at a right angle to his body. He lay on the deck, face down, unmoving. The smoldering length of spar sat within inches of his head.

Roz stumbled forward, then screamed and shrank back as a piece of the mainyard crashed down to her right. She had to get to Kit. Gathering her skirts tightly around her, she skirted the mast and spar until she reached him.

He stirred and groaned as she pulled at him urgently, too frightened to be gentle. "You must come," she moaned, scanning his body for damage. An ugly burn marked his shoulders where the spar had struck. Her hand tightened on him as she saw the back of his head was covered with blood.

"Go without me, Rozalinde. I cannot . . ."

Kit's eyes opened, and he stared into her face, his gaze blue as the Dorset sea.

"No! You must get up. Please, Kit." She tugged at him irrationally, unwilling to admit he was incapable of rising. He was too big, too strong to be felled by a spar. For the first time, she saw his left foot lay at a strange angle.

He must have broken it in the fall, she thought unemotionally. She would have to get help. Whirling about, she scanned the deck, which was littered with burning rubble. To their left, they were surrounded by an inferno.

"Save yourself."

Kit's words drifted to her as if in a dream through the crackle of fire and smothering smoke. Roz heard him as she navigated the hazards on the burning deck, making doggedly for the ship's bow.

"I'll be back!" she cried to him, putting the full force of her lungs behind the reassurance. Two cables off she spotted *The Raven*, heading their way to take up the men of the *Swiftsure*. "Courte!" she screamed, waving her arms and jumping up and down desperately. "Courte! Help!"

He had to see her. He could not fail to notice that she and Kit were not aboard the two longboats. With a savage rip, she tore off one of her two petticoats, hoisted the white linen over her head like a banner and waved.

Courte saw her. Or someone did. She didn't care who it was as long as he came to their aid. She waited just long enough to see him vault over the side of *The Raven* and into one of the *Swiftsure*'s now-empty longboats. Turning, she sprinted back to Kit.

His cheek was cushioned against one arm and he lay motionless near the burning spar. His eyes were closed. He had given up.

Fury seized her. "Damn you, Christopher Howard. Sit up and help me get you off this ship." She gathered her skirts close and eyed the burning spar. The flames had grown higher since she left him. Could she leap it without catching fire or must she waste precious minutes going around?

Troth, there was no time to debate the issue. Grabbing a nearby coil of rope, she beat its mass against the spar, temporarily extinguishing a portion of the blaze. A narrow path lay open for her to pass. Wrapping her skirts tightly around her body, she made the leap.

She didn't question how she got to Kit safely. Hastily she knelt over him and squeezed his arm.

His eyes opened. He stared at Rozalinde, dazed.

"I'm not going without you," she told him fiercely. "So you might as well cooperate unless you want us both to die. And I won't do it. Do you hear me? I won't, Christopher Howard." She spoke vehemently as she worked. Grasping him by the hip and shoulders, she pushed and pulled him onto his back, then she supported him into a sitting position. Anger made her strong, and she half dragged, half bullied him until he rose to a crouch on his one good foot. He leaned against her heavily, and she slung his left arm around her shoulder, insisting he move forward. Guiding him toward the starboard, she frantically hoped Courte would be there.

By now the other dry timbers of the ship had caught, but most of the deck was still clear. All those weeks of devoted swabbing by the men had kept the boards wet. They couldn't support fire, Roz noted with satisfaction. Now if they could just avoid falling masts and spars, they would make it. She urged Kit to the rail and peered over the side.

Courte Philips thought he was in hell. The three men he'd brought in the longboat tried to hold it steady. He was surrounded by ships that burned or spewed cannon fire. The shouts of men attacking, the screams of men dying, filled his ears. Before him, the earl's beloved ship, the *Swiftsure,* blazed.

In agony, he scanned the sheer side of the ship, wondering what had become of the countess. If she didn't hurry, the ammunition might explode. Just then, her face appeared above the wales. She waved, but realized at once she had his attention. Her face disappeared.

Christ's wounds, should he climb up? A rope ladder dangled further down the way. Tersely he directed the rowers to approach it. When they were near enough, he caught it with both hands.

A boot appeared over the side of the ship, then the rest of a leg. It was joined by its mate, and Courte could see Kit support himself with his arms, lower himself onto the rope ladder. His left leg dangled oddly. Courte gripped the rope ladder tighter to keep it steady.

With painful slowness, the two figures above inched their way down, Kit first, followed by the countess. Kit's injured foot was practically useless, and seconds ticked away as he shifted the good foot from one rung to the next.

"I can't help him from here," Rozalinde cried to Courte. "I'm afraid he'll fall."

"I'll get him." Shouting for his men to hold the longboat against the ship, Courte stepped onto the ladder and climbed, just as Kit missed a rung.

Rozalinde shrieked. Courte braced himself for the impact of Kit's fall, but it didn't come. Looking up, Courte could see Kit had caught himself. He clung to the ladder, head hanging, eyes closed. Clearly he struggled against the pain of his injuries to remain conscious. The ship rose on a wave, made them sway precariously.

Somehow, Kit climbed lower. Courte reached out to help him, then he and the others supported him into the longboat.

"My lady, sit you down. We will place his head in your lap." Courte motioned for Rozalinde to hurry, and she hopped from the last rung of the ladder. Heedless of the muck in the bottom of the boat, she scrambled into position, sat, and held out her arms.

They lowered their master into the bottom of the boat as gently as possible, knowing he was now unconscious. That done, Courte motioned the men to the oars.

They rowed hard for the shore, their four oars making a desperate rhythm in the tide-driven water. When the water grew too shallow to row, Courte shipped his oar and leaped over the side into the calf-high water. Grasping the rope at the bow with the others, they raced for land, passing soldiers and townspeople on their way out. When he felt the boat scrape on the sandy bottom, Courte turned to look back. He wished to see the *Gran Grifon* captured. The soldiers should be taking prisoners by now.

To his astonishment, two ships blazed on the water behind him. One had to be the *Swiftsure,* but the other was evidently the *Gran Grifon.* The wind must had shifted. The flames from the fireboat blew southwest. The *Gran Grifon* was lost.

Even as he watched, a blast of thunder rocked the Zuider Zee. Everyone ducked as the *Swiftsure* exploded into a million pieces, raining the sky and water with debris. The small longboat bobbed and rocked from the shock waves.

Anger flooded Courte's mind, and he wheeled around to look at Kit. His friend's eyelids were closed, looking like dark smudges set deeply in their sockets. He gave no sign of knowing that his prized possession had just disappeared from the face of the earth.

Rozalinde bent over him, crooning, her hair singed and

dirty, her face smeared with soot. She swayed her upper body back and forth, as if in mourning. "Never mind," he heard her whisper fiercely. Tears made distinct paths down her dirty cheek. "Never mind, Christopher. Never mind."

Epilogue

The Dutch won a great victory that day in October. The admiral of the Spanish fleet, none other than Count von Bossu, was captured along with his flagship. Four other major ships of the Spanish fleet surrendered to the Dutch, along with a half-dozen smaller vessels. The triumph secured the safety of the Zuider Zee and established the supremacy of the Dutch in the vast realm of the North Sea.

Rozalinde heard none of this until the next day. Her first action after rescuing Christopher was to convey him to the town of Enckhuysen and to find a physician to treat his wounds. The broken foot was set, his back smeared with healing salve. The burn covered a good portion of his shoulders, but by good fortune it was not severe. Though it would pain him considerably due to its position, it would not endanger his life.

The blow to his head concerned Rozalinde more. Kit had been knocked unconscious by it, and they could not tell immediately if it had affected his wits. For the rest of the day and through the night, he drifted in and out of awareness, sometimes talking wildly, other times wrestling with the sheets. Throughout, Rozalinde remained doggedly at his side, refusing to sleep, seeing to his needs, no matter how humble.

On the morning of the next day, he opened his eyes and looked into hers. She had been leaning over him, sponging his forehead with cool water, hoping he would wake.

Suddenly his lids rose. His deep blue eyes focused on hers.

"I'm here," she whispered.

Kit stared, not sure for a minute where he was or who ministered to him. Then he realized it was Rozalinde, for she smiled that dazzling smile of hers, a smile so rich because she gave it so seldom, and he reached up to touch the never-ending, lyric curve of her lips. "You stayed behind for me," he said wonderingly. "Why?"

"Such a question." Rozalinde tossed a rough answer at him as she shifted on the bed, returning the sponge to its basin. "Because I love you. Under no circumstance could I be forced to leave you if you needed me, Kit. Didn't you understand?"

"No. Forgive me." He closed his eyes as moisture welled under his lids. He felt weak and foolish, lying here wounded in bed while others finished the battle for him. He was embarrassing himself, but it couldn't be helped. He'd found his salvation. Clasping Rozalinde's hand, he held it to his cheek, his grip fierce.

"I thought women were delicate and helpless," he managed in a strangled voice.

"Some of them are." One of Rozalinde's braids had come loose, as usual, and she pushed it over her shoulder impatiently, her face suddenly gone solemn. "But I'm not like your mother. *She* had the disadvantage from the beginning, being married to Henry Howard. She couldn't change that." She leaned forward to smooth an unruly lock of hair from his forehead. "Can you find it in your heart to forgive her?"

Kit moved his head in the smallest of nods, remembering the look on Rozalinde's face when he'd opened his eyes on the burning deck of the *Swiftsure*. It was much like the look on his mother's face, that day when his father caught her giving him the present. The pain assaulted him again, and suddenly he remembered everything from that day. Not just how it felt when his father disciplined him. Not just his mother's tears as she watched. In his mind's eye, the scene recreated itself. His father had entered the room, seen the toy, demanded it be put away. Kit made his statement of defiance. The hated cane rose in the air, propelled by his father's powerful arm, and broke the marvelous top into a thousand pieces. Again the cane rose. It cut into Kit's thigh. And then ...

... his mother launched herself at his father with a scream that tore the air. She hit him squarely on the right arm, sent him reeling across the room while the cane flew from his hand and he lost his grip on Kit.

Kit had scrambled away, crawled under a table to watch from safety while his mother defied his father. With all the wiles she possessed, she confronted him. She argued with him, challenged him, berated his manner of bringing up their children. For an interminable stretch of time Kit watched and listened to their verbal battle. For a fleeting second, he thought his mother might win.

Ultimately, she hadn't. His father lost patience and rang for the servants. They came running at the uproar, and his father bid them restrain her while he administered the appropriate punishment to his disobedient son. Kit had been hauled out from under the table and struck with the cane five times. It was always the cane for defiance, one blow for each of his years. Forever he had remembered those wounding cuts, but somehow he'd forgotten his mother, begging her husband to stop.

Her words, the raging fury in her voice, floated to the surface of remembrance, and Kit winced sharply. She had fought valiantly for him that day, but his father was the master—firm in his belief that fear of God must be taught. The coldest man alive. The servants held his struggling mother while his father beat him, and Kit had blocked her futile defense from his mind, recalling only his hatred and pain. A small moan escaped him. She had fought for him many times before that. Now he remembered. But her husband held the power. Easily he removed the children from her jurisdiction. Rozalinde was right. She had no way to fight back.

"Thank you for that."

The sound of Rozalinde's voice burned through Kit's memories, bringing him back to the present. He blinked, focusing on her. "For what?"

Rozalinde's face had grown soft with tenderness. She touched his cheek with one hand. "For giving me the chance to convince you. For the sake of your mother's memory, I'll try never to let you down."

"No," he said, remembering again the courage and love in her face when he'd opened his eyes on the burning deck of the *Swiftsure*. "I don't think you could."

Kit's recovery was rapid after that. Within a day he was up and about, hobbling with a crutch on his one good foot.

Rozalinde stayed beside him without ceasing, and where once he would have complained and sent her away so he could be alone, now he kept her near and let her do what she would. It felt astonishingly good to be coddled, knowing she had no greedy motive behind it. This woman served him out of affection, not out of desire for what he could give her. For the first time in his life, he believed it.

The day he was able to go out, he requested a coach to drive them. But first he did what was long overdue—he dispatched a special messenger to Rozalinde's family in England to inform them of her safety and their marriage. She had been too busy caring for him to see about obtaining the money or a man to deliver such a message. After receiving her grateful thanks, he assisted her into the coach and directed the driver to the quay.

"Rozalinde, there is *The Chalice.*" He indicated the ship with his crutch when they arrived. "I want you to see to its unloading and the sale of the cargo. I agree to accompany you. But I warn you, you must decide everything for yourself."

Rozalinde had beamed at him, then gone to work, realizing this was his way of saying he would not usurp her position as head of her father's business. He gave her permission to be herself, let her know he would support her. He would be present if she wanted him, but he would not deprive her of her power.

By nightfall, Kit was sorry for his promise to accompany her. She'd led him on an exhausting day, dragging him through one warehouse after another, then to the marketplace where the merchants haggled. She was such a clever bargain maker, by the time they returned to their quarters, she'd made a comfortable profit for her father's business. The wool broadcloths on *The Chalice* were all promised to buyers and she had a goodly stock of items selected for sale in England. They would be loaded as soon as *The Chalice* was unloaded and made ready for the return trip.

That night, in their rooms at the merchant's establishment, they made love for the first time since before the battle. Kit's broken foot and the burns on his back made things difficult, but Rozalinde slipped into bed beside him where he lay on his side and made love so gently, so sweetly to him, he groaned with pleasure before, during, and after. Especially after, when she lay against him beneath the coverlet and continued to tantalize him with her body.

"I'm a wounded man," he protested as he felt himself harden for a second time that night. "Leave off, or you'll injure me further."

Rozalinde put on a look of insult, but she couldn't maintain it. She grinned. "I'll not injure you. I'm relaxing you. Can't you just accept and let it be?"

He laughed at that and pulled her closer. "Roses," he growled, nuzzling at her neck. "You smell like roses."

"Blast the roses," she chuckled, easing herself down on him again. "I don't care about them. I care about you."

There was a celebration in the town hall the next day, where William of Nassau, Prince of Orange, received his faithful followers and decorated the admiral of the Sea Beggars with a special medal struck in honor of the Victory of Enckhuysen. The room was crowded with soldiers, burghers of the town with their wives and children, and all the other townspeople, who cheered and clapped each speech and toast with jubilation.

Then the prince called Lord Christopher Howard, the Earl of Wynford, to stand before him. Kit left Rozalinde with Courte Philips on one side and the Count of Hoorne on the other and went to bow before the prince.

"Lord Christopher Howard," said William, his voice ringing clearly so all could hear him in the huge hall, "we owe you a debt we can never repay for your courage and devoted service which have aided us in winning this victory. You have made a great sacrifice on behalf of our nation. May God bless you and your queen and all the people of England for your support."

The crowd applauded wildly. But then the prince did something unexpected. "I would also like to call upon the Countess of Wynford, Rozalinde Howard, to come forward to receive our thanks."

Standing beside the Count of Hoorne, Rozalinde's mouth fell open. She was so astonished, her legs could scarce carry her forward, but she managed to move through the crowd toward the dais where the prince waited. Kit was grinning at her proudly as she came to a halt at his side.

"Without the aid of the countess," Prince William continued, "and her expert deciphering of the Spanish code, we would not have known about the surprise attack planned on our navy. We are eternally in her debt."

Amid thunderous applause, the prince presented Kit and Rozalinde each with medals showing the Lion of Holland joined with the Tudor roses of Queen Elizabeth. Though Rozalinde smiled and curtsied, pleased to receive the prince's praise, her heart went out to Kit for his sacrifice in rendering this service. She knew how he felt about his ship, knew its loss pained him deeply. And although she felt in a mood to celebrate, she left him alone that afternoon instead, to hobble along the quay with Courte and remember.

Besides, now that the battle was won, now that Kit was up and about, she had another task. In Phillipe's company, she took herself to the city garrison where prisoners were kept. But in response to her questions, no one knew of an Englishman taken prisoner off the *Gran Grifon*. All prisoners had been Spanish, and among them there had been no English citizen named George Trenchard, nor anyone answering to his physical description.

Rozalinde returned to Kit afterward, deeply puzzled. It was not her imagination that George Trenchard had sailed on the *Gran Grifon*. Had he managed to escape both the burning, sinking ship and the Dutch soldiers? In the chaos of battle, it was possible. With this disquieting thought to haunt her, Roz packed her navigation instruments in her trunk, arranged the new garments Kit had bought her in another, and prepared for their return to England.

Kit, too, had many tasks to perform before departure, but the most important one he saved for last. He went to call on Phillipe where he lodged at the Hotel de Ville, along with the Prince of Orange.

"I must return to England for now. But I'll be back to see you and aid the Netherlands. I promise."

Phillipe embraced him heartily. "You are a married man now, Christopher. You must stay at home and beget your heirs. I won't hear of you endangering your life chasing Spanish communiqués. In fact, I forbid it."

"But the Spanish still trouble you. They trouble both our countries."

"We will launch a new initiative," Phillipe insisted. "One that does not require your active presence."

Kit shook his head, not believing such a thing possible, but he embraced Phillipe in return and whispered, "*Duizendmaal dank, mijn vader.*"

Phillipe looked at him, a spark of pleasure danced in his eye. "Have you decided, then, on our kinship? I have never been so sure."

Kit looked away, embarrassed. "No. I've decided it doesn't matter what the reality might be." He turned back, determined to speak his heart. "You are as a father to me, and since I have no other, I thought . . ."

"I understand."

Once again Phillipe enfolded Kit in his massive, warming embrace, and the two men clung to each other in farewell. Kit felt much of the troubling pain from his past lift from his shoulders, and he returned to Rozalinde, feeling more joyous of heart than he had in years.

Back in West Lulworth, there was great jubilation at Roz's homecoming. Her father, looking more fit than he had in months, met them at Poole and bore his daughter home with great ceremony and excitement. There she was greeted by four squealing youngsters and her mother, all of whom hung on her and demanded the story of her adventures. Jonathan's greeting was more restrained, though no less loving. But Rozalinde thought he looked tired and worn. When she had a chance, she took him aside.

"You have had much to bear in my absence?"

He nodded, not meeting her eyes.

"All is well with the shop? Mother and Father? The children?"

They were well. She realized the trouble lay not there.

"Margaret?"

Jon's face changed, and Rozalinde knew she had found the cause of Jonathan's dispirited expression. Margaret's father had finally died, she learned, and Margaret had been spirited away by her mother to live with relatives in the north. Roz strove to comfort her brother for the loss of his sweetheart, but she was required to journey to London with Kit almost immediately. There she settled the business of her father's company debts while Kit visited the queen, for he still required her permission to marry.

The queen didn't approve his choice, naturally. At least not until Kit knelt before her.

"Your Majesty, I wish to take a wife, so that I may get heirs to my family name and have a woman to comfort me in my old age."

"Old age," Elizabeth snorted. "He talks of old age. When you are twice the age you are at present, you may speak of such things. But very well, I shall look about me and choose you a wife."

"I have already chosen her, Your Majesty. Her name is Rozalinde Cavandish."

The queen's eyes narrowed. The corners of her mouth turned down. "Many eligible daughters of my nobles want for husbands. I will choose you one of them."

To which Kit had replied nothing. He only placed in her lap a carved, wooden box and, opening it, displayed for her amazed yes a hundred shining pieces of gold. "There are more where those came from." He motioned to his servant, who left the chamber and returned with a companion, both groaning under the weight of gold equalling two thousand English pounds. "The Spanish," he explained, "no longer had use for it."

Elizabeth's face changed suddenly, for her treasury was ever bare and she did not scorn to take income from any reasonable source. She smiled on him an indulgent smile. "Good, my lord, and you wish the wedding to be soon?"

"I do," he answered, glad he had not mentioned that he and Rozalinde had already wed.

"I shall send you a gift," Elizabeth decided, "and I shall stand godmother to your first child."

"We would be honored, Your Majesty."

The visit to London was not all pleasant, however. One day Rozalinde returned to the Howard town house to find Kit frowning over a letter.

"Bad news?" She couldn't imagine what else might happen to mar their happiness.

"Trenchard," Kit answered.

The name caused Roz's smile to fade. She felt the blood drain from her face. "I never did understand why he risked everything to sail into battle with the Spanish," she began.

"He could have stayed in Lulworth and his traitorous ways would not have been discovered. As it is, he cannot return to England."

Kit looked up from the letter. "That depends entirely on the future, as this letter reveals. I am on friendly terms with Francis Walsingham, Her Majesty's secretary. He has men in many foreign places who find out information important to England. In response to my inquiries, they bring word of an Englishman who has taken up residence at the court of Philip, King of Spain. He appears to be a favored advisor."

Rozalinde blanched further. "And it is Trenchard?"

"He is called by a different name, but the description leaves no doubt whatsoever as to his identity." Christopher studied his wife for her reaction.

Worry creased Rozalinde's forehead. "But why would he go to live there?"

"To understand that, you must think using his logic," Kit answered dryly. "First of all, when he gambled on the Spanish winning the Battle of Enckhuysen, he thought the odds were in his favor. The Spanish are strong. And he knew that if they won, I was the one who would not return to Lulworth. Thus, there would have been no one to prevent his return, no one to betray him or prevent his continued work for both countries. He intended to win a great victory and rid himself of me in one stroke."

"I would have betrayed him," Roz declared indignantly. "I would have opposed him at every turn."

Kit scoffed. "To him, that meant nothing. Once you were his wife, he would have been free to make up any story he wished. And if you will remember, he was good at them. If you didn't obey him by agreeing, he could have had you flogged, imprisoned, clapped up in a mad house, anything he wished. The Spanish must have promised him much, for he took a great risk, but apparently even though the Spanish lost the battle, Trenchard did not lose in like measure. He seems to have gained."

"But his house in Lulworth," Roz protested, "and his shop. He's lost those."

"He was never stupid." Kit tapped the letter. "Walsingham's men learned that the business was sold in the last week, for a tidy sum, and the funds invested in a foreign venture. All perfectly legal."

Roz sighed deeply. "He is clever. What about the house in Lulworth?"

"Rented," Kit told her crisply, slapping the letter down on the table and pushing himself away with both hands. "At a pretty price, with word given out that the owner has gone abroad for his health."

"But the Privy Council can take away his property," Rozalinde argued, thoroughly aggrieved by this news. "They can confiscate his land. And what about his appointment as deputy-lieutenant?"

"They can't take his land until after a hearing in the courts. And Trenchard has hired a very good lawyer to represent his interests in his absence. Without Trenchard present to prosecute, there is no solid proof of his guilt. He claims to have gone abroad for his health. It could take years to untangle through the law. And he very neatly sold his appointment."

Rozalinde groaned with frustration. "How can he advise the Spanish king? What does he know that's so valuable, he receives favored treatment?"

"He knows the best way to invade England." Kit shook his head ruefully. "Such information is valuable. But never mind, Rose. Let us forget him. He can't reach you here and that's the important thing. If in future he should return to trouble us, we will deal with him then. Right now, we must concentrate on the part of English law that will get us legally wed."

Kit's arms encircled her, and Roz let herself lean against his broad chest. She nodded, willing for once to give in to his demands. Trenchard was as good as dead in her life.

And so Kit and Rozalinde were married for a second time before the parish priest of West Lulworth, so that in the eyes of their family and neighbors they would be truly joined. After Kit placed his ring on Rozalinde's finger and the priest pronounced them wed before man and God, she knelt before him and he set on her shining braids the heirloom coronet of the Countesses of Wynford. And all the congregation cheered until the sound echoed through the vaulted stone church and out into the streets of West Lulworth.

Rozalinde was pleased to note that none cheered them more vigorously than the former dowager countess of Wynford, who attended the ceremony with her new husband, a rich knight from the north. Not only was the Lady Mary happily wed, Kit pointed out to Rozalinde, but she was already growing great with child—a blessing that had never been bestowed on her by his brother.

A mighty feast took place in the great hall of Lulworth Castle that night, with many toasts drunk and dancing and music. At one point during the revels, Rozalinde's father assembled the immediate family in a private chamber to make an announcement.

"I have changed my will," he indicated, smiling upon his newly wed daughter and her husband. He linked arms with his wife, who leaned against him affectionately. Her belly had grown larger during Roz's absence with the newest member of the family. "It's not quite what I originally planned," he went on, "but at the urging of your mother and my new son-in-law, I have made certain changes." Here he took a deep breath, then continued. "Upon my death, as is right and natural, my wife will inherit her one-third portion in the form of this house and other property. But with Rozalinde now one and twenty and a married woman, she will be specified as heir to all my business holdings. She would also act as guardian to her brothers as long as they are underage. When her brothers reach their majority, they can elect to become partners with her or receive a share of profit from the business, according to their desires. Your mother wishes it thus, don't you, my dear?" He patted Joan's hand. "She says she has no head for such things."

Rozalinde looked at her father and mother in astonishment. Then she stared at Kit. "You urged this? This is wonderful."

He grinned at her mischievously. "It's you who loves the business. Not Jon. Eh?"

Jon nodded vigorously in agreement.

"And the others are too young to know for sure," Kit finished.

"I don't love it, either," Charles volunteered loudly to everyone present. "She can have my share and welcome. I'll take the gold."

His elders chucked at his openness. "You must wait to decide when you're older," Rozalinde told him, caressing his hair. But a smile hovered on her lips and she was vastly pleased at her father's words.

After that, Rozalinde was able to watch her father enjoy the revels, knowing she had put his mind at rest. He at last had an acceptable guardian for both family and business should he pass away. Perhaps for that very reason he looked healthier and happier that night than he had for some time. And Roz's mother was all smiles, knowing that her daughter would continue to run the business the way she had, so her husband could rest. Even Jonathan, who made no secret about disliking drapery, had been a diligent manager in Roz's absence, running the business competently for his father. And though he now put on a sober face on life due to his loss of Margaret, he seemed all the more trustworthy because he had no distractions. Roz tried for a while to cheer him, but before long she gave up and sent him off at Kit's suggestion to sit with Courte Philips and listen to the men tell stories about the Battle of Enckhuysen. It was a tale that would be repeated for years to come, embellished with each telling.

Despite these distractions, Kit found he had eyes only for Rozalinde, and sitting beside her at the high table, he leaned near and whispered to her. "We're not to have this nonsense of a bawdy bedding. You are to slip away quietly when I give you the signal. I'll join you after, as soon as I can."

Kit was as good as his word, and at last they were alone in Kit's chamber, sitting in the great curtained bed with the clamor of the guests still resounding below.

"My sweet." He took her in his arms. "I never thought the day would come when I would look upon the woman in my bed as my bride."

Once Roz would have taken offense, but now she laughed and pressed herself against him. "How do you find your bride? Old and ugly? A shrew?" She nipped his neck with her teeth.

Obligingly he wrestled her to the bed in mock anger, all the while indulging his eyes on the feast of her body—slim white hips and thighs, sweetest of lush young breasts. With one hand he explored those lovely breasts until a sigh escaped her lips and she confessed her love.

It lit his blood like flame put to a brazier, that confession. With a groan he fell upon her, covering her body with his own, parting her legs with eager hands. He had not meant to use haste, but suddenly it seemed he couldn't possess her soon enough.

"Old and ugly, indeed, my Rose," he whispered as he slid into the depths of her. It made him remember the night in his cabinet, when she had come to warn him, and his blood soared again like on that night, singing with desire for her. He began to move within her, carefully at first, then more quickly as she met his thrusts.

"Ah, Rozalinde," he said afterward, when it was over. He brushed the hair from her damp face. "How long I have loved you."

"Love?" Rozalinde smiled up at him, obviously delighted. "Did I hear you say love, Christopher Howard? I thought you didn't know the word."

"Oh, I know it," he chuckled, cradling her cheek with one hand. "I learned it from someone just recently. I won't say who."

"Tell me," Roz coaxed, opening her eyes wide and feigning innocence. "Who would have taught you such a thing?"

But Kit grew thoughtful, his expression turned serious. "I learned it when I was young from my mother. What a tragedy that I stopped believing in it as I matured. And how strange it is that here I am, once again understanding. It's a miracle, really."

"Not so strange," Rozalinde countered, turning his hand to kiss the palm. "I think you were not meant to be deprived of it forever. That would have been a cruel fate."

"You are right in that. I wouldn't want *my* son to grow up without it." Kit caressed her belly. "Our child will be a son, you know."

Rozalinde stared at him, astounded. "Son? Just what makes you think—"

"Consider the date," he answered, smiling in a superior manner. "Either our son has already set up housekeeping in your belly, or your body behaves in a manner not the least natural to women. With a mind as mathematical as yours, you should have realized that."

Roz thought about the date she had set sail from West Lulworth, then realized he was right. She should have had her monthly courses by now, but none had come. "You may be correct, Lord Howard," she told him saucily. "But you need not consider yourself so wondrous clever. You've become a hopeless romantic if ever I saw one, babbling about love and babes. Is there a shred of logic left in you?"

"No," he teased back, seeking her face to kiss her. "I have accepted the idea that I am all passion. I willingly leave the logic in the family to you."

And at this Rozalinde laughed and settled more comfortably in his arms, secure at last in the knowledge that this man loved her, equally secure in the belief that he granted her power over her own destiny—allowing the two things she wanted most in life to coexist.

Glossary

duizendmaal dank—a thousand times thanks
dochter—daughter
geliefde—beloved
goeie hemel—by heaven
heel bekoorlijk—very enchanting or pretty
lieveling—sweetheart
mijn or *m'n*—my
niet gij—not thee
onervaren—inexperienced
rozekleur—rose
Sakkerloot—good heavens
uiterst kostbaar—most precious
vader—father
vriend—friend (male)
vriendin—friend (female)

Historical Note

Sixteenth-century England, the time of Queen Elizabeth, was a fascinating period, full of change in many areas—in religion, in manners and customs, and in roles for men and women. Known as the Early Modern Period in history, it is a time that holds a vast appeal to me and to many readers, with its mingling of the medieval age—when knights still rescued fair damsels—and the dawning of the new age—when women could throw off the shackles of chatteldom and emancipate themselves by owning property, inheriting wealth, and governing their own lives. I have tried, in portraying the story of Rozalinde and Christopher, to convey some of the excitement of the age. I sincerely hope you enjoyed it.

I wish to thank Dr. Harry Vredeveld, professor of German at the Department of Germanic Languages and Literature at Ohio State University, for checking the accuracy of my Dutch usage and suggesting appropriate phrases.

In terms of historical accuracy of the story, the Sea Beggars, or the Gueux de Mer, were real sixteenth-century outlaws, given letters of marque by the rebel Prince of Orange to fight for their country's freedom from Spain. And the Count of Hoorne was a real noble, though history tells us King Philip of Spain successfully beheaded him in the town square of Brussels.

As for the emancipation of the Netherlands from Spain, sadly, the valiant Prince of Orange did not live to see that day. After many unsuccessful attempts on his life, Spain at last triumphed. In 1584 when he was fifty-one, William was shot by an assassin as he sat at dinner with his wife and children. Despite this, the heroic leadership of William the Silent, Prince of Orange, paved the way for others to continue the battle. But it wasn't until January 1648 that Spain

formally recognized the independence of the Netherlands
at a treaty signing known as the Peace of Westphalia. The
Dutch Eighty Years' War is considered by some historians
to be the precursor to both the French and American
revolutions.

As to the question of nobles marrying into merchant
families as Christopher did in this story, it is true that such
intermingling of the classes was looked upon with disfavor
by many people of the time. Despite this, exceptions exist
in any period of history, and there were always those ready
to challenge the opinions and attitudes of the establishment. Scholarly historians of the sixteenth century document a number of marriages between noblemen and either
widows or daughters of rich London merchants. Reading
about one such marriage piqued my interest in a noble/
merchant union; thus the relationship between Kit and Rozalinde was born.

If you enjoyed reading about Kit and Rozalinde, I hope
you will look forward to my next historical romance, which
tells the story of Jonathan Cavandish and his sweetheart,
Margaret. It will be published by Topaz in the winter of
1996.